RECLAIMED *Love*

Tha..., I hope you enjoy's! The Saga Continues! Love, Ramona

RAMONA FLIGHTNER

Ramona Flightner/Grizzly Damsel Publishing
P.O. Box 187
Boston, MA 02128
www.ramonaflightner.com

Cover design by Derek Murphy

Publisher's Note: This is a work of fiction. Names, characters, places, and incidents are a product of the author's imagination. Locales and public names are sometimes used for atmospheric purposes. Any resemblance to actual people, living or dead, or to businesses, companies, events, institutions, or locales is completely coincidental.

Ordering Information: Quantity sales. Special discounts are available on quantity purchases by corporations, associations, and others. For details, contact the "Special Sales Department" at the address above.

Reclaimed Love/ Ramona Flightner. — 1st ed.

Print ISBN: 978-0-9860502-3-7

eBook ISBN: 978-0-9860502-4-4

RECLAIMED Love

RAMONA FLIGHTNER

Mum,
You ensured I never went to bed
Without a bedtime story.
Thank you for your boundless
Enthusiasm for the ones I create.

CAST OF CHARACTERS

BOSTON

Clarissa Sullivan: teaches school in the West End of Boston, a suffragette, lives in the South End,

Colin Sullivan: Clarissa's brother, a blacksmith

Sean Sullivan: Clarissa's father, a blacksmith, from Ireland

Mrs. Rebecca Sullivan nee Smythe: Clarissa's stepmother, has social aspirations

Agnes Sullivan nee Thompson: Clarissa's mother, deceased

Savannah Montgomery nee Russell: Clarissa's cousin and confidante, recently married to Jonas Montgomery, lives in the Back Bay

Lucas Russell: Clarissa's cousin, works at his father's linen store, "Russells," is a talented piano player

Martin Russell: father to Lucas and Savannah, uncle to Clarissa, owns and runs the linen store, "Russells," store and home in the South End, near the Sullivan home

Matilda Russell nee Thompson: Savannah's mother and Clarissa's aunt, sister to Agnes and Betsy

Betsy Parker nee Thompson: childless, lives in Quincy, married to a wealthy man, free-thinking, cryptic comments, Matilda and Agnes' sister, Clarissa and Savannah's aunt.

Richard McLeod: Gabriel's middle brother, a blacksmith, friend to Colin

Jeremy McLeod: the youngest McLeod brother, in the Army, fighting in the Philippines

Aidan McLeod: uncle to the three McLeod boys

Ian McLeod: father to the three McLeod boys

Geraldine McLeod nee Sanders: wife to Ian and mother to the McLeod boys

Patricia Masterson nee Sanders: sister to Geraldine, aunt to the McLeod boys, helped raise them.

Henry Masterson: cousin to the McLeod boys

Nicholas Masterson: cousin to the McLeod boys

Florence Butler: orphan teacher who works with Clarissa in the West End

Sophronia Chickering: feisty suffragette who befriends Clarissa, lives on Beacon Hill, distantly related by marriage to the piano Chickerings

Jonas Montgomery: wealthy New Yorker, Savannah's husband
Cameron Wright: a suitor for Clarissa's hand
Mrs. Wright: Cameron's mother
Maid Mary: Clarissa's maid who is loyal to her
Maid Bridget: the other maid in the Sullivan household, more loyal to Mrs. Sullivan (Smythe)
Maid Polly: Uncle Martin's maid

IN THE WEST

Gabriel McLeod: the eldest McLeod brother, a cabinetmaker, starting a new life, devoted to Clarissa
Matthew Donovan: befriends Gabriel in Chicago and convinces him to travel to Butte; friends with Ronan
Ronan O'Bara: Matthew's friend who works in the mine with Liam
Liam Egan: Irish miner, married to Amelia
Amelia Egan: married to Liam, was a schoolteacher
Nicholas Egan: son to Liam and Amelia
Niall O'Donnell: works with Gabriel at the Thornton
Larry Ferguson: works with Gabriel at the Thornton
Morgan O'Malley: works with Gabriel at the Thornton
Jeffers: supervisor at the Thornton
Jedediah Maloney: friendly porter at the train station
Mr. A.J. Pickens: works at the Book Depository
Mrs. Bouchard: works on the Library Committee with her sister; considers herself a great arbiter of fashion
Mrs. Vaughan: works with her sister, Mrs. Bouchard, on the Library Committee
Sebastian Carling: mill foreman, befriends Gabrie

CHAPTER 1

Boston, March 1900

"WHAT DID YOU THINK would happen, my girl?" Sophronia Chickering asked, raising an eyebrow. "You gallivant about unchaperoned, spend time with him alone in his warehouse allowing God-knows-what liberties to be taken to your person. How did you expect your father to react?"

I blushed a rosy red at her comments. I had decided to visit Sophie, my opinionated friend and fellow suffragette, for tea rather than return home after school. We sat in her upstairs parlor with white wainscoting and soothing yellow wallpaper in her house on Beacon Hill overlooking the Boston Common.

"I knew he would be upset," I said with a long sigh. "I never expected him to act in a way that would lead to Gabriel's banishment." I stared at the sole painting of a mountain glen over the fireplace, wishing the bucolic scene would infuse me with a similar sense of peace.

"He's a man. You can only imagine what he envisioned. You must try to see things from others' perspectives, Clarissa. It will help you outmaneuver them in the future." Sophie sat with impeccable posture, her shoulders back and feet crossed at the ankles tucked under her chair. Her gray hair was pulled back in an elegant chignon while her cobalt-blue silk dress with its lace collar highlighted the mischief in her aquamarine eyes.

"Sophie, Gabriel always acted as a gentleman," I protested. "Nothing happened."

"Well, I can see you enjoyed yourself. Clearly something occurred or you wouldn't be uncomfortable," Sophie said with a gentle cackle as my cheeks continued to redden. "Besides, for my part, I hope a little something did happen to keep the fires of your romance fanned during his absence. I fear it may be a long one."

"I don't know how I will bear it," I whispered. "I need him to come home now."

"When men are off adventuring, they rarely think of returning. You must continue to write him to remind him of what he left behind."

"I will, never fear."

"How is your stepmother, my girl?"

"The same. Insufferable. Overbearing. Insisting that I am home more because of the upcoming birth of my brother or sister." I punched at a small settee pillow in frustration.

"Have you learned what you needed from her?"

"There is nothing she knows that I could possibly benefit from learning."

"Oh, but there is," Sophie countered. "How to manipulate people to see your version of events. How to act in such a way that people do what you want them to. How to ingratiate yourself to someone even if you loathe them."

"So—"

She held up her hand toward me to forestall any argument. "No. Listen, Clarissa. She would have you learn how to brew a pot of tea properly and laugh at a pleasant volume to stroke a man's ego. However, the true lessons you need to learn are subtler. Start paying attention and learn from a master." She harrumphed once, although I could not tell if it was with displeasure or not.

"Why would I want to do any of those things? It's what I most dislike about her."

"Because, as you must realize by now, your life will not follow the simple path you had envisioned for yourself as a child. You should learn all your lessons, the good and the bad. Sometimes the bad ones can be the most enjoyable." Sophie smiled at me with a wicked gleam in her eyes. "And as for your Gabriel, I'd dream of my return to him."

***

I DEPARTED SOPHIE'S with few options to avoid increased interactions with Mrs. Smythe, my meddlesome stepmother of a year. I resolutely refused to call her Mrs. Sullivan when I thought of her, although I tried to remember to address her by her appropriate name when I spoke of her or with her. I had received too many blistering lectures on treating her with respect to wish to receive another. My cousin Savannah had yet to return from her prolonged honeymoon, but I decided to walk to her parents' linen store, Russell's, to visit with my late mama's sister, Aunt Matilda.

As I entered the store, the memory of the stormy day when I had stumbled into and onto Gabriel flitted through my mind. I remembered the agony of watching him tumble off the ladder, of falling on top of him, the amused glimmer in his eyes from the beginning when he watched me. I recalled his deep voice as we had spoken later while he rested, recovering from the head wound I had caused. I took a shuddering breath, trying not to focus too much on him and the past for fear of weeping.

I glanced toward the main area of the fine linen store, hopeful to speak with Uncle Martin. Instead, my cousin Lucas stood behind the glass-encased counter with his back toward me. He called out, "Be with you in a moment." He folded a cloth, placing it in one of the many shelves behind the counter.

"Lucas," I said, "who is here today?"

"Clarissa, it's been too long since you called." He came out from behind the counter to clasp my arm. "Savannah is still away with Jonas, but Mother is sipping tea by herself. You just missed the grandparents."

He raised an eyebrow and winked at me as my eyes widened, my only outward reaction to Lucas's news and my near encounter with our grandparents. I turned to smile at Aunt Matilda as she entered the storefront.

"Clarissa," she said with a sniff of disdain. "You've decided to come for tea?" She walked toward me, gripped my elbow and hauled me out of the storefront. I waved a good-bye toward Lucas with my free hand. Aunt Matilda dragged me through the back hallway reserved for family, passing the closed door to Uncle's study and the darkened formal parlor. We moved without speaking, climbing the newly carpeted stairs to the second-floor family parlor.

She released me upon entering the upstairs parlor filled with stuffy formal furniture, and I saw a fresh tea tray had just been delivered. Faint light entered the front windows, the light and view now partially blocked by the construction of the elevated streetcar line. "I'm sorry to interrupt if you were expecting someone else for tea," I said.

Aunt Matilda gave a small *humph* of disgust and sat elegantly on her favorite lady's chair. I chose the uncomfortable rococo camelback settee because it reminded me of Savannah. After a few moments of awkward silence, during which Aunt Matilda failed to serve me tea, she expelled a pent-up breath of air.

"Clarissa," Aunt Matilda hissed, "what could you possibly be thinking?"

I watched her, uncertain as to the thrust of her argument and the cause of her displeasure. I shrugged my shoulders by way of acknowledgment.

"I would think you would have learned by now that different groups do not mix," she seethed.

I squinted at her, hoping I had misunderstood her.

"You heard me, Clarissa," Aunt Matilda continued. "Why do you think the Italians live together in the North End? The Irish in South Boston? The Chinese in Chinatown?"

She raised her eyebrows at me as though expecting a response. When I failed to respond, she flushed with anger.

"Like marries like. Like associates with like. It's the way of the world. It's how it has been and how it will continue to be. You will marry a man of your class, not a poor laborer." By now her bosom heaved with her proclamations.

"Aunt Matilda," I began after a long pause, carefully choosing my words. "Why are you upset now? Gabriel is far away in the West."

"You have rained shame and infamy on the family again. Why can you never act with grace and decorum as Savannah does?"

"Aunt Matilda, please," I whispered.

"Please what, Clarissa? Please forgive you for your unsupportable fascination with a disgraced laborer? Please forgive you for the shame you have brought to our family name? Do you realize we are once again the talk of the town? Tell me, which one of those should you be forgiven for?"

I stared into her irate eyes as my own anger began to simmer. "What would you have me do, Aunt Matilda? Marry a man I do not love? Consign myself to a life of tedium and monotony for the sake of the family's reputation?"

"I expect you to act as your mother would have taught you. With decorum and an acknowledgment of societal rules."

"Don't bring my mama into this. She would have wanted me to marry for love, just as she did. Just as you did," I retorted, my cheeks reddened with anger.

Aunt Matilda sat back in her chair, lips pursed, glaring at me, as though biting back bitter words. "How—" Aunt Matilda abruptly stopped as the parlor door flew open.

"There she is!" Uncle Martin called out, striding toward the settee. I barely had time to stand before he enfolded me in his strong arms. When he released me, he beamed down at me, his brown eyes glowing with pleasure. "I thought you'd never come to visit," he reproached me, gripping my hand. "Will you stay for supper, regale us with school stories?"

"I'd love to," I said, squeezing his hand.

"I am not sure that is wise, Martin. I wouldn't want to vex Mrs. Sullivan when she is in such a delicate state," Aunt Matilda said.

"Well, not tonight then, Clarissa, but another day soon," Uncle Martin said after sharing a long glance with Aunt Matilda. "Let me see you out."

I smiled toward Aunt Matilda, her rigid stance forestalling any attempt at an embrace. Uncle Martin shook his head, sighing in exasperation as we descended the stairs. "I haven't seen her this angry in years."

"I'm sorry, Uncle."

"It's not your fault. She is very upset by recent visits from your grandparents."

"Uncle..."

"There's no need to say anything to me." We shared a meaningful look. He leaned forward, kissing my forehead. "We will have you over again soon for supper."

"Thank you, Uncle Martin," I murmured.

I walked as though in a trance from Russell's linen store toward my home on Union Park in the South End. The late summer air was filled with the smells of a long, hot summer, and I longed for a heavy rain to wash away the stench of horse dung and refuse. I strolled along tree-shaded streets and attempted to focus on the cloudless day, the children laughing in a nearby park, and the birds flying freely above me. However, my mind continued to return to the scene with Aunt Matilda. Why was it crucial to her that I improve the family name by marrying well?

I thought of Gabriel. Proud, loyal, kind Gabriel. I had never thought to meet such a man, and yet I had. I paused on my walk home as I remembered his gentle embraces, his soft kisses. His desire to understand me as I was, not as he wished I were. The amusement mixed with tenderness and love he always had in his eyes when he watched me.

His banishment from my life two months ago had been the worst period of my life. I had previously thought Cameron's abandonment of me at the altar or my mama's death more than I could bear, but now I knew better. Now I knew what it was to live with my heart elsewhere. Now I knew what it was like to live in daily fear that what I had experienced with Gabriel was an illusion. A lovely dream. I had not heard from him since he had left, and his silence frightened me. Every day I did not hear from him, my faith in our future diminished. Why didn't he write?

CHAPTER 2

THE LURCHING, WHISTLING HALT to the train's forward momentum jerked Gabriel McLeod from a dazed stupor. Hissing steam obstructed his view of Butte, Montana, but he had glimpsed enough from the mountain pass as the train traveled down the winding tracks to know this town was unlike any place he could have imagined. Happy to stand after the long train ride, he stood, gathered his belongings and clambered down the steps after Matthew Donovan.

"Why did you ever convince me to come to this barren wasteland?" Gabriel asked Matthew. He arched his long back, stretching muscles cramped from the journey. A faint breeze ruffled his ebony hair.

"Ronan told me the first impression of Butte is the worst. You'll love it here!" Matthew said as he moved into the waiting crowd. His shorter stature allowed him to navigate the mingling crowd with nimble grace.

"Ronan must be blind," Gabriel muttered as he glanced around, trying to locate a porter. He followed Matthew's serpentine pattern through the people milling about, keeping Matthew's tan-colored bowler hat in sight. "Matthew, do you see him?"

"Not yet."

"I just hope he was able to secure us a place to stay," Gabriel said.

"At least our trunks made it just fine," Matthew said as he and Gabriel walked off toward their luggage stacked near the redbrick wall of the platform under a heavy awning. Gabriel peered into a nearby door and saw a large, well-lit waiting area filled with sturdy benches.

"I hope we don't have to spend much time waiting in there," Gabriel said.

"We won't. Ronan'll be here soon. You'll see," Matthew said, his pale blue eyes lit with excitement. He picked up a discarded newspaper and fanned himself as he leaned against the wall. "I never thought it would be so hot high in the mountains."

"I meet you in a hotel in Chicago, and, the next thing I know, you're dragging me into this godforsaken part of the country," Gabriel said. "I should have insisted we travel to San Francisco." He hailed an approaching porter for help and only mustered a half smile as the middle-aged man neared.

"Welcome to Butte, America!" The porter grunted as he helped Matthew and Gabriel lift their heavy trunks onto his carriage. His black suspenders stretched taut over his protruding potbelly, and he moved with an offbeat gait.

"You seem out of sorts, young man," the porter said Gabriel's way. He spat a stream of tobacco juice onto the boardwalk, leaving a chickareed-colored splat on the ground. "Where're ye headed?"

"I think downtown," Gabriel replied after a long pause.

"Well, seeing as you're in downtown, you might want to rethink that," the porter replied with a chuckle. They moved through the waiting room and out to the front of the station into the bright sunlight. "In this city, all good places are up." He pointed toward the hill, causing Gabriel to turn and stare at the steep streets. They seemed to go up and up for as far as the eye could see.

"This is an upside-down kind of place, young man. Uptown is our downtown." The porter chuckled. He glanced at Gabriel. "Now, if you've come here for mining, I fear you'll find it difficult work for someone so tall. Although the Swedes seem able to adjust just fine." He spat again, barely missing Gabriel's shoe.

Gabriel scowled at the man. "We're newly arrived and uncertain where to go. A friend was to meet us, but he hasn't arrived. We are undecided if we should wait for him here or find a place to board for the night."

"I'd find a place to board. If he's on his shift, he's hours yet 'til he's free. Leave his name with me, and, if he comes looking for you, I'll send him in the right direction," the porter said. Gabriel glanced toward Matthew to find him nodding in agreement. "Now, if you was to ask me, I'd recommend a few nights at a hotel near the train depot. Take the time to find where you'll be working and then find lodging near your mine. It's best to live near where you work. The days are long, and the weather can be vicious."

Gabriel grunted as he looked around at the early September sunshine.

"You look doubtful now, son. But you'll know what I mean come No-vember. If you last that long." The porter chuckled once more to himself. "Now, am I to take this to the Northwestern Hotel?"

"Is it affordable?"

"Not so much as a boardinghouse, but it's better than a hotel in Uptown. At the McDermott, you'd pay a right pretty penny."

"We are much obliged for your help, sir," Gabriel said.

"You're welcome, son. My name's Jedediah Maloney. Jed to my friends. You seem like a good-enough sort. I see your type all the time," he said. "As for him, he's all starry-eyed now. Just wait 'til he has to go down the cage the first time." He shook his head ruefully at Matthew's wide-eyed wonder.

They traveled to the nearby hotel with Gabriel helping to push the heavy cart. Gabriel grunted a few times as his side of the cart became lodged in a rut in the unpaved road. He had to exert extra force to propel the cart forward rather than heave its contents to one side and risk the trunks tumbling into the street. A raised boardwalk lined each side of the street, with carts, horses and electric streetcars vying for space. Spindly electric poles sprouted up in front of every other building, with electrical wires connected to each structure. A light strung from sturdy electrical wires hung at every intersection. Gabriel thought the lampposts of Boston were more practical but soon focused on pushing the cart to the nearby hotel.

After obtaining rooms for the night at the three-story Northwestern Hotel, Gabriel helped Jedediah carry the heavy trunks to his room on the second floor. The smells from the kitchen below wafted up to tempt Gabriel as he studied his room. It was large enough for a single-paned window, a cot pushed into the far corner across from the door and a bureau. A green-and-white ceramic pitcher and chipped basin sat on the bureau. After stacking the trunks at the base of his bed, Gabriel collapsed onto it, thankful to be able to lie flat after that train ride. He rolled over to riffle through a small traveling case to extract a letter from Clarissa, the woman he loved who had remained in Boston. Throughout the journey he had found letters from her hidden in his luggage, easing the ache of their separation. He caressed her handwriting, imagining her penning these positive, loving letters in the days before his departure.

"Gabe!" Matthew said as he opened Gabriel's door. "Good God, man, are you reading her letters again?" At Gabriel's silence, Matthew sighed with frustration. "I say we wash up and then explore this town."

"I say any exploration can wait for tomorrow."

"You have no idea what you'll have here until you've experienced some of this city."

Gabriel smiled at his friend's optimism. "Let me wash up, and then we'll see what we find."

After a quick bath in a bathing room down the hall and a change into fresh clothes, Gabriel wandered downstairs to wait for Matthew. His boot heels sounded on the polished wooden floors as he peered into the doors off the lobby. One led to private living quarters for the owner, while another led to the saloon and restaurant. Late afternoon sunlight streamed into the tall front windows, limning the bare brick walls. A large oak desk greeted guests at the main double-door entrance.

Gabriel moved toward the unlit fireplace to sit in a wingback chair but paused as he saw Jedediah arriving.

"Hello, Jedediah," Gabriel said as Jed entered with a short brown-haired, brown-eyed man who wore a light-gray, faded three-piece suit. A tarnished pocket watch chain dangled from his waistcoat pocket.

"Gabriel, just the young man I was looking for. I found him searching for a friend who had arrived on the westbound train," Jedediah said, his right cheek protruding like a beaver's. He turned to look for a spittoon and grimaced when he saw none in sight.

"Are you Ronan O'Bara?" Gabriel asked the stocky man with a thick beard.

"The one and only. I'm looking for Matthew Donovan."

"You're in the right place." Gabriel nodded to Jedediah as he left.

"Ronan!" Matthew said as he came down the stairs. "It's good to see you. How are you?"

"Better now that I've found you. I was working and couldn't meet your train when it arrived. How was your journey?" he asked as he and Matthew shook hands and clapped each other on the shoulders.

"Long," Gabriel answered.

"How are things here in Butte, Ronan?" Matthew asked.

"Better than in other mining towns. The work is steady, and the pay is good," Ronan said. His deep brown eyes studied Gabriel.

"Ronan, this is Gabriel McLeod, a friend I made in Chicago."

"It's nice to meet you, Gabriel," Ronan said. He motioned for them to leave the hotel.

"Is it always this light so late?" Gabriel asked.

"Enjoy these days now while you can. Winter can seem endless. And whatever light you have now will be darkness come January," Ronan said. He glanced back at the hotel. "How long are you staying here?"

"We did not commit to any length of time," Gabriel said.

"Good. I have a place for you up at the Mullin House in Centerville, Matthew," Ronan said.

"What about Gabriel?" Matthew asked.

"I didn't know about him, but I can see if there is a room available. It's full of miners. Most of us work at the Mountain Con." Ronan paused for a moment as he studied Gabriel. "Mountain Consolidated Mine. Do you need a job too?"

"No. No, I am a cabinetmaker. I will look for other work."

"You shouldn't have any difficulty. Butte is booming with construction projects. And, if you have skills, you'll be wanted," Ronan said with a smile.

"That is good to hear," Gabriel said trying not to pant from the thin mountain air as they slowly climbed Main Street toward Uptown. The main thoroughfare of Butte was lined with brick buildings. Painted signs on the sides of the businesses proclaimed the benefits of shopping at this grocer or sipping that brewer's beer. As they crossed Galena Street, the air became redolent with the smell of fried noodles.

"Is there a Chinatown in Butte?" Gabriel asked.

"You bet," said Ronan. "It's the place to get your clothes laundered cheap."

"I never would have thought they'd be here, so far away from civilization," Gabriel said as they continued their walk up the hill into the central business district.

"Well, they're good businessmen, and this is a great place to make money. Even if you're not into mining," Ronan said with a smile. "And this *is* civilization, Montana style. High in the mountains."

Gabriel nodded, gasping a little as they made toward their destination. As an electric streetcar roared past them, he glared at Ronan. "Any reason we aren't in a streetcar?" Gabriel paused to look around the valley below him and then glance up the steep street.

Ronan eyed him. "You should accustom yourself to the altitude. It's a bit different when you're a mile high, isn't it?" He grinned at them. "Besides, I like being outside."

"Even though you can't see the mountains, and it stinks like rotten eggs?" Gabriel asked.

"The smell means the mines are running well," Ronan said. "And we just have to hope a good breeze comes along to push it out. The air's been a bit still the past few days."

"What else is there in Butte besides mining?" Matthew asked.

Ronan laughed. "Butte *is* mining, and hopefully the veins never run dry. And if the miners are happy and well paid, then the rest of the town prospers."

Gabriel grunted his understanding as they continued their climb.

"Where're we headed, Ronan?" Matthew asked.

"Let's go to the Curtis Music Hall for some songs and dancing. If we become bored, we can always go to one of the nearby saloons."

"What time does it close?" Gabriel asked.

"Nothing closes in this town, Gabriel," Ronan said. "You'll learn that after a while. Especially a bar."

"You mean I could wander in at five in the morning?" Gabriel asked and shook his head in disbelief at Ronan's nod.

"Yes, and get a pint with your eggs," Ronan said with a grin.

"This is my kind of town!" Matthew exclaimed as they entered the roaring crowd at the music hall.

***

WITHIN A WEEK, Gabriel knew his way about town. He wandered out of the Mullin House. He looked along Main Street in Centerville for a few moments and decided to walk up the hill toward Walkerville rather than take a streetcar. As he acclimated to the thin mountain air, he passed the whitewashed St. Lawrence O'Toole Catholic Church. He crested the hill and glanced down to the small hamlet of Walkerville, a thriving independent town bustling with saloons, boardinghouses, grocers and mines.

He turned away from Walkerville to study Butte below him. A gusty breeze blew the pervasive soot and smoke from the valley allowing him a good view of the city. His perusal took in numerous smokestacks and mine head frames on the hill, sprouting out of the earth like quills on a porcupine. The bare hills were no match for the wind and small dust funnels which formed in places.

He looked toward the left and saw the seven distinctive smokestacks of the Anaconda Company's Neversweat Mine pumping ash into the sky. It was one of the 400 mines in Butte employing over 13,000 men. Gabriel shook his head in wonder at the number of men burrowing underground as he stood enjoying the sunny day.

His glance continued from the barren backbone of Butte toward the Uptown area and its imposing brick buildings. He marveled that the fine buildings sat juxtaposed to the city's slum known as the Cabbage Patch and were separated by a mere block or two from the red light district. The steam from a train's engine caught his eye as it slowly made its way down the mountain pass toward Butte, and he imagined the emotions the travelers felt upon their first view of the city. The overwhelming palette was somber. Gray and black soot spilled from tall smokestacks. Brown tailings surrounded the buildings and mines. Gabriel squinted in an attempt to see the distant valley, but thick clouds of pollution obscured it.

"What an amazing city," Gabriel murmured.

He began the long walk down Main Street toward the Uptown part of Butte, passing the church and his boardinghouse. Although he could have eaten at any number of saloons and cafés in or near Centerville, Gabriel wanted to eat lunch at a restaurant Ronan had mentioned recently. He continued his descent into Uptown Butte, walking past the Miner's Union Hall and crossed Granite Street. The Hennessy Building filled half a city block, its red brick gleaming in the sunlight. A never-ending stream of customers entered and exited its large mahogany doors. After crossing Broadway and foregoing the bustling M&M saloon, he turned right onto Park Street.

As he made his way down the street, he searched for the café. "Excuse me, is this the Chequamegon Café?" he asked a man exiting a single-storied, whitewashed brick building near the Curtis Music Hall. Large front windows faced the street, and the door stood propped open in the warm late summer air, obscuring the name written on it.

"The Chew Quick and Be Gone Again?" the man asked with a smile. "Yes, this be the place. I'd get in and find a seat while you've a chance."

Gabriel nodded his thanks and entered. Four rows of tables for two filled the crowded restaurant. Some of the tables were crammed together for larger parties, causing serpentine aisles throughout. Along the right wall a large mirror reflected the room and the light from the windows overlooking the street. Overhead a tin ceiling gleamed.

He found a small table with a crisp white tablecloth to one side near a window, ordered a meal of fried chicken and potatoes, and watched the patrons come and go.

"You new here?" asked the man sitting next to Gabriel.

"Yes, sir."

"Well, enjoy the food. It's good and plentiful. It's why the copper kings come here to eat when they've a chance. Though none are here today."

Gabriel nodded. "What do you do, sir?"

"I'm in construction, currently working on a building on Main Street."

"Would you know of anyone hiring finish carpenters or cabinetmakers?"

"I'll be hiring in a few months, but if you want something now, I'd go to the Thornton Block, down Broadway near the McDermott. Ask for Jeffers. If you've the skills, he'll be eager to hire you. Can't seem to keep able-bodied men healthy on his site."

"I don't know as that is a recommendation," Gabriel said.

"His workers keep injuring themselves in bar brawls."

"I thank you for the advice," Gabriel said as the other man paid for his meal and prepared to leave.

"Tell Jeffers that Cassidy sent you."

"I'm obliged," Gabriel said with a nod.

"Welcome to Butte, young man."

***

"HEY, MATTHEW!" Gabriel called out at the Never Dry Saloon on Main Street in Centerville just down from the boardinghouse. The din from conversations among off-duty miners almost eclipsed the sweet music from the fiddle player tooling away in the corner. He was taking requests but only agreed to play songs that he liked. Some patrons tapped their feet on the plank wooden floors.

The tables were three-quarters full, and two bartenders were busy with the patrons crowded along the long oak bar. The majority of the area behind the bar held casks of gin and whiskey stacked nearly to the ceiling. One small area was framed by intricately carved mahogany columns.

Gabriel set aside the paper after reading about two miners who had been blown up past recognition in one of the mines. He shivered as he recalled the frank description of the bits of red-and-blue cloth and body parts found at the scene.

"Hi, Gabe. Didn't see you there," Matthew said.

"You look like hell."

"Oh, I'm fine, don't worry about me," Matthew said, his hand shaking so hard beer spilled from his glass as he attempted to take a sip. He quickly wiped away the beer, then swiped at beads of sweat from his forehead. His black hair was rumpled, and, in his agitation, he continually ran his fingers through it. He seemed to have lost weight, his lanky frame now bordering on wiry.

"Matthew, what happened?" Gabriel demanded.

"I had my first underground shift at the Mountain Consolidated Mine today, Gabe," Matthew murmured. "By God, I tell you, when I stepped onto that cage and realized seven other miners were to be crammed in there with me, I almost begged to get off. Before I had the courage to speak up, the cage jolted into motion, and we were belowground. Then I realized it would be twelve hours until I could get out of there."

Gabriel quelled a shudder at the thought.

"I knew the ride only lasted a few minutes, but it felt an eternity. The man across from me hadn't bathed in days and had eaten onions recently. When I finally arrived at my level, I soon understood why the seasoned miners laughed as I got off. My level is known as purgatory, 'cause it's so hot that we must be at risk of going to hell. And the smells were worse than I could have imagined. You think it stinks aboveground?" Matthew shook his head from side to side. "The stench from the mules, the men not using the piss pots, and all of us crowded together in so tight a place for hours on end. You have no idea what it's like.

"The light from the candle on my hat did little to illuminate my way, and I stumbled into the wall. I could barely see where my partner wanted me to drill. Somehow I got through the twelve hours, my partner ensuring I didn't get blown up. But, I tell you, Gabe, I've never been more afraid than when we were told to go back to dig out the blown-up ore when we hadn't heard all the charges go off. I thought for sure I was going to be the one to pick at the pile with the unexploded dynamite. Instead, Tim Daly did."

Gabriel listened, understanding Matthew's need to talk.

"Oh, Christ, Gabe. The blood. His screams. And it took forever to get the cage to our level. By the time he left, he was comatose. They don't think he'll make it."

"Jesus," Gabriel muttered.

"Oh, God, I don't want to go back down again," Matthew murmured, pinching the bridge of his nose and closing his eyes in despair.

"Then don't," Gabriel said.

"This is what I do, Gabe," Matthew said. "Or what I want to be. A hard-rock miner. I—"

"Hey, Matthew, great job today," Ronan said as he slapped Matthew on the shoulder and raised his pint to him. "Thought we might lose you as the cage started down, but you did well enough."

"It was fine," Matthew said with false bravado.

"I hope Liam treated you well," Ronan said.

Matthew snorted. "He's a surly bastard, and I can't imagine why you'd think he'd be a good partner for me."

"Well, I don't know what else you'd expect. He just buried his best friend last week, and, instead of getting a seasoned miner, he's saddled with you. Don't worry. I'm sure you'll earn his respect soon enough," Ronan said. "You're lucky to be working with him. He has a lot of experience and will teach you what you need to know. Keep your mouth shut and listen, mind."

Matthew nodded.

"How are things for you, Ronan?" Gabriel asked.

"Fine enough. I'm working on a good drift, so that helps the day go by."

"A drift?"

"It's like a side channel from the mine shaft, goes off to one side. You carve them out, looking for the vein," Ronan explained.

"Don't you worry about rocks falling on your heads?"

"A duggan," Matthew murmured.

"A what?" Gabriel asked with a shake of his head.

"Makes you wish you were one of us so you knew what we were talking about, doesn't it?" Ronan said with a laugh. "A duggan's what we call a piece of rock that falls on you, and then we have to call Duggan, the undertaker. Only bad things come from falling rock."

Gabriel shook his head again at the morbid humor.

"Where is this Liam?" Gabriel asked.

"He's off with his wife and son. He likes to spend as much of his free time with his family as he can, though he does come to the pub for a pint once in a while," Ronan said.

Gabriel glanced at Matthew, who continued to look into his drink, as though searching for comfort, and then at Ronan with exasperation. Gabriel cocked his head toward Ronan and pointed his chin toward Matthew.

"He'll be fine," Ronan murmured. "Happens to all of us the first few times down. And I heard what happened to Tim. Bound to shake anyone up." Ronan cleared his throat, speaking loudly. "How are you, Gabe?"

"Well enough. I have a lead on steady work that I'll be looking into tomorrow."

"Good for you," Ronan said. "Think of us while you enjoy the daylight every day," he murmured with another lift of his pint. Gabriel raised his in salute, wishing his friends could find another way to earn a living.

"Any word from your lady, Gabe?" Matthew asked, emerging from his stupor.

"No, nothing."

"Well, I am sure a letter will arrive any day now. We've only been here a little over a week. Can't imagine letters traveling so fast," Matthew said.

"I'd keep writing her, Gabe," Ronan said. "She's one beautiful-looking woman from that photo in your room. One of us should have a chance with a woman such as her." He winked at Matthew.

"Her beauty is the least amazing aspect of her. She is intelligent, kind…" He broke off as Ronan and Matthew rolled their eyes and waved their arms about as though conducting music. "If you, *when* you, meet her, you'll understand," he said laughing at their antics. He gave Matthew a nudge in his shoulder, enjoying Matthew's return to good humor.

"What do you think of Butte, Gabriel?" Ronan asked as he looked around the bar full of miners, tapping his fingers absentmindedly to the fiddle player's music.

"I still think it is the ugliest place I have ever seen. How can people survive in a city with no trees?" Gabriel asked as Ronan shrugged. "And yet, as I walk the city streets, I realize how extraordinary it is. I never thought to see blocks filled with brick buildings, theaters, banks and stores in a city so far from anywhere. And the streetcars. I can't believe there are electric street-cars here! Or that you made us climb the hill the day we arrived."

Ronan laughed and slapped Gabriel's back.

"Have either of you been into Hennessy's?" Gabriel asked.

Ronan and Matthew shook their heads.

"It's a beautiful brick building on the corner of Main and Granite with prism glass that causes the sunlight from outside to sparkle and spread inside the first floor. It's so fancy that I didn't know if they'd let me in, but I went in anyway. As I entered, I realized it's a store that sells anything you could imagine wanting. And things you didn't even know you wanted or needed. They have a Moorish room that made me imagine what a sultan's room would look like from when I read *The Arabian Nights*. And the woodwork is extraordinary. The staircase and the displays…" He shook his head in wonder. "It rivals anything I saw in Boston."

"So are you saying that you are beginning to like it here?" Ronan asked with a hint of a smile.

"Yes," Gabriel admitted.

"Have you been to a Finnish steam room yet?" Ronan asked as he scratched his thick beard. He leaned back in his chair, stretching his short legs in front of him and crossing his feet at the ankles.

"No, though I haven't been working so I've no real need of one."

"It's almost worth living in Finntown just to be able to board at a place where you could get good food and a steam in the price of boarding," Ronan said. He closed his sherry-colored eyes as though imagining the relaxing heat from the steam rooms.

"But it would be too far from the mine," Matthew argued.

"Yes, it would, especially in the winter. I'd hate to have to walk any farther in the cold than is necessary," Ronan said, opening his eyes again. "As for you, Gabriel, you might look for another place to board that's not so full of miners, and where you can have your own room."

"I don't mind sharing with Matthew," Gabriel said. "I'm used to sharing space with my brother."

"Well, when that lovely lady of yours comes here, that will have to change," Matthew said.

"Yes, when she joins me, all will be different," Gabriel murmured attempting to envision Clarissa living in Butte.

CHAPTER 3

GABRIEL ENTERED THE DOORWAY to the imposing five-story red-bricked building with black wrought-iron balconies that stood diagonally across the street from the McDermott Hotel on Broadway. Hammering, sawing and a good deal of swearing were heard as he walked into the main floor work space. Rough wooden planks covered the floors and clusters of workbenches and carpenters were scattered around the room. Frames for smaller rooms were slowly being raised or created, breaking up the cavernous space. Gabriel asked for the foreman and then scanned the room, searching for him.

"Excuse me," Gabriel said as he stopped next to the man. The foreman turned toward Gabriel with inquisitive, piercing blue eyes. His rail-thin frame seemed barely strong enough to allow him to stand, and yet he met Gabriel's look with frank interest.

Gabriel doffed his hat and stood tall as he met the foreman's eyes. "Hello, sir. My name is Gabriel McLeod, and I am looking for work. A Mr. Cassidy told me that you are the man I should speak with."

"You don't sound like an immigrant," he drawled. "Are you one of them Irish? No, your last name don't sound right."

"Of Irish heritage, but from Boston."

"Hmm ... wonder what you're running from out there," he said as he spat a wad of chewing tobacco into a nearby spittoon.

Gabriel raised his eyebrows in surprise at the man's perfect aim. "Nothing, sir. I just dream of a better life. I heard you had work here."

"Well, there's plenty of work for those who want it. But I bet there's more to your story than you're lettin' on. Bet you got in a bar brawl and are in trouble with the law."

"That might be someone else's tale, but not mine."

"Don't tell me you're one of those temperance folks? I can't be working with one of them."

"No, sir, I like a pint after a hard day's work."

"Hmm ... well that's good. That's proper."

"Sir, about this work—"

"You need to be a carpenter. If you want the higher paying work, you should be able to do the finish work. I already have a few who are quite skilled in that but wouldn't mind a few more to help complete the project on time. Harmless, Hapless Harvey has left us for a spell after breakin' his hand." He paused, shaking his head. "Stupid idiot. Getting in a bar brawl about politics. If you're going to fight, might as well fight over something worthwhile, like a woman."

Gabriel nodded. "I am a cabinetmaker. I can do whatever finish work you need."

"La-di-da, a cabinetmaker," he said with a long, high-pitched whistle. "And can you prove this claim?"

"My work will prove what I say."

"My name's Jeffers. Just Jeffers, no *mister*. I come from the South, so some think I'm a bit dim 'cause I talk slow, and I like my bourbon and beer. I wouldn't make that mistake if I was you."

"Of course not, sir."

"Never thought I'd hire a Yank from Boston, but I guess that sort of thing don't matter so much here in Butte," Jeffers said with a long intense glance. "I'll show you 'round."

They approached a small group of men who were reviewing plans.

"Morgan, Niall and Larry, this is Gabriel. He'll be working with you." Jeffers glared at all three before he spun on his heel and moved to another area.

"I'm Larry," one of the men said, his russet-colored hair and brown eyes inquisitive as he studied the newcomer.

A man with a commanding presence and dull blond hair turned toward Gabriel. His faded light-blue work shirt strained at the shoulders, emphasizing their breadth and strength. "How'd you talk him into giving you a job? He's miserly as hell and would rather work us to death than hire anyone new."

"I'm not sure. I just asked for a job."

"How do we know he'll be able to do the work? Just shows up with no proof he can actually do anything. We can survive until Harvey comes back," hissed the third man with raven-black hair and green cat-colored eyes. He was nearly as tall as Gabriel although lankier. He prowled around Gabriel as though examining him for any defect.

"Niall, we should at least give him a chance," Larry said.

"Where are you from?" Niall demanded. He stood in front of Gabriel, almost eye to eye.

"Boston."

"Boston! Listen to the likes of that, lads. We have a rarefied one from Boston," Larry said trying to mimic what he imagined to be a Bostonian accent.

Gabriel smiled as he murmured to Larry, "Too many Rs," before he turned away from Niall and included Morgan in the conversation. "Listen, I don't want any trouble. I'd just like some work. And I am skilled. I think I will be an asset to this project."

"You are a true cabinetmaker?" Larry asked. At Gabriel's nod, he asked, "Why work here with us? Why not on your own?"

"I was told there was a lot of work to be done, and I didn't want to have to search for work or clients over the winter," Gabriel said, answering part of the question.

"Smart man," Morgan said with a small smile and a nod to Niall. "My friends call me Mete-It-Out Morgan."

"Why the nicknames?" Gabriel asked.

"Everyone has a nickname of sorts here. You'll have one after a while," Larry said. "Even if you don't earn it."

"Don't believe him," Niall said. "He's earned his ten times over. He's Loose-Lipped Larry," he said in a lilting Irish accent with a tap on his nose. He reached out his hand to shake Gabriel's. "I'm Never-Enough Niall."

Gabriel shook his and the others' hands feeling like he had passed a secret test. "What exactly are we building?"

***

THAT EVENING GABRIEL LAY on the cotlike bed in the room he shared with Matthew, thinking about the day. Trying not to think about Clarissa and the fact that there had been no letter again from her. He had written every day for the past two weeks, and her continued silence worried him. As he lay on the narrow bed in the cramped room staring at the ceiling, all he saw was Clarissa. Her beautiful, expressive blue eyes, her chestnut-brown hair falling out of its pins. Her exuberance as she spoke about her day. An insistent ache settled in a small corner of his heart. In the beginning the letters she had hidden in his trunks with his brother Richard's help had aided in soothing the pain of their parting, but now he needed news of her.

The pounding on his door snapped him from his reverie. He rose from the bed and in one stride opened the door. "Larry, nice to see you. I didn't know you boarded here."

"I don't, but I learned that you do and wanted to invite you down to the pub with the rest of us."

"Thanks," Gabriel said as he turned to reach for his jacket. It hung on a peg to the side of the door, at the foot of his bed. His bed lay along the same wall as the door, while Matthew's was separated from his by a small table. A shared bureau stood at the foot of Matthew's bed. A miniscule window over the bureau let in a faint light.

When Gabriel turned back to leave, he found Larry peering around his room, studying everything he could see. "Who's the fancy piece?" Larry asked, his gaze focused on the only adornment in Gabriel's part of the Spartan rented rooms. It was a picture of Clarissa propped up on his side of the nightstand, taken in all her finery at Savannah's wedding. She looked the part of a haughty and unapproachable society woman, a woman who would never notice him, unless someone looked closely at her eyes. He saw a hint of the vivacious woman he loved in those eyes.

"A friend from home," Gabriel said.

"Seems a bit above the likes of you," Larry said with a good-natured snort.

Gabriel grunted his agreement, not wishing to test the accuracy of Larry's nickname. "Let's go," Gabriel said, pushing him out of the room.

They headed down the hill toward the Uptown section of Butte. "Why in God's name do you live in Centerville?" Larry asked.

"I made a friend on the train, and he lives up here because he works in one of the mines. And it's cheap."

"Well, that's one way of looking at it. You should think of moving to Dublin Gulch. That's where we all live."

"Why would I want to live in a gulch rather than at the top of a hill? I like the view."

"As if you can see the mountains or the valley below through the smoke. Besides, it's where the Irish live without having to put up with the Cornish. You'd feel at home, I would think," Larry said with a raised eyebrow. "Think about it, Gabriel."

Gabriel shrugged his shoulders by way of response.

"We decided to meet at a bar nearer to you rather than our local," Larry said as they entered the Owsley Bar, pushing into the crowd. Announcements for the latest vaudeville shows were tacked in a haphazard display behind the barman. Off-duty miners made up the majority of the men who stood jammed along the long mahogany bar, sipping pints. Tables sat to the side and back of the room, spittoons scattered about and in frequent use. Mirrors on the back wall reflected light, making the room seem brighter and longer. After Larry and he collected their drinks, they made their way to a small side table where Morgan and Niall sat with pints in front of them.

"What do you think of the work, Gabriel?" Morgan asked after Gabriel took a sip of his drink.

"It seems an ambitious project, although I don't know how Jeffers thinks it'll be completed in time without more carpenters."

"As you aren't the foreman, I don't see how your opinion holds much sway," Niall said with a frown.

"I know if you want quality, you don't attain it by hoping rough carpentry can take the place of finish work."

"Who are you to imply...?" Niall began with flashing green eyes but was cut off by a severe look from Morgan.

"Whatever you might think, we are finish cabinetmakers," Morgan said as he nodded to the three of them around the table.

"But the others aren't," Gabriel argued. "Four of us will be unable to complete all of the fine carving and finish work by May."

Morgan sighed. "I fear you are correct. If Harvey hadn't been so high-strung as to get in a bar brawl..."

"What was it over?" Gabriel asked.

"Politics," Niall said. "The *eejit* doesn't know to keep his mouth shut. Why in God's name go into a bar in Butte promotin' McKinley? We're all W. J. Bryan men."

Gabriel suppressed an amused grin. "Is that a requirement for me to work with you?"

"No, though don't go talking to us about it if you aren't. I can't stand another four more bloody years with that man," Niall said with a long sigh. "Promotin' the likes of Amalgamated and big business over the common man."

"Did you see what they did in Pennsylvania?" Morgan asked as he flicked a copy of the day's newspaper, *The Anaconda Standard*, onto the table.

Gabriel read the headline proclaiming the strike of ninety thousand coal miners in rural Pennsylvania. "That's a lot of men! How long do they expect the strike to last?"

"No one knows. But it'll be winter soon, and more expensive coal is not something that any of us needs," Larry said.

"Though we should support them," Niall argued as he leaned toward Gabriel to read the article. "Who would've thought that many men could organize?"

Morgan nodded. "Makes you wonder, doesn't it?"

Gabriel lowered his voice to barely above a whisper. "Would the miners here strike?"

"Who's to say? But they make a good wage. Much better than most." Morgan picked up the paper and folded it on top of the table. "What I hope is that actions like this will help Bryan. Show the American people that the likes of McKinley and his 'full dinner pail'—"

"What a bunch of malarkey," Niall muttered.

"—is nothing more than a slogan. That the majority of Americans aren't any better off than before, and his support of the trusts is only hurting the common man."

"Some would argue McKinley and his policies have led to economic stability," Gabriel argued. "Folks aren't making runs on the banks like they were back in the mid '90s."

"Are you saying you support the man?" Niall demanded.

"No, I've no love for the man who's sent my brother to the Philippines. Nor for the man he's chosen to run with."

Larry snickered. "There are many who like Teddy Roosevelt and his expansionist views." He, Morgan and Niall watched Gabriel's reaction closely.

Gabriel merely studied them.

"What brings you here from Boston, Gabriel?" asked Larry.

"A change in circumstance," Gabriel said.

"I wonder if it has anything to do with the photo of that fancy piece in your room?" Larry mused.

Gabriel took another sip of beer. "I have always wanted adventure, and Butte seemed the perfect place."

"Don't worry, I'll get the story out of you one way or the other," Larry said with a laugh.

"Are you ever serious?" Niall demanded. "Here we were, about to start a good discussion on politics, and all you can think about is some photo of a pretty girl you saw in his room."

Larry shrugged his shoulders.

Niall shook his head in disgust but not before Gabriel saw his lips quirk with a smile.

"Well, it's a damn sight more interesting than listening to you yammer on night after night about the same thing," Larry said as he took a swig of his ale.

"McLeod. McLeod. Hmm..." Niall said. "You claim you're Irish, but your last name doesn't sound Irish to me. It sounds more Scotch-Irish. Protestant. Like Clark."

"Clark? The Copper King, W. A. Clark?"

"Yes. He's running for US Senate again. Although if our Marcus Daly has his way, he'll never make it to Washington," Larry said.

"Marcus Daly. The Irish Copper King?"

"Yes. He owns the Anaconda Copper Company. Well, now it's the Amalgamated. But we all think of it as Anaconda," Niall said. "So, are you Irish or not?"

"Well, my da always said he came from Ireland, and I believed him."

"Why would anyone claim to be from there when they're not?" Larry asked, earning him a kick in the shins from Niall.

"Why don't you write your da and ask him to clarify?" Niall asked.

"Seeing as he's been dead fifteen years, that might prove difficult."

"Leave off, Niall," Larry said. "If he says he's Irish, then he's Irish. Just not off the boat like you."

"Are you at least Catholic?" Niall asked.

Gabriel paused to study Niall, suddenly thankful that he had allowed

Matthew to badger him into attending Mass since his arrival. "Yes," Gabriel said.

"You don't seem too sure on that."

"Well, I haven't gone to church regularly until recently."

"Which church do you go to?"

Gabriel watched the threesome, unease filling him as they continued to pepper him with personal questions. "St. Lawrence O'Toole."

"Ah, that's a lovely church. Built by the miners own money, mind," Niall said.

"Gabe!"

He looked up to see Matthew approaching them. "Matthew, I am surprised to see you here."

"Well, I thought I'd get out, see a bit more of Butte. And tomorrow's my day off, so I don't have to worry about an early start." He looked around the table at Gabriel's acquaintances, smiling in a friendly manner, waiting for an introduction. He stumbled as another saloon patron jostled him on his way to the bar. The man weaved for a moment, slapped Matthew on the back by way of apology and continued on his way.

"Matthew Donovan, this is Niall O'Donnell, Larry Ferguson and Morgan O'Malley."

Niall nodded, his green eyes serious, while Larry smiled and Morgan raised his pint to Matthew.

All three studied Matthew as Gabriel continued to speak. "I began working with them today at the Thornton Block."

"That's great, Gabe," Matthew said with a wide smile. "Do you mind if I steal you away for a few moments? I want to introduce you to my mining partner."

Gabe nodded to the three men as he rose to follow Matthew, carrying his pint with him. When the rowdy crowd had engulfed them, Gabriel murmured, "Is there really someone for me to meet?"

Matthew said with a knowing nod, "There is, though it seemed like you weren't too eager to stay in their company."

"They're a bit too curious about me."

"Well, most people here are interested in newcomers, Gabe. You have to accustom yourself to answering a few questions."

"I don't like having to work in a group," Gabriel muttered.

"You'll find that you'll do a lot better in Butte if you become more social and community focused, Gabe."

"How do you know this already? We arrived on the same train."

"Well, you don't have to go down a mine shaft each day and depend on others to come out again," Matthew said. "If you did, you'd learn about your dependence on others." He reached out to slap a burly auburn-haired man on his shoulders. "Here's the man I wanted you to meet."

Gabriel nodded as the short, stocky man turned toward him. Bushy eyebrows framed hazel eyes, and a thick walrus mustache tickled his nose. "Aye, Matthew?" he said in a thick Irish brogue.

"Liam Egan," Matthew said, "this is my good friend, Gabriel McLeod. He's from Boston."

"But he's not a miner," Liam said.

"No, I'm no miner," Gabriel said. "I am not that brave." He gave a salute with his pint.

"So what do you do in this town as a newcomer then?" Liam asked.

"I'm a cabinetmaker, and I just found work today that should keep me busy throughout the winter," Gabriel said.

"Ah, you have a trade then. One of the lucky ones," Liam said.

Gabriel laughed. "I have a trade until the machines take it over for me."

"Ah, the bloody machines," Liam said with a shake of his head. "I'm just thankful that the mines still require men. But a day will come when the machines'll take over there too."

"Not while we're alive!" Matthew said.

"No, it probably won't affect us. But someday, lad, you'll see," Liam said. "Now, Mr. McLeod, are you married? Did you leave family behind before you came out here?"

"No. No to either question."

"Ah, that's too bad then. I'll have to have you over to meet my Amelia and little man," he said with a soft smile at his wife's name.

"How did you meet her, Liam?" Gabriel asked.

"Ah, 'tis a grand story. And deserves telling more than the one time." He gave a quick wink to Matthew. "We met when I was in Leadville. That's in Colorado, in case you didn't know. Another mining town, way up in the mountains. We should never have met. Me, a rough Irish miner, and her, an educated woman. She was the teacher, mind. But, I can only be thankful she's not sensible and decided to marry me anyway," he said with a grin.

"How long have you been in Butte?" Gabriel asked trying not to think of Clarissa and the parallels in his own romance with her.

"We decided to come up about a year ago. I had a good friend here, Jimmy McManus, God rest 'im, who recommended me to one of the bosses at the Mountain Con. We were both members of the AOH, and, with that recommendation, it was easier to find a job. I wanted to have steady work to support my Amelia, and there seemed more consistent work here than in Leadville. And the pay's good."

"The AOH?"

"The Ancient Order of Hibernians. A grand group of lads."

"Does your wife like it here?" Gabriel asked.

"A mining camp's a mining camp, though this is one hell of a town. Wouldn't you agree?"

Gabriel and Matthew nodded.

"Though I think she likes it. She's got no family so she left no one behind. She misses teaching, but, of course since marrying me, that is closed to her now." He laughed. "If you asked her, all she'd talk about would be the smells and the smoke and the constant soot and dirt."

"Gabe, you have family in Boston. And a sweetheart," Matthew said.

Gabriel glared at Matthew for bringing up the topic. "I have brothers, yes. And I did leave … someone special behind in Boston."

"So you're not alone in the world? That's grand. What does your sweetheart do?" Liam asked. He took a sip of his pint and then wiped at his long mustache as he watched Gabriel.

"She's a schoolteacher."

Liam smiled. "Ah, well, I hope she finds her way out here to you."

"As do I."

"Now we have to find someone for young Matthew here," Liam said with a slap on his back. "You need to settle, find yourself a good woman and have yourself some babies."

"You know that's not likely here, Liam," Matthew protested.

"There's a dance coming up at the Hall. Sure we'll be able to find you someone there," he said. "We just need to find you a woman who's not set on an aboveground man. Some women are becoming set against marrying a miner. I'll talk to my Amelia about it. See what she thinks. In fact why don't you come by the house now?"

"Oh, I wouldn't want to impose." Gabriel said.

"Sure, 'tis no imposition when you've been invited. No, Amelia loves company. And she hates it when I spend too long at the pub. Time to be gettin' home anyway," he said, swallowing the rest of his pint in one big gulp and signaling for them to join him.

Gabriel glanced toward Morgan, Larry and Niall, waving his departure with Matthew and Liam. He followed them into the crisp night air, shuddering at the sudden drop in temperature.

"Winter's on her way, and it'll be a beast," Liam said.

"It can't be worse than what I lived through in Ohio," Matthew said.

"You might have known snow there, but you'll never have known a cold that goes to your bones and doesn't leave you for months like you do here," Liam said. "I'd buy some new clothes if I were you."

They began the slow walk up Main Street toward Centerville. "Why don't we take the streetcar?" Gabriel asked. The streetlights at the intersection of each street flickered on providing faint illumination. Men wandered in and out of bars, cafés and boardinghouses as they continued up the hill. Thick clouds along with the normal soot and smoke prevented any stargazing.

"It's good exercise, and I spend enough of my time unable to see the sky," Liam said. "Matthew, that brick building over there is our Miner's Union Hall. I'm sure you'll spend some time inside. Our next meeting is in a few days." Liam nodded to a brick building with floor-to-ceiling windows on the first floor and long arched windows on the second.

"I'll be there, Liam," Matthew said.

Upon their arrival in Centerville, they turned down La Platte Street toward a row of identical one-story stuccoed homes with small front porches.

"Here we are, then," Liam said at number six. "Amelia, I've brought some friends home to meet you," he called out as the door swung open.

A loud child's cry rent the air followed by a soft cooing noise.

"Nicholas, you mind your mum!" Liam said as he entered the small hallway.

A small naked boy ran toward Liam on short, chubby legs hurling himself against Liam's calves.

"Nicholas!" a woman's breathless voice called out from the kitchen area. She stood in its doorway at the edge of the dining area, exasperation evident in her expression. "You will have your bath," she said severely. She marched over to Liam, plucked little Nicholas away from Liam's ankles and carried him, kicking and screaming, back toward a tub in the kitchen.

"If this is a bad time," Gabriel began.

"No, for Pete's sake, stay. It'll calm her to have to entertain," Liam said. "That's Amelia," he said with a quick wave to the woman making a hasty retreat.

"Are you sure about that?" Gabriel asked as he watched large droplets of water flying freely from the vicinity of the kitchen.

"Give me a moment. I'm just going to give her a hand and put the kettle on," Liam said. He left them in the living room. "Nicholas Patrick Egan, if you don't start behavin'..." Liam began.

"Hush, love," Amelia murmured. A few whimpers and then the sound of Nicholas being lifted out of the water to be dried. "Now it's time for bed, little man, and no tomfoolery, as your da would say." She emerged with his swaddled form and carried him to a small room off the dining room.

Liam returned to find Gabriel and Matthew studying the small living room, trying not to focus too much on the goings-on in the next room. Filled with mismatched furniture, the living room had two upholstered chairs and a settee with one leg made out of a pile of books. A rocking chair sat in the far corner next to a reading lamp set on an overflowing bookshelf. Fading wallpaper adorned the walls, its once-white background now resembling weak tea with the rose-colored flowers faded to puce. A small throw rug lay between the chairs and settee.

"Please, you are very welcome," he said, pointing to the living room. He sat in one of the upholstered chairs covered in threadbare red velvet with half its stuffing missing. "Ah, domestic bliss. Sure'n you don't want this?" he said with a broad smile.

Gabriel laughed. "It reminds me of my home when I was a young child." He sat in the rocking chair while Matthew sat in the other upholstered chair.

"Are you not married then?" Amelia asked as she reentered the room. "I'm Mrs. Egan."

Gabriel stood. "Ma'am, I'm Gabriel McLeod." He towered over her as she barely reached midchest.

"Matthew Donovan."

"Delighted. Tea will be ready soon," she said with an informal smile, settling her small frame on the arm of Liam's chair. "Mr. Donovan, are you my

Liam's new partner? It's lovely to meet you at last."

Matthew blushed and bobbed his head.

"And neither of you are married?" She pinned them with her almond-shaped hazel eyes. She brushed at her honey-blond hair, falling free after the exertions of Nicholas's bath.

"No, love, though Gabriel left a sweetheart in Boston," Liam supplied, reaching up to hold her hand.

"Boston. Well, then, we'll have to see about getting her out here. Not good for a big strapping man like you to be all alone," Amelia said. "But there's no one waiting for you at home, Mr. Donovan?"

"No, ma'am."

"The fall dance is coming up, isn't it, Liam?" At his quick nod, she continued. "We'll see about finding you a nice bride."

"Now I'm not so sure I am ready to settle down just yet," Matthew said with a note of panic in his voice.

"Isn't that what all men say, and then they find it's to their liking?" Amelia asked. She elbowed Liam in his shoulder, and he grunted his agreement. "'Tis true," she said with a pointed glance as the kettle squealed, and she rose to fill the teapot.

"Mr. McLeod, which mine do you work at?" she called out from the kitchen.

"I don't work at a mine, ma'am. I am a cabinetmaker, and I just began work at the Thornton Block today."

"Now that is something. But you chose to come to Butte? Even though you aren't a miner?"

"Matthew convinced me it was the place to be between San Francisco and Chicago," Gabriel said. "Though I had been planning on settling in San Francisco."

"And San Francisco might have been a more appealing city for your sweetheart. It's hard to convince women to come to Butte," Amelia said.

"I have begun to fear that," Gabriel said.

"The soot, the dirt. It's not all that attractive a place to look at."

"Amelia…" Liam said with a note of warning.

"You tell me, Liam Egan, if this is your version of paradise? It surely isn't mine." She turned back to address Gabriel and Matthew. "Though you won't find a better place for community and supportive neighbors."

"You have to admit, the gardens are a nice addition," Liam said.

"They are, and thankfully there is a streetcar that will take us to them."

Matthew and Gabriel shared a quick glance. "The gardens?" Matthew asked.

"Columbia Gardens. One of those copper barons, Clark, set up a park that is gloriously different from the rest of Butte. Green, with a creek rolling through it. It's wondrous. We like to go there when Liam has a day off and take Nicholas, so he can romp around in fresh air," Amelia said as she passed out cups of tea.

"We'll be headed there tomorrow, won't we, Amelia?" At her quick nod, Liam continued, "Why don't you come with us?"

"I would, but I must work," Gabriel said.

"I'd love to," Matthew said.

"Well, you'll have to come with us next time, Mr. McLeod. We try to go there as often as we can as the weather is changing. It will be winter again soon."

CHAPTER 4

I PAUSED OUTSIDE of Savannah's new home, momentarily taken aback by the imposing building. The four-storied redbrick home with black shutters and mansard roof—over twice as large as the neighboring homes—was situated on a corner lot on Marlborough Street in the Back Bay. The front garden bloomed with late season dahlias, their bright and varied colors a contrast to the austere red and black of the house. I approached the black walnut door, large enough for a horse to enter, and rapped the brass knocker. A circular window above the door allowed light to enter the two-storied entrance hall.

A distinguished butler in formal black and white welcomed me inside. I tripped as I stepped from marble to hardwood floors covered in plush red Turkish carpets. The butler gripped my arm, frowning his disapproval at me as I removed my coat. The front hall had a large coat rack, and a small table and mirror. On the table an iridescent turquoise vase held a large bouquet of ruby-red dahlias. I peered down a long hallway that led toward the back of the house but was escorted to one of the two doors that opened directly onto either side of the front hall. The ornately carved staircase had two landings leading to the upper floors.

"Savannah!" I exclaimed as I entered the formal living room, elated at seeing her for the first time since her wedding over three months ago. Savannah watched me as she approached at a sedate pace and held out her hands. I thought of our reunion last spring when she had flung her arms around me in a fierce hug and given a whoop of joy to see me. And that had been after a visit to Aunt Betsy's for a few short weeks, rather than a three-month separation.

I studied Savannah, upset to see that she held herself rigidly, as though she feared placing a foot out of place. Her strawberry-blond hair was tied back in an intricate chignon. Clothes from her trousseau hung on her, a clear indication she had lost more weight since her wedding. Most alarming was the cold, disinterested look in her eyes. I felt like she could have been interviewing a new maid for all of the enthusiasm she showed. I dropped my arms and clasped her hands, fighting tears at her welcome.

"This is quite a house, Sav," I murmured. "Very imposing."

"Yes, well it's what Jonas wanted," Savannah replied as she turned toward a seating area in the formal parlor. I stifled a groan to find Jonas awaiting our arrival. I had hoped to have time alone with Savannah after so many months.

"Hello, Jonas," I said with a small smile, determined to be outwardly friendly.

"Clarissa." He refrained from standing but gave a mere hint of a nod in my direction. He wore an impeccable slate-blue suit with matching waistcoat and pristine white shirt with stiffly starched collar and cuffs. Ruby cuff links matched a pin on his lapel. His short muddy-brown hair was parted to one side with an excess of pomade to keep it in place.

I studied the room as I sat in stiff formality on one of their new lady's chairs covered in cream-colored silk. The front wall consisted of bow-fronted windows with a comfortable-looking bench nestled next to the windows. I imagined myself curling up there in the sun to read on a lazy day. The fireplace with red and gray marble inlay was opposite the doorway. The far wall was not connected to the dining area, and along it there was a large portrait of some important ancestor from Jonas's family. The wood parquet floors gleamed, and the areas not covered by expensive Turkish carpets had a mosaic pattern of delicate rosewood.

The room was formally furnished, with pictures of faraway lands, thick ivory-colored wallpaper, plush blue velvet curtains, numerous chairs, tables and settees. There was even a grand piano in the far corner, under the ancestor's photograph, although I knew Savannah refused to play. Thankfully the curtains were pulled open, allowing sunlight to stream into the room and illuminate it.

"How was Paris?" I asked, more for a topic of conversation than out of true curiosity.

"Mr. Montgomery was correct of course," Savannah replied. "It was the perfect place to honeymoon. Such well-dressed, elegant people. I could never have imagined such refinement. And the new boulevards are glorious." She sighed in apparent contentment though her eyes remained detached.

I continued to search for the old Savannah but could not find her.

"Yes, I wanted Mrs. Montgomery to know how I envisioned our lives. Nothing but the absolute best for our branch of the family," Jonas intoned.

"Savannah…"

"Don't ever use that name again in my presence," Jonas hissed.

"Why should Savannah's name be offensive to you?"

"It is not a proper name for a woman of high society in New England," Jonas replied in a tone that said he would brook no argument.

"I disagree. Savannah's name is good and proper, given to honor her father's uncle Mortimer, who died in the War Between the States near Savannah, Georgia. I should think even you, Jonas, would honor the dead."

"I know what is best for *my wife*, Clarissa. Don't you dare contradict me."

I looked toward Savannah, and, for the first time, I saw emotion in her sky-blue eyes. She sat motionless with perfect posture, by all appearances at ease, but her eyes pleaded with me to stop engaging Jonas. I hated the defeated, fearful look in her eyes but knew I would do what she asked. I nodded to Jonas, not because I agreed, but because I wanted to prevent any lasting repercussions for Savannah.

We sat in the formal parlor in an uncomfortable silence. Savannah pleated and repleated the same part of her sea-blue linen skirts over and over again. Jonas crossed his legs and held his trim body in tight control except for the slight tapping motion of his foot dangling in midair.

"It seems you are incapable of remaining scandal-free, Clarissa," Jonas said, every line of his body expressing his contempt.

"I don't know to what you refer," I said.

Jonas snorted his disgust, watching me with intense eyes. "First the debacle at our wedding, where the entire newspaper notice was wasted on an attendant's lack of composure and grace rather than on the elegance and good breeding of the groom and his chosen bride."

I blushed, grimacing as I recalled my flight through the air at their wedding when I tripped while walking off the altar.

"Your grandmother Thompson was correct in advising Mrs. Mont-

gomery to choose a new attendant. From now on we will follow their es-
teemed advice," Jonas continued.

I bristled at the mention of my grandparents but refrained from speaking.

"But, no, Clarissa." He said my name with absolute derision. "I am talking
about the scandal with the poor cabinetmaker. I shouldn't be surprised,
knowing you and your family, that you would choose such an inappropriate
man. An oafish oversize ogre with no idea as to the proper ways of society?"
Jonas raised an eyebrow.

My heartbeat raced, and a fierce anger filled me, preventing me from
speaking coherently.

"I would think you could have chosen someone better, someone like
Cameron," Jonas said, watching me closely.

I glared at him upon hearing Cameron's name.

"As for the poor cabinetmaker, good riddance. Hopefully we will never
hear from him again. You have yet to receive a letter from him?" Again the
raised eyebrow.

I attempted to take a calming breath but instead felt as though I were
hyperventilating.

"Maybe there was a train accident, and we are well rid of his regrettable
presence."

I gasped in horror.

Jonas smiled. "Ah, you are still foolish then and pining for a man who
left you."

I blinked away tears, bristling as I looked toward Savannah for help, but
she only watched me with sorrowful eyes. "At least I know what it feels to
truly love and be loved. I do not regret a moment of the time I spent with
him," I blurted out.

"*My* only regret is that we have that sideboard he made. I dislike having
anything associated with that scandalmonger, and yet it is a rather decent
piece," Jonas said. "I had thought to rip it apart and use it for kindling, but
we may keep it for now."

"You can't," I protested. "That was a wedding present from her father.
It should be cherished."

"Much should be cherished that isn't," Savannah whispered.

Jonas stiffened, glaring in her direction.

"Could I have a tour of your new home, Savannah?" I asked.

"*Mrs. Montgomery* is too busy today to show you through our house. As am I," Jonas replied for Savannah. "She will send you a note when you may call again. Please do not call if you have not been invited. We are quite occupied with our new lives to entertain, well, you, Clarissa, whenever you feel like calling. This isn't like before her marriage when you could stop by whenever you wanted."

"Sav?" I whispered.

A flicker of a joyless smile moved over her features before she looked away.

I nodded. "I may not be welcome here, but you are always welcome at my house," I said. I reached out and gripped her hands.

She gave my fingers a gentle squeeze and then turned toward Jonas to stand beside him.

Jonas barely nodded his good-bye to me.

I stumbled out of their ornate entryway and walked down their cobbled street. I decided to forgo the pleasure of seeing the late-season roses in the Public Gardens to meet the mailman.

I walked toward my neighborhood in the nearby South End. When my parents had purchased our family home with my mama's dowry, the South End had been a prestigious neighborhood losing its bloom. Now its luster was almost completely tarnished as it became increasingly working class. Many of the once-private homes were filled with boarders renting rooms, and Boston's first apartment building, the St. Cloud, had been constructed near my home. My street was like an oasis with an oval park down the middle with bow-fronted homes lining the park, although few of the houses surrounding the park remained single-family residences.

As I reached Union Park, my street in the South End, I saw our mailman, Mr. Curtis, on his rounds. His mailbag bulged with letters to deliver, although I knew that, if I were inclined to visit with him, he would spend time every day talking with me about my family, work or the latest political intrigue. I quickened my pace.

I arrived home, panting, to hear him say to Mrs. Smythe, "Another one for Miss Clarissa from Montana. Wouldn't that be something to receive mail from such a far-off place?"

At hearing the word *another*, I suddenly comprehended that Mrs. Smythe had stolen my mail as she had earlier in the summer. I reached for the letter, ripping it out of Mrs. Smythe's hands.

Mr. Curtis turned toward me with an open, friendly smile. "Ah, eager to hear the news. Can only mean one thing. Love is in the air! Good afternoon, ladies." He nodded before turning past me to walk down our front stairs to continue his rounds.

"Give me that letter this instant, Clarissa," Mrs. Smythe hissed, one hand on her pregnant belly.

"No, it's mine," I snapped. I moved into the house. "How dare you keep my letters from me!"

"You have formed a regrettable attachment, and I aim to see you recover from it," Mrs. Smythe snarled. She reached again for my letter, but I firmly held onto it, over my head.

As she stood on her toes, reaching for the letter, she tripped on the edge of the carpet, which hurled her into me. Neither of us were in a position to catch our balance, and we landed in a heap on the floor. I nearly bashed my head against the base of the staircase, and Mrs. Smythe landed on top of me. One of her legs nudged the front hall table, knocking over a new blue crystal vase. I watched in horror as it tumbled to the ground and splintered apart.

"Now look what you've done," Mrs. Smythe wailed, holding her belly.

"What? I've made you act like me?" I asked, trying not to chuckle.

"No, you've hurt the baby," Mrs. Smythe gasped.

"I've done no such thing," I argued. "But we'll call for the doctor." I saw Bridget, Mrs. Smythe's faithful maid, standing in the hallway and instructed her to fetch the doctor.

I extricated myself from Mrs. Smythe's clothes, stood and heaved her off the floor. However, Mrs. Smythe retained her focus and reached for the letter. I realized her intent too late and pulled it away from her just as she grabbed it, causing it to tear in two. She held onto the larger portion of the letter, including the corner with the return address.

"No!" I yelled. "No!"

"You are so naive, Clarissa," Mrs. Smythe simpered with a triumphant smile. She waddled into the parlor, no pain evident in her movements. I rushed after her, determined to retrieve that portion of the letter to piece it together, only to watch her throw it in the smoldering grate of the fire.

I collapsed onto a settee. I sat near her, in her favorite section of the parlor near the door. The furniture was newer, freshly upholstered in gaudy gold satin. I looked toward the distant part of the parlor, envisioning my evenings last summer with Gabriel as we sat by the piano or next to each other by the window, on the settee far from Mrs. Smythe.

"Why?" I asked, though I knew it was a futile question. She did not like me, loathed Gabriel and would do anything to keep us separated. I should have suspected she would do something like this.

I heard the commotion at the front door and sat mesmerized by the sight of Mrs. Smythe transforming herself into an injured woman. She leaned into her favorite lady's chair and began to moan and twitch as though she were in paroxysms of agony. Tendrils of her previously tidy dyed-blond hair stuck to her forehead and trailed down her arm as her chignon came loose. She wiped at her forehead as though at sweat, and her small frame looked even smaller as she curled into her chair, clutching her belly. I watched the doctor's solicitude, his concern for the baby and his abject disapproval of me.

"I would think, young lady," Dr. Mitchelson said with a fierce frown, "you would have more common sense than to rile your stepmother at this late stage of her delicate condition."

"She landed on top of me, and I think I provided a good cushion for the baby," I said.

"There should have been no need for her to fall," the doctor said. "I am sure your father will have quite a bit to say."

***

THAT EVENING, after a scathing lecture from Da over treating Mrs. Smythe with the respect she was owed as my stepmother, I escaped to my bedroom to weep in private. Da seemed much less concerned that she had been intercepting my post and had in fact destroyed one of my letters in front of me.

I lay curled on my bed, crying, imagining what Gabriel would have written me when a loud knock sounded on my door.

"Rissa, come to the parlor," Colin, my middle brother, commanded.

"Go away, Col," I called back. I sniffled but hoped he didn't hear it.

"I think you will be sorely disappointed if you don't come down, Rissa," he said with a hint of the old humor in his voice.

I sighed, rose from my bed and washed my face. I studied myself in the mirror in my mama's vanity and was thankful I had not wept for long and that the aftereffects of my crying jag were not overly evident. My topaz-blue eyes showed very little red, and I had no swelling under my eyes to indicate my recent tears. I repinned my waist-length chestnut hair into a simple bun, brushed down my pale blue skirts and took a calming breath at the thought of having to spend time in the presence of Mrs. Smythe.

Upon entering the parlor, I saw Richard McLeod, one of Gabriel's brothers, sitting companionably beside Colin on the medallion-style sofa near the fire discussing their blacksmithing projects. "Richard!" I exclaimed with delight.

"Hello, Miss Sullivan," he said with the open warmness he had always shown me. "It is nice to see you." He stood to his full height, nearly as tall as Gabriel at over six feet. His icy-blue eyes lit with warmth and concern as he studied me.

I blushed, hoping he would be unable to discern that I had been crying.

I sat in a chair near them. "Have you heard from Gabriel?" I asked, interrupting their conversation.

Colin laughed and gave me a wink, a lock of wavy auburn hair falling over his forehead and past his eyebrows. He reached up with hands battered from years working at the forge and pushed his hair out of his light blue eyes.

"Yes, and he is doing well in Montana," Richard said, watching me intently.

It was a searching look, similar to the look Gabriel had used with me, and the memory made my throat tighten. "Montana?" Then I remembered what the postman had said today. "But he's supposed to be in California."

"Well, he met someone in Chicago who talked him into going to a booming mining town in the wilds of Montana called Butte."

"Butte?" I asked. "Why on earth would he want to go to a mining town?"

"I guess for the adventure. Though I think he's been asking himself that question since he arrived," Richard responded with a wry smile. "But, now that he's there, he's got to stay for a while. He doesn't have enough put by to be traveling here and there whenever the mood strikes."

"Does he have work?" I asked.

"I'm surprised you know nothing about Gabe, Miss Sullivan. He writes you a few times a week, if not more." Again the questioning look.

I took a deep breath in an attempt to calm my anger. "I have not received a single letter. They have been, ah, intercepted for lack of a better word and have not been delivered to me." I tilted my head in Mrs. Smythe's direction.

"Ah, the meddling stepmother," Richard said, nodding his understanding.

"I learned today that she is intercepting my letters and destroying them."

"Well, then, it's a good thing Gabriel has a suspicious nature because he envisioned just this type of scenario," he said with a wide smile and handed a sealed envelope to me.

I gasped with joy, snatching it out of Richard's fingers. I traced Gabriel's bold handwriting, feeling a connection with him after all of these weeks.

"That smile is thanks enough," Richard said. "I think Gabriel will continue to send your letters to me, and I will deliver them to you, if you find that acceptable, Miss Sullivan."

"I do. Exceedingly acceptable. Thank you, Richard," I said.

"Rissa, Rich and I were in the middle of a serious discussion about bellowing techniques at the smithy," Colin said with a smirk. "Would you mind giving us a few moments alone?" He tilted his head toward the piano and a quiet part of the room.

I smiled again, rose and walked toward the piano stool. I rarely sat in this part of the parlor as it held so many bittersweet memories for me from the summer when Gabriel and I officially courted. The final memories—his telling me that he would leave and then giving me his locket—were too painful to relive.

However, tonight I sat on the piano stool, determined to remember the joy and happiness of Gabriel's visits. I carefully opened his letter, reading the return address.

September 23, 1900

My darling Clarissa,

Over three weeks have passed since I left Massachusetts, and yet I have heard nothing from you. In my weaker moments, as I lie awake at night, I feel like I will drown from an overwhelming loneliness. I worry that you have had a change of heart. When I think about your life, during the day while I work, I know that your stepmother most likely causes your silence. Please write me. Please tell me that your feelings have not changed. It is the dream of us being reunited that makes the struggle of living in a mining town worthwhile.

If you have not received any of my letters, you may be surprised to learn that I am in Butte, Montana, rather than San Francisco. I met a young man named Matthew Donovan in Chicago who was headed to Butte. I decided to join him as I thought it would be better to have a friend than go to a place where I knew no one.

It would take a magician's wand or a blind man's optimism to say that Butte is an attractive place. There are smokestacks everywhere pumping ash constantly into the sky. So much soot falls to the ground that many can't even raise a garden. The surrounding mountains and hills have been stripped of trees for the mineshafts, and there are piles of dirt and tailings everywhere you look.

On the bright side, the Uptown part of Butte, which we would call downtown, is a fancy area with good shops, restaurants and hotels. The manners might not be quite as formal as Boston, but the people are as fancily dressed.

I am enclosing this letter with Richard's. If it is as I suspect and you have not been receiving my letters, I will continue to send my letters to you with Richard's aid.

I miss you, my love.

Gabriel

I held Gabriel's letter to my heart, joy filling me and banishing all doubts. I glanced toward Richard and Colin to find them watching me closely. I rose, walking to join them again.

"Did you finish your bellowing discussion?" I asked as I again sat on a chair near their sofa.

"Oh, yes. We were comparing notes on how loud we had to yell to get our youngest assistants to do anything," Colin replied with a wink.

I laughed.

"Good news then, Miss Sullivan?" Richard asked.

I nodded. "Although I hate that he had reason to doubt me due to my silence." I glared in Mrs. Smythe's direction and met her scrutinizing glare. "Richard, please continue to visit whenever you have a letter or any news of Gabriel. I enjoy seeing you."

"That would be very nice, Miss Sullivan. I find the house to be too quiet now with Gabe gone."

"Have you received much news from him?"

"Yes, Miss Sullivan." On a long sigh and with an impish smile, Richard said, "Gabriel lives in a boardinghouse, filled to the brim with miners. He has found work at a hotel where they need to have a lot of finish work done. Seems there's a lot of money out there from all those mines, and people want fancy houses and hotels. He's begun to make friends, though mainly with a group of miners he met through his friend, Matthew Donovan. He's just becoming acquainted with his workmates."

"I am glad he is making friends and has a good job," I said. "I never thought a mining town would be that prosperous."

"It seems that this one is different in that its fortunes aren't as fleeting as most."

"I can't imagine living in such a place."

"I think Gabe is still reconciling himself to it too," Richard said with a small laugh. "I should leave you. I will call again when I have another letter."

"Please call whenever you would like. Your company is most welcome," I said.

"You are very kind, Miss Sullivan."

I watched Richard leave. "Why on earth would he go to a mining town?" I asked as I turned to face Colin.

"Makes one reconsider the future, don't you think, Rissa?"

I studied him, not wanting to think too much about Colin's words. He gave me a quick kiss on my forehead as he rose to leave the parlor.

CHAPTER 5

GABRIEL KNOCKED at the Egan's door as a cold, brisk wind helped clear the valley of the ever-present pollution. Gabriel shivered. He paused on their doorstep, enjoying the view of the valley and distant mountains normally veiled by smelter smoke.

"Coming!" a soft female voice called out, then the door was opened. "Mr. McLeod! It's wonderful to see you," Amelia said as she let him in.

He handed her a loaf of fresh bread and a fruitcake that he had bought at the baker's.

"You didn't need to bring anything," she chided him, although she smiled as she reproached him. "This bread seems fresh. It will go well with dinner. I hope you like stew," she said as she made her way to the small kitchen.

"Yes, that's fine, ma'am," Gabriel replied as he wandered toward the bookshelf in the living room. A gentle light shone from two end lamps on either side of the settee, casting a welcome glow over the room. On the bookshelf he saw many of his old favorites, picking out books at random to peruse. As Amelia reentered the room he said, "I beg your pardon. It's been a while since I've seen this many books."

"Well, I am glad someone appreciates them. Liam did no end of bellyaching to have to bring them all the way from Leadville. But I would not leave them behind. Many of them I inherited from my mother and grandmother. They were learned women and encouraged me to become a teacher."

"Were they disappointed you had to give up your career when you married Liam?"

"Well, they both died in an influenza outbreak a few years before I met Liam. But I believe they would rejoice in my life and my family. They ensured

I had the ability to make a good living, if I were never to marry, but they always wanted me to live the life I desired."

"You sound like Clarissa," he said.

"Hmm, the mysterious woman you left behind in Boston."

"Not mysterious. Just … special. Sometimes I think she wasn't real. That I imagined her out of my loneliness," he murmured and then flushed.

"Well, I am sure she is real, as you don't seem like a lunatic. I'd hate to see you end up in Warm Springs."

Gabriel shook his head at the thought of the mental hospital twenty-five miles from Butte. "No, I know she was real. Though I am guilty of having conversations with her in my head now."

"Still no letter?"

Gabriel shook his head. "I hear there's a good library in town," he said by way of changing the conversation.

"Yes, there is. I would take out a membership seeing as you like books so much."

Gabriel nodded as the front door swung open to welcome Liam, Matthew and Ronan. Amelia leaned in for a quick embrace from Liam, his hand resting for a few moments on her belly.

Matthew's eyes lit up when he saw Gabriel. "Look what I found when I went by the boardinghouse on my way here," he said. "The man at the desk said he forgot to give it to you." Matthew waved a letter in front of Gabriel's face that Gabriel quickly snatched out of his hand.

"Clarissa," Gabriel murmured, tracing her writing with his fingers.

"She's finally written then. Why don't you take a moment and read her letter while we, ah, set the table," Liam said as he gripped Matthew by the shoulder and pushed him toward the dining room table. Ronan chortled and followed them.

Gabriel barely heard them as he collapsed into one of the dilapidated easy chairs.

October 2, 1900

My darling Gabriel,

Oh, to finally receive a letter from you! I have missed you more than I can say, and not receiving word from you has caused such torment. I discovered today that Mrs. Smythe has been intercepting my mail and destroying your letters.

I thought my heart would break with no word from you and no way to write you. Thankfully you had sensed things were not as they should be and had sent another letter for me through Richard. Thank you, my darling! Just seeing your handwriting has brought me a measure of peace. I have been taunted by those less charitable that misfortune had befallen you or that you had forgotten me. However, to receive a letter from you, even though it is from a mining town, is more wondrous than I can say.

I miss you. I miss our walks, our talks, your smile. I miss everything about you. I worry that you will become as a ghost to me, a wonderful memory, but something that was never truly real. Please tell me that you will return to me soon.

I enjoy teaching, though every time I hear a creak at the doorway after hours, my heart leaps at the thought that it might be you, leaning against the door frame, watching me with that mix of amusement and deep interest. I know it is foolish of me, and yet I cannot force myself to stop imagining you, here with me.
Write me often. Tell me of your life in Butte. Is it very different from Boston?
Ever Yours,
Clarissa

"Gabe, is all well?" Matthew asked from the dining room. He sat with his jacket slung over the back of his chair and his shirtsleeves rolled up as he held Nicholas on his lap, playing horse with one of his legs.

"I don't know," Gabriel said. "I think so. She writes that her stepmother had been intercepting my letters. And that she dreams of one day being reunited with me. I wish she had written more."

"Hmm…" said Liam.

"Mr. McLeod—" Amelia said.

"You should really call me Gabriel."

"Yes, well, Gabriel then, I am sure she'll write more soon. It is just one letter."

"I know. But it is hard not to be disappointed when it's the only news I have had from her in over a month."

"Give her time to write you. Soon you'll find she has written you such detailed letters that you will long for the shorter ones," Amelia said.

Gabriel smiled, placing Clarissa's letter in his inner jacket pocket. "How are things at the mine?"

"The usual. Long days, but steady pay," Liam said, clasping Amelia's hand.

"One of the damn mules died today. I thought it would make us late to dinner," Ronan said as he stuffed a piece of bread in his mouth. He wiped away crumbs from his mouth and rubbed at his beard. The patch on the left elbow of his brown jacket was fraying, and Nicholas lost interest in Matthew's game and instead pulled at the strings.

"The poor creature," Amelia murmured.

"Put out of its blind, cantankerous misery," Ronan said as he grabbed at Nicholas's hands and then tickled him. "Ah, the poor beast just gave out on us when it was hauling its heavy carts full of ore."

"I told you that last cart should have been split in two," Liam muttered.

"I know, but Devlin McDermott wanted all his ore on one cart," Ronan said, as Nicholas squealed with laughter and burrowed into Matthew to escape Ronan's tickling. "Didn't want any of us to receive credit for his work."

"Selfish bastard," Liam said. "He was still only going to earn his $3.50 a day. Didn't need to kill the mule over it."

"I thought they would refuse to move if the load was too heavy," Gabriel said. "That's what the lads at the pub tell me."

"Well, maybe it wasn't too heavy, and it was this mule's time. But Devlin should know that he won't be made foreman by making the rest of us look bad," Liam growled.

"We still met our goals, Liam," Matthew argued.

"Yes, but barely. We are supposed to work as a team, and that man is going to get us into trouble."

"What other news?" Amelia asked with a bright smile as she clasped Liam's hand.

"Young Johnny Fitzgerald had his leg crushed by one of the carts today," Matthew said, settling Nicholas onto the floor to romp around. "They're not sure as they might have to amputate."

Liam glared at him.

At Gabriel's hiss, Ronan's "For the love of God," and Amelia's grimace, Matthew looked chagrined. "But, I'm sure he'll be taken care of by the Company."

"I hope so. It's just unfortunate he's not a member of the Hibernians," Liam said, picking up young Nicholas to sit on his lap. "They'd help take care of him. That extra $8 a week until his leg healed would help, surely." He paused for a moment to watch Matthew. "I'd see about joining if I were you. If you plan on staying here and working in the mines, that is."

"Let's talk of lighter things," Amelia said. She moved toward the cramped kitchen area and began to ladle out stew. "Mr. ... Gabriel, how is your work?"

"It's good work, and there is plenty of it. The pay's decent, though not miner's wages, and it's regular. I'll be able to put some by each month. The boardinghouse is a little expensive," Gabriel said.

"It would be to you," Ronan said. "It's based on miner's wages. You're making a little more than half what we do, I'd imagine." At Gabriel's nod, Ronan sighed. "Well, hopefully you'll make more soon."

"Once I've been here a few months and Jeffers approves of my work, I'll earn fifty cents more a day," Gabriel said.

"You seem preoccupied, Liam," Amelia murmured as she moved to sit. She stroked his shoulder in an attempt to ease his tension.

"I am. One of the men from another level, Brian O'Shaughnessy, didn't pick up his tag today."

"His tag?" Gabriel asked.

"When we go down the mine, we put a metal tag in a bowl to show we are working. When we end shift, we pick our tag out of the bowl so everyone knows we are..."

"Safe," Amelia murmured with a gentle squeeze to Liam's shoulders.

"Yes," Liam said as he reached up to grip her hand. "When we left, they were looking for him."

"All we can do is pray they find him, healthy and whole," Gabriel said.

"Aye, 'tis all we can do. But it always makes me wish there was more I could do other than go to the wake and pay my respects."

After an awkward pause, Gabriel spoke. "Amelia, can you tell me about the upcoming fall dance at the Hibernian Hall?"

She smiled as she settled into her chair. "Yes. We will have the McNamara band, and there should be plenty of dancing. I have heard that there will be a number of eligible women there, Matthew." At Ronan's snort, Amelia arched an eyebrow at him. "And what has you amused, Ronan? You just might find a woman who interests you."

"Set your trap for wee Matthew here," Ronan said as he attempted to mimic Liam, "but I have no interest in a wife and responsibilities. I am too young to contemplate anything so drastic as marriage."

"Many would argue you are nearly decrepit at twenty-eight," Liam said.

"Seeing as I've used up half my mining years, yes, I can see that," Ronan said with a laugh.

"Half your mining years?" Gabriel asked.

"Most say our work expectancy is short. We'll only ever put in about fifteen years in the mine. It's part of the reason we're paid so well. Besides, there are too many women I have yet to meet on a certain street," Ronan said with an impish smile as he referred to Mercury Street and Butte's Red Light district.

"Don't you dare mention that name in this house," Amelia said with a tap to his hand.

"In fact, maybe my unencumbered friends would care to join me tonight? Matthew? Gabe?" Ronan looked toward them as he finished his stew.

Gabriel shook his head in denial, but Matthew jumped up to join Ronan. "I thank you for a delicious meal, Amelia," Ronan said.

"Ma'am," Matthew muttered, flushing red. They left, allowing in a blast of cold air.

"Liam, talk some sense into that partner of yours," Amelia demanded as she washed the dishes.

"He's young and unmarried in a city filled with ample opportunity for … adventure, love," Liam said with a roll of his eyes toward Gabriel. "How d'ye expect him to act?"

"More like Gabriel!"

"Now, 'tisn't fair, as the man's got his woman," Liam said with a nod in Gabriel's direction. "She might be across a great continent. But sure, he's still got his woman." When Amelia opened her mouth to argue, Liam set Nicholas down, rose and covered her lips with his fingers. "What Matthew didn't tell you is that the ore cart that got Johnny Fitzgerald was meant for him. He jumped out of the way just in time. The lad needs somethin' to take his mind off of nearly dyin' today."

***

GABRIEL LEFT THE EGANS and decided to go to the local pub. He had no desire to sit by himself in the small room at the boardinghouse. As he entered, he noted that a button accordion player had joined the fiddler tonight with most conversation at a low din out of respect for the music.

Gabriel collected his pint and found a seat at an empty table a short distance from the music. Round tables and chairs scattered around the room were filled with off-duty miners. Spittoons sat near the foot of each table. Men leaned against the long wooden bar. Knicks and scratches from the multitude of drinks and patrons scarred the oak wood surface. The burly barman had a towel tied to his waist, and he washed glasses in a sink behind the bar when he was not busy serving customers. Gabriel settled in, absently listening to the men around him marvel at the ongoing coal strike in Pennsylvania. They grumbled at the rising price of coal but seemed to support the miners' efforts.

"I'd like to think they'd support us if'n we ever had need of a strike," one man muttered. A hearty round of ayes followed that comment.

"I wonder what the wee buggers are eatin'," another said. "They can't have enough put by to last weeks with no pay." The men around him continued to murmur.

"You new around these parts?" A small man with powerful shoulders sat next to Gabriel. "I don't remember seein' you at the Mountain Con."

"I don't work there, but I'm bunking with a friend who does. I'm Gabriel."

"Nice to meet you. My name's Red."

Gabriel stared at him for a few moments, taking in the man's pale complexion and raven-black hair.

"Ah, a man who doesn't ask too many questions. I like that. No, I'm Red 'cause I have a fiery temperament."

Gabriel nodded.

"Some say I should work in a smelter so my work would match my spirit."

"But then you wouldn't live in Butte."

"Exactly. I have no desire to live in Anaconda, although Daly built a beautiful town there." He said Daly's name with reverence.

"If Daly built Anaconda, the smelters there must only be for his mines. Where do the other mines send their ore?" Gabriel asked.

"The non-Anaconda? They send theirs to a smelter in Great Falls. There's plenty of water there from the Missouri River, though it's a fair distance from Butte."

Gabriel nodded. "I haven't had the chance to travel to Anaconda yet, although I know it's close. Great Falls seems too far away."

"Aye, that it is. Now, Anaconda might be a place to visit on a free day. It's only about twenty-five miles from here. All the ore from Anaconda mines are brought there to the smelter. One of the lads has a brother-in-law who works at the smelter, and he told us about this long process of separating the copper from all the other metals. Sounded like magic when he talked about it, conjuring the copper from the other metals." He snorted once. "Though he used fancy scientific terms, something to do with gravity. When it's all over, they have a nice copper pig."

Red raised one black eyebrow at Gabriel's snicker.

"Copper pigs?" Gabriel repeated.

"Yeah, bars of copper," Red said. He took a sip from his pint, his toe tapping to the lively reel.

"From what you say, it sounds like working in the smelter would be an easier job than working belowground," Gabriel said as he took a long swallow from his pint.

"I wouldn't start thinking like that, Gabriel. Working in a smelter is hard. That machinery is tough. Any small accident and…" Red shook his head. "They're as tough as any of us." After a moment's pause, he added, "You sure you have no interest in mining? You'd make better pay, and you seem strong enough for it."

"No, I do well enough right now."

Red nodded in agreement and sat for a few minutes, listening as the musicians moved from a reel to a slow waltz.

"Ah, the music's lovely tonight. Glad these lads have chosen our pub to play in," Red said as he rose to move to another table. "'Twas nice meeting you, Gabriel. I hope to see you again."

Gabriel nodded, enjoying the rest of his pint and the music.

CHAPTER 6

WE SAT IN THE PARLOR, the room illuminated in a soft glow from the gaslights. A small fire crackled in the marble-topped fireplace, the new fili-greed fire grate preventing wayward sparks from singeing Mrs. Smythe's re-cently purchased oriental rugs. The orange in the rug clashed with the rose wallpaper, although I had seen enough wallpaper patterns around to know that it, too, would soon be altered.

"Richard?"

"Yes, Miss Sullivan?"

"I don't want to hurt you," I began, biting my lip. I played with the but-tons adorning the skirts of my navy dress.

"But you still want to tell me something," he said with wary amusement. He sat across from me in the chair Da usually sat in. The plush red velvet wingback chair with wooden wings and woven cane work had recently been reupholstered.

"Yes." I sighed. "I want you to come to my school. I have a good friend there who I think once used to be a … an acquaintance of yours."

"I highly doubt a school marm is any friend of mine," Richard contra-dicted with a laugh.

"Her name is Florence Butler," I whispered, watching him. He stilled, as I imagined an animal becomes motionless to prevent detection from its prey. His eyes betrayed him, a deep flash of emotion sparking in their icy-blue depths at her name.

"Florence?" he murmured.

"Yes, I thought you should know…" I stopped speaking when he held up a hand, silently asking me to desist.

"I would think she hates me," Richard said, a deep note of mourning in his voice.

"I can't answer for her, Richard. But from what I do understand, from what I have heard from her and pieced together from her interactions with Gabriel…" I paused for a moment as his eyes narrowed. "I believe you should speak with her. Try to overcome what happened in the past."

"Gabe has seen her? Knows where she works?"

"Yes. It's why we had to write letters in the spring. I didn't want Florence to become uncomfortable with visits from him."

Richard sat in shocked silence, his eyes distant, unfocused. He finally raised haunted eyes to me. "After all I did to help him with you, why wouldn't he help me?"

I reached out to grip his hand. "Richard, it was never my intention to harm your relationship with Gabriel. He has only ever wanted to protect you."

"Protect me from the woman I love? Separate me from her?" Richard asked in an anger-laced voice.

I held onto his hand, refusing to let go. "Richard, please. You must understand Gabriel's animosity toward your aunt Masterson. Well, try to at least. I didn't understand how awful she was until this summer.

"Gabriel has such strong memories of your life with your parents. He would remember and compare those memories to the home, barren of love, provided by your aunt. He would dream, every day, of the life that had been lost. And feel the burden to make everything better so that you and Jeremy could have the life your parents dreamt of for you."

"You really love him, don't you?" Richard asked, letting out a long, shaky sigh, the anger seeming to evaporate.

I nodded with a tremulous smile.

"Then why didn't you tell him you loved him before he left?"

"He knew how I felt, Richard," I whispered, releasing his hand and sitting against the back of my chair.

"So it would appear from your frequent letters." Richard paused, watching me a moment. "He told me, one evening as he prepared to leave, how he had told you that he loved you, but you didn't say it back."

"Would he have stayed if I'd said the words?" I gasped, dread filling me.

Richard shook his head, unwilling to answer an unanswerable question.

I sat, stunned into absolute silence. I looked toward Richard without seeing him, reliving scenes in my head. I quickly shook off the memories. "You're very cunning you know," I accused.

"Why?"

"I won't allow you to make me forget our original topic," I said, raising an eyebrow toward him.

He smiled. "Yes, Florence." He patted my hand a few times. "Let me think about it a while. There's a good chance she won't appreciate your meddling."

***

A FEW DAYS LATER, I prepared for a formal dinner at Savannah and Jonas's. My maid, Mary, spent extra time on an elaborate chignon. My burgundy velvet dress was fitted through the bodice yet full at the waist and through the skirt. Although mid-October, I gave thanks to the mild weather as I glanced in the mirror at the three-quarter-length sheer lace sleeves. I bit my lip as I studied my reflection, fingering the decorative flower at my left shoulder. I turned, picked up my light wrap and took a fortifying breath that I would survive a party at the Montgomery's home scandal free.

I arrived at Savannah and Jonas's house a few minutes late, worried that Jonas would be annoyed at my tardy arrival. However, as I exited the hired carriage and stepped onto the cobblestone sidewalk ineffectually lit by a dim streetlight, I noted other well-dressed guests entering the house.

I followed them to the hallway, awed again by its splendor. The immense oak staircase, wide enough for three to walk abreast, was ornately carved in the decorative rococo style. I glanced toward the ceiling to marvel at the decorative plaster medallion encircling the chandelier. White wainscoting on the walls enhanced the sense of light in the windowless room.

I handed my light wrap to a waiting maid, smiling my thanks. She bobbed and turned to the guest behind me. Upon glancing into the formal parlor, I was surprised to find only a dozen or so people present. Satin-covered chairs and settees were arranged in informal clusters in an attempt to entice guests to sit and converse. However, most remained standing, moving from group to group so as to speak with all present. Waiters in impeccable formal livery walked through the room, discreetly inquiring about before-dinner drinks. I placed a hand on my stomach, trying to calm the fluttering in my belly that I would be expected to interact with the exquisitely dressed members of society.

I slipped into the parlor, hoping to speak with Savannah. She wore a stunning aquamarine satin charmeuse gown with a design of ink-pressed flowers etched into the delicate fabric. A softer aquamarine tulle border highlighted the scalloped neck of the gown and Savannah's trim waist. Beginning at the waist, a black lace cutout overlaid the body of the dress in a delicate leaf pattern sweeping from midwaist across her hips to the floor. The dress just touched the floor in front, with a slight train in the back.

I did not wish to interrupt her, as she was deep in conversation with a tall, dark-haired man in a formal black suit with white tie. Savannah looked up, noticed me standing near the doorway and motioned for me to join her.

"Clarissa," Savannah said by way of including me in her conversation. "I am having the most fascinating conversation. Please join us." She held out her hand to me as I walked toward her. She squeezed my hand in welcome, and I examined her. Her eyes held an impenetrable sadness, but only if you looked deeply and knew that she had not always been this way.

"Mr. McLeod, might I introduce my cousin, Miss Sullivan?"

"Mr. McLeod?" I repeated.

"Yes, ma'am. Mr. Aidan McLeod. It's nice to meet you," he said, nodding his head. He looked around the room at the other guests as though looking for someone more interesting to speak with.

"Brother to Ian McLeod?" I asked.

His gaze jerked back toward mine, his intense blue eyes now fully focused on me. He squinted and faint lines around his eyes crinkled. "What did you say?" he whispered.

"Are you Ian's brother?" When he remained silent, I continued. "Uncle to Gabriel, Richard and Jeremy McLeod?" His blue eyes blazed with emotion, and I worried I had erred in saying their names.

"How do you know about them?" he asked, tilting his head to the side as I had seen Gabriel and Richard do so often.

"Gabriel speaks of his uncle Aidan, who was an adventurer. I doubt Gabriel could have imagined a well-dressed society man such as you. If you are his uncle," I said with a questioning look.

He nodded a few times, appearing at a loss for words. "Yes, yes, I am."

At that moment, Jonas joined us. "Ah, Aidan, I see you have had the pleasure of meeting Mrs. Montgomery's cousin. Let me introduce you to the other guests." He walked away, expecting Aidan to follow him. However, Aidan hesitated.

"Will I be able to speak with you again?" he asked.

"We'll find a way," I said with a warm smile. I watched him join Jonas to meet a group of businessmen.

"Sav, how?" I asked.

"Jonas shared the guest list with me. I had hoped, rather than knew, that he might be a connection with your Gabriel," she said with a small smile. "It's why I insisted on inviting you tonight."

"Sav, Jonas will wish to keep me separated from him. I must have an opportunity to talk with him." I watched Aidan surrounded by men dressed in starched suits discussing trades on the New York Stock Exchange and other business transactions. I could not imagine interrupting such a group.

"Don't worry, you will," Savannah said with a cryptic smile before leaving me to greet other guests.

I spent the time in the parlor before dinner examining the portraits on the wall rather than openly studying Mr. McLeod. On the few occasions I glanced in his direction, I found him watching me. He stood as tall as Gabriel, although he was not as broad shouldered. His raven hair had begun to turn salt-and-pepper. I glanced again and caught him smiling. My breath caught. It was Gabriel's smile.

As we were called into dinner, I discovered Savannah had risked Jonas's wrath by having Mr. McLeod accompany me into the dining room and seating him next to me. I saw Jonas's censorious glare in her direction and smiled my thanks toward her. For the first part of the meal, I tried to feign interest in the business concerns of Mr. Marday. I soon realized I needed to give little input other than a well-timed "Oh, really?" or a "How interesting," when he paused for breath. I wondered how Savannah managed to survive these mind-numbing events.

Finally Mr. Marday turned to his other dinner companion as a new course was served, and I focused on Aidan.

"Mr. McLeod, please pardon the impertinence, but I am very curious about you."

"And I, you, Miss Sullivan," he said.

"Why did you never visit your nephews after their parents' death?" I asked.

A flash of pain sparked in his eyes as he spoke. "I did come to Boston. I was informed the entire family had perished in the fire," he murmured.

"Who would say such a cruel thing?" I asked. "Mrs. Masterson?"

"Yes, exactly," Aidan replied in a grim tone. "Do you know where my nephews are now?"

"Gabriel is in Montana, Jeremy is in the Philippines, and Richard lives here in Boston."

"Will you introduce me to Richard?" Aidan asked, unable to hide the eagerness from his voice.

"Of course," I said. "Will you call tomorrow evening? I will invite Richard."

"Of course. You have no idea what it means to realize, in an instant, that you have family again," Aidan murmured. "I have thought for so long that I was completely alone in this world."

***

THE FOLLOWING EVENING I sat in the parlor next to Colin, waiting for Richard and Aidan McLeod to arrive. I squirmed on my once-favored chair, now lumpy and uncomfortable. It was also tea stained, the rose floral ecru no match for my clumsiness. I looked at the ornate gold-gilted clock on the mantel every few minutes, suddenly thankful for one of Mrs. Smythe's extravagant purchases. Mrs. Smythe watched me although she kept her silence. We had reached a fragile truce that could persevere only if we refrained from speaking to each other.

At the heavy knock on the door, Mrs. Smythe frowned. "Who would have the gall to call at this hour?" she asked, though it was only a little past seven. She fanned herself and her protruding belly as she neared the final month of her pregnancy.

Bridget entered the room and addressed Da. "There be a Mr. McLeod here to see the family, sir," Bridget said.

"There can't already be another letter," Mrs. Smythe snapped. Da threw her a warning glance.

"Please show him in," Da said.

Aidan followed Bridget into the room, pausing at the entranceway. The crisp black of his evening jacket and the stark white of his tie enhanced his salt-and-pepper hair. The well-tailored black pants partially covered black leather shoes polished to a high sheen.

Da stood, tugging on his waistcoat as he reached out his hand. "Mr. McLeod?" he asked in confusion with a glance in my direction.

"Yes, sir. Aidan McLeod of San Francisco. I believe you know my nephew, Richard."

"Aye, and Gabriel too. You are very welcome," he said motioning for Aidan to enter the room.

"Miss Sullivan, it is a pleasure to see you again," Aidan said.

"Colin, this is Aidan McLeod, Gabriel's uncle," I said. "Mr. McLeod, Colin Sullivan. And my da and stepmother."

Aidan nodded. "It's very nice to meet you. Has Richard not arrived?"

"No, but he will soon," I said, shooting Mrs. Smythe a censorious glare as she sniffed again at Richard's name.

"Do you mind me asking why you are having a meeting of sorts in my drawing room?" Da asked as he settled on the settee next to Mrs. Smythe with Colin seated across from them.

"Da, both Richard and Gabriel believed their uncle dead or lost to them in some way after the fire that killed their parents. And Mr. McLeod was led to believe that they too had died in the fire. He did not know until last night that they were still alive."

"Imagine that. But who would tell such lies to family?" Da asked.

"Mrs. Masterson," I said.

"Now stop right there, young lady. I will not have you maligning my good friend when she is not present to defend herself. How dare you besmirch her good character, after all she has done for this family? I would think you would give thanks to her. Instead, you try to find fault," Mrs. Smythe bellowed, finally pausing for breath and blushing as Aidan studied her. She continued to fan herself as she rubbed her belly.

"Ma'am, she has never done right by my family. I find it hard to believe she would have done right by yours if my nephews were involved," Aidan said in a firm, unyielding tone.

"Well, I never! And you just arrived into my home. If this is the sort of hospitality they show in the West, then I am thankful I shall never have to travel there." She pursed her lips and snapped her fan closed, heralding her displeasure.

"They are actually quite friendly in the West. Though there is more of a belief of 'live and let live.' Do you know what that means, Mrs. Sullivan?"

"I am sure it has nothing to do with me," she said.

"I think it has everything to do with you and your good friend," Aidan said. His attention was turned as Richard entered the room.

I stood, walking quickly toward Richard. He spoke before I could tell him the news. "Miss Sullivan, I received your message to call tonight. Is everything all right? Have you had concerning news from Gabriel?"

"No, Richard. Please forgive me for alarming you. I have wondrous news and wanted to tell you in person." I placed my hand on his arm and led him toward Aidan.

"Richard, I would like you to meet Aidan McLeod."

Richard shook his head from side to side as though trying to discern what I had said. "You must be mistaken. He … died." His hungry gaze took in Aidan's tall frame, broad shoulders and long limbs.

"I did not die, Richard. And you didn't either," Aidan said with a broad smile.

Richard took a step back at the smile, shock and unease flitting across his face.

"Richard, what is it?" I asked.

"You look like my da," Richard gasped out. "Just like him, when you smile."

Aidan gave a half smile again, watching Richard. "And you look like Ian when he was young."

"You're really my uncle Aidan?"

"Yes."

Richard reached out his hand but was caught in a strong hug by Aidan. "God, it's good to know you boys are alive!"

Richard stepped back with a dazed expression on his face. "Wait 'til Gabe hears. He'll be overjoyed and then distraught that he missed meeting you."

"Mr. Sullivan," Aidan called out to Da who sat avidly watching the reunion. "Do you mind if we sit and converse here for a while longer?"

"Of course not. The McLeods are always welcome in my home," Da said.

"Miss Sullivan, thank you," Richard said to me, gripping my hand for a moment. I smiled and led them to the comfortable area of the sitting room near the piano, listening to them learn more about each other as Colin rose to join them.

"You live in San Francisco?" Richard asked.

"Yes. It's a lovely city by the Bay. I run an import-export business."

"And by all appearances, a quite successful one," Colin said.

"I've done well professionally."

"San Francisco," Richard murmured, cutting off anything more Colin might have said. "If only Gabe had known, he would never have gone to Butte."

"I think he is coming to like Butte," I interjected.

"That's because you are an optimist," Richard said. "And so is Gabe. But he only went to Butte because he had made a friend on the train, and he knew he wouldn't be alone there. If he had known you were in San Francisco…"

"Well, there's nothing to be done about it now," Aidan said. "Though I will see if he would like to join me." After a short pause, he said, "Butte? Montana?" At my quick nod, Aidan murmured, "I've always wanted to go to Montana."

"It seems you haven't lost your adventuring ways," I said.

Aidan laughed. "No, if there is an adventure to be had, I will try to join in."

"I fear Gabriel takes after you," I said with a wry smile.

"What do you do for a living?" Aidan asked, focusing on Richard.

Richard held up his battered hands that still appeared dirty. "I'm a blacksmith."

"A wonderful profession," Aidan said with a nod of approval.

Da grunted his agreement and relaxed against his chair.

Aidan looked to Colin and Da. "You're all blacksmiths, aren't you?"

"Yes, sir, we are," Colin said. "Well, except for Rissa."

Aidan smiled toward me. "Have you had any word from Jeremy?"

"The last we heard, he was ill in the Philippines," Richard said. "We haven't any further word in months."

"Well, I just pray he returns home safely," Aidan whispered. He stared at Richard for a moment, a deep emotion glinting in his blue eyes. "Ian would have been so proud of you three boys. Grown men with professions."

Richard nodded, appearing overcome and unable to speak.

Aidan glanced around the parlor. "I fear we may overstay our welcome. Would you mind if I walked home with you, Richard? I'd like to see where you live."

"That would be fine, Uncle," Richard said.

Da led them out and then retired to his study.

After they left, Mrs. Smythe speared me with a glare. She tapped the fingers of one hand on the arm of her chair before settling against the back of her lady's chair. Her golden brocade dress with lace overlay shimmered as she settled. The gold of her dress enhanced the dyed-blond color of her hair. "In the future, Clarissa, if you are thinking of inviting such people to our home, I believe you should warn us."

"They are upstanding gentlemen who are friends of this family," I argued.

"Clarissa, you must begin to accept how little you understand society. Neither of those men will ever be considered upstanding, and there is nothing gentlemanly about them. Proper clothes and an attempt at social niceties do not make the man. Only good breeding suffices."

"If that is how you truly feel, I'm surprised you deigned to marry into this family," I said.

Mrs. Smythe's smile set my nerves on edge. "All in good time, Clarissa. All in good time," she said smugly as she waddled out of the room.

CHAPTER 7

"HEY, McLEOD!" NIALL CALLED OUT at the end of the workday. "We're heading out for a drink. Why don't you join us?"

Niall, Morgan, Larry and Gabriel formed a unit working on the fine cabinetry and finishing details for the public areas of the hotel, including the restaurant and saloon. They each had their own workbenches where they studied drawings, drafted ideas and then created ornately carved finished products. Around them, men hammered and sawed, completing the rough-finish work. As Gabriel glanced about, he envisioned the completed space, gleaming with highly polished mahogany.

Gabriel looked up from tracing a piece of wood to carve to find Niall, Morgan and Larry waiting. "I am to have dinner tonight at the Egans' home, but I have time for a drink or two before then," Gabriel said with a quick stretch to his shoulders. He set aside his pencil and the piece of wood, and rose, pulling on his coat.

"We can talk about that fancy photo I saw in your room," Larry said with a wink as they made their way onto the street. "Let's head to Daly's Place."

As they walked down Broadway, they passed a building covered in election posters.

"Interesting how McKinley's posters continue to be plastered over by Bryan's supporters," Gabriel said as he stopped to study them.

"What a load of malarkey. Would you look at the likes of this?" Niall said pointing to McKinley and Roosevelt's poster. "They've 'kept their promises'? To whom? The bankers and money-grabbin' robber barons?"

"Do you believe Bryan's promise of 'justice, liberty and humanity'?" Gabriel asked.

"I'd believe him more 'n the other two," Larry said. "Those aren't words I'd use for Roosevelt."

Gabriel grunted his agreement. He studied the two posters. McKinley's poster highlighted the differences between 1896 and now, with American rule in Cuba, bank stability and prosperity under Republican leadership. Bryan's poster showed his belief in "equal rights to all, special privileges to none."

"I like the octopus," Gabriel said with a chuckle as he stared further at Bryan's poster.

"Well, it shows how big business has tentacles everywhere. I like the lady in white there about to lop them off with her hatchet proclaiming 'Democracy,'" Morgan said as he pointed to the woman.

"It's just too bad the coal strike ended last week," Niall said. "If it had lasted just a bit longer, then Bryan would've had a better chance."

"Well, it's a moot point now," Larry said as they continued their walk toward the pub.

"Is this Marcus Daly's pub?" Gabriel asked as they entered.

"No, another immigrant with a similar name. He's really O'Daly, but calls his bar *Daly's Place*. It's the largest bar in Butte," Morgan said.

"The largest in Montana," Gabriel said as he peered down the length of the seventy-five-foot maple bar. Mirrors mounted on the wall behind the bar reflected the room and more casks of liquor than he had ever seen. The men elbowed their way to the bar to order their pints.

"A bit tense tonight, eh, lads?" Niall said in a hushed tone.

They all continued to speak to each other in voices barely loud enough to be heard over the din of other patrons' conversations.

"What do you expect, with the election in a few days?" Morgan murmured.

"I shouldn't think you'd be tense. You know you're going to vote for Bryan," Gabriel said.

"That's not what has us on edge. It's whether or not to vote for Clark as our senator," Morgan whispered. "And whether or not we'll get the eight-hour day."

"Why would you vote for a man who was already thrown out for corruption?" Larry asked.

"All politics is corrupt," Niall muttered. "Although I'd never vote for that man. Not when Daly hates 'im."

"Would you still be paid the same for an eight-hour day as for a longer day?" Gabriel asked.

"Yes," Larry said as he eyed the restive crowd. "And the good bosses, like Daly, are proponents, as they know it'll lead to healthier workers."

"And less turnover so they save money," Niall said. "We may not be miners, but the law would affect us too."

"But I thought Daly was now with Amalgamated, and they didn't support the eight-hour day in the beginning," Gabriel said. "And that Clark supported it from the start."

"That was Amalgamated speaking, not Marcus Daly. He's a man for the working classes," Niall said.

"This is a Daly-supporter bar," Morgan said in a low voice. "Clark's people know better than to come here."

"Is Clark as bad as they say?" Gabriel asked as he looked around.

"Gabriel—" Morgan began with a note of warning in his voice, but it was too late. The men standing around them had heard their conversation.

"If you have to ask, you don't know what yer talking about," a brawny man next to Gabriel hissed.

Gabriel nodded, taking a sip of his beer. "I meant no offense. I want to better understand..."

"Understand this. Any man who doubts Marcus Daly is a worthless son of a bitch. He doesn't like Clark, and you shouldn't neither."

Gabriel nodded, looking toward Morgan, Niall and Larry. He saw them go rigid as they watched the men around him. He turned back toward the large man.

"And where are you from? You sound foreignlike," the man said.

"Boston."

"Boston?" Another man with a fiery glint to his alcohol-dulled eyes turned toward Gabriel. "You out here to spy on us for Amalgam?"

"No, no, not at all," Gabriel said.

"You expect us to work here, dying in the mines, having our lungs rot 'n getting miner's con, just so you can ship those profits home to your cronies?"

"I don't—"

"You bastard," the large man said. He reared back, fisted his mallet-size hand and began to pummel Gabriel with a series of well-timed, sharp jabs to Gabriel's jaw and right eye.

Gabriel fell to the floor, both from the blows and to escape the beating. He looked up to see an enraged man the size of a giant looming over him, waiting for him to rise.

"Damnation," Gabriel muttered. A pair of hands helped pull him to his feet, and he swayed as he attempted to regain his equilibrium. He held one hand to his tender eye, noting that the majority of the patrons in the bar had given him a wide circle of space as though expecting him to fight his attacker. He glanced behind him to see Larry, Niall and Morgan standing with their fists clenched as though ready for battle. He shook his head from side to side, and then groaned with the pain that movement wrought. "I have no fight with you. I am a cabinetmaker. Trying to make my way here, same as you."

The other man merely shrugged, turning back to his friends and his drink. Gabriel jerked as Morgan grasped him on his shoulder. "We told you not to speak about politics after Jeffers got so irate yesterday," he snapped. "You really are an ignorant Northerner with no common sense if you don't know when to keep your mouth shut."

"Especially if you don't know what you're talking about," Larry muttered. "I knew we should have talked about that photo from your room instead. You'd be in a damn better condition than you are now."

"I was just trying to figure it all out. Montana politics is almost as confusing as Boston politics," Gabriel said as he poked at his tender right eye.

"If you have questions, ask us at the Thornton when Jeffers is on break. Don't bring the wrath of men like Cu Chulainn down on you again," Niall said.

"*Cu* who?"

He rolled his eyes. "A strong Irish fighter. Someone you could take lessons from," Niall said. "Let's get you out of here before someone thinks it's a good idea to hit you again."

"How would I go about meeting this *Cullan* person?" Gabriel asked.

"For the love of God, do you know nothing about your heritage? He's one of our mythical men. Read a book, talk to one of the storytellers. They'll tell you all you'd want to know about him." Niall pushed him in the back, helping to propel him onto the boardwalk.

Gabriel paused outside the bar, the cool air a balm to his throbbing jaw and eye. "There's no need for me to ruin everyone's night. I'll make it home fine." He waved at them as he crossed the street to catch a passing streetcar. As he boarded it, he ignored the stares of curious passengers and settled into one of the rear seats for the short ride up the hill. He closed his eyes for a few moments as he fought dizziness from the lurching movement of the streetcar.

After disembarking, he stopped in at the boardinghouse, picked up a letter from Richard and decided to go to the Egans' house early. He attempted to ignore the insistent ache in his right eye, but, as the throbbing steadily increased on the short walk to their house, he hoped Amelia would know what to do to help ease the pain.

"Coming!" Amelia called out after he knocked. He heard a patter of footsteps at the door and little Nicholas answered.

"Hello, Nicholas," Gabriel said. Nicholas shrieked, turning to flee toward his mother.

Gabriel touched his eye. "Amelia," he said as he glanced in her direction. "I'm sorry I scared your boy."

She glanced up from comforting Nicholas to study Gabriel with wide hazel eyes. "Oh my," she said, biting her lower lip. "I hope the other man looks worse." Wisps of honey-colored hair framed her face, her bun always loose after a day of chasing Nicholas. Wet splotches marred her ivory-colored apron and covered the front of her buttercream-toned wool dress.

Gabriel laughed. "I doubt it. He caught me off guard and knocked me down before I knew what had happened." He patted his eye, grimacing at the light touch.

"Sit, Gabriel," Amelia said as she pushed him toward the living room. Gabriel collapsed into the partially stuffed chair. "Nicholas, stop it. Gabriel's been in a fight and must be tended to."

"Where's everyone else?" Gabriel asked on a groan as he laid his head back against the chair, closing his eyes for a moment.

"They had a meeting at the union hall, then went by the pub with the hopes of meeting you there," Amelia said.

"Well, we didn't go to the local tonight. The men I work with wanted to go to Daly's Place, and it was crazy." Gabriel sighed as Amelia placed a cool, wet cloth to the right side of his face.

"I wish I had ice," she murmured.

"This will help."

"What'd'ye do to earn a facer?" Nicholas asked, as he climbed Gabriel's leg like a tree branch, excited energy running off him. His russet-colored hair formed a riotous halo of curls around his head, and his dark brown eyes watched Gabriel with intense curiosity.

"I'm not sure. One moment I was talking about politics, next I was on the floor."

"People take their politics seriously around here," Amelia said.

"I'm learning that," Gabriel muttered. "God, this hurts almost as bad as when Clarissa bashed my head open."

"She did what?" Amelia asked with a hint of a laugh in her voice.

Gabriel opened his good eye to watch her. "You may find that funny, and I guess it is now, but that's how we met," Gabriel said with a broad smile as he closed his eye again. "I was on a ladder, and she stumbled into it and me. Felled me like a pine tree..."

"Timber!" Nicholas called out gaily in his youthful voice.

"And when I came to, my head was bashed open, and this small, magnificent woman was there," he said. "How could I not love her?"

Amelia laughed, unable to hide her mirth. "You are a wonder, Gabriel. Most men would want their woman to have some grace."

"Her clumsiness is almost graceful."

"Have you heard any more from her?"

At this, Gabriel frowned. "Very little of consequence. Ramblings about the weather or school, but nothing about how she truly is. I worry about what is happening, and yet there is nothing I can do."

"Why are you worried? She is with her family."

"Yes, and with her stepmother and near my aunt. Two truly evil women."

"Surely your brother would tell you if anything were occurring."

"I would hope so," Gabriel said. "Though he is very angry with me at the moment."

"You live a complicated life, Gabriel. One I do not envy," Amelia said as she patted Nicholas's head. The door flew open, and Liam, Matthew and Ronan entered.

"Shut that door! You're letting all of the heat out," Amelia admonished.

"Sorry, ma'am," Ronan said as he closed the door. "Have you seen..." He glanced around the room and saw Gabriel sprawled in one of the chairs.

"Gabriel?" Matthew finished the sentence. "What in damnation happened to you?" He unbuttoned his thick wool coat, untied a gray scarf from around his neck and took off a wool hat. He ran a hand through his black hair, setting the short strands on edge before he patted them down.

"Matthew!" Amelia scolded his language as Liam nudged him in the side with a nod toward little Nicholas.

"We hoped to meet you at the pub," Liam said. He brushed his long mustache as he studied Gabriel and the nascent bruises forming along his jaw.

"I was invited—"

"Coerced more like," Ronan muttered as he took in Gabriel's swollen face.

"—to go out with the men I work with. They wanted to spend some time with me outside of work."

"*Eejits.* They think having a bar brawl is a bit of entertainment for them?" Liam asked as he studied Gabriel. "Did you hurt your hands?" He relaxed at Gabriel's shake of his head.

"It's my own fault. I got this for my remarks about politics. Though I'm still unsure what I said that was so offensive."

"What were you talking about?" Ronan asked. He hung up his jacket alongside Matthew's and rubbed his hands together to warm them as he moved into the living room.

"The upcoming Senate election," Gabriel said, opening his left eye to watch his friends.

"Did you mention Marcus Daly?" Liam asked.

"Probably."

"Well, that's why you look like you do. Those loyal to him are a bit testy at the moment," Matthew said.

"And I thought politics in Boston was complicated," Gabriel said on a groan.

"Don't you read the local papers? *The Reveille? The Standard?*" Liam asked. At Gabriel's quick shake of his head, Liam said, "Well, I'd start reading them. Then you'll have a better idea what's going on and what not to talk about."

"Why is Daly so against Clark gaining the Senate seat?" Gabriel asked.

"I can't be sure why they loathe each other. Maybe it's because one's Catholic and the other isn't," Liam said as he settled into the other dilapidated chair in the room.

"Or maybe it's because some men can never share success," Amelia muttered. She grabbed Nicholas and carried him toward the rocking chair where she sat to rock him.

"At any rate, there is great animosity between the two men, and they'll go to great lengths to beat the other," Liam said.

"It's why Helena's the state capitol and not Anaconda," Ronan said. "Daly wanted Anaconda. Clark didn't want him to win just to be ornery. Buckets full of money were spent, and, in the end, Daly lost." He eyed the settee with Matthew sitting on the side with one leg made from books and opted to sprawl on the floor.

"So now Daly is intent on preventing Clark from obtaining what he wants?" Gabriel said.

"So it seems. Though by all accounts, Clark will be our next senator," Matthew said. "Even if he is a bit corrupt."

"That's like saying the pope's slightly Catholic," Liam muttered. "The man's not had an altruistic thought in his life."

Gabriel chuckled. "Tonight I think they were most upset that I was from Boston. There's nothing I can do to change that."

"There are many here who are none too pleased with the Amalgamated takeover of Anaconda. They have ties to Boston. And you can't help sounding like you do," Liam said.

Gabriel rolled his good eye at that comment coming from Liam in his thick Irish accent.

"Yeah, like you've lost your Rs every time you speak," Matthew teased.

"I do not," Gabriel said.

"Say bar, horse, fork," Ronan taunted. "Please, especially fork."

"Ronan!" Amelia admonished him with a tap on his head. "No need to taunt the poor man after he's already had his head bashed."

"Well, you don't have to be so forthright about where you are from, Gabriel," Liam said. "Say something vague."

"I am proud to be from Boston," Gabriel protested.

"That's all well and good, but I would think you wouldn't want too many more facers just now," Matthew said.

"Here, this is what got them so riled," Ronan said. He rose and pulled out a copy of *The Butte Miner* from his jacket pocket. He handed it to Gabriel. "It came out today."

Gabriel groaned as he looked at the cartoon of a fat milking cow fed by Montana labor, but being milked by Wall Street with men in suits from Boston and New York walking away with the profits.

"Damn," Gabriel whispered. "*Fed in Montana, Milked in the East.* Who writes this stuff?"

"Whether you believe it or not, it's how most feel out here, Gabe," Liam said.

"And I chose the worst day to admit to being from Boston," Gabriel said.

"Yes, though we know you aren't profiting from it," Matthew said. "Otherwise, you'd never bunk with me." He made Gabriel laugh.

"You weren't at the bar alone, Gabe. Didn't your work friends stand up for you?" Ronan asked.

"They helped me up and stood by me once I got myself off the floor, and then ensured I wasn't further attacked as I left the bar."

"At least they helped you a little," Matthew said.

"Why didn't they clobber the man for you?" Ronan demanded from the floor. He had collapsed onto it again to play marbles with Nicholas who had squirmed down from Amelia's lap as she rose to work in the kitchen.

"I think they were waiting to see if I were insane enough to fight him."

"Big lout, was he?" Liam said with a laugh.

"Monstrous. I wasn't that stupid. Niall compared him to Cu Chulainn."

"Well, then count yourself lucky to still be with us," Liam said with a wink.

"I will. And I think I'll avoid Daly's Place from now on."

"Could you be any more dense, man?" Ronan moaned. "What in God's name possessed you to talk about politics in a place like that?"

"I thought we were having a quiet conversation as I learned more about the ways of Montana politics. I never imagined everyone around us was listening in and ripe for a fight."

"Gabriel, you seem intelligent. And I hope for your Clarissa's sake you are. But don't go stirring things up on the eve of an election in one of the copper king's bastions of support."

Gabriel nodded. "Believe me, I've figured that out."

"The last thing you'd want to happen is to hurt your hands so you couldn't work. You wouldn't want to end up in the Cabbage Patch," Liam said. They all grimaced.

"None of us will ever end up in Butte's slum," Matthew vowed. All of them nodded their agreement and pledge to each other.

Amelia called out from the kitchen where she was placing the finishing touches on dinner. "Did you know Gabriel's Clarissa bashed his head open? That's how they met."

"So you're used to this kind of treatment?" Ronan asked with a laugh. "That's good to know."

"Leave off, the lot of you," Gabriel said, though he could not refrain from joining in their laughter.

"What news from your letter, Gabriel?" Amelia asked. "You know how we all wish we received mail as regularly as you."

"Give me a little time, and I'll tell you the latest," Gabriel said, settling back to read the letter from Richard. After a few moments he muttered, "Holy hell."

"Gabe?" Liam asked.

Gabriel waved away the concern, intent on the news.

After a few more moments he whispered, "My uncle is alive." He looked toward them, awestruck. "My uncle whom I haven't seen since I was twelve. I thought he was dead. He thought we were dead. He met Clarissa at a function at her fancy cousin's house, and she introduced him to Richard." He paused.

"Gabriel, that is wonderful! To have family where you thought you didn't. I envy you," Amelia said.

"I remember him well, my seafaring uncle. He was so like my da."

"What does your brother say about him?" Ronan asked.

"That he reminds him of Da, but that he can't remember Aidan."

"Maybe he's not your uncle," Matthew said.

"Why would he claim to be my uncle if he weren't?" Gabriel asked. "He has nothing to gain from an association with my brothers and me. And by all accounts, he is a very successful businessman. Besides, Richard says he reminds him of our da."

"Well, then this is a reason to celebrate!" Amelia said. "Though it is only a simple meal, it should suffice."

CHAPTER 8

I STOOD ERASING THE DAY'S LESSON from the chalkboard when I heard heavy footsteps approaching. I twirled. My breath caught and my heart skipped a beat as I saw the tall, dark-haired man in the doorway.

"Richard," I said, expelling my pent-up breath. "Wonderful to see you." I collapsed into my chair out of fear of fainting.

Drawings from my students decorated the wall to one side of my cluttered desk, and I had managed to erase only half of the day's lesson. Bright light streamed in through the only window on the other side. I took a deep breath, battling memories.

"Are you all right, Miss Sullivan?" he entered the room, crouching in front of me and taking hold of my hands.

"I'm sorry," I whispered. I attempted to feign a happy smile but knew I had failed miserably.

Richard studied me. "You thought I was Gabe," he murmured. At my swift nod, he squeezed my hands. "Sorry to disappoint."

"Clarissa, do you have any—" Florence called out as she entered the room but stopped abruptly near the doorway.

Richard stood, dropping my hands, all of his focus on Florence across the room. "Florence," he breathed. He studied her from head to foot as though cataloging the changes in her.

Florence paled and then flushed red. She watched him with wide eyes through her glasses, mute. Her curly black hair had escaped its tight bun while numerous curls framed her round face. She wrapped her arms around her middle, effectively covering the stains to her gray cotton shirtwaist dress received during the day's penmanship lesson.

I rose, walking toward her and looped my arm through hers to drag her farther into the room. I did not want her to escape.

"I'm sorry to have interrupted," Florence choked out.

"I came to see you," Richard murmured. He reached out to touch her but dropped his hand as Florence flinched away.

"How could you?" Florence glared at me.

"She did the right thing, Flo," Richard said. "I have wondered for too long what happened to you. Where you went when old Mrs. Kruger died. How you were." He watched her. "How are you, Florence?"

"I'm fine," she said with only a slight tremble in her voice to betray the lie.

I let go of Florence's arm reluctantly, wanting to give them a bit of privacy. But as I eased away, Florence gripped my arm, forestalling any movement. "No. Stay, Clarissa. You wanted this to occur and must be curious to know what would happen."

"Florence, it's not like that at all. Well, not solely for that reason. I want to see you happy."

"You can't even see to your own happiness. Why should you think to suddenly try to look after mine?" Florence spat out.

I recoiled as though I had been struck, freed my arm and moved a few paces away from her.

"Florence, that's not like you," Richard murmured. "There is no need to lash out at Clarissa. She has been a good friend to me with Gabriel gone." Richard reached out to her, clasping her arms. "Florence, I know that you and I've had a few rough years. I know that you think you have a reason to cling to bitterness. But you don't. Not any longer."

"You don't know me, Richard McLeod," Florence said. "If you had…"

"I don't know who you are now, Florence," Richard agreed. "But I know who you were. A loyal, lovely, kind, intelligent woman struggling for a better future. Just like I was struggling. I had no right to allow myself to be torn away from you without speaking with you. Will you speak with me now?"

Tears silently coursed down Florence's cheeks. "Why are you here? Why are you doing this to me?"

"I am here because I have never truly been happy without you," he murmured, tenderly brushing her riotous black curls behind her ear. "I am here because, no matter how hard I tried, no matter how hard Gabriel tried to make me, I couldn't forget you."

"You are only interested because you are all alone now."

"There will never come a time when I don't want you in my life, Florence. I knew that from the moment we met."

"Why wouldn't you talk with me? I begged you ... I *begged* you, and you wouldn't." She sobbed.

Richard shook his head, regret and hurt in his eyes. "I saw you with Henry, and I imagined the worst. You were pouring tea for them, my hated aunt Masterson and cousin. And they knew more about your true past than I did."

"If you would have let me explain..."

"I know now. *I know*. But, then, all I felt was a fool. And hurt."

Florence stepped away from him, scrubbing the tears from her eyes. "It's going to take more than a few sweet words to convince me," she said with a glower.

Richard smiled. "If it were any other way, I would be disappointed." He glanced toward me, and I saw true happiness flit across his face. "Join me for tea, Flo?"

"I will not. You seem to be under the impression that I am free whenever you want to see me. I have a life and responsibilities."

"Tomorrow?" he murmured.

She watched him with a glimmer of joy in her eyes, and I realized their dance had begun again. "I might be free tomorrow."

"Good. Then I might call for you here at the end of the school day. If you will excuse me, I must return to the smithy," Richard said with a jaunty smile as he turned to leave.

After a few moments of silence, Florence glared at me. "How dare you, Rissa?"

"What? Want to see my dear friend happy?" I said with a broad smile. "For you will be happy with him."

"If he is constant."

"Florence, you know he will be. You know why he reacted the way he did."

"I may know why, but that doesn't mean I understand. There's still a lot of hurt that needs to be resolved, Rissa."

"I know, but at least you have the chance now," I said, drawing her into a quick embrace. "I'd wear the pretty light-purple dress tomorrow with an extra petticoat."

"Rissa!" Florence laughed, sounding young and carefree. "I agree."

***

"CLARISSA, LOOK WHO has called for tea," Mrs. Smythe called out.

I looked up from my book, *The Wonderful Wizard of Oz*, with no real interest in the new arrival. I turned toward the door, the book lightly clasped in my hands. It fell with a thud as my eyes bulged at the visitor. Mrs. Smythe tittered as she welcomed Cameron into the parlor, patting the space next to her for him to seat himself. He looked toward me for a moment, and I was thankful I sat in a chair rather than my now customary settee.

I glanced from him to her then back to him again, sure that he must be an apparition. However, he stood in the doorway, as proud as could be. His golden-blond hair was shellacked into place with a thick coating of pomade, and a well-tailored suit and waistcoat covered his tall, narrow frame. I frowned at the exultant gleam in his honey-brown eyes.

"Come, Clarissa welcome our guest." She glared at me as I continued to stare dumbly at Cameron.

"Hello, darling Miss Sullivan. It is such a pleasure to see you again." He sat gracefully next to Mrs. Smythe.

"I'm glad one of us is happy."

"I thought you were too lonely, dearest Clarissa," Mrs. Smythe said as she patted his arm a few times. "I hate to see you pining so, losing your bloom in your prime. Such a sad thing to behold in a young woman."

"As you can clearly see, I am not pining away. I continue to teach. Continue with activities that truly matter to me."

Mrs. Smythe fluttered her hand in the air, disregarding my words. "Well, believe what you will, dearest. I can see how you have suffered since your horrible abandonment. Yes, abandonment. Oh, my poor darling. And now, here is your old beau, come to reacquaint himself with you."

"We are as acquainted as we need to be," I hissed, rising to leave the room.

"Clarissa Sullivan, you will remain in the parlor and be kind to our guest."

"I will not."

I turned, fleeing the room for my bedroom, although not before I heard the triumphant murmur of his voice.

***

"WHAT'S GOT YOU so riled, Rissa?" Colin murmured from the chair next to mine. "You'd think you were reading about the disaster near Nova Scotia." He carefully folded the evening paper, his battered hands almost scrubbed clean after a long day in the smithy. I sat on a camelback settee next to Colin's gentleman's chair near the door. A fire gilded the far side of the room with flickering light. Lit gaslights on the end tables cast a warm glow to the rose-colored wallpaper.

I glanced around the room, thankful Da and Mrs. Smythe appeared deep in conversation on the medallion-style sofa close to the fireplace. "Do you know who called today?" At Colin's nearly imperceptible shake of his head in denial, I breathed, "Cameron."

He gripped the paper so hard he tore it down the middle, ruining any possibility of anyone else reading it. "Colin, what can you be thinking?" Da called out. "You know I was to be the next to read that."

"Sorry, Da," Colin said with a quick glance toward me with a raised eyebrow.

I shrugged my shoulders in resignation.

"I was simply shocked to hear who called on Clarissa today."

"Who would that be now?" Da said, rising to move toward us. I saw Mrs. Smythe try to hold onto his hand, but he gently disengaged himself from her as he approached us.

"Cameron," I said in a strong voice.

Da stopped moving, looking from Colin to me then back again. Finally he turned toward Mrs. Smythe. "And you allowed such a man into my house?"

"Now, Sean—"

"Don't you 'now, Sean' me, Mrs. Sullivan," Da ground out. "I know good and well I told you that man was never to be welcomed into my house. How could you have misunderstood?"

"Your house? Your house? Isn't this my house too? Shouldn't I be able to invite those I want, welcome those I want, into my house?"

"Now, Rebecca—"

"How dare you try to dictate who can call here during my afternoon teas? If you only knew how hard I have had to work to have any decent sort of people even want to call after that disastrous daughter of yours wreaked such scandal this summer. And now, now that a young man of good family and breeding wants to grace our home, yes, *our* home, you won't even allow me that. It's too much to be borne."

"Now, Rebecca—"

"Why marry me if you do not want my guidance, my expertise in the gentler aspects of life? Why not allow me to help your daughter make a respectable match?" She held onto her pregnant belly, her breaths heaving.

"Mrs. Sullivan," Colin said. "If you for one moment believe that Cameron is a decent match for Clarissa, then—"

"Of course he is a decent match. He's attractive, attentive—"

At this I sputtered in disbelief.

"—intelligent. I don't know what more a woman could ask for."

"Except for constancy and an ability to keep a promise," I muttered.

"Well, I shouldn't think you'd continue to hold his minor lapse of judgment against him when you clearly show continuous poor judgment in your choice of men. It's not as though Mr. McLeod is beating down the door to drag you to the altar, is it?"

"How dare you?" I exclaimed.

"How dare I try to find you a man who is actually present? How dare I try to find you a man who wants to live in Boston and not in some godforsaken mining town? Yes, how terrible of me to treat you so poorly, Clarissa."

"Enough!" Da roared. "I've told you enough times, Rebecca. Cameron will never be welcomed into my home. He shamed Clarissa, disgraced our family and is not welcome here. I expect you to heed me on this. And you," he said toward me, "will begin to show Rebecca, Mrs. Sullivan, the respect she is due as your stepmother. If she has guests, you will not leave the room until you have been excused. Do you understand, Clarissa?"

"Is this not also my home, Da? Do I no longer have the freedom to come and go as I would like?"

He sat heavily next to me on the settee. He heaved a lusty sigh and then shook his head. "No, you don't. Not anymore."

I sat, as still as a stone pillar, barely able to breathe from the shock of Da's words.

"You have had entirely too many freedoms. I see that now."

"What do you mean, Da?" Colin asked. He reached out to grip my hand, giving me a gentle squeeze in support.

"I mean that Clarissa needs to spend her time at home. Helping Mrs. Sullivan to run the house. To begin to take things over as Mrs. Sullivan's time nears so that the home will continue to run smoothly after the baby is born. As you said, Clarissa, this is your home too. Now start acting like it."

"Da!"

"You need to learn how to run a house. You need to learn how to be a woman of society. I have taught you neither of these things. Mrs. Sullivan can. These are things that you cannot learn teaching at a school," he said, watching me. "Or taking tea with suffragettes."

"No!"

"Yes, Clarissa," he said. "No more school. No more suffragist meetings. Your place is here, at home, learning to run it. If young, upstanding men, as your stepmother calls them, are reluctant to court you, you must learn what is needed. I want to see you settled. It's what your mum would have wanted."

"Da, no. I need to work. I need to have a purpose to my day. To my life." A hot tear escaped, coursing unheeded down my cheek.

"No, Clarissa. I have come to see the error in my ways in granting you so much freedom. You suffered near total disgrace this summer. Your step-mother has shown me it was due to your headstrong, liberal ways, and my indulgence of them. Your mother would want more for you than to risk ru-ination and a life lived as a spinster. Be thankful you will have your step-mother to guide you."

"Da, that's not fair."

"If your Gabriel doesn't return to you, you need to prepare yourself for a life here," Da said.

***

A WEEK LATER I sat in the parlor, ignoring Mrs. Smythe as she prattled on about the redecoration of the parlor. At the knock on the front door, I tilted my head to listen for who had called.

"Now stop your timidity, girl. You know Clarissa would want to see you." I heard Sophronia's commanding voice in the hallway speaking to her hesitant companion. I stifled a *whoop* of joy and rose, walking to greet them with a lightness of step.

Sophronia, attired in a burgundy wool dress with black cotton soutache trim along the bodice, hem and wrists, marched forward with determined steps whereas Florence hung back a pace. Sophronia wielded a walking stick, although I suspected it was more to badger people out of her way than for any true need.

"Sophie! Florence!" I shrieked. "How wonderful to see you. Tea will be bearable because you are here," I whispered to them as we walked toward the parlor.

"Clarissa, my girl, it is about time we saw you," Sophronia said.

"Clarissa, how good it is to see you. School is dreadful without you," Florence said. "The children miss you terribly and even mean old Mr. Carney has said he wishes you back."

I gripped her hand at the thought of my students and the principal, and teaching again, and led them into the parlor to a frowning Mrs. Smythe.

"Mrs. Sullivan, a pleasure to see you again," Sophronia said.

"I am glad one of us finds pleasure in it," Mrs. Smythe snapped. She stared at Florence, taking in her disheveled appearance, riotous mass of curly black hair and stained, faded forest-green wool dress. "Who might you be?"

"Florence Butler, ma'am," Florence said. "I teach school with Clarissa."

"I see. As I suspected, they have a penchant for hiring undesirable women in the hopes of giving them some sort of future."

"Mrs. Smythe!" I gasped.

"It is why I wish for Clarissa to remain at home. She has many attributes that will be valued by upstanding young men who would not think of frequenting such a school. Surely you agree with me, Mrs. Chickering. Clarissa's future must be of our utmost concern."

"Her future happiness is never far from my thoughts," Sophronia murmured as she sat on a chair near Mrs. Smythe. "I doubt, however, you give much thought to her emotional state when you ponder her life."

"You have no right! To come into my home and make such assertions. I care for that girl as though she were my own."

"Well, then let us hope you have a son," Sophronia said with a small smile in my direction.

"I refuse to sit here and be insulted in my own sitting room. If you will excuse me?" Mrs. Smythe rose to storm out of the room in all of her pregnant glory.

"Nicely done, Sophie. Though I am sure I will have to hear a lecture tonight from Da about respecting her." I rose to shut the door for privacy.

"At last! We can have some peace without her around," Sophie said. "And as for you, Florence, don't give credence to one word she said. She doesn't know about Richard, does she?"

"Florence! Tell me more. What has happened?"

Florence bit her lip for a few moments as she gathered her thoughts. "I have seen Richard a few times and…"

"Do you think there is a future between you?"

"I hope so, Rissa. I dream of one every night, though I tell myself not to."

"Why, Florence? Dreams are what help us to continue when the drudgery of life seems unbearable."

"It was easier not to dream because then I never had to worry about the inevitable disappointment. The fear that he will change his mind again."

"Oh, Flo," I said. "I can only imagine the heartbreak you have gone through. And yet I know it is better to be able to envision a happy future."

"We are meeting almost every day for tea or supper. And it seems so much like old times. I had forgotten how nice he is and interesting."

"Has he written Gabriel?"

Florence's shoulders hunched together before she straightened. "Yes. Gabriel thinks him a fool. Gabriel believes that once a liar or a deceiver, always a liar."

"That doesn't sound like Gabriel."

"It does with regard to me," Florence murmured. "And yet Richard doesn't seem to care. He is incredibly angry with Gabriel for knowing where I was all last spring and not telling him. Richard feels deceived by him."

I sat back in my chair, sighing. "They certainly know how to complicate something that should be simple."

"My thoughts exactly, my girl," Sophronia said. "I should think two orphan boys should have the sense to know good fortune when they see it."

I gripped my friend's hand. "Florence, this simply means you must learn to trust him again. That takes time. And he must learn to trust you."

"Will you trust Gabriel again when you see him?"

"He's given me no reason not to trust him."

"Except leave you here."

"Well, yes, but I know he wants me in his life."

"Won't you have to learn to trust that he won't leave you again?"

"Flo, please," I said as I closed my eyes for a moment. "I can't doubt what I have with Gabriel. If I do that, I'll go mad. It is the only thing that gives purpose to my life, now that I can't teach or take part in the suffragist movement."

"Well, my girl," Sophronia said. "It's good to have a purpose in your life. Although I worry when it is based on a man. You need to continue your activities with us, even though they will need to be clandestine out of necessity with that stepmother of yours."

"What do you suggest, Sophie?"

"You should continue to read the newspaper and correspond with us as much as possible. We will call for tea once a week to keep you abreast of developments and to provide needed distraction from your stepmother and her ilk."

"She would destroy the paper if it were delivered here, Sophie," I protested.

"I will ask Richard to deliver it to you with Gabriel's letters," Florence said. "He will enjoy irritating her as much as possible."

"Whatever you do, Clarissa, I want you at that convention in May," Sophie said.

"Convention? What convention?"

"The National American Woman Suffrage Association's annual convention will be held in Minneapolis at the end of May. I want you to attend with me. Florence will be unable to join us due to her school duties. However, you will be free."

"I highly doubt Da will allow me to attend a meeting in Minneapolis when I am not allowed to sip tea with you in Boston."

"Then you know what your task is. Find a way," Sophie said, piercing me with her aquamarine eyes.

I nodded in agreement before jumping with a start at the soft knock at the sitting room door.

"Miss Sullivan, there is someone calling for tea," Mary said.

"Send her in," I said. I turned to Sophie and Florence. "At least you will be here to help me."

"I had hoped by now you would know how to pour a cup of tea, Clarissa," Cameron said from the doorway. He posed for a moment, one leg bent at the knee with a hand in his pocket, the gray linen of his suit tailored and ironed to show off his tall, lean frame. A crisp white shirt and collar, navy blue waistcoat and ruby cuff links completed his ensemble.

I gaped at him for a moment, surprised at his gall. "Mr. Wright, how ... interesting you have decided to call again. May I introduce you to Mrs. Chickering and Miss Butler?"

"Enchanted," Cameron said with a quick bow. "No Mrs. Sullivan today? I had hoped to speak with her about something I read recently in the paper."

"I wouldn't expect her to know to what you are referring," I said, watching him take the seat nearest me. "She rarely reads."

Sophie snickered, muttering, "It's not rarely, but barely."

"How cruel you are, Clarissa," Cameron chided. "I am sure your stepmother is very knowledgeable." He glanced from Sophie's imposing figure in burgundy wool to Florence's faded green wool, then back to me. "I hadn't realized I was interrupting a hen party."

"I can't imagine you would expect anything different, young man," Sophie barked. "This is tea time after all. A time when women call on each other."

"I..."

"I would think you would have something worthwhile to fill your time rather than listening to our mindless chatter," Sophie said with a fierce glower.

"If there is one thing I have learned, ma'am, it is that women rarely partake in mindless chatter. I find myself fascinated by whatever they find interesting."

"Meaningless prattle," Sophie said. "I had hoped you would be a young man of some intellect who endeavored to do something worthwhile with his days."

"As my family is wealthy, I have no need of work."

I watched as Sophie flushed red. "Have you no need of purpose? No need to help those less fortunate?"

"I should think you, out of all of those present, Mrs. Chickering, would understand my responsibilities start and end with my family. And those I hope to make part of my family."

I shared a quick, horrified glance with Florence.

"You have no sense of noblesse oblige then?" Sophie demanded, as she fanned herself furiously.

"I have no obligation to anyone but myself, no," Cameron said.

"You may find, young man, that, one day, no one has an obligation to you either."

"Come now, this conversation has turned too serious," Cameron said after an awkward silence. "Clarissa, I was afraid you would be out this afternoon."

"I have nowhere else to be," I said with a wan smile.

"I agree. Your place is here, learning how to properly run a home. I am just thankful that Mrs. Sullivan is here to help you." Cameron brushed a piece of lint off of his pant leg.

"I should think that woman would limit Clarissa's horizons, not expand them," Sophronia barked.

"How do you know Clarissa?" Cameron asked as he leaned back in his chair with his legs casually crossed, a dainty teacup balanced on his knee.

"We are suffragettes," Sophronia said with a proud tilt of her chin. "We met at a meeting this spring."

"I am surprised one such as you from a distinguished family would be involved in scandalous endeavors," Cameron said.

"It is only by actions, scandalous or otherwise, that women will advance," Sophronia said.

"If you truly believe that, I can understand why the estimable Mrs. Sullivan is reluctant to have you as a guest in her parlor."

"Any woman, any *man*, with any sense would agree with me."

Florence and I exchanged amused glances. "What is it that amuses you, Clarissa?" Cameron asked.

"I find this conversation enlightening," I murmured. "It is as though I had never really seen you before now."

"That is because you rarely saw me interacting with those of equal social standing as myself," he said.

I shared an amused smile with Sophie and nodded my agreement.

CHAPTER 9

November 18, 1900

My dearest Gabriel,

Just writing your name brings me solace. Things are horrible here. I am incapable of writing an upbeat letter right now. I miss you so much I sometimes feel I cannot catch my breath for the pain your absence brings. I wonder that life seems to continue on as usual as everything is far from normal.

Mrs. Smythe (I refuse to write her married name) treats me like a servant. My da now listens to her counsel, and I am no longer allowed to teach. I am expected to sit at home, learning from her how to run a proper home. Although no one seems to understand I have no interest in learning such a skill. Never fear, darling, I am capable enough for a simple home. It's just that I do not see the importance of knowing the use of four different forks at dinner or how to prattle on meaninglessly to flatter a man's ego as I sit through an eight-course meal.

I feel abandoned by Colin as he is rarely home anymore. He told me that he didn't like being around that much tension. Why do men have the freedom to go where they want, when they want, but women must sit at home, doing nothing except waiting for the men to return?

It's as though I have lost everyone: you, Savannah, Colin, even my da. Why is there a limit to the amount a person can love? Why isn't there enough love to go around to include me?

I miss you with a never-ending ache, as though a part of me is dormant, waiting to come alive again.

Ever Yours,

Clarissa

***

November 24, 1900

My darling Clarissa,

I just received your letter, and it made me want to board the next available train to Boston. I wish I had the fare saved! Oh, darling, I am sorrier than I can say that you continue to suffer due to your stepmother's actions. I hope Richard is present a few evenings a week to bring you company.

You deserve kindness, love, warmth and understanding, darling, rather than the contempt of a woman who belittles such qualities. I only hope that when your baby brother or sister is born, you will find joy in him or her.

My dearest Clarissa, you must know how much you are loved. You have not lost any of us, my darling. Love is not finite, but infinite. Remember, the more you love, the more that love is returned to you.
Gabriel

***

November 28, 1900

Dear Gabriel,

How does one write to a beloved nephew who he had thought lost to him? How can I ever express my joy to realize that you boys are alive and thriving? I have told myself that I will not bemoan my lost time with you, but I find that challenging.

The last time I saw you, you had dreams of becoming a lawyer. I hope your work as a cabinetmaker has proven to be as rewarding. From what I have heard, you are very much like your father. Ian never failed to show me loyalty and love. You have shown the same to your brothers. Your father would have been very proud of you.

My business is growing, and I look to expand to Boston and New York. Mr. Montgomery seems the perfect business partner for my new ventures, though I would like your insight as your Miss Sullivan's cousin is married to him.

If it is agreeable with you, I would like to travel to see you in the spring. I am sorry I will not be with you during the holidays. I wish you a holiday filled with joy, Gabriel.
Your uncle,
Aidan

***

December 13, 1900

My dearest Clarissa,

I am writing this letter in mid-December in the hopes that it will arrive before Christmas. As I sit in my cramped room, writing by candlelight after a power cut, I think back on the past year with wonder. I have trouble believing in all of the changes that have occurred in my life. The most wondrous change was meeting you. You saw me, a simple cabinetmaker, and were able to look below the surface. Such a rare, priceless quality. You listened to my stories, accepted them and then helped me to believe in a future between us. It is a future that I still see and dream of.

My loyal, kind, intelligent, beautiful, vivacious Clarissa. Know that you are cherished for who you are. Who you truly are.

Clarissa, I know I am far away and that the immediacy of others may dim my memory. However, never doubt my love for you or my constancy.
Merry Christmas, my Clarissa, my love.
Gabriel

***

"I HOPE I'M NOT LATE," Gabriel called out as he pushed open the door. "Oof," he said as Nicholas threw himself at his knees. Sticky hands clung to his legs, marring his newly cleaned, black suit pants. "Easy, Nicholas," he said with a laugh as he hauled him up to carry him on his hip.

Gabriel glanced around to see wrapped presents stacked in one corner of the living room near the rocking chair. Pieces of evergreen covered the small side tables, the air redolent of a pine forest. A red cloth covered the dining room table, although rough, everyday white napkins sat at each place.

"We've been waiting so long," Nicholas said as he wrapped his arms around Gabriel's neck. "Where've you been?" Tears glistened on the edges of his eyelashes although he was not crying. His curly, russet-colored hair was snarled in places, and he still wore his nightclothes.

"It's barely seven in the morning, Nicholas," Gabriel said. "I'm sure St. Nick brought you plenty."

"Mama said that St. Nick would fly over us and go to children who need him," he said as his bottom lip trembled a little at the thought.

"Never fear, little man," Gabriel said sharing a smile with Liam and Amelia. "I saw the reindeer last night, and I am sure I saw him stop here. I'm surprised you didn't hear him. He made quite a racket."

"Gabriel, don't start," Amelia warned.

Nicholas squirmed so much that Gabriel had to set him down. When he was on the ground again, Nicholas began to leap about. "I knew I heard something, Mama!" He raced toward her, dragging her toward the corner of the room where the small pile of presents awaited them. "Can we open them? Can we?"

"Not yet. Ronan and Matthew aren't here," Amelia said. She brushed at his curls, trying to bring some sense of order to them. She sat in the rocking chair in a thick evergreen wool dress, her small belly bump proclaiming her pregnancy barely visible.

"But, Mama!"

"Mind your mum, young man," Liam said. Although early, he wore his best suit. He had visited the barber's yesterday. His walrus mustache had been tamed, and his shaggy auburn hair trimmed.

Nicholas collapsed in front of the presents on the verge of tears.

"Did your mum or da read you *A Visit from St. Nicholas* last night?" Gabriel asked after he had hung his jacket on a peg by the front door. He moved toward a chair near Nicholas.

Nicholas looked up toward him with desolate eyes. "No."

"Then come here, and I'll tell it to you. My mum used to tell it to me every Christmas Eve. You're only a few hours late, and you can hear what St. Nick was doing last night," Gabriel said as Nicholas clambered onto his lap.

"'Twas the night before Christmas," Gabriel began.

He closed his eyes as he held Nicholas in his arms and recalled the poem his mother had told him. He knew he wouldn't remember all the words correctly, but Nicholas would not care. The ache at remembering past Christmases eased as he said the familiar words.

Gabriel glared at the door as Matthew and Ronan barged into the room. "Sorry to be late!" they called out in their booming voices. "Hey, Nicholas! Merry Christmas!"

"Amelia, we went to the bakery and bought povitica," Ronan explained.

"We listened to men in the mine talk about it enough the past few weeks, we decided to buy one so we could see why they're so popular," Matthew said.

"We were told it is a traditional bread to eat at Christmas," Ronan said as he shrugged out of his jacket, hanging it by the door.

"Povi what?" Gabriel asked

"Povitica," Matthew said. "I guess it's some sort of nut roll that is special to this time of year. The bakery was crowded this morning before it closed for the rest of the day. We wanted to buy one fresh."

"Thank you," Amelia said. "It should make a lovely dessert."

At this point Nicolas threw himself on the floor and chanted the word *presents*.

Ronan watched him with fond amusement. "Amelia, why don't we have breakfast and coffee before we do anything else?"

Liam started coughing as he choked on a laugh. "A sound plan, Ronan. A sound plan."

"Da!" Nicholas wailed as he rolled around on the ground as though in agony.

"What are you going on for?" Liam asked him in mock exasperation.

"Pre…sents," Nicholas said through tears.

"Ah, ye wee *eejit*, we're just having a go at you," Liam soothed as he picked him up and wiped his face. "Of course it's presents time. I'm dying to know what's wrapped up in that large blanket."

"Come on, everyone, grab your coffee. Let's open presents before Nicholas does himself bodily harm," Gabriel said with a wink to Nicholas.

Gabriel remained seated in one of the chairs, Liam sat in the half-stuffed chair, and Matthew and Ronan collapsed onto the settee. They held their breaths to see if the books forming one leg were sturdy enough to hold their weight, and, when they did not crash to the floor, they leaned back with a sigh of relief. Amelia relaxed in her rocking chair with Nicholas sprawled at her feet. After everyone had settled, Amelia doled out the small cache of presents. "There's not much to go around this year, so I thought if we all opened our presents one at a time, it would make it last longer," she said.

"A grand idea, darling," Liam said, taking her hand and kissing it.

As the gifts were opened slowly, Gabriel unwrapped a burgundy-colored scarf from Amelia, a packet of writing paper from Matthew and Ronan, and a chisel from Liam.

Gabriel sat fingering his scarf, watching Ronan and Matthew open similar presents, but in forest green and cobalt blue.

Nicholas ripped open paper with abandon, delighting in every gift. "Look, Mama, Da, a horse!" he said as he pulled out the hand-carved horse Gabriel had made him. "Thank you, Gavriel!" He said as he launched himself at Gabriel for a quick hug. In a matter of seconds, he was on the floor, playing with it.

Amelia chortled as she opened her gift from Ronan and Matthew. "Look what the boys gave me. *The Fannie Farmer Cookbook*." They all laughed.

"At least you'll have more recipes to try for us, darling," Liam said.

"And we didn't want Gabe to miss any of the recipes he's accustomed to," Ronan said.

"Ah, yes, *The Boston Cooking-School Cook Book*," Matthew said. "You Bostonians have a tremendous opinion of yourselves to think we all want to be like you."

"Well, you must, as you bought the book," Gabriel replied as they all laughed.

"Oh, Gabriel, you shouldn't have," Amelia said as she unwrapped the large present covered in a blanket. "Liam, look what he made us." She reached out her hand to Liam as she continued to pull off the blanket with her other hand to reveal a well-hewn baby's crib.

"I made it big so the baby can grow into it. And it's made of sturdy maple so it will last," Gabriel murmured.

"Thank you, Gabriel," Liam said. "We could never have bought such a well-made piece."

Amelia nodded and smiled her thanks through her sniffles as she continued to trace the simple, elegant curves of the crib.

"I'm just looking forward to seeing what kind of mischief the new baby brings," Gabriel said.

"Gabriel McLeod, careful what you wish for!" Amelia said with a laugh.

"What did your lady love send you, Gabe?" Matthew asked as he tied his new scarf around his neck.

"She sent me a pair of socks she knitted herself. And a sweater that she bought."

"Those socks will be mighty welcome as winter drags on," Ronan said as he reached out to tighten Mathew's scarf, nearly choking him in the process.

"You would think. Clarissa's not the most talented woman when it comes to the domestic arts. They look more like mittens, and my feet won't fit into shoes when I have them on."

"Consider them slippers then," Liam said with a wink.

"I'd be thankful she didn't decide to knit you a sweater. You might have ended up with three sleeves," Ronan joked.

"I was very happy to see she purchased the sweater."

"And she wrote you a lovely letter," Amelia murmured.

Gabriel flushed. "Yes."

"Nicholas, you must change. Now. We have to go to Mass, and then we can return for the meal." She stood leading Nicholas away from the room. "This won't take long. Start bundling up for the walk." They nodded, stood and donned their coats and other winter wear to withstand the cold for the walk to church.

***

"GABE, YOU AWAKE?" Matthew mumbled.

"Yeah."

"It was a good day. I didn't miss home as much as I had thought."

"Nor did I," Gabriel admitted. "It helped to be with all of you. Did you hear from your family?"

"No, none of 'em can read or write. I knew when I left I wouldn't hear from them again."

"You could still write them, Matthew. Tell them how you are."

"I do. About once a month. And I hope they find someone to read it to them. What did your lovely lady have to tell you, Gabe?"

"She missed me and wished me home."

"But you aren't going back," Matthew said on a loud yawn.

"No, I'm not. Somehow I have to explain that to her."

"She'll grow to like Butte."

"Maybe. But she'll like all of you," Gabriel said with warm affection in his voice.

"Without a doubt. Night, Gabe," Matthew said.

A few moments later, Gabriel heard a soft snoring. Gabriel lay on his cot rereading Clarissa's recent letter.

December 17, 1900

My darling Gabriel,

Merry Christmas, dearest! I wish you were here to celebrate the holiday with me. We could go for long walks, warm up with hot chocolate and finish the perfect day of my imaginings with a kiss (or two!) under the mistletoe. Know that you are never far from my thoughts.

We have begun to decorate the house. There is beautiful holly this year, and I have placed it in lovely vases throughout the family parlor. I have also strung boughs of evergreen around the fireplace. The stockings have been hung, and we now await the arrival of St. Nicholas. The decorations are rather simple, but I enjoy them.

My baby sister, Melinda, will be one month old on Christmas day and gives us something more to celebrate. It is a marvel to watch her grow and change every day.

Thank you for your letters. I would be lost without them. Never fear that the sweet talkings of those present would ever cause me to forget you. I simply act as I know is expected of me, smile when I should, think my own thoughts and dream of you.

Enclosed you will find something that I labored to make for you. Hopefully you will find it useful during the next few months. My darling Gabriel, I wish you a very Merry Christmas and a Happy New Year. May this be the last holiday that we spend apart.

Your Clarissa

CHAPTER 10

I FROWNED AT THE DOOR at the gentle, insistent tapping that intruded upon my quietude as I rocked in my chair overlooking the back garden.

"Rissa," Colin called out. When I didn't answer, he poked his head in, rolling his eyes to see my distant gaze. "Daydreaming again?"

I raised my eyebrows at him by way of answer, waiting for him to speak.

"Richard's here with a surprise."

I bolted up, breathless.

"Rissa, don't," Colin warned. "It's not what you think."

I nodded. "Of course. How silly of me," I choked out.

Colin moved toward me, taking my face in his hands. His thumbs rubbed my cheeks, forcing my eyes open. "Rissa, it's acceptable to miss him. To wish him here. If I had ever loved like that, I'd cling to it. Fight for it."

"Let's go see Richard," I said, attempting to fake a smile.

"Someday I'd like to see that smile reach your eyes."

I shrugged as I shook myself free of his hold, brushing past him and making my way downstairs.

"Richard!" I called out as I entered the parlor. I stopped short as two tall, dark-haired, broad-shouldered men turned toward me. The man beside Richard watched me with piercing green eyes and his black hair gleamed in the lamplight. He leaned on a cane held in his left hand and reached up with his free hand to swipe away at a fine bead of perspiration from his brow. He grimaced at the slight movement.

"Miss Sullivan," Richard said with a beaming smile. "May I present my brother, Jeremy?"

"Jeremy!" I exclaimed, reaching out to clasp his arm that felt almost skeletal. In my exuberance, I nearly missed his cringe at my touch. "I beg your pardon," I said, moving away and feeling chastised. I saw Richard watching Jeremy but sensed more concern than annoyance.

I motioned to the chairs and settee nearer to the piano and fire, and farther from Da and Mrs. Smythe who sat near the door this evening. Colin joined us sitting next to me on the medallion sofa covered in a pale gray damask, the sofa named for the three circular pieces framing its back. Richard sat on a chair next to Colin. Jeremy limped and leaned heavily on his cane as he moved toward Da's red velvet gentleman's chair near the fire and next to Richard. After a few moments, the tightness around his mouth eased as he relaxed into the comfortable seat.

"Tell me about your homecoming," I said after I settled the skirts of my dusted-rose wool dress.

Jeremy just shook his head, refusing to speak. He closed his eyes for a moment, like a cat basking in the warmth and glow of the fire. The tension continued to seep out of him, and he appeared more and more relaxed with each passing moment.

"I was working at the smithy yesterday when Tommy said someone was looking for me. I thought it was ol' Cousin Henry, but, when I turned away from the forge, I saw Jer," Richard said with a big smile and a catch in his voice. "I…" He shook his head, unable to say more.

"I think he was disappointed I wasn't Gabe," Jeremy said in a deeper voice than either Richard or Gabriel. His black hair, cut in a short military style, showed signs of slowly growing out. He made fleeting eye contact with deep green eyes.

"Never," Richard said. "All that matters is that you are home. Safe, healthy and whole."

"Well, I'm safe at least," Jeremy said with a lopsided smile.

"I hope you soon find the health and happiness you don't already have," I said.

"From your mouth to God's ear," Jeremy replied, reminding me of Gabriel.

"What do you plan on doing, Jeremy?" Colin asked.

"I'm not sure. I just arrived and I have few … skills." He ruefully shook his head. "I am really not prepared for much of anything useful other than…" Another shake of his head came as he stopped speaking.

"Gabriel will be very excited," I said in a gentle tone, sensing a deep emotion. "I hope you have written him." At his small nod, I beamed at him. "He will be saddened that he was not here to welcome you home. To have the three of you together again."

"He wrote me about you, Miss Sullivan," Jeremy said. "It's nice to see you are as kind as he described."

"Thank you."

"Is Gabriel's workshop let?" Colin mused aloud as he lounged on the settee next to me with his long legs stretched in front of him.

"No, no one has been interested in it. And if I'm truthful, I haven't wanted to take the time to clear out all the tools he left behind," Richard said.

"You could always work there. Try your hand at building something," Colin said, watching Jeremy's reaction. "And I imagine a little solitude would be welcome."

"I could. If you don't mind, Rich."

"Not at all."

"Richard," I said as the conversation lulled. "How is Florence?"

"She is fine. Still a bit prickly, but enjoying our sojourns, as she calls them. I'll wear her down."

"Good," I said.

"Florence sure misses you at school," Richard said.

"And I miss her. She doesn't visit nearly enough. Though, if I know she is busy with you, that helps." I smiled at him. "Oh, it is so good to have you both here. I just wish…"

"We do too, Miss Sullivan," Jeremy murmured.

"And with that, we should go," Richard said. "Lest I forget, here is a letter for you," he said with a wink as he handed me an envelope with Gabriel's bold handwriting.

"Thank you, Richard," I whispered.

"You are very welcome, Miss Sullivan," he murmured, grasping my shoulder as he passed to leave the room.

I sat next to Colin in silent wonder. Finally, I spoke. "Can you believe it?" I whispered. "Jeremy is home, and Gabriel's not here."

"It's a terrific irony," Colin agreed.

"I wonder if this will convince him to return."

"Clarissa," Colin said, gripping my hand, "at some point you may have to accept that he's never coming back." At my deep inhalation, he murmured, "Which doesn't mean you won't be together again."

***

"YOU ARE THE INFAMOUS McLeod brothers," Sophronia said. "Although it appears the most important one is absent."

We sat in our parlor a few weeks later at an impromptu soiree of sorts. The furniture had been rearranged to accommodate everyone as we sat in one large group.

Da sat to one side whispering in Mrs. Smythe's ear. She sat with her body vibrating with anger at Da's harsh words. I could hear some of them as he grew excited. "Bar that man ... not allowed ... against my wishes." Through it all, Mrs. Smythe maintained a brittle smile as she watched the room from her seat. Although she sat near the edge of the group, she managed to listen and see everyone in the room. A flush from her chin down to the scalloped neckline of her pink satin evening dress was the only sign of distress at Da's words.

"I am thankful to have been allowed admittance," Cameron said with a small nod toward Mrs. Smythe. "There are those among us who would have preferred my absence." He sat next to me on an increasingly shrinking settee.

Sophronia sat in my once-comfortable chair to my right while Colin lounged to her right. Richard and Jeremy, in rough wool pants and jackets, were ensconced in older gentlemen's chairs set higher off the ground with sturdy arms, high backs and light-blue velvet upholstery. Their dull blue shirts showed evidence of many washings, and Richard needed a patch on the right elbow of his jacket. I glanced toward Cameron, noting the sparkle from his diamond cravat pin. I edged further away from him, leaning toward Sophronia.

"Depends on who you speak with, ma'am," Jeremy said with a quirk of his eyebrow, ignoring Cameron.

"I beg your pardon?" Sophie asked. Her eyes flashed, their aquamarine color enhanced by her irritation.

"Florence might disagree that the most important one is missing," Richard murmured with a quick smile.

"At any rate..." Cameron said.

"Harrumph," Sophie said, interrupting Cameron. She grumbled a moment before a chuckle escaped. "You're Jeremy," she said with a pointed glance at his cane.

"Yes."

"You must feel tremendous pride in having fought in such an important war. Bringing Christianity to those poor heathens and ensuring their continued safety from despotic rulers. Such a valiant endeavor."

"If you weren't there, ma'am, I wouldn't assume anything about the war."

"As Elizabeth Cady Stanton said, 'I have no sympathy with all the pessimistic twaddle about the Philippines.'"

"Again, ma'am, not wishing to be rude, but I wouldn't presume to know what it was like or whether the battles were glorious without having been there."

"Surely, man, you must take pride in quelling their uncalled-for rebellion? As if those savages would ever know how to rule themselves," Cameron said with a quick shake of his head.

Sophie glared at Cameron for a moment. "I hate to say that I agree with anything Mr. Wright says, and yet I must at this time. I admit myself confused, young man. I should think you would feel honor for having fought for your country," she said addressing Jeremy.

"Then you would presume wrong," Jeremy said as he rose and limped toward the door, leaning on his cane. He nodded toward me, and paused for Richard to join him.

"Miss Sullivan," Richard said as he strode after Jeremy.

Cameron reached for my hand, clasping it tightly before I could evade him. "Be thankful you are no longer aligned with that family, Clarissa. He is clearly unhinged, and I can't imagine any woman wanting to bind herself to a man whose brother is mad."

I tried to pull my hand away, but he kept a firm hold on it.

"I think…"

"I am thankful that I am once again in your life, Clarissa. When I realize now what type of life you might have had to live if I hadn't returned, it is unbearable. I know you, too, realize your good fortune."

"Yes, a life lacking purpose and full of indolence is the life I have always imagined for my girl," Sophie said.

"Oh, a life with one such as me will have meaning, Mrs. Chickering," Cameron countered. "She will need to spend more time at the shops for her wardrobe is shabby. She will spend her afternoons at important teas with the opportunity of joining committees acceptable to a woman of her standing in my world. She will have my home to run, my children to rear. I see that as a life of tremendous purpose."

"That sounds more like a gilded cage than a life for a free-spirited woman," Sophie said.

"Isn't it just the sort of cage that you yourself entered?" Mrs. Smythe asked with a bite to her tone.

"No, Mrs. Sullivan. I entered no cage, as I have always had a purpose to my life. I married for love, had children with a man I loved and now have the freedom to pursue the interests that are important to me."

"Though you married into a wealthy family," Mrs. Smythe argued.

"I had the fortune of loving a man who did not have to struggle to survive, yes. Though I would not have married him had I not loved him."

"Pshaw. So you say now. I imagine, at the time, his money was as much an inducement to marriage as his handsome face, the cut of his clothes or his pretty words. You are a hypocrite, Mrs. Chickering."

"I am no such thing, Mrs. Sullivan. I am able to adapt to the times I live in, rather than desperately cling to a bygone era in the hopes that my perceived life will be deemed important."

"You have no right to fill my dearest Clarissa's head with such foolish notions."

"I have done no such thing. I believe they were already filled by the time I met her," Sophie said with pride. "She will determine her own future in a way that neither you nor I could ever have imagined."

"Now you speak absolute nonsense. Her future has been known for years. She will marry an acceptable man, live in a good home and have children. That is her destiny."

CHAPTER 11

"WHERE'S AMELIA?" GABRIEL ASKED as he, Matthew and Ronan settled at the Egans' dining room table for an impromptu poker night. Nicholas was in bed, and Liam had agreed to watch him while Amelia was out. Ronan rolled up his shirtsleeves to mimic the time he had won $5, Matthew had donned his lucky hat, Liam stroked his walrus mustache for a "little help from the faeries" and Gabriel wore Clarissa's Christmas sweater.

"That's a pretty sweater, Gabe, but it won't help you win," Ronan taunted as he waited for Liam to deal the cards.

"She's at the Hall, preparing for the St. Patrick's Day celebrations. Hard to believe 'tis in a few days," Liam said as he answered Gabriel's question. "And I don't see how rolling up your sleeves will make ye more apt to win, ye luckless bugger." He winked at Gabe as he dealt.

"I'm surprised you'd let her go with the Ghost on the loose," Ronan said. He glared at Liam as Liam dealt.

Gabriel wasn't sure if Ronan's glare was due to his cards or Amelia being out with a purported ghost haunting the citizens of Centerville, determined to frighten everyone with whom it crossed paths.

"And I'm the only one among us who's won at cards. A bit of superstition will bring me luck," Liam said.

"It won't bring you a big payday as Gabe refuses to play for anything worthwhile. Pennies." Matthew sighed as he threw one into the ante and then stared at his cards before looking at Liam. "Are you mad? Even if Amelia has an escort, she won't be safe. It didn't stop a group of men from nearly jumping out of their skins the other evening."

Ronan grunted in agreement.

Matthew tipped back his bedraggled bowler hat as he studied his cards again.

"And when was the last time I was successful in denying anything to my Amelia?" Liam asked with a long-suffering sigh. "I tried to make her see sense, you know? But she trammeled my arguments and continued on her way out the door."

"Last I looked, I thought you were her husband," Matthew said. He glanced toward Gabriel with a mischievous smirk.

"Sure you can say that to me when you have your own woman to contend with. They've minds of their own, and, if they're happy, they want to do as they please."

"But surely not if she is in danger?" Gabriel asked.

"Now, would you be telling your Clarissa what she could or couldn't do?" Liam raised an amused eyebrow in Gabriel's direction. At Gabriel's shake of his head, Liam chuckled. "I didn't think so. Womenfolk like a man around to help at times, aye. But other times, they want to be free to do what they will."

"Even if they're making a mistake?" Ronan asked. "Then why marry if not to have a man's support and listen to his counsel?"

"Ah, that's the grand part of it. She knows she has my support, and I am fortunate she feels free enough to tell me what she wants. Besides, 'tis a sure thing, too soon she'll be tied to the wee babe, unable to enjoy time with her friends."

"Who'll see her home?"

"I'd hoped to, if you'd stay with little Nicholas while I went by the Hall."

At his friend's nod of agreement, they began the serious work of playing poker.

"Gabe, you seem distracted," Matthew said. "Is that lady of yours finally coming out here?"

"No, but I just received word that Jeremy is finally home from the Philippines!"

Liam slapped his cards onto the table and clapped Gabriel around the shoulders. "Fantastic news, Gabe. How is he? Will he join you out here?"

"I think he is recovering from malaria and a wound to his leg. And, no, I doubt he'll travel to Montana."

"He'll live with your other brother, I'd imagine," Liam said as he rose to find his stash of liquor. He pulled out four small glasses and clunked them on the table. "This calls for a celebratory dram." He poured a sip into each glass and raised his in a toast. "To Gabe's long-lost brother, home at last. May he find peace and health. May you see him soon."

They all raised their glasses and nodded their agreement before drinking down the whiskey. "Jesus, Liam, where'd you get that stuff?" Ronan groaned as Gabriel and Matthew coughed uncontrollably.

"One of the old-timers said he brought it with him from the old country," Liam said, seeming unaffected by the harsh flavor of the *poitín*.

"Tastes more like moonshine than whiskey," Gabriel choked out, wiping tears from his eyes. "You could have warned us what we were getting."

"Well, 'tis a bit rough, and I fear the man may have tried to make it himself, but I thought you were all strong enough to handle it." He watched them with a hint of amusement.

"Are you trying to kill your best mates?" Matthew asked.

"Some welcome home for my brother," Gabriel said.

Liam finally let out a chortle of laughter. "Well, you know Amelia doesn't like to have alcohol in the house. 'Twas the only way she'd allow it in, if it came from Seamus O'Donnell coming back from Ireland."

"Even then, I doubt she was pleased," Gabriel whispered. "Especially if she knew the caliber of the drink."

"She knew I wouldn't be tempted to have too much at one go," Liam said with another chuckle. "Ah, but at any rate, your brother's home safe, Gabe." He glanced at the clock. "And I should be away to the Hall to check on my Amelia."

"We'll stay here with Nicholas. Never fear, we'll drink you dry," Ronan said.

Liam laughed as he donned his coat, hat and scarf before departing into the cold night air.

Liam and Amelia returned nearly an hour later to find Gabriel, Matthew and Ronan playing five-card stud. Gabriel shivered at the cold breeze that entered with the opened door. A sole lamp limned the table with faint light, casting long shadows over the room and players. Through the open bedroom door, Nicholas's gentle snore could be heard.

Gabriel threw down his cards in disgust. "Thank God we're only playing for pennies," he said as he glanced up to smile a greeting to Amelia and Liam. Then he glared at Ronan and Matthew. "You're both cardsharks."

"We've had our share of matches," Ronan said as he pulled his winnings toward him. "Though I won't get rich off you miserly——"

"No ghost tonight?" Matthew asked. He took off his hat and tossed it on the table before leaning back in his chair, his arms behind his head.

"No, and I'm not sure I believe in the ghost nonsense," Amelia said with a smile to Matthew, Ronan and Gabriel.

"Mother of God, woman. Are you trying to get yourself cursed?"

"Liam..."

"You know better than to doubt the spirits, love." He shivered once before collapsing into the chair he had vacated over an hour earlier.

Amelia glanced around the table, glaring for a moment at the bottle of *poitín*. "I see you're set on killing yourself and your friends aboveground, Liam."

Gabriel laughed. "I thought I would die after one sip of that swill. God help the Irish if that is the best you can do." Gabriel winked at Amelia.

"You know bloody well we make some of the best spirits and ales you'll ever be fortunate enough to drink," Liam said.

"How's the Hall looking, Amelia?" Ronan asked. He stretched in his chair.

"As my darling husband would say, 'grand.' We could have used your help, Gabriel, hanging the decorations."

"I would have——" Gabriel began before Liam cut him off.

"You're the one insistent on banning men from the goings-on tonight, Amelia. Wanted some sort of hen party. Should have realized we have our uses." Liam smiled.

"Incorrigible," she said as she brushed his auburn hair off his forehead. She looked toward the others. "I'll see you at the party?"

"Of course," they said in unison.

"Then I wish you good night."

***

A FEW NIGHTS LATER on St. Patrick's Day evening, Gabriel followed Matthew, Ronan and a stream of men and women into the Hibernian Hall. Some of the men listed from side to side, the St. Patrick's Day celebrations having begun that morning with the parade down Broadway. Gabriel ascended the steps into the well-lit Hall to the sounds of a lively reel.

"It seems John McNamara and his lads have already started playing," Liam said from behind. Gabriel turned to smile at Liam and Amelia. Amelia waddled from the increasing weight of the baby and had begun to pant from the exertions of the short walk from their house.

"Evening, Liam, Amelia," Gabriel said as he turned back into the room and scanned the area. "I think there's a chair over there by the windows, Amelia." Gabriel nodded toward the opposite wall. The Hall glowed from the electric lights. John McNamara and his band sat on a small raised dais off to one side, playing rousing Irish and Western tunes. Green banners were strung overhead, forming a complex pattern similar to that of a spider's web. The wooden floor shook from the dancers' feet.

The line to obtain a pint seemed to grow every minute. Ronan and Matthew joined friends from the mine, and Gabriel heard the beginnings of a tall tale as he moved past them to enter farther into the room. The punch bowl sat on the opposite side of the room.

"I don't want to spend the evening sitting down," Amelia protested. "This is one of my last nights out before the baby comes. I want to dance and move about, speaking with my friends."

"No need to be foolish, love. 'Tis best to have a place to sit if you become tired. And you're tired now," Liam said with a pat to her hand looped through his elbow. He led her toward a free chair near the back wall. Gabriel stood behind her, leaning against the wall, watching the room.

"I hate it when you're right," Amelia grumbled as she collapsed into the chair, giving her belly an affectionate pat.

"Who's taking care of Nicholas tonight?" Gabriel asked.

"Thankfully, our neighbor, Sheila, was willing to care for Nicholas. I could not have stood missing this party." Amelia sighed as she tapped her feet to the rhythm of the music.

"Hey, Liam," Matthew said as he rejoined them. "Here's a pint for you." He handed him one of the two he carried. "The brewery's been stockpiling kegs for the celebrations, but I bet we still drink 'em dry by the end of the night." He grinned as he took a long swallow from the dark brew.

"It's a lucky thing the brewery's in the Hall's basement," Gabriel said with a laugh, accepting a pint from Ronan. "No need for transportation costs."

"Who're you going to dance with, Matthew?" Ronan asked as he eyed the few single women standing near the punch bowl.

"I doubt they'd dance with a miner," Matthew muttered.

"I heard they might, especially since you've been taking those dancing lessons," Amelia said.

"Dancing lessons?" Gabriel asked, biting down a laugh.

"I've helped him a time or two, before he met you all at the pub," Amelia said.

"I thought you were writing letters home to your folks!" Gabriel said.

"Well, go on. Show us what you learned," Ronan said as he chortled with laughter. He gave Matthew a gentle push toward the single ladies.

"I'd go with him, Ronan," Liam said. "They like to move in packs. So should we."

"Liam!"

Ronan winked at Amelia, put down his nearly empty pint glass on a nearby ledge and pulled on Matthew's arm, skirting the dancing crowds and pulling him toward the waiting women. Gabriel shook his head at his friends.

"You should dance too, Gabriel," Amelia murmured.

"The only woman I want to dance with is thousands of miles from here. I have no need of dancing."

"You don't dance, do you?" Liam asked with a laugh.

Gabriel grinned. "Not well. Thankfully that was never something I had to do with Clarissa."

"Well, I do dance. And as they are playing a sweet waltz, I want to dance. Liam?" Amelia asked as she heaved herself to her feet.

"Of course, darling," he said as he took her hand.

"Hello, Gabriel," Morgan said, standing with Larry and Niall who both seemed to weave in place. Niall's green eyes were duller than usual from drink while Larry's cheeks were a rosy red.

"If you weave much more, Larry, you'll be flat on your face," Gabriel said.

"I know," he slurred. "Been too damn good a party. Beg pardon, ma'am." He turned bleary eyes toward Amelia and nodded.

"Liam, Amelia, these are the men I work with," Gabriel said. "Larry Ferguson, Niall O'Donnell and Morgan O'Malley."

"Nice to meet you," Niall said. "Quite a celebration. The parade this morning was better than last year's." He waved toward the room, his jerky movement almost causing him and Larry to tumble to the floor.

"'Twas," Liam said. "Nice turnout from all the members of the AOH. Always nice to hear our marching bands playing for some joyful reason."

"I agree," Niall said.

"Well, lads, I'm going to dance with me wife." Liam clasped Amelia's hand and led her onto the dance floor where another slow song, an air, had just begun.

"They seem like nice people," Morgan said. Of the three, he seemed the most sober. His sharp gray eyes watched the room, noting partygoers' interactions. His gaze settled on a group of single women across the room.

"The best," Gabriel said as he watched Amelia laugh at something Liam whispered in her ear. He saw Ronan coax a bashful black-haired young woman to the floor. Soon Ronan had her chattering away in his ear. Gabriel looked for Matthew and found him speaking with a pair of women, although he made no move toward the dance floor.

"We'll see you tomorrow at work, Gabe," Niall said as the three of them wandered toward the punch bowl and the single ladies. Gabriel watched as they joined Matthew. He saw Matthew tilt his head to one side as the music changed and then ask one of the women to dance.

"Oh, that was lovely," Amelia said as she and Liam returned from the dance floor. "I just wish I could dance every dance."

"I doubt the doctor would approve of you dancing jigs, love," Liam said as he stood behind her and rubbed her shoulders.

Gabriel smiled as he watched their byplay. He turned to watch his friends on the dance floor, Ronan now with a different woman. Gabriel relaxed against the wall. His mind filled with images of Clarissa and dreams of holding her in his arms again.

CHAPTER 12

I STOOD IN MELINDA'S NURSERY, rocking her to and fro as I walked from window to window. "Shh ... little sister, don't cry so. Whatever it is, it can't be that bad." I kissed her forehead. "Although I'd cry as much or more if I had your mother, so maybe a good cry is called for."

She calmed with my voice so I continued to speak in a soothing tone. "Yes, my little darling. Hopefully you will sleep soon and give me a moment's respite. I want to venture outside into this beautiful spring day. We don't have many of them here in Boston, as you will learn. You must take advantage of them as often as you can."

I continued to stroke her forehead and sway side to side as I looked out the window to the sunny day.

"Clarissa! Clarissa Sullivan quit your hiding this instant!"

"Shh ... little love, don't let the monster awaken you," I whispered as I laid a now dozing Melinda in her crib and softly closed her door.

I descended the carpeted stairs, my hand resting on the oak banister. When I reached the first floor hall, I noted a light gray wool coat with gold-colored buttons on the hallstand. I turned toward the parlor and straightened my shoulders. "You desired my presence, stepmother?"

"Do you realize you are eighteen minutes late for tea? And we have a very important guest today who has patiently waited your tardy arrival. You selfish, unfeeling girl." Mrs. Smythe sat on the edge of her chair, her posture impeccable. Her copper-colored satin dress shimmered with her movement as she motioned for me to sit.

"I was—"

"What are you wearing? Have you listened to nothing I have taught you these past months? Why do you continue to thwart me so, Clarissa?"

"It is because she takes after her mother."

I spun to the guest in the room and blanched. "Mrs. Masterson. I had not hoped to see you again." Although I had not seen her in months, I recognized her instantly. Her black satin dress with gray ribbon around the waist highlighted her emaciated form. Her hair was pulled back in a tight bun, enhancing her pronounced forehead and the frown lines around her mouth.

"Apparently. Is that a new perfume you are wearing?" Her turquoise eyes shone with derision.

"Yes, eau de spit-up." I sat with a *thunk* in my lumpy refurbished lady's chair and squirmed to find a comfortable position. I patted down the skirts of my blue-gray wool dress and tucked my feet under the chair. My hair was anchored in a loose chignon, and I feared it would tumble down at any moment.

"Clarissa!"

"I was tending Melinda. She has colic and needed to be held. I thought something dire had happened and came to see you when you called, Stepmother. I did not wish for your voice to wake her once she had finally settled."

"You spoil that girl to no end. She will learn to soothe herself if you will leave her be." Mrs. Smythe glowered at me. "And that is no excuse for your dreadful attire."

"Your daughter is barely four months old. She needs to be held when she is upset," I argued.

Mrs. Smythe shared a smirk with Mrs. Masterson. "When you have a child, Clarissa, I will readily accept your criticism and advice. Until then, I expect you to do as I ask. No more coddling of her. The child must learn to be self-sufficient."

"It is the problem with children these days. We spoil them and then wonder why they are such a disappointment to us. It was the same with my nephews. They came to me ruined by their parents. I had no way to undo the damage already wrought by the indulgences of such ignorant people." Mrs. Masterson sighed.

"I understand completely." Mrs. Smythe nodded in my direction causing me to stiffen. "My only hope is that some good can come from my influence. I continue to pray that dearest Clarissa will make a good marriage." Mrs. Smythe looked toward me with pity.

"I hear that Mr. Wright has again taken an interest. You are most fortunate." Mrs. Masterson watched me over the rim of her teacup.

"We are, although Sean would like to ban him from this house. As though such a fine, upstanding young man should not be allowed entrance! Can you imagine the disgrace?"

"Really, Rebecca. I would think by now you would have him under control. He is only a blacksmith after all and ignorant of the ways of the world. You must continue to exert your influence. Do not let him be persuaded by the feelings of others."

"I agree. Mr. Wright is the only decent man who would ever want her. But does anyone listen to me? No. They are focused on the past and imagined slights. He is here, now, desirous of her. It's more than can be said of others."

"Ah, the young. They fancy themselves in love, but often fashion themselves glass castles that are no more than an illusion. I fear your stepdaughter has done just that. For Gabriel is as fickle and feckless as his father. He'll come to ruin and be unable to provide her with the life she deserves. She'll walk the streets in rags, starving, too proud to beg for food," Mrs. Masterson said with scorn and a small amount of glee.

"How can you say that about your own nephew? He's a talented cabinetmaker! He'll always have a good profession." I gripped the arms of my chair in my agitation.

"If you knew anything about him, you'd know he is never coming back for you. He will have forgotten you. I wouldn't be surprised if he doesn't already have another woman, more beautiful, demure and ladylike in whatever dreadful place he has found himself in. It is the McLeod way, after all."

"That's not like Gabriel. Or Richard."

"You believe you know them better after a year's acquaintance than I do? Half of which has been spent sending letters back and forth? You really are a foolish girl." She leaned forward and tapped me on my knee with the tip of her walking stick. "You need to follow the advice of those who care for you and desire for you to have a prosperous future."

"And that would be the two of you?" I asked with a raised eyebrow. "The two who forced the man I love out of this city in disgrace? Never."

"You will never find happiness, Clarissa, until you accept you will marry Mr. Wright. Cameron is an estimable young man. You will live a life similar to Savannah's. How could you want more?" Mrs. Smythe asked.

"Accept the truth that my disgraceful nephew is never to return to you. You never were and aren't that important to him. You are bound to be alone, forever, if you do not accept Mr. Wright. Is that the sort of future you want? Tending other women's babies because you were too proud to accept the advice of those more worldly than you? Living off the charity of your family because you didn't have the sense to marry? Eking out a living at that miserable school, teaching worthless immigrant children when you could have had a better life?"

"You're wrong!"

"Ah, even you lack conviction," Mrs. Masterson said with a smug smile as she heard the tremor in my voice. "I can see my nephew is as fickle as I always thought." She shared a triumphant smile with Mrs. Smythe. "I look forward to reading about the forthcoming marriage in the papers."

I shook my head in denial.

"Has that Mr. McLeod ever once indicated he wants you with him? Has he invited you to join him?" As I paled further, Mrs. Smythe smiled with satisfaction. "Of course he hasn't. Because he never believed in a future with you. Only you were foolish enough to continue to fashion such a future in your dreams. My poor Clarissa. How you have suffered."

I rose from my chair. "If you will excuse me?" I rushed toward the door, almost tripping in my long skirts in my haste.

"Give my regards to Mr. Wright the next you see him, dear," Mrs. Masterson said.

I left the room to the sound of their laughter.

CHAPTER 13

"YOU SEEM WORRIED, GABRIEL," Amelia said as she moved around the kitchen preparing dinner. While she chopped vegetables, cleaned dishes and checked the bread baking in the oven, Gabriel leaned against one wall, sipping a cup of tea. He shrugged his shoulders a few times to ease the tension after a long day bent over a workbench.

"I ... it's nothing."

"It's clearly more than nothing. Aren't we friends? You keep me company as I wait to see if Liam comes back to me. Let me offer you the same support," she said.

"I worry about them too, you know," Gabriel said. "I hate them having to go down into the mines, spending their days in darkness. I wish..."

"So do I, but there's nothing more we can do but wait and pray that today is not the day for them."

"You feel a little hopeless though, don't you, Amelia? I mean, I wish there were more I could do than pray."

"Well, you can entertain me with whatever it is that's bothering you so I don't have to think about it," she said with a small laugh as she stirred the stew pot. She swiped at her fine honey-blond hair curling around her face, pushing long strands behind her ears. Nicholas played with marbles in the living room, shouting his joy every few minutes.

"It's nothing," Gabriel said again.

"Are you worried about your Clarissa?"

"Yes. I'm also worried about my brother Jeremy. Ever since he got back from the war, he's different."

"Different. In what way?"

"Well, I haven't seen him, so it's just perceptions, but Jeremy was always the gentlest of us all. Never wanted to hurt anyone. And then, because he wanted adventure and to escape our aunt's home, he left Boston, ended up in the Midwest. He got caught in the fervor for the war spreading through the country and enlisted. He wrote me once that he didn't know what else to do, and he thought joining the army seemed like a good decision. I worry he got more adventure than he bargained for in the Philippines."

"Why do you say that?"

"He's not as open as he used to be. As though he's afraid of saying too much or…"

"Getting in trouble?"

"Maybe, I don't know. It would be much easier if I could see for myself that he is well."

"Well, that's one of your concerns. Why are you worried about Clarissa? What does she say?"

"She's as positive as ever, although I can't imagine her life—sequestered at home with her miserable stepmother, forced to care for her infant sister—would bring her much joy. When she writes to me, she talks about how much she misses me and dreams of us being together again."

"That all sounds positive, Gabriel. Why would you be worried by what she has written?"

"I worry that she will be convinced I am no longer acceptable."

"Why?"

"I know I'm not. It's why I'm here. I was banished from her life, and then her stepmother and my aunt worked together to ruin my business. I left to build a life for myself with the dream of reuniting with Clarissa again one day."

"Well, it seems she continues to share that dream with you, Gabriel. Now all you need to do is find a way to reunite."

"I have trouble imagining her here, Amelia," Gabriel said with a sigh. "It's so different from Massachusetts."

"In what way?"

"There's water everywhere with the harbor and the river. There are green parks and promenades lined with trees. I used to walk by the harbor just to inhale the briny smell of the sea."

"You miss it," Amelia murmured.

"I'll always miss it, even if I never return," Gabriel admitted.

"It sounds lovely, but it couldn't be any more different from Butte."

"That's what concerns me," Gabriel said with a sigh.

"Have you written her, asking her to join you here? To journey to you rather than have her continue to hope for your return?"

"I'm afraid she'll say no."

"The longer you wait, the more likely you are to lose her. Write her, Gabriel."

Amelia removed the cooked bread from the oven, stirred the stew pot once more before turning it down to low and moving toward the living room. She sat, letting out a low groan.

"I can't wait for this baby to be born. I know the doctor says April, but it seems like any day now." She gave her protruding belly an affectionate pat.

"Is it worth it? Giving up teaching? Forgive me my bluntness. I wonder because of Clarissa. If she would find contentment in homemaking."

"I can't answer for your Clarissa. I can say that, for me, I find tremendous joy in my life with Liam. He is a good man and a wonderful father. He treats me well, and that's something that cannot be overlooked."

"Of course he does," Gabriel sputtered.

"There's no 'of course' about it, Gabriel. When a woman marries a man, she has to have tremendous faith that he'll treat her well. Or believe that the life she will live with him will be better than the life she is leaving behind."

"Liam would never harm you."

"I know. And that is my point, Gabriel. Liam is a wonderful man, and I am very fortunate. But not all women are."

"You sound like Clarissa when she becomes passionate about her suffragist cause."

"Well, to my way of thinking, suffragism is an extension of wanting women to have rights and protections equal to what a man has. And I would have to agree with that."

"You never seemed ra…"

"Radical?" Amelia asked amused. "Well, in one way, I am not, as I am a contented wife and mother. In another sense I am, because I foresee more for women than what they are currently living."

"And does Liam know your views?"

"Of course. He might not agree, and he encourages me not to be too vocal in certain spheres, but he always listens to me. That is one of his greatest gifts to me."

***

"RONAN," MATTHEW SAID as he poked his head into the Egans' house. "It's your turn to watch Nicholas."

"Right," Ronan said. He gripped Liam's shoulder and called out to Nicholas as he grabbed his jacket. "Let's play marbles!"

Liam watched them leave and began to pace. "It's grand of you three to watch him for me today."

"You knew we would," Gabriel said as Matthew collapsed into a chair. Gabriel wiped his hands as he came out of the kitchen. "That's the last of the dishes. I cleaned up the one that broke when the pains started."

Liam nodded his thanks.

"I never realized the little tyke had so much energy. How does Amelia do it all day?" Matthew wondered as he laid his head against the back of the chair.

"Why is it taking so long?" Liam muttered as he continued his pacing. He walked to the dining room table and back, six steps covering the entire distance. "When it started, I thought it would be a matter of an hour or so."

"These things take time," Gabriel said. He settled on the other chair, having no desire to test his luck on the rickety settee.

"And I'm fortunate it started on my day off, but I can't be missing work tomorrow," Liam said.

"Surely you could miss a day or two," Gabriel argued.

"A day, maybe," Liam said. "But I need to work."

"Are there no women who will help her?" Matthew asked.

"There are a few from the Ladies Guild, but everyone's their own family, you know? I wish one of you were married and your wife could help here."

Matthew and Gabriel shrugged. Whatever might have been said was interrupted by a fierce scream followed by a weak baby's wail.

"Amelia," Liam whispered, white as snow. He moved toward the door, but Gabriel rose, gripping his arm.

"You might not be welcomed in there, Liam."

"That's my wife. I should be with her," Liam said watching the door as he heard muttered curses from behind the closed door.

"Let the doctor and midwife help her. They know what they're doing," Gabriel urged.

"She's bleedin' worse than a stuck pig."

They heard through the door the doctor's bitter exclamation.

Liam broke free of Gabriel's grasp, flinging open the door. The midwife turned toward him, aghast and then with relief as she thrust the mewling baby in his arms. "A girl," she said as she turned toward the doctor and Amelia. She pushed aside the doctor and took control of the situation.

Gabriel poked his head in, blanching at the smell and the overwhelming sight of an excess of blood, with fear in his heart at Amelia's limp, ashen form on the bed. He blinked to see the midwife bent over Amelia, one hand between Amelia's legs. He jerked his vision to look at the doctor.

"Don't they teach you anything?" the midwife rasped. "You have to massage the uterus. It helps stanch the bleeding."

Amelia moaned and then slowly calmed before arching in pain again.

Gabriel gripped Liam's shoulder as he stiffened in agony watching his wife.

"It's all right, little mother. We'll help stop this bleeding, and then we'll get you all cleaned up to meet your daughter." The midwife continued her ministrations, relaxed and in control.

"Come on, Liam," Gabriel said, gripping his arm.

"Here, take the baby," Liam said, pushing the infant into his arms. "I need to be here with Amelia." He moved toward the head of the bed and knelt on the floor by her. He took hold of her hand, wiped her forehead and began whispering in her ear.

Gabriel moved to the living area, holding the squirming bundle.

"Is that the baby?" Matthew asked in awe.

"Yes, and I think she's hungry," Gabriel said as he saw her opening her little lips and making smacking noises. He used a piece of the blanket to wipe the baby's face clean. He traced her cheek, making cooing noises as he held her in the crook of his arm and swayed gently from side to side. He held out his pinkie, and she suckled. After a few minutes he walked around the room, telling her stories about how he had met her father.

"She's not going to care, Gabriel," Matthew said from his chair.

"I know, but it keeps my mind off of what is going on in there," Gabriel said with a quick nod to the bedroom. "And I think my voice soothes her."

"I wish Amelia had made it to the hospital in time," Matthew said.

"I guess it all started so suddenly they didn't have time to get her there," Gabriel said.

"And then it turned as slow as molasses," Matthew muttered.

"Shows we're not in control, doesn't it?" Gabriel said as he stared at the baby, now limp in his arms with sleep. "She's beautiful, isn't she?"

"She is," Matthew said as he rose to look at her. "It's my turn to hold her." Gabriel passed her carefully to Matthew's arms but continued to pace.

The doctor and Liam emerged from the room. "Amelia?" Matthew and Gabriel asked at the same time.

"She will be weak for a while, but she will recover. Thankfully the midwife was here to lend her expertise as the need arose," the doctor said. He turned to Liam. "I shall return tomorrow to examine her."

"Yes, Doctor, thank you," Liam said.

He showed the doctor out then collapsed into his dilapidated chair. He sat with his head in his hands, massaging his scalp.

"Liam, do you want to hold your daughter?" Matthew asked.

"Aye, I would," he said, trying to calm his shaking. He reached for the baby, settling back into the chair and holding her in the crook of his arm. "Hello, darling," he crooned and kissed her forehead.

"How is Amelia, Liam?" Gabriel asked.

"Alive but for the grace of God. And the midwife," he said, looking at them with terror-filled eyes. "If she hadn't been here…" He broke off, shaking his head.

"But she was, Liam," Gabriel said. "Focus on that."

"I am. It's why I want to name the baby Anne after her. Because if she hadn't been here, my Amelia would be gone," he said. "Because of Midwife Anne, we have a future as a family."

"Liam, what can we do to help?" Matthew asked.

"I'll need to be out of work a few days. This nearly killed her, and she can't be expected to care for two little ones in her condition. I need to find someone to come in to help for a bit," he said. "Lord, I'm so tired."

"We can bring food in so Amelia doesn't worry about that," Gabriel said as Matthew nodded.

"That would be grand," Liam said.

"Mr. Egan," a commanding voice from the doorway boomed.

Gabriel and Matthew stood to attention, and Liam sat upright although he did not stand due to the baby in his arms.

Midwife Anne had removed her blood-soaked apron and stood watching them in a clean navy shirtwaist. Her black hair was pulled back severely in a bun, and her serious gray eyes watched Liam as he held the baby.

"Yes, ma'am?" Liam asked.

"Mrs. Egan is resting but would like to see the baby," she said. "I will be back later this evening to see how she does and again every day until I think she no longer needs me."

"Thank you. I will never be able to thank you enough," Liam said as he struggled to a standing position with the baby in his arms.

She smiled. "It is one of my greatest pleasures to help keep a family whole." She motioned Liam into the bedroom but remained in the living area to allow them time alone. "I will see myself out," she said to Gabriel and Matthew as she left.

***

GABRIEL RETURNED to the boardinghouse later that evening to find a letter from Jeremy. He washed and changed for bed. He turned on the bed-side lamp, and leaned against the pillow and wall before opening the envelope, studying Jeremy's handwriting for a moment.

April 3, 1901

Dear Gabe,

I have been working at the workshop you left in Boston. It is a good space, with plenty of light. I am trying to remember all that you taught me before I went to war, though I have mangled many pieces of decent wood. I wish you were here to help me.

I enjoy the solitude of my work, but wonder how I will ever support myself. Richard has been understanding, but, if he becomes serious about Florence, I wouldn't want him to have to worry about me as well. I doubt I will ever be fit for acceptable society again. I fear the war killed all that was good in me.

I miss you, Gabe.

Your brother,

Jeremy

CHAPTER 14

"WAIT UNTIL YOU SEE who has accepted an invitation for tea today, Clarissa," Mrs. Smythe said. She fidgeted in her seat in anticipation, patting at the skirt of her plum-colored velvet dress. "It is quite a coup, and I am sure you will be impressed."

"Of course, Stepmother."

"Though you never seem to be awed by anything truly remarkable. You would rather discuss the horrid newspaper stories and twaddle about women's rights than concern yourself with your role as an upstanding woman of society."

"As you say, Stepmother."

"It's not like you to be meek, Clarissa." She slapped her hand onto the mahogany arm of her chair. "Is it that you have finally seen sense?"

"Of course, Stepmother."

"Or is it that your insolence knows no bounds and you refuse to pay me the attention I am due?" She hissed, slapping my knee with her fan.

I flinched and focused on her.

"What have I been saying these past minutes, Clarissa?"

"Your dress is one you are proud of."

"No, you shameless girl. Wait until I speak with your father about your actions toward me."

"I can hardly see where you have a reason for complaint. I am sitting here, in as uncomfortable a dress as I can imagine, waiting for another of your spoiled friends, rather than doing anything of actual import with my life. I care for your daughter, although you'd rather have her cry herself to death than have one iota of love shown to her. So, Mrs. Smythe, I do not know why you'd have a reason to complain to my da."

"Your lack of respect for your elders. For your betters. You have no regard for those around you. You think you are so superior. But you will receive your comeuppance one day. And one day soon, my girl. For that worthless laborer is never coming back to you. He never truly wanted you. You will spend your life alone and miserable, if you do not begin to heed my advice."

"You say the same, day in and day out, Mrs. Smythe, and yet I will never believe you."

"Where is your letter inviting you to join him? I am no longer intercepting them, thus you know, deep inside, that he hasn't asked you. That he doesn't want you." She sighed and paused for a moment before beginning to speak again.

"Do you want to be poor? Dependent on the charity of your family? What will you do when your father dies? For no one will have any reason to care for you. You will be destitute with no children and no home of your own. Only bitter memories of your folly as a young woman for not heeding the advice of those who knew better."

A gentle knocking at the front door forestalled any further conversation. I sat straight in my chair, pleating and repleating the rose-colored wool of my skirts. I glanced toward the door and blanched, becoming paler than the ivory-toned shirtwaist I wore.

"Mrs. Wright!" Mrs. Smythe simpered. "How lovely to see you again. How gratified I am to have you visit me for one of my teas."

"I would have preferred you visit me, dear Mrs. Sullivan. The South End isn't what it used to be. I can't imagine having to live in such a neighborhood. So many immigrants and workers. How you must worry about your safety." Mrs. Wright sat on the settee between Mrs. Smythe and myself. A roaring fire added a gentle glow to this part of the room. A small table in front of the settee held the tea tray, cups, and a plate full of sandwiches and cakes.

"If that isn't just what I say to my dear husband. But he is insistent that this is a reputable neighborhood and a decent home. Oh, how I worry about my daughter growing up in such a place." She placed a hand to her heart.

"Clarissa, girl, it's good to see you again," Mrs. Wright said. "I may still call you, Clarissa?"

"Ma'am, nice to see you. It's been a few years." I nodded my agreement to her question.

"Yes, since my foolish son failed to marry you. I am hopeful that the situation can be rectified to everyone's liking. I hear he has been welcomed back into your home again."

"Oh, he has. He is always welcome in the Sullivan household," Mrs. Smythe simpered.

"Hmm … although it seems he isn't welcomed by all who live here." A searching look in my direction came.

"Much time has passed, Mrs. Wright. Life continues. I hope you wouldn't think me so weak a woman as to spend years pining for him." I smiled toward her as I handed her a cup of tea. I then prepared and passed a cup of tea to Mrs. Smythe.

"I had heard you were amenable to his suit until another took interest. Although I hear the other man is no longer … in the picture, shall we say?" Mrs. Wright took a sip of her tea. "Ah, lovely, Clarissa. You remembered how I like it prepared."

"Clarissa is most attentive to everyone. Why she is a wonderful sister to my daughter. You should see how she dotes on her."

"I have never doubted she would be a wonderful match for my son, dear Cameron. I am hopeful you will make me a happy old woman soon, Clarissa. You know how fond I was of you, and I still am. I would like nothing more than to welcome you into our home on Commonwealth Avenue."

"Commonwealth Avenue! Can you imagine such a fine address? Oh, how fortunate a girl you are," Mrs. Smythe fawned.

"I recall your concern for your French porcelain miniatures at the prospect of my marriage to Mr. Wright," I murmured, setting my cup of tea on the table in front of me. "I don't recall any great urgency from your family for Mr. Wright to marry me."

"Be that as it may, I'm sure we remember the past in different hues. Yours would be tinged with bitterness, of course."

Her placating smile set my nerves on edge.

"As for now, I am aware there are certain … formalities that need to occur. However, I have every faith in your common sense, Clarissa, and that you will soon join me and my estimable family."

"You have given me much to consider, Mrs. Wright."

"I would hate to see a woman such as you, Clarissa, already beginning to lose the bloom of youthful beauty, forego an opportunity at happiness and harmony that marriage to one such as my son could bring." She watched me with sharp, hawklike eyes. "For these types of opportunities will not be plentiful for a woman like you."

"I understand, Mrs. Wright." I clenched my hands in the folds of my skirt, my tea sitting in its teacup, untasted on the low table in front of me.

"Excellent. I am glad we are in agreement." She shared a triumphant smile with Mrs. Smythe. "I shall tell my son to call within a few days. I am sure he will be most eager to speak with you, Clarissa."

CHAPTER 15

"CLARISSA!" MRS. SMYTHE'S VOICE screeched up the stairs.

I rose, slowly making my way downstairs. I paused near the bottom of the stairs and gripped the oak balustrade for a moment to paste on a placid smile before descending the remaining few stairs and entering the parlor.

"Ah, there she is," Mrs. Smythe simpered as I entered the parlor. "Clarissa, how fortunate you are to have Mr. Wright call."

I forced a smile as I faced Cameron. "Hello." I sat on a nearby lady's chair, having no wish to sit next to Cameron on the settee. Cameron wore an impeccable black suit with indigo waistcoat and white shirt. Emeralds glinted from his cuff links and a gold pinkie ring caught the late afternoon sunlight.

I wrinkled the skirt to my gray-blue velvet dress with pearl buttons down the front in my agitation at listening to Cameron and Mrs. Smythe's conversation. Mrs. Smythe sat in her comfortable satin lady's chair, her tan brocade dress highlighting her figure, once again trim after the birth of her daughter five months ago. We sat in the central part of the room, near the fireplace, away from the door.

I attempted to take calming breaths as Cameron and Mrs. Smythe spoke around me about mutual acquaintances. After a few minutes Mrs. Smythe rose on the pretense of finding a recipe for Cameron's mother. I turned to study Cameron, a fissure of unease running through me at our isolation at the front of the house with the staff in the basement and Mrs. Smythe absent.

"Ah, darling Clarissa, it is wonderful to have time alone with you at last," he said with a broad smile. "I am hopeful that soon we will have a life to fill with such moments. I heard about the delightful tea you had with my mother a few days ago."

"Cameron, I'm sorry if you have the impression I would be amenable to a suit—"

"Don't you see, Clarissa," Cameron said interrupting me, "we will have a perfect life. You will make me an ideal wife. We will have an inviting home with presentable children."

"Cameron, you know I am not that woman. I do not see myself at home, waiting for you, idly passing the day. I need a purpose to my life."

"You will have one," he argued. "Our life. Our family. Our home. You will ensure I want for nothing. Isn't that what you desire?"

"No, not with you," I said.

"It's not as though you would want to continue with those suffragettes or your teaching. Your life will finally have the purpose it was meant to have. As my wife, and as a mother to my children."

"You must desist speaking in such a manner. We are not to marry."

"I can't imagine any woman, given the opportunity to live a conventional life, would want to continue on the dangerous path you have started down, Clarissa," Cameron said. "I can't imagine what your father was thinking, condoning such behavior. He waited for too long to heed Mrs. Sullivan's faultless advice."

"I believe he was concerned for my personal happiness."

"As if that path ever leads to lasting happiness. You must realize by now that it is best to allow men to ponder the truly weighty matters of the world. It does you no good to worry about what you cannot change."

"But it is acceptable for you to worry about such things?"

"Of course. I have the mental capacity and preparedness from years of study and cultural advantage."

"One could argue that I have studied extensively," I said.

"Yes, but only on a limited amount of subjects. You should never overtax your tender sensibilities. I would hate for you to have an attack of hysteria," he intoned.

"Cameron, you must realize I am not as weak as you portray me."

"You are a woman, thus you have delicate sensibilities. I am surprised your stepmother, the estimably proper Mrs. Sullivan, hasn't taught you this. I must know, Clarissa, that we are of one mind on this. It is paramount that, as my wife, you agree with me on all things." He watched me closely, studying my reaction. "You will marry me, won't you?"

"Then I'm afraid you will be disappointed on a daily basis," I snapped. "I will not be told what to believe, how to act, or with whom to associate. I will have my own thoughts and ideas." I took a deep shuddering breath. "And, no, I will not marry you."

"Ah, Clarissa, that is one of the reasons I love you. Your naive optimism that life will continue as you wish." He rose and moved to the door. I sighed with relief that he was leaving but rose from my seat in alarm as he shut and locked the parlor door.

"Cameron, you know this is improper and you must leave. Now," I insisted, hating that my voice wavered.

"No, Clarissa, I mustn't," he said as he walked toward me. "What I must do is ensure that you understand I am your only option."

"Cameron." I tried to evade him, but he reached out and clasped my arms in a painful grip, tugging to hold my hands behind my back with one of his. His other hand grasped the side of my neck, preventing any movement. I tried to break free, but his hands were like steel manacles.

"I have spent months attempting to show you how well we suit. Yet you cling to your disgraced carpenter. I am disappointed in you, Clarissa. I thought you had more sense. He's never coming back for you. He doesn't want you. He probably never did." He gripped my chin in a painful grasp between two of his strong fingers and his intense brown eyes gleamed with lust. "*I* want you."

"How dare you speak of Gabriel in such a manner?" I said wriggling in an attempt to free myself from his tight grip of my arms as I fought panic. My futile movements only pushed me off balance and made it easier for him to maneuver me toward the settee.

"I would like to have a summer wedding. In order to not cause a scandal, we must become engaged soon, Clarissa. It is April," Cameron said as he pushed me onto the settee.

A few of the buttons from the front of my dress popped free from the pressure he exerted, and I struggled against him. I tried to twist, to turn, but had no ability to move. Finally I bit him on his nose, which earned a grunt of displeasure from him and the tightening of his hand at my neck to the point I almost blacked out. His hold on my arms did not lessen.

"You will be mine, one way or another," Cameron growled. When he relaxed the hand from my neck, I lay pliant, gasping for air. I was enveloped in his cologne, a deep bay rum, and I tried to turn my head to escape the scent. As he gripped the neck of my dress, more buttons were torn away. "What the hell is this?" he demanded as he saw Gabriel's necklace and grasped it.

"A gift from a friend," I said, grimacing as the chain bit into my neck. "Please, stop, you are hurting me!"

He succeeded in tearing it from my neck and threw it onto the floor. "You'll have no need of that necklace, nor of any memories of that worthless laborer after this afternoon."

"Cameron. Cameron, no!" I pleaded, unable to yell through my tears and sore throat.

"Soon you will realize I am your only option," Cameron ground out. He reached toward his throat, pulling off his tie. He jerked me to a sitting position and lashed my hands together behind my back with his tie. Now that he had both hands freed, he thrust me backward and attacked my dress in earnest. I opened my mouth to scream, but he covered my mouth with his.

I bucked and sobbed, trying to push him off me in any way possible. He chuckled as he raised his mouth and stuffed his handkerchief into my mouth. I nearly gagged. I focused on breathing, on trying to stop crying so I could still inhale through my nose.

I flinched as I felt his hands on my breasts, pinching and bruising. Tears fell unheeded as he lifted my skirts and pushed apart my legs. I heard a ripping sound as he tore my drawers followed by an unzipping. I bucked, using all my meager strength to force him off me.

"Stop fighting me, Clarissa," he rasped. "You must learn to accept your destiny." He pressed his forearm against my throat, stilling any further movement on my part as he cut off my access to air.

I tried to meet his eyes, to beg him in any way I could to not do this to me, but he would not be deterred. I felt him poking and prodding at me until I arched in agony as I screamed to the point I thought I would remain hoarse forever. Through it all, I heard his voice.

"You are mine now, Clarissa. No one will ever want you but me."

***

THE FIRST FEW MOMENTS after Cameron's attack were chaotic. It seemed as though they were happening to someone else, although some part of my mind recognized I was present. Cameron collapsing on top of me afterward with a sigh of contentment and a kiss to my temple. Me bucking so hard that he finally fell off me. The eventual untying of my hands, the rush to push down my skirts and refasten my bodice. Tumbling off the settee in my desire to flee and finding that my legs had no strength. Seeing the smear of blood on the new upholstery. Watching as Cameron left with a jaunty lope to his step and a contented smile.

Seeing his happy smile brought me back to myself for a moment as anger and shame roiled inside me. As I pushed myself to a standing position on rickety legs, I picked up the settee cushion and flipped it over. Thankfully it was a perfect match to the other side and no one would be the wiser for a while. I walked with an unsteady gait, as though I had injured my hip. I gripped the banister with both hands, heaving myself upstairs with all of my strength.

I passed no one in the halls, and I entered my bedroom with no witness to my bedraggled appearance. The door closed with a soft click behind me, and I locked it before collapsing onto the floor. Tears leaked down my cheeks and soon uncontrollable sobs burst from deep within me. I curled into myself on the floor as I gave myself up to my grief.

After a few minutes, my crying abated, and I rose from the floor. I glimpsed myself in my mama's vanity and a few more tears fell. I did not recognize the ashen woman with destroyed blue eyes standing in front of me. My dress was torn in numerous places with the buttons misaligned from my frantic refastening in the parlor. I fingered my neck, flinching at the light touch as I traced the bruising.

I turned away from the mirror, walking toward my privacy screen and washbasin. I unbuttoned my dress, in an instant frantic to have it off of me. I heard seams rip and buttons pop as I freed myself from my clothes. I wanted everything from this afternoon far from me. I stood, naked behind the screen, scrubbing myself until I felt my skin rubbed raw. Until I understood no amount of scrubbing or washing would ever remove the memory of Cameron's touch.

***

"CLARISSA, ARE YOU ALL RIGHT?" Colin asked that evening in the parlor. His light blue eyes watched me. Although I sat across from him near the fire, I shivered and pulled my shawl more firmly around my shoulders.

"I'm fine, Col," I whispered.

"You don't look fine," Colin said. "You look like hell." His auburn hair glinted red in the firelight. I could not bear to look in his direction, not at that settee. And yet I had sat here because I could not have borne to sit near Mrs. Smythe.

"Clarissa," Da called out from the other side of the parlor. "Mrs. Sullivan tells me Cameron called today." He watched me with stormy brown eyes, as though daring me to confirm what Mrs. Smythe had said. His muscular shoulders and arms tensed underneath the fine cloth of his evening suit, waiting my response.

"Yes, Da," I said in a weak voice. I watched as his face became blotchy as he glared at Mrs. Smythe.

"Did you discuss anything of interest?" Mrs. Smythe asked. She raised an eyebrow expectantly, her brown eyes lit with satisfaction.

"No."

"Are you sure?" Surprise laced her voice. She sat forward and began to fan herself.

"Yes. After you left us alone in the parlor, we did not speak of anything of interest."

"You left my Clarissa alone with that man?" Da asked with a growl. "What could you have been thinking?"

"I had been under the impression he was to ask her to marry him. And that she was to be a very fortunate young lady."

"The only good fortune I would have would be to never see him again," I said as I attempted to stifle a sob.

"Clarissa, you must begin to show reason and realize that he is your only sensible option."

I blinked furiously in an attempt to prevent myself from sobbing. "No, I never will. I'll never marry him! Not if he were my only option. I'd rather be alone than with … than with…" I clasped a hand over my mouth to swallow my sob.

"Now, darling," Da said as he rose and walked toward me. "If you don't want the man, I understand. I imagine you still love your Gabriel."

"Yes," I whispered. "But even if I didn't have Gabriel, I would never want a man such as Cameron."

"Then that is that," Da said as he glared at Mrs. Smythe. "The man is not wanted here and will not be welcomed here for tea or of an evening. I thought I had made myself clear months ago."

"I cannot agree with that, Sean. Your daughter must begin to show some sense as to her future. Does she want to spend the rest of her life living off the charity of her family? Does she want to become the spinster aunt pitied by the rest of the family because she spurned her only chance at marriage? Does she want to die alone and unloved?"

"How dare you?" I screeched. "How dare you presume to know anything about me and what I dream about?" I took a deep breath as I attempted to calm myself. I looked toward Da. "I'm sorry, Da," I whispered as I flung myself into his arms. "I can't remain here. I can't live with her anymore. I must be free to live my life the way I wish to live it without the interferences of a woman who has no true regard for my well-being. I will miss you." I clung to him for a moment.

"Now, Clarissa, don't do anything out of haste," Da said as he stroked my back.

"No, Da. I can't. Not anymore. Not after today." My voice broke and tears coursed down my cheeks. "No more." I fled the parlor, racing upstairs to my room, the stairs and hallway a blur through my tears. I entered my room, collapsed on the seat in front of my mama's vanity and realized I might never see it again. One of my connections to her would be severed with my flight from home.

Colin entered my room without knocking. "Rissa, what's going on?"

"I must leave, Col."

"Yes, and about time. But why now?" he asked.

I shook my head in refusal as I turned to face him.

He nodded. "Where will you go?"

"To the Russells," I said. "I know Uncle Martin will take me in."

"Yes, he will. I'll walk there with you tonight once you are packed," Colin said. "I found this on the floor. Care to tell me how it got there?" He held out my necklace, its chain snapped.

"My necklace," I whispered.

"Let me put it on you," Colin said.

"You can't. The chain's broken," I protested but Colin was already pushing aside my collar as though to place the necklace around my neck. He hissed as he saw the red gouges and bruising along the side of my neck.

"The bastard," Colin growled. "I'll kill him if I see him again."

"No, you can't," I protested as tears coursed down my cheeks again. "I need you to help me."

"In any way I can," he whispered as he knelt beside me, pulling me into a long hug.

"Help me go to the Russells. Convince Uncle Martin and Aunt Matilda that I should be welcomed."

"Of course." He studied me for a moment, his gentle hands rubbing up and down my arms. "Are you going to write to Gabe? Tell him what's happened?"

"No, I couldn't," I whispered.

"He'd want to know you're leaving your father's home. He'd want you to come to him."

"He should already want that!" I leaned forward unable to fight my tears as my shoulders heaved with sobs. Colin pulled me into his arms, and I soaked his shirtfront. "Why didn't he ask me to go to him months ago? He had to have known I'd travel to him."

"He wants you in his life. Look at how many letters he writes you."

"But never the right one," I whispered.

Colin pushed me back from his shoulder and cupped my face. "Rissa, did Cameron do more than rip a necklace off your neck?"

"I don't want to talk about it," I said, refusing to meet his eyes.

"Rissa?" Colin asked with deep concern in his voice.

I finally looked up and allowed him to see the devastation in my eyes. I nodded once before I burrowed back into his arms. Colin groaned. "I will kill him and then Mrs. Smythe."

"No, Col. I couldn't bear it if you went to prison. He's not worth it."

"You are, Rissa." All humor and teasing absent from his face, I had never seen Colin so serious. "We have to hope you do not find yourself bound to Cameron." He raised one eyebrow, the intensity of his gaze unnerving me.

"I'll never be bound to him."

"You might already be," he said as gently as possible.

"No, never. I'll find a way," I declared. "I'll find a way so that I'll be able to travel to Gabriel…"

"When he writes."

I stared at Colin, a horrible bleakness in my gaze. "Yes, when he writes."

***

I TURNED THE DOORKNOB at Russell's linen store, only to find it locked. I looked toward Colin in frustration, and he winked. He pounded on the door so hard it rattled in its hinges.

"Coming!" Lucas called out. He unbolted the door, his glower turning to concern as his quick glance took in my bedraggled appearance. A faint light shone behind him, casting the store in shadows. He wore a fine white long-sleeved shirt and well-tailored black pants. His brown hair was ruffled, a sign he'd been playing the piano. "Rissa! What happened?"

He reached out to grip my arms as I stumbled forward toward him, causing him to nearly lose his balance. He grunted in protest before chuckling as he regained his equilibrium. I burst into tears as he pulled me into his arms.

"Shh … Shh … It's all right. Whatever happened, it's all right," Lucas said. His strong arms enveloped me, giving me the sensation of safety. He crooned a gentle song as he held me, rocking me and caressing my back.

I calmed, the sobs turning into hiccupping gasps.

"Come in, Clarissa, Colin," Lucas said, leaning away from me, my hand clasped in his as he led us into the store, down the darkened hallway and up the stairs to the family parlor. Colin followed us, carrying my heavy bag.

"Lucas, who was it?" Uncle Martin asked.

"Hello, Uncle Martin," I said. The area near the piano was brightly lit with pieces of paper scattered around the base of the piano. A pencil lay on the floor next to the overturned piano bench. Gaslights on side tables enhanced the shadows in the far corners of the room and highlighted the fading upholstery. Aunt Matilda sat near the door, as far as possible from the piano while Uncle Martin had pulled his gentleman's chair next to the piano. As I entered the parlor, Colin stood behind me, nodding his hello to Uncle Martin and Aunt Matilda.

"Clarissa, dear, what are you doing here so late at night?" he exclaimed as he strode toward me to grip my shoulders, his eyes turning to a deep, in-scrutable brown. He wore no waistcoat, jacket or tie, his crisp cotton shirt unbuttoned at his wrists. He studied my face a few moments, attempting to discern the cause of my distress. He looked toward Colin for answers, but Colin shrugged his shoulders.

"Absolutely not. I forbid it!" Aunt Matilda called out from her stiff lady's chair. She vibrated with displeasure, a red flush rising up her neck and cheeks.

"What exactly are you forbidding, Mother?"

"She's seeking refuge. Look at her—hair askew, eyes red from crying over her inappropriate behavior and Colin lugging her traveling bag."

Uncle Martin raised an eyebrow, silently seeking my response.

I let out a sigh. "Aunt Matilda is partially correct. I would like to stay here for as long as necessary. I plan to travel to Minneapolis for the suffragette convention in May, and I do not plan to return to my da's house before then. I can assure you, I have not left my da's house due to any impropriety."

"Then from what?" she demanded.

"From a desire to live my life as I wish to live it," I said on a stuttering exhalation. "I can no longer live under Mrs. Smythe's dictates."

"You will not stay here. I will not allow it. What would the grandparents say?"

"I would think they would approve of your charity toward family, dear," Uncle Martin said. "Clarissa is always welcome here. For however long she needs to stay."

"Martin…"

"No, Matilda, that's final. Clarissa will be made to feel welcomed, and she will have the freedoms she has been denied for so long."

"You wish to bring scorn and ridicule down upon this house? Upon your business?"

"No, Matilda, I choose to support my niece rather than sacrifice her for the sake of propriety. Something I failed to do for my own daughter."

"Martin, you know we were in agreement with the grandparents…" Aunt Matilda began but cut herself short as she saw Uncle Martin's glower.

"No, Matilda, I never agreed. I had hoped you were correct. I see now I was wrong. And I refuse to allow the same misfortune to befall Clarissa. I am only surprised you lasted so long," Uncle Martin murmured as he turned toward me.

"Thank you, Uncle." I attempted to smile but tears escaped instead.

"There, now. Let's have none of that," he said with a tender smile, wiping away a few tears. "We'll have you settled in no time."

"Uncle, if I may," Colin said. "Cameron should not be allowed to visit Clarissa. She has no desire of his company. He should not be welcomed here. Not even for tea." He shared a long look with Uncle Martin.

"It is unusual for a woman's beau to be banned," Aunt Matilda protested. "What will people say?"

"Let them think what they will," Colin said in a hard voice. "Never alone."

I nodded my agreement.

"Of course, Colin," Uncle Martin murmured. He embraced me and whispered into my ear, "Courage, Clarissa darling, courage."

CHAPTER 16

I AWOKE THE FOLLOWING MORNING disoriented and confused. The paisley wallpaper and dark wood furniture were unfamiliar to me. I remained cocooned under the blankets as I tried to remember why I was not in my own bed in my da's house. I stretched and groaned in pain as every muscle in my body seemed to protest movement. My thigh and shoulder muscles were the sorest.

I rolled over and covered my head with my pillows in an attempt to bury the memories that flashed through my mind. Cameron looming over me. The sound of ripping material as I fought him. The pain as my arms were lashed behind my back. The horrible pain as … I forced my eyes shut and took deep breaths, chanting "No, no, no." As I turned onto my side with tears pouring from my eyes, I knew that no amount of wishing could undo what had been done.

I pressed my hand against my lower belly and the insistent chant of "No, no, no," would not stop playing through my head. I had been in too much shock, as well as defiant, to fully heed Colin's words last night. Now a cold dread pierced me at the thought of the potential repercussions. I had no one to turn to for advice, and I had never felt more alone. What could I do?

***

A FEW DAYS AFTER ARRIVING at my aunt and uncle's house, I slipped out the servant's entrance. Another tea with Aunt Matilda loomed, and I could not face her probing questions and insinuations as to my presence in her house. A trolley approached, and I hastened my steps to board it as it was about to leave.

With no clear destination in mind, I considered riding the streetcar for the better part of the day before returning to my aunt and uncle's for dinner. However, as the route wound through Boston and approached Haymarket Square, I rose to disembark.

The bustle of Haymarket had not changed since my previous visit last summer. I scurried across the square to the side, escaping an approaching delivery cart weighted down with kegs of liquor. I began a slow walk down Canal Street, noting that bananas were the fresh fruit offered in today's cart. I paused, glanced at Gabriel's old building, took a deep breath and pushed through the doorway to begin the climb to his workshop.

"Mr. McLeod," I gasped on a huff as I paused at the workshop doorway. "Do you mind a visitor?" I entered before giving him the option of barring me entrance.

As I stepped into the workshop, the memories of my visits with Gabriel assailed me, with Jeremy looking similar enough to Gabriel to cause my breath to catch. I closed my eyes as I remembered Gabriel's smile, his cajoling voice, his gentle embrace.

I looked around the workshop, cataloguing changes. The workbench remained but few tools were scattered on its surface. Scrap pieces of wood lay in the corner where Gabriel had stored oak, mahogany and rosewood. The small stove continued to radiate heat, and the table was still covered in a fine sheen of wood dust. My throat constricted as I saw my rocking chair.

"Miss Sullivan," Jeremy said with a wisp of a smile. "Please, do come in."

I wandered toward my rocking chair, patting the arms before easing into it with a sigh. I glanced up to see Jeremy watching me.

"Now I know why that chair was not sold," he murmured. "It seems it was made for you."

"It was."

"Hmm..." he said as he wiped at the sweat on his forehead. "Please make yourself comfortable," he said motioning for me to remove my jacket, scarf and hat. "It has become rather warm in here today with the stove."

After unpinning my hat and setting it on the table, I peeled off my gloves, shrugged out of my jacket and loosened my scarf but left it hanging around my neck. I rocked, the soothing motion of the chair a balm to my bruised spirit.

"Are you well, Miss Sullivan?"

"I believe I will be well soon," I said.

He raised an eyebrow at my response.

"Have you had any recent word from Gabriel?" I asked.

"No, but he seems to enjoy life in that wild mining city. He's got good friends there, and for that I am grateful. One of the men's wives just had a baby, and he's enjoying watching her grow."

"You worry for him the way he worried about you."

"I hope Butte isn't as dangerous as a war zone, though, with the stories Gabe tells, you never know."

"What were the Philippines like?" I asked.

"Hot, humid, wet," he said as he closed his eyes. "Terrible."

"What happened there, Mr. McLeod?"

"You would never understand what it was like. What war does to a person. Turns you into someone you never thought you could be."

I rose, moved toward the small stove and began to prepare a pot of tea. I worked in silence, waiting for him to speak with me.

"I've read in the newspapers how we needed to go there, calm the natives and bring them Christianity. That they would be unable to rule themselves," Jeremy said, walking with less of a limp as he moved and forgoing his cane to sit at the table across from me.

"Are they wrong?"

"Yes, on all counts. They're already Christian. They have a group that would be willing and able to lead them. But we have turned them into rebels, calling them insurgents as an excuse to kill those who refuse to be subjugated to our rule."

"Was the fighting terrible?" I asked and then winced.

"Worse than you could imagine," Jeremy murmured as his eyes took on a distant look. He spoke as though in a trance. "Waiting for battle to begin, often waist high in brackish water, is the hardest time. You don't know what to expect, how the enemy will respond. Once you're fighting, instinct takes over. I found I was quite good at killing.

"You look at me, see my height and strength, and think of my gentle, caring brother, Gabriel. I'm nothing like him," he said, as he looked at his hands in abject misery. "I held men down, pried their mouths open, helped as others forcibly bloated their bellies with water to the point they thought they'd explode. All in the hopes of garnering a little bit of information. My commanding officer was always quite pleased with my group because our informants took the least amount of time to break." He closed his eyes in agony. "Where is the honor in that?"

"Jeremy," I whispered, reaching out to take his hand.

"Forgive me. I should never have said that." He opened haunted eyes, unable to hide his anguish.

"You need to share it with someone. And I like to think we are friends."

"I can see why Gabriel loves you, Miss Sullivan," Jeremy said with a faint smile.

"I miss him," I whispered. "I fear he is never to return to Boston."

"If he doesn't, what are you to do?"

"I do not envision living my life alone, away from the man I love."

He smiled, squeezed my hand and rose to move toward the workbench.

"What are you building?"

"I am practicing carving," Jeremy said. "I just wish Gabe were here to help me."

"Did you spend time here with Gabriel before you joined the army?"

"I would come here on afternoons when I had nothing better to do and pester him into teaching me things. I would razz him, saying that what he did was boring, but I was fascinated that he could make beautiful things from pieces of wood."

"How much did he teach you?"

"Just the basics. I was restless, didn't want to spend the time on an apprenticeship to become a Master like him, and I wanted to do something different than my brothers."

"You succeeded."

"All too well," Jeremy murmured. "Now I wish I had stayed, with my greatest worry suffering a splinter. Forgive me my impertinence, Miss Sullivan, but I believe I have earned it after answering your questions." At my quick nod he continued. "If you don't like being separated from Gabriel, why don't you do something about it?"

"Things are never as simple as we would like, Mr. McLeod."

"And never as complicated either. Don't go twisting things around until you've entered the world of the imponderables, as my da would say. Just do the thing that's in your heart."

I glanced up to find him studying me the way Gabriel used to. "What really worries you, Miss Sullivan?"

"What if I were to travel there and he no longer wanted me?" At his continued silence, I forged on. "What if … things have happened to change his feelings toward me?"

Jeremy cocked his head to the side, his intense stare nearly unnerving me. "I think you are allowing fear to dictate your actions. And that's a shame. I've never seen Gabe around you. I've only read his letters about you. But Rich has, and he told me that he'd never seen our composed, controlled brother as miserable as when he'd thought he'd lost you. And then he'd never seen him as happy as when he was allowed to court you. And I can think of nothing, not even you marrying another man, that would stop him loving you."

I blinked back tears, flushing at his words. "Thank you." I fingered the ends of my scarf absently.

"What happened to your neck, Miss Sullivan?" he asked as he moved toward a bench near the rocking chair.

I stopped rocking, watching him with wide eyes. I gripped both sides of the scarf, wrapping it tightly around my neck. "Nothing. Nothing. I should go," I said, refusing to meet Jeremy's eyes.

He reached out, steadying me in the chair by holding onto my arms, but also not allowing me to rise. "Are you well, Miss Sullivan?"

"As well as is possible," I choked out.

"Are you safe, Miss Sullivan?"

"Yes, I am … now."

"May Richard and I call on you soon?"

"Yes, please," I rasped as I gripped his hand. "I am now with my aunt and uncle at Russell's in the South End. Richard knows where it is."

Jeremy nodded as he continued to watch me. He caressed my arm a moment as though to calm me before helping me to a standing position.

"I hope you call again, Miss Sullivan."

***

"YOU LOOK TERRIBLE, my girl," Sophronia intoned as she relaxed on a comfortable lady's chair in cream-colored damask in her soothing yellow parlor overlooking the Boston Common. I sat on a matching camelback settee gazing into the scene of the mountain glen illuminated by a soft light.

"I'm fine," I whispered.

"Save that useless twaddle for someone who barely pays you any mind. Like you aunt or stepmother," Sophie snapped. "I was very disappointed to hear you had left your father's house last week."

I jerked to meet her serious gaze, her aquamarine eyes filled with censure. "Sophie, I had to."

"Of course you did. But what I will never understand is why you didn't come to me." She *harrumphed* her displeasure. "I had to learn of your flight during an exceedingly dull tea with your grandmother and Mrs. Wright yesterday."

I paled at the mention of Mrs. Wright.

Sophie continued to speak. "They seemed to be under the impression that a very important announcement was soon to be pronounced." She speared me with an even more severe glare. "I thought you were more intrepid than to become caught in their snare, my girl."

I closed my eyes as I fought memories of that afternoon. "Some snares are impossible to escape." I met her eyes, for a moment allowing her to see my devastation and despair.

Sophie squinted at me for a moment, and, as she sighed, it was as though her anger evaporated. In its place, I saw a tremendous sorrow. For a moment, the weight of her sadness stripped her of her essential vitality causing her to appear old and helpless. "I see. I see, my girl." She rose, and I feared she was going to ask me to leave.

"Please, Sophie. Let me explain."

"There is nothing to explain, Clarissa." She looked at me with a defiant tilt to her chin, the action banishing the image of an old woman. She strode toward the door and flung it open.

I stood and bowed my head. "I'm sorry, Sophie," I whispered as I moved to walk past her.

"Where do you think you are going?" She gripped my hand and prevented me from slinking past her. "Sit down this instant." She put her finger under my chin and made me meet her worried gaze. "Let someone who loves you take care of you."

I blinked away tears as I nodded. I moved toward the settee and collapsed onto it. I heard Sophie muttering something to her maid, but I could not make out the words. After a few moments Sophie rejoined me, sitting next to me on the settee. The parlor door had been firmly shut behind her.

She leaned toward me, speaking in hushed tones to the point I had to lean in or not hear her. "I fear you have been treated very poorly by some in your life, Clarissa."

"Yes."

"And that you now fear there may be an ... unfortunate event." She met my shocked gaze with frankness.

"Yes," I whispered as tears escaped and trailed down my cheeks.

"From what I understand, from what I have been able to piece together from the few clues you have given me, you still desire a future with your Gabriel. Is this correct?"

I nodded, failing to meet her eyes.

"It is still possible to have a good relationship with a man even after ... unfortunate events have occurred." She took a deep breath before clasping my hand and prying open my fingers. She placed a small sachet into my palm.

"What is this, Sophie?"

"A tea. A potentially potent tea called pennyroyal. One that you must decide if you want to drink. I may be wrong in what I believe was done to you, my girl, but I don't believe I am. If you desire to go to your Gabriel with piece of mind, I would drink a cup of this tea every morning until your monthly comes."

I gaped at her, as tears flowed unheeded. "How—?"

"I was married to a physician. Not all aspects of life are savory, my dear. When I began to suspect what had occurred, I badgered one of his old colleagues until he gave me the information I requested. He was none pleased with me, but that is immaterial." She met my sorrowful gaze with a determined one. "I know what it is to have those around us believe they can take away our choices for us. I want you to continue to have the ability to live the life you want."

I sobbed, and Sophie enveloped me in her embrace. "You are not alone, my girl. And those of us who truly care for you will not turn away from you."

"It's my fault, Sophie."

"Did you encourage him?"

"No!"

"Then how could this be your fault?"

"I didn't fight hard enough," I said.

"How are you to fight off a grown man, my girl? No woman could. Men made up those mythical Amazonians to make themselves feel better as they carry out just such actions as this against us." Her aquamarine eyes held a fiery glint. "To ensure you feel guilty for their irredeemable behavior."

"What will Gabriel do?"

"If he loves you, he will treat you with respect and compassion. As any man worthy of you would."

"I'm so afraid, Sophie." I gripped the sachet of tea tightly in my hand.

"Don't let fear dictate your actions. Always know what you desire and do what you must to obtain it. If you don't know what it is you want, you must not want it very badly."

CHAPTER 17

GABRIEL WORKED AT HIS BENCH in the Thornton Block, sanding wood. The walls for the individual rooms were up, and he, along with Larry, Morgan and Niall, worked at a feverish pace to complete the carving and finish work. The elaborately carved bar for the saloon was only a quarter completed, and, with every day that passed, the foreman Jeffers became more agitated. However, today Gabriel knew that he did not have the ability to concentrate on carving. His mind was full of the letter he had received yesterday from Jeremy.

> *I saw Clarissa recently, and she did not look well. She has lost the sparkle that seemed to light her from within, and I worry for her. Has she written you recently about any troubles in Boston?*

"Mr. McLeod, you must come quickly. Mrs. Egan has sent for you!" A young man in faded blue overalls with windblown brown hair gasped as he bent over to lean on his knees, exhausted from his run across town.

"Mrs. Egan?" Gabriel asked as he glanced at the clock. Three o'clock. "What is the matter?"

"Sir, I think it best if she explains," the boy said.

Gabriel looked toward Morgan, Niall and Larry, noticing their interest. "I will be back as soon as possible."

"We'll cover for you as long as we can with Jeffers," Morgan said, his shoulders tensing at the prospect. He raked his hands through his dull blond hair, shaking out wood dust.

"Thanks."

Gabriel left, striding down Broadway toward a streetcar stop on Main Street that would take him to Centerville. After a ride that lasted only minutes, but which seemed like an hour, Gabriel alit at Platte Street. He could not remember any of the passing scenery as the brick buildings, storefronts and homes blurred together in his agitation.

"Amelia!" he called out as he knocked on the door. When there was no answer, he eased the door open. "Amelia?"

Gabriel entered the house, noting the pile of dishes on the dining room table. He poked his head into the kitchen, finding numerous dirty pots on the stove. Gabriel frowned at the mess as Amelia always kept a tidy house. Just then Nicholas bolted from the back room, throwing himself against Gabriel's legs.

"Hey there," Gabriel said as he squatted down to meet Nicholas's eyes, taking his arms gently into his hands. "Where's your mother?"

"The mine," he mumbled out.

"Why'd she leave you behind?"

"I won't go there! You can't make me!" He started to scream, trying to break from Gabriel's now firm grip.

"I will not force you to do anything, Nicholas," Gabriel soothed. "I need to know why your mother is there."

"My da is not dead," he sniffled with a defiant lift of his chin.

All breath left Gabriel in a *whoosh*, and he sat back on his heels for a moment. "God, I hope not," he breathed, pulling Nicholas in for a tight hug. "Please, God, no."

He broke the hug to rub away the tears from Nicholas's cheeks. "I need to be there with your mother. She needs our support, Nicholas." At Nicholas's nod, Gabriel scooped him into his arms and walked toward the mine.

A group of women and children stood huddled near the gates. The large gallows frame of the Mountain Consolidated mine gleamed in the late afternoon sun while the small smokestack pumped ash in the sky. A light breeze blew, and the distant mountains were visible through a thin haze of smoke. The gates to the mine yard were closed, and, every time a man inside was visible, a woman yelled at him for information.

Gabriel scanned the crowd, looking for Amelia, finding her sitting on a nearby boulder with baby Anne in her arms, rocking in place. She wore a tattered brown cotton shawl around her shoulders against the chill of a spring breeze, and she had not removed her apron before racing out of the house. The gray cotton covered most of her everyday sky-blue shirtwaist.

"Amelia!" he called out as he rushed toward her. "Amelia, what have they told you?" He reached for her hand as he sat next to her, hoping to impart comfort. Nicholas squirmed to the ground and huddled against his mother's skirts.

"Only that there has been a collapse, deep in the mine. And some of the men are trapped. They don't know, or won't say, who," she said on a sob, turning her face into his shoulder for comfort.

"Then there is hope," Gabriel said.

"The men who could escape, did escape, Gabriel. And Liam wasn't among them."

"And Matthew? Ronan?"

"I haven't seen them," she said.

"Could they all be trapped?"

At her nod, Gabriel groaned and leaned forward, trying to calm his fears.

As the hours passed, Gabriel alternated from sitting to standing to pacing. He found the most solace in pacing, and Nicholas clung to him like a bur as he walked back and forth in front of Amelia. He wished he had thought to bring a few marbles to keep Nicholas entertained. Finally as dusk approached, Gabriel crouched in front of Amelia. She sat pillarlike, not having moved for hours.

"Amelia," Gabriel coaxed. "We should bring the children home." Nicholas was a dead weight in his arms.

"No, I will not leave here," Amelia said. "If I leave, I am admitting that I think they are lost."

"You are not," Gabriel countered. "You are being sensible and continuing to care for your family as Liam would want you to."

"Of course," she whispered. "I ... I can't ... I ..." She broke off unable to finish her sentence.

"I will keep vigil with you tonight if you want," he said. She looked up at him with grateful eyes.

"Thank you, Gabriel. I can't imagine being alone. Not yet," she said in a small voice.

"Give me a moment," Gabriel said. He wandered over toward a man who had appeared at the mine's gate. Gabriel spoke with him for a moment before returning to Amelia.

"What did you give him?" Amelia asked.

"I asked him to inform us whenever there is any news and gave him a little something to ensure he didn't forget," Gabriel admitted. At Amelia's weary nod, Gabriel helped her from her seated position, and they started the short walk to her home on Platte Street. Amelia stared straight ahead, whereas Gabriel nodded toward the neighbors sitting on their front porches or steps.

Gabriel helped put Nicholas to bed and left the room so that Amelia could feed and settle Anne. He entered the kitchen, took off his jacket, rolled up his sleeves, gathered the plates and began to clean out the sink.

"Gabriel, you shouldn't be doing that," Amelia admonished him when she entered the kitchen a short time later.

"I wanted something to do, and washing a few dishes is good for the soul," Gabriel said with a quick smile. "Sit before you collapse, Amelia. Tea is about ready. Do you want anything to eat?"

"No, I couldn't," she said.

"I didn't think so, but here's some soda bread. You need to eat to keep up your strength," Gabriel said as he placed a small plate of bread on the table. He found mugs, filled them with tea and handed one to Amelia.

"Thank you, Gabriel," she said. When he watched her questioningly, she clarified, "For coming when I asked you to. For being so good to Nicholas. For doing the dishes." She waved around the house. "I can't be alone when…"

"Enough of that talk," Gabriel said as he set down his mug with a *thunk*. Bile rose in his throat at the thought of his friends, lying hurt in a mineshaft deep below him. He tapped out a nervous rhythm with his fingertips on the tabletop. "We'll wait for news before making any judgments."

Amelia finally went to bed. Gabriel roamed the small sitting area, perusing the bookshelf. He decided to read *A Connecticut Yankee in King Arthur's Court* because it reminded him of Clarissa. When he read it, he heard her animated voice reading passages to him and saw her sitting in the rocking chair he had made her in his workshop in Boston.

As dawn approached, Gabriel fell asleep, the book open on his chest. He bolted awake at the harsh pounding on the front door at a little past eight. He wiped his face for a moment, disoriented as to his surroundings. As he rushed to the door, he hastily rolled down his shirtsleeves.

"Yes?" Gabriel said as the door opened with a loud creak.

"I have news for a Mrs. Egan," a young man in a dark formal suit said. Gabriel tensed.

"I am Timothy Flynn."

"Please come in. I will wake her," Gabriel said. He approached the back room, knocking gently on the door. "Amelia? There is a man to see you."

"I'll be there in a moment. I'm tending to Anne," she called out.

"She has a baby," Gabriel said by way of explanation to the young man. "Would you like coffee?" he asked as he headed to the kitchen to put on the kettle.

"No thank you, sir." Mr. Flynn remained, standing stiffly by the door.

"No one is going to attack you, man," Gabriel said as he moved back into the dining room area. "We have a good idea why you're here."

"Doesn't mean it makes the job any easier," Mr. Flynn murmured, his eyes turning mournful.

"Do you have news of Ronan O'Bara or Matthew Donovan? They were good friends of mine. Of the Egans," Gabriel said. He gripped the back of a chair as Timothy Flynn flipped open a small notebook he carried.

Timothy cleared his throat, shuffling his feet before finally meeting Gabriel's eyes. "I, ah, I, no," he said.

"No, what?" Gabriel said. "I am afraid I am going to need you to speak plainly to me."

"They didn't make it," Timothy said.

Gabriel bent over to his waist, feeling as though he had received a crushing body blow. Only this attack was to his spirit, and he had no way to prevent the overwhelming pain from seeping in. He looked up to see Amelia studying him, her pale face becoming ashen as she braced herself for the news.

"Amelia," he murmured.

"Tell me," she said in a hard voice, turning to Timothy Flynn. "Tell me so that you can continue with your day."

"Mrs. Egan," Timothy Flynn said as he cleared his throat and squared his shoulders. "We are sorry to inform you that there has been a minor accident at the level of the mine where your husband worked. He died there yesterday."

"A minor accident? And yet he died?" Amelia said. "How?" At Timothy's blank face. "Tell me how he died," Amelia demanded. "Was he crushed? Did he suffer an injury?"

"Yes, ma'am," Timothy said as he cleared his throat. "The area that he and a few other men worked in collapsed, crushing some of the workers. I was told they died instantly. They didn't suffer much."

"Shut up, man!" Gabriel said as he took a swaying Amelia into his arms. He glared at Timothy Flynn while he held Amelia as she slowly crumpled to the ground, Gabriel following her down.

"Gabriel," she whispered. "Ronan? Matthew?"

"They were together," Gabriel said. "At least they weren't alone."

Her harsh sobs shook his body as he held her while she keened. "Is there a body?" Amelia asked. "I need to see him again."

Gabriel glanced up at Timothy. "Well, is there? Is there a body? Can we bury him properly?"

"Yes, yes, of course. It will be delivered to the undertaker. To Duggan today. You can make arrangements as you please for the wake," he said. "And since you were good friends of the other two, will you want to wake them also? We weren't sure what to, ah—"

"Yes, we will see to them," Gabriel hissed. "They were members of the AOH. All arrangements will be covered for them by the group. Please be on your way. I am sure you have plenty of other important duties to attend to." He glowered at the young man's relief at being able to escape their misery.

CHAPTER 18

April 24, 1901

My darling daughter,

 I hope you are settled at your uncle's, and I have every faith that you are well cared for. I have waited the last weeks for you to come home. I am surprised you have remained away for so long.

 Clarissa, darling, you are my daughter, and I want you home. Safe in my house. I want to see you at my dining room table, hear about your day, listen to you and Colin arguing in the sitting room. I do not like having my family separated.

 Your continued silence has shown me how much I have hurt you, Clarissa. I see the error in my ways. Please, come home.

Your Da

As I swiped away a tear, I glanced up to see Florence hovering at the Russells' parlor door. "Florence, I am surprised to see you." Her untamable, curly black hair defied being tamed by its pins, and her lavender shirtwaist had a large ink stain at the left cuff.

"Why?"

"I thought you were spending most of your free time with Richard."

"I do. But I want to see my good friend who hasn't been writing me as frequently as before." She sat on a chair next to my settee. "I was surprised when Jeremy told us you had moved here." Her gray eyes roamed over the dimly lit room, the gaslights already on in midafternoon. Faint hammering and men's voices yelling at each other could be heard from outside as the elevated streetcar construction occurred farther down the street from Russell's.

"I needed a change of scenery."

Florence raised an eyebrow at that. "Evidently. You look dreadful."

"I'm fine."

"What happened?"

I shook my head but reached out to grip her hand. "I can't … I can't talk about it. But…" I broke off, releasing her hand to brush at the tears that streamed down my cheeks. My eyes burned as I attempted to hold back more.

"Does Gabriel know?"

"I have written what I can. Some things must be discussed in person," I whispered.

"Gabriel loves you, Rissa."

"How is Richard?"

She flushed, unable to hide a contented smile. "Wonderful. As I remembered him from before our … misunderstanding. I can't tell you how extraordinary it is, Clarissa, that he is again a part of my life."

"I am very happy for you, Florence. You deserve happiness." At my words, she seemed to pale and to pleat her skirts. "Florence?"

"Oh, Clarissa, the worst has happened all over again!"

"What do you mean?"

"I've lost my teaching post," Florence whispered in a tear-thickened voice.

"What?"

"I swear we weren't indiscreet!" She swiped at the tears that escaped. "We met for tea, talked. It was wonderful. I saw Jeremy again." She paused, clearing her throat.

I waited.

"A few days ago, Mr. Carney called me into his office to inform me that he couldn't abide having a teacher of loose morals instructing the impressionable minds of Boston's youth and that I should be ashamed of myself." She paused on a stuttering sigh. "I should have known better. I know that. After they did the same thing to Ursula last year, but I couldn't help myself, Clarissa. I had to see Richard."

"What does Richard say?" I asked in a gentle murmur.

"I haven't told him."

"Florence," I said, shaking my head as she interrupted me. "Your misunderstanding years ago began because you did not talk to each other. You must speak with him now. Explain to him what has happened."

"I don't want him to offer for me because he has to. I want him to propose because he *wants* to."

"Well, as Sophie would say, sometimes we don't always get what we want in life. And sometimes, dearest Florence, sometimes when we are doing what we have to do, it transforms itself into our heart's desire."

Florence nodded but seemed unconvinced.

"If you believe that, what are you doing to attain your heart's desire?"

"I'm working toward it, Flo."

"Well, I hope it's not too long in coming and that soon you are your healthy self again. You're too pale by half." She reached out to clasp my hand.

"As for you, you need to speak with Richard. Tell him the truth. And if he is anything like his brother, he will do what is right. What is proper."

"I don't want to be a burden," Florence choked out. "Teaching was to be my way to independence."

"Flo, you need to tell Richard."

"Tell Richard what?" a deep voice asked from the doorway. The two tall McLeod brothers, nearly the same height, filled the doorway. Richard gripped the doorjamb, the blue of his eyes startling for their coldness. Jeremy stood a step behind Richard, his pose more relaxed but alert.

"Richard!" Florence gasped.

I smiled toward both him and Jeremy.

"Hello, Florence," he said, watching her closely, a guarded expression flitting across his face. "Miss Sullivan." He nodded in my direction.

"Richard, please join us," I said, waving him into the room.

"I am sorry to interrupt," he said in a voice tinged with bitterness. "I hate to think I'm interrupting the sharing of any secrets." At this he cast a sharp glance toward an ashen Florence. He turned toward me. "I have a letter for you from Gabriel. It came a few days ago. I'm sorry I haven't delivered it until now."

"Oh, thank you, Richard," I said as I fingered the envelope. I wanted to rip it open and read it, but, more than anything, I knew I needed to focus on Richard and Florence. Jeremy entered the room, sitting next to me on the settee. He no longer needed a cane and moved with the silence of a cat.

Richard turned toward Florence and focused on her. "Flo, any news? How was school today?"

Florence threw a baleful glance in my direction, although I only smiled encouragingly. She shook her head as though mute, her eyes filling with tears.

"Florence?" Richard asked. He moved toward her chair, crouching by her side, taking one of her hands into his. "Please tell me. I've suspected for some time that something was wrong."

"Richard, I'm sorry," she whispered.

"Why, darling?"

"I haven't taught in nearly two weeks. I have no way to pay my boarding fees. And no one in Boston will hire me as a private tutor or as a teacher again because my reputation has been ruined."

"How?"

"I spent time with a man not of my family. The school board does not want a woman of such loose morals to influence the minds of the next generation."

"What rubbish," Richard said. "And who told the school board?"

Florence whistled in a breath, shaking her head. "One of the teachers who wanted a promotion. But it's my fault, Richard. I knew the rules. I knew I needed to guard my reputation." She paused, taking another stuttering breath. "It's just…"

"It's just what, darling?"

"I needed to see you again. Dream again," Florence whispered.

"There is only one solution," Richard said as he cupped her cheek with one hand.

"No, Richard," Florence wailed.

"Florence, you know I love you. We were working our way toward this before you were forced out of your job. It will simply be sooner than I had thought. The apartment is small, but I imagine it's better than a boarding-house. Jeremy will enjoy having a sister, won't you, Jer?"

"I can imagine no better woman for Richard than you, Florence," Jeremy said with deep sincerity.

"Marry me, Florence. Marry me and let me keep you safe," Richard coaxed.

"I don't want you to marry me out of duty," Florence said through her tears.

"Well, it is a duty. To you, because you are the woman I love. But to me as well. I'm not happy without you. Surely you understand that?" He smiled, raising her hand to kiss her palm. "Ah, it is a duty, but seeing as this is my greatest desire, it will be no hardship." At her continued silence, Richard said, "Marry me, Flo. Have children with me. Give me a daughter with curly black hair like yours." He reached out to touch one of her curls.

"Rich." Florence sobbed as she fell into his arms, the two of them kneeling on Aunt Matilda's thick Aubusson carpet. I gripped Jeremy's arm in my excitement for Florence.

"Someday you will have this too, Miss Sullivan," Jeremy whispered.

"Thank you." I sighed.

"Isn't this a touching scene?" Cameron asked as he strolled into the room. His blond hair was held in place with pomade while his impeccable clothes proclaimed him a man of wealth and society. He fiddled with his cuff links, the emerald ones he had worn that day in my sitting room. I fought memories as I inhaled the scent of his bay rum cologne.

I started at his unexpected arrival, with Polly nowhere in sight, and grasped Jeremy's arm with such force he grunted in pain. "Cameron, what are you doing here?"

"No need to show such enthusiasm, Clarissa," Cameron chided.

Richard, who continued to hold a sniffling Florence in his arms, looked from Cameron to me, concern flitting across his expression. "Mr. Wright. I had hoped not to see you again."

"The sentiment was mutual," Cameron snapped as he glared at Richard and Jeremy. "I had hoped to sit next to my betrothed." He hovered over Jeremy and me, raising one eyebrow as he looked toward Jeremy. "Would you please move to another seat?"

"No," Jeremy said in a hard voice as he glared at Cameron. "Miss Sullivan?" he murmured as he leaned toward me but did not take his gaze off of Cameron.

"We are not betrothed," I said. "We are nothing to each other."

"You wound me, dearest Clarissa. I thought we'd come to an understanding last time we met in your sitting room. From your actions, I understood you to agree to my proposal. I, for one, enjoyed our interlude."

"The only understanding we reached was that you have a fanciful imagination," I gasped. "And for my part, little enjoyment was found."

"Oh, I no longer need to imagine much," he said in a low silky voice that caused me to shiver. "In fact, I brought you a gift to replace the worthless bit of tin you wore last time I called."

"You no longer wear Gabe's necklace?" Richard asked from across the room.

I felt Jeremy flinch next to me and heard him say, "Ah," as Cameron leaned over me. I focused on breathing as his scent, his warmth, his nearness enveloped me. His emerald cuff links twinkled at me, mocking me. "Go away," I urged as my hands gripped the seat edge of the settee, my nails gouging into the dulled, gaudy fabric.

"Never, darling Carissa. You will never be free of me." He reached for the neck of my gown as though to open it. I jolted and squirmed, bumping into Jeremy.

Cameron reached for something in his pocket, and I jerked farther away, leaning as far into the back of the settee as possible, battling memories. After a moment, I freed my hands from their tight grip on the settee and pushed at his shoulders with all my strength. "Go away!" I yelled. He stumbled back, nearly falling onto his backside.

When he rose from his crouched position by my side, he smoothed down his jacket and hair. A red flush highlighted his cheekbones and agitation.

"I believe Miss Sullivan would like you to leave," Jeremy said.

"I would think you would know better than to interfere in matters that do not concern you. Although seeing as you're related to that worthless laborer, I shouldn't be surprised you don't know your place."

"He's worth ten of you," Jeremy snapped, rising to his imposing height, towering over Cameron. "If you will follow me out, sir, Miss Sullivan has made it clear she has no interest in seeing you."

"How impertinent! Who are you to order me about?"

"I don't care who you think I am, and I don't really care what you think about my family. But you are through hurting Miss Sullivan." Before I knew it, Jeremy had grasped Cameron's arm and wrenched it behind his back, immobilizing him. Cameron gave a shout of pain as Jeremy hitched his arm a bit higher up, causing Cameron to bend forward. "You are no match for the likes of me. You have no idea what I am capable of. Don't test me." He pushed Cameron in the back and propelled him out of the room.

"Bravo," Lucas said as he plastered himself against the door frame as Jeremy forced Cameron out of the room. "I couldn't have done better myself."

"Clarissa?" Florence asked from Richard's embrace. "What did Jeremy mean?"

Lucas looked into the parlor at Florence's voice, and saw Florence and Richard sitting on the floor near a chair by the piano. He tugged on his dusty gray waistcoat and shrugged into the matching jacket he had been in the process of shedding. As he brushed his light brown hair out of his eyes, he turned to me with inquisitive amber eyes. "I hadn't realized we were entertaining the McLeods tonight." He raised an eyebrow.

"Lucas, could you play for us?" I asked, thankful for his arrival and distraction from Florence's question and ignoring the implied question from Lucas.

After he studied me for a moment, he said, "I'd love to. Seems a celebration of sorts is in order for the removal of such a rodent." He sauntered toward the piano in the corner of the room, sat and played "Für Elise."

Jeremy entered and stood in the doorway transfixed by Lucas's music. Lucas continued to play songs in the same vein as Jeremy eventually sat in a nearby chair, though he continued to focus solely on Lucas's playing.

After a while, Lucas finished and smiled toward me. "Any requests, Rissa?" He continued to play random, harmonious chords as he awaited my response.

"Can you play 'Maple Leaf Rag' for us?" I asked.

"With pleasure!" Soon the room was filled with the sounds of his joyous playing. The song was bittersweet as it reminded me of last year when I was with Gabriel. I saw Richard settle Florence into his arms as he leaned against a chair. Jeremy now watched Lucas play with rapt fascination.

When Lucas finished, we all burst into applause. "Have you ever considered performing?" Jeremy asked. "You are extraordinary."

"No, no need to perform when I have a good, steady job here at the linen store," Lucas said. Jeremy looked to be about to argue with Lucas when he was interrupted.

"Lucas!" Savannah exclaimed from the doorway. "I am thankful I heard the end of that song. You play it so well, and I haven't heard you play in too long." She rushed into the room to embrace her brother.

"Sav!" I said, jumping up to hug her. "What are you doing here? It's wonderful to see you."

"I had thought I would call as it has been a while since my last visit. Mr. Montgomery likes to keep a very busy social calendar. And I heard that you were staying with Mother and Father now." We studied each other.

I noted her gaunt features and listless hair. Her stylish cream-colored brocade tea dress with fine machine lace overlay hung on her. No amount of corseting could enhance curves that had disappeared. As I studied her, I could only imagine what changes she saw in me.

"Savannah, may I introduce you to Mr. Jeremy McLeod and Miss Florence Butler? I am sure you remember Mr. Richard McLeod. Florence and Jeremy, this is my cousin, Mrs. Montgomery."

"Pleasure," Florence and Jeremy said in unison.

"Clarissa, what did Jeremy mean by not allowing Cameron to hurt you further?" Florence asked.

"Cameron was here?" Savannah asked as Lucas frowned at me from his piano bench.

"Yes, he was," I said as my mind raced to concoct a suitable excuse.

Lucas spoke up as he continued to play. "I would think Clarissa wouldn't want much more to do with that rat after he abandoned her almost three years ago. Why would she allow herself to be hurt by him again? She's smarter than that."

"Exactly," I said.

Florence and Richard seemed unconvinced, and Jeremy shook his head in silent disagreement but said nothing else.

"Mother would be scandalized to find the pair of you sitting on her parlor floor. Why don't you sit on one of the settees?" Savannah asked Richard and Florence.

"We are quite settled where we are," Richard said as he snuggled Florence closer to him.

"And the settees aren't all that comfortable," Lucas said.

"Lucas!" Savannah chided.

"Well, they aren't, Sav. Besides, they just became engaged. They want some time together, I imagine," I said with a wink to Lucas.

"Oh, engaged. How lovely. Let's call for a bottle of champagne to toast your future."

"Sav, I doubt Uncle Martin has champagne waiting for a visit from you." I shared an amused smile with Lucas as Jeremy shook his head at the thought.

"I will think of something," she said as she rose and walked to the door. After a few moments, she returned. "This reminds me of a party I attended recently. It was a grand affair on Newbury Street. We must have drunk fifty bottles of champagne. What an evening."

"I'm surprised at you, Sav," I said. "I thought you were more of a temperance-movement wife."

"Jonas doesn't approve of the movement. Thinks that individuals, rather than any governmental decree, should decide for themselves what they should and shouldn't drink. I, of course, believe as my husband does."

A few moments later, Polly entered with another maid carrying a tray with glasses and two bottles of white wine. "It's not champagne, but it will suffice to toast the newly betrothed," Savannah said. She raised her glass. "To Richard and Florence! May you have a lifetime of love, health and prosperity."

"Hear, hear," we all said in unison.

After the toast, Savannah noted the time and rose to depart. I walked Savannah to the front door. "You are happy here, Rissa?" Savannah asked.

"Yes, I am. Much more so than at home," I said. "I needed more freedom."

"I don't see you missing Mrs. Smythe, although I feel badly for your father."

"I do too, but that couldn't be helped."

"Are you feeling well? You're quite pale."

"I'm just a little under the weather. I am sure it will pass soon," I whispered. Savannah studied me for a moment before nodding her agreement.

"Take care with Cameron. He is set on you and will not be easily thwarted."

"Sav?"

"Be sure to call for tea soon," she whispered as she leaned in for a hug.

I closed the door behind her and moved toward Gabriel's glass-case displays. I needed to feel close to him tonight, and I wanted to read his letter away from the sitting room and curious eyes.

April 19, 1901

My darling Clarissa,

I write with news that may distress you. I know that for some time you have believed that I would return to Boston. I must be honest with you. I will never return to Boston to live.

Boston is my past, darling. Life in Montana is my future. Would you con-

sider traveling to me? I have friends here who would welcome you. I know it is not the same as having family nearby, but I believe we can become family for each other, wherever we live. I have steady work, and my reputation as a reliable finish carpenter is growing.

I miss you, my darling, and want nothing more than to be reunited with you. Please come to me.
I miss you, my love,
Gabriel

I stifled a sob as I kissed his handwriting. Finally I knew where I was headed: toward my heart's desire.

CHAPTER 19

"GABRIEL, I DON'T FEEL strong enough to go to Duggan's. Will you…
" Amelia stopped speaking, biting her trembling lip as tears fell. Her honey-blond hair was pulled back severely into a tight bun, and she wore a dated black satin mourning dress with puffy sleeves.

"Of course," Gabriel soothed. "Do you still wish to have the wake here?" he asked as he looked around the cramped living room. His crisp black pants had creases down the front, thanks to the meticulous laundering from the Chinese laundry. The indigo of his shirt enhanced the blue of his eyes.

"I want my Liam home, even if it's only for the wake. And Matthew and Ronan were our good friends. They should be together."

"I understand, Amelia," Gabriel said. He gripped her arm as he left to travel to Uptown Butte. Not wishing to dirty his clothes for the wake, he rode the streetcar for the short trip to the undertaker's in Uptown. A faint breeze blew, allowing him to see the valley and the mountains in the distance as the trolley descended the hill. He disembarked at Copper Street walking the short distance to Duggan's.

Duggan's funeral parlor consisted of a small brick building with potted plants in the front. Gabriel glared at the flowers, at anything attempting to brighten his mood. As he entered the dimly lit foyer, he doffed his hat. Soon his nose itched from the hint of incense and he wanted to flee as he heard the faint wails of another's grief. After waiting a few moments, he spoke with a chubby middle-aged man.

"I'm terribly sorry for your loss," the man said as he wiped perspiration from his forehead with a crisp white handkerchief. "The … ah … well, they are waiting for you over here." He held out his arm and led Gabriel to a small room adjacent to the main entranceway.

Upon entering, Gabriel noted that the coffin covers were closed. He did a quick double take when he saw two coffins. "Excuse me," he said to the man as he took his leave. "There were supposed to be three."

"Only two were delivered, young man."

Gabriel collapsed onto a nearby chair. "Are you saying that one of them survived?"

"I couldn't say. What I can say is that we prepared two bodies for you for burial. And we'll transport them to the widow's home when you like. Now, if you'll excuse me for a moment, we've been terribly busy of late."

"Of course." Gabriel sat, leaning forward with his elbows braced on his knees, staring at the coffins. He took a deep breath, stood up and slowly approached the caskets.

He exhaled, reaching out to the first coffin, grunting with the weight as he heaved it open more brusquely than he would have liked. He looked down into Matthew's peaceful face and sighed.

After carefully lowering the casket cover, he moved to the other one. Prepared for the heavy weight of the lid, he opened it more smoothly. "Liam," he murmured.

He collapsed onto the chair, staring at the two coffins. "How I will miss you," he whispered to his friends. He rose to speak to the portly man for a moment.

"Sir, can you deliver them to Mrs. Egan's on Platte Street in Centerville? We will wake them from there." At the man's nod, Gabriel hurried toward St. James's Hospital to search for Ronan.

He walked down Main Street in a daze, barely noticing the men loitering outside the bars. He turned right onto Galena where the rich scent of sesame seed oil and exotic smells of garlic, chili peppers and ginger filled the air and tantalized him, causing him to emerge from his trancelike walk and notice his surroundings. Miners and businessmen formed a constant flow of customers in and out of laundries. Men and women scurried to and fro from the Chinese groceries and herbalist pharmacies, in search of fresh produce and alternative remedies to common health ailments. The noodle shops were filled to capacity. Gabriel continued toward Idaho Street, turned left and approached the hospital at the corner of Silver Street.

Upon his arrival at St. James's Hospital, he entered under an arched doorway with a large cross overhead. He spoke with an orderly, who found a nurse dressed in a nun's habit.

"I don't have time to show you the way. He's up there," the nun said pointing toward the stairs. "Second floor."

Gabriel took the well-lit stairs two at a time, ignoring the antiseptic smell, and paused when he arrived at the top. He decided to peer into each room in the hopes of seeing Ronan. Finally, at the fifth room, he saw him in the far bed near the window.

"Ronan," Gabriel murmured as he sat by his bed. Ronan opened his eyes, his head swaddled in crisp white bandages. A large bruise marred one side of his face, continuing down to his neck. He wore a white gown and was tucked into a bed with white sheets. Five other men shared the room with Ronan, and Gabriel gave thanks that Ronan was situated near the window. Small wooden trays that could be wheeled to any bedside stood in one corner of the room. A sink, pitcher and towel rack were in the far corner to the right side of the door. The whitewashed walls nearly blinded Gabriel in their intensity, the bright May sunlight streaming in with no curtains covering the windows.

"Gabriel," Ronan rasped as he squinted at him. "Where have you been?"

"I had no idea you were alive. We were told you were dead."

"Matthew? Liam?" he asked. "They won't tell me where they are. Are they here? Is Liam at home with Amelia? They haven't visited me either."

Gabriel cleared his throat. "Ronan, they died," Gabriel said in as gentle a manner as possible. "They…"

"They couldn't have!"

"We were told they were crushed by the falling rock," Gabriel whispered.

"They can't be dead. Not Liam. Not with a new baby. What is Amelia going to do?"

"I don't know."

"The Hibernians will help her some," Ronan said, his eyes roaming over the room as though his mind were racing. "But she needs to marry again. Needs protection for herself and the children."

"She's a long way from considering that, Ronan." Gabriel massaged the back of his neck. "How long 'til they let you out of here?"

"I don't know. I still get dizzy if I sit up fast, and I see double."

"You're concussed?" At Ronan's nod, Gabriel said, "I'd think they'd let you home to recover."

"It's not just that, Gabe. I can't feel my legs. I ... I can't really remember, but I think I was thrown against something sharp, my back burned and then nothing." Ronan turned fiery brown eyes toward Gabriel. "I never thought I'd never feel nothing ever again."

"Ronan," Gabriel said. "Maybe they're wrong."

"They've had a team of doctors in, and they all agree," Ronan said. "And how am I to be paying for the hospital?"

"We'll take up a collection," Gabriel said. "And I've some money put aside. We'll take care of you, Ronan."

"How will I be anything but a burden?"

"We'll think of something," Gabriel murmured. "As for me, I best be getting back to warn Amelia as she is expecting three caskets for the wake today."

"I wish I could be there."

"I'd rather have you here than trussed up by Duggan in a casket." Gabriel squeezed Ronan's shoulder as Gabe rose to leave. "I'll be by tomorrow, if not sooner. Do you need anything?" At Ronan's weary shake of his head, Gabriel attempted a half smile and departed.

***

"AMELIA." GABRIEL PAUSED. "Amelia, I need a moment before the wake begins." He glanced around, noted the living room cleared to make space for the caskets.

"Gabriel, I don't have time for a chat now. I must finish cleaning and preparing for the guests who will arrive."

"They can wait. Sit," Gabriel commanded, pushing gently onto her shoulder so she sat in one of the few remaining chairs. "I have news, and I am sorry to upset you."

"Gabriel?"

"I went to Duggan's, like you asked, and was brought into the room with the coffins." He gripped her hand as she struggled not to cry. "There were only two. It appears Ronan survived the blast but no one bothered to inform us."

"Ronan survived?" At his quick nod a flush rose up her neck. "Are you sure just Ronan?"

"Positive."

"How are you positive?"

"I looked in the caskets, Amelia," Gabriel said with a grimace. "I saw Matthew and … Liam." He gripped her hand as tears dripped down her cheeks.

"How fortunate for Ronan."

"Amelia!" Gabriel admonished. "Yes, he is fortunate, though he is most likely a cripple. And while you have every right to mourn Liam, I hope you will never wish anyone dead."

At this Amelia crumpled, curling into herself and sobbing. "I'm sorry. I just want Liam."

He pulled her into his embrace. "I know, Amelia, I know," Gabriel cooed, gently caressing her back.

Eventually her crying stopped, and she swiped her cheeks with erratic, brusque movements. She rose, moving to the kitchen to prepare for the mourners.

Gabriel became distracted with the arrival of the undertakers from Duggan's. They placed the two caskets in the living room, filling the entire living area. So, as mourners trickled into the room, they paused in front of each casket to say a prayer and then moved toward the dining room.

The women, carrying food, immediately headed toward the kitchen and conversed with Amelia. Gabriel smiled toward those he knew, nodded to those he didn't and stood in the only free space in the living room near the bookshelf. A keg was sent from the brewer under the Hall, and soon all had a glass in their hands. Toasts were made to Liam and Matthew, the Irish, all miners and the AOH. John McNamara's fiddler arrived and began to play soul-achingly mournful music. Soon the house was bursting with people and had overflowed to the street.

Gabriel imagined to himself what Liam or Matthew would have said had they heard such music and half smiled. *For God's sake, man, do you want more than the two dead an' gone with that depressing music? Sure'n you could find another way to keep the priest occupied.* Gabriel heard Liam's voice as though he were standing next to him. He wandered outside to escape the oppressive atmosphere inside the house.

"Gavriel!" Nicholas cried, launching himself at Gabriel's legs.

Gabriel picked him up, cuddling him as the young boy shivered. He stroked Nicholas's uncontrollable curls in an attempt to soothe him.

"What's the matter, little man?"

"I want Da," Nicholas said through his tears.

"I know, Nicholas." Gabriel hitched him a bit on his hip, moving through the crowd outside. He walked up and down the street, ignoring the pitying stares of the Egans' neighbors as he attempted to calm Nicholas. A soft breeze blew, the warm spring weather a harbinger of hot summer days to come.

"Where is he?"

"He's in heaven, little man. Looking down on you, making sure you're all right."

"But I want him here," Nicholas wailed.

"I know, Nicholas." Gabriel sighed and pulled him close for a hug. "I want him here too. But he is with Uncle Matthew too. And they won't be coming back to us," Gabriel said in a raspy voice as he fought tears.

"Why did they have to go away?"

"I don't know, Nicholas. I don't know."

Nicholas whimpered in his arms but eventually settled and fell asleep.

Gabriel walked around the mingling crowds, nodding to the few men he knew. Most would be from the mines, although some he recognized from the pubs.

"Gabe!" Larry said as he clasped him on the shoulder. "Sorry to be late."

Gabriel half smiled toward Larry, Morgan and Niall. They were formally dressed in suits, waistcoats and ties with no sign of wood dust. "Thanks for coming. It will mean a lot to Amelia."

"Who's the wee chap?" Niall asked.

Gabriel twisted around a bit so they could see Nicholas. "This is Liam and Amelia's son, Nicholas."

"Poor creature looks worn out," Niall said. He reached out to stroke Nicholas's back in a soft caress, not waking him.

"What would you expect?" Morgan said. He nodded his thanks as a pint was passed to him. "Good turnout," he murmured around his first sip.

"Yes, though I think it is mandated by the Miner's Union that they all show for the wakes and funerals of the deceased," Gabriel said.

"Makes sense," Larry whispered. "They never know when it will be their turn."

"How are things at the Thornton?"

He saw the three of them exchange a long glance. "Testy," Morgan said after a few moments. "Jeffers is none pleased with you."

"He knew I'd be out."

"Well, there's a difference between askin' to be away and tellin' the man you'll be out, Gabe. You could've used a bit more tact with the man," Niall said with a frown.

"I'll explain when I am back. Work extra hours to make up the time," Gabriel said.

"We'll do what we can to calm the man down, but he's been on a tirade lately. Seems we're behind schedule, and you not being in isn't helping. By the way, Harvey's back," Larry said. He waved to an acquaintance before turning to watch Gabriel with a frown.

"That's good."

Morgan shook his head. "Maybe not for you, Gabe. Come back to work as soon as you can. Jeffers can be mean, and you don't want to get on his bad side."

Gabriel nodded.

"Who's keeping vigil?" Niall asked.

"I will," Gabriel said.

"You know these things go on for two or three days, Gabe?" Larry asked. "You can't be out that long. Be here today. Come back for the funeral, but don't miss so much work."

"I will do what I must to honor my friends."

Niall grunted. "Loyalty is good, Gabe, but not if you sacrifice your future for it." He nodded to Larry and Morgan. "We should pay our respects to the widow." They clapped Gabriel on the back as they moved into the house.

***

May 3, 1901

My darling Gabriel,

Please forgive my recent silence. I know I have not written as often as I should have, and I worry that you will fear I have had a change of heart. Nothing could be further from the truth. Life has become increasingly difficult in Boston, and I can no longer envision a future here.

I have news for you, darling, and I believe from your recent letter that this is news you will rejoice in. Colin and I will travel to Montana after my convention with Sophronia and Aunt Betsy in May. We will leave Minneapolis on the 6th of June and travel to Butte. Will you meet me at the train station? I can no longer bear our separation and want to be with you.

I miss you, my darling. It is hard to believe that, soon, our separation will be at an end.
Ever Yours,
Clarissa

CHAPTER 20

"SAV, WHY ARE WE in the front parlor?" I asked.

Bright light streamed in the front windows, a nice change from the dim family parlor in my aunt and uncle's house. However, no amount of sunlight would convert the parlor into a pleasant room with the imposing rosewood furniture polished to a high sheen preventing any true sense of welcome. Savannah had seated us in matching taupe-colored striped silk and satin chairs near the fireplace. They were situated far from the open door with an overflowing tea tray set in front of us on a low table.

Savannah waved away the question. "Keep your voice down, Rissa," she commanded. "I don't want Jonas to know you are already here." Her strawberry-blond hair shone today, and her yellow day dress enhanced her skin's subtle glow. I wondered for a moment what could have brought about the change but then focused on our conversation.

"Why?"

"Because there is much to gossip about."

"Sav, I really don't feel like idle gossip about faceless society matrons," I complained, unable to hide my exhaustion before the upcoming trip to Minneapolis.

"I think gossiping about you will keep us plenty busy," Savannah said with a quick smile. "So, are you are going to marry Cameron?"

"No, of course not. What I don't understand, Sav, is why he's insistent on marrying me. Why does Mrs. Smythe like him?"

"What is the greatest motivator in life, Rissa?"

"Love?"

"No, not for those with honor, for the rest?"

"Power?"

"Yes, and money," Savannah said.

"But I have no money."

"So you think."

"Sav, please tell me what you know."

"We have, or I should say, you have and I had, dowries. Set up by our grandparents. To ensure that we would make good matches. When our mothers made disastrous marriages, in their opinion, they wanted to ensure that we could marry well and restore family honor."

"But why didn't we know about it until now?"

"They decided our parents would never be able to determine a good match having descended too far from the upper class. Therefore they set out to choose our ideal husbands."

"What?"

"It's no coincidence Jonas and I met at their house for tea," Savannah said with an irate sniff. "They arranged the entire thing. And Jonas only became wealthier with my dowry."

"But it's yours. You should be able to do what you want with it," I argued.

"In theory, Rissa, but not reality," Savannah said. "And I would have greater control of it if it were actual property rather than money. As it is, Jonas controls it."

"Then what use are the marriage rights laws for women?" I asked. "Why bother writing laws, saying they are going to protect the rights of women, and then ignore the laws they write?"

"Rissa…"

"You know as well as I do that the marriage rights laws were written to protect a woman's property from their spendthrift husbands. That women were to be able to maintain control or title to whatever property they brought into a marriage. It was to help prevent women and children from becoming destitute and at the hands of creditors if they were to become widows, all because they couldn't own or have the rights to property." I snorted in disgust. "And yet the courts won't uphold their own laws," I hissed.

"You are taking a very one-sided view," Savannah said.

"Of course I am. You should have control of your dowry, not Jonas. It's yours, not his." I took a deep breath, hoping my anger would dissipate. "You have had your dowry taken from you and are now trapped with such a man. Of course I am going to take your side."

Savannah smiled and gripped my hand. "Rissa, I understand your need for suffragist politics, but today is not the day. Listen. Cameron knows about your dowry. It's what he wants. Not you."

I sat back against the settee, feeling winded. "And Mrs. Smythe?"

"She gets a portion of the dowry for smoothing his way."

"How?"

"Why do you think he disappeared after my wedding?" She watched me closely. "Yes, I saw him there, taunting you. Why did he then miraculously reappear this fall after Gabriel was gone?"

"You can't mean..." I asked, unable to continue.

"Yes, she advised him to give her time to ensure Gabriel's absence."

"How could she? She knew what Cameron was, and yet she encouraged him?"

"I imagine all she cares about is the money. And will do whatever she deems necessary to obtain it."

"Even sacrificing me to someone like him," I choked out.

"He has hurt you?"

"Terribly," I whispered.

"I imagine he believes you are now bound to him?"

"But I'm not," I said with a desperate defiance in my voice. "I made sure of it."

Savannah watched me with sad eyes before nodding. "You aren't yet, Rissa," Savannah agreed. "You must ensure that you continue to evade him."

"Sav, how do you know this?"

"The family parlor is fairly easy to eavesdrop on, which is why Jonas prefers me to entertain you there. He likes the maids to listen for any pertinent gossip and report back to him," she said with a glower toward Jonas's closed library door. "My maid, the only one in the house loyal to me, finally admitted it to me a few weeks ago even though she was terrified to do so."

"Terrified?"

"Yes, for fear of being fired. She has to send money home to her family in Ireland."

"Well, now that you know, you should say you prefer this parlor," I said. "What did you learn when you eavesdropped?"

"I learned all about our dowries. About how the money almost compensated for having to marry so far below Jonas's expectations," Savannah said with a catch in her voice. "And I heard him encouraging Cameron to continue to pursue you even if he had to give a portion to that 'dreadful' woman."

I glanced quickly at the door, saw no one nearby and heard no one approaching. I leaned in toward Savannah and breathed, "I have known for some time that I must leave."

"Take care with those whom you trust, Rissa. You don't want to be prevented from fulfilling your dreams."

"Why didn't you tell me before about what you had learned? You've known for a while now."

"Jonas restricts who I can see and where I may go. When I called last week at my parents' home, there were too many present to have a decent conversation. Jonas and I had a vicious argument yesterday about you calling today. I am sorry, Rissa, but I didn't trust writing such information in a letter."

I clasped her hand, my anger rising at the clues to her married life. "Please don't worry. I know now and that will help me. Why don't you want me to make a marriage like yours?"

"Because I realize I was maneuvered into a sham of a marriage. To a man who has no true regard for me. Into a world where I will never be accepted. Where people will always whisper about my shopkeeping beginnings. Where I understand now that even my mother used me to further her social standing and relationship with the grandparents."

"Sav, Aunt Matilda loves you."

"Not enough, it seems," she said. "Though you should know, if you don't marry someone acceptable, you may lose the dowry."

"I don't want their money."

"You are so much braver than I am."

"What..." I stopped as I heard footsteps approaching.

"Clarissa, how bereft I am to realize your visit is nearly over, and I have only just greeted you," Jonas said.

"I did not wish to interrupt your important work," Savannah murmured.

"I called to discuss the exciting news," I said.

"Oh?"

"Yes, my travels to the suffragist convention in Minneapolis. I leave in a few days with Aunt Betsy and Mrs. Chickering."

"Of course," he said. "I had hoped you had rid yourself of such tendencies. Though I am certain, should you have the good sense to marry Cameron, you will be cured of such notions."

"It's not an illness."

"Be that as it may, we shall be able to readily welcome you into our home when you have married an acceptable man," Jonas said.

"I had hoped I would always be welcomed here," I said with a lift of an eyebrow.

"Do not flatter yourself."

"Jonas!" Savannah said.

"Don't worry, Savannah, we understand each other," I said.

"As long as you realize Cameron also understands you," Jonas said in an ominous voice. "Has Mrs. Montgomery told you our news?"

I shook my head in denial, concerned for Savannah as she paled. "She will give birth to my son in six month's time."

"Your son?" I asked as I shared a quick glance with Savannah. "What about your daughter?"

"Mrs. Montgomery knows better than to give birth to a mewling girl."

"She might have less control over the outcome than you think," I said as Savannah paled further.

"Nonsense! Mrs. Montgomery knows she needs merely to focus to produce my heir. She knows what is expected of her and what shall happen should I be disappointed."

"I give you my congratulations. I hope both mother and child have a safe and healthy time," I said. I turned toward Savannah, searching for a spark of joy in her eyes. Instead, I saw overwhelming sorrow.

"I must leave you, Sav," I said, choking up. I reached toward her, grasping her in a tight embrace. "Take care of yourself," I whispered. She clung to me for a moment before releasing me.

"Jonas," I said as I walked from the room with only a quick glance in his direction.

Outside I paused, closing my eyes, inhaling the scent of freshly tilled earth from their side garden, the loamy scent soothing me. I glanced to see red, purple and yellow tulips in full bloom, the beds recently weeded. I took a calming breath as I faced returning home for the first time since the day of Cameron's assault.

***

I STOOD AT THE FRONT DOOR of my father's house, fidgeting. Lucas sensed my mood and looped his arm through mine in an attempt to bolster my lagging spirit. I stared at a new gold knocker, the size of Uncle Martin's large fist, fastened in the middle of the black door. Uncle Martin winked at me as he reached for it and rapped loudly on the door.

"It works well enough," he said with a quick smile.

The maid Bridget answered the door. "I am unsure if they be acceptin' callers," she said.

"Nonsense," Uncle Martin said as he pushed past her into the house. "I'm certain we are welcome." He took off his hat, hung it on a peg on the hallstand, brushed at the sides of his trimmed brown hair, and walked into the parlor with Lucas and me in his wake.

"Sean, good to see you!" Uncle Martin exclaimed. I peered around the doorway of the parlor, hoping to see changes. However, Mrs. Smythe had done no redecorating in my absence, and the room was exactly as when I had left.

"Martin!" Da called out. He rose from his chair to shake Uncle Martin's hand and to clap him on the back. "Lucas, you are very welcome." He shook his hand, but continued to glance toward the doorway. I finally entered the parlor, and he said, "Ah, there she is. My girl, home at last." He enfolded me in a warm embrace. He smelled of fresh soap and shaving cream. Smells that would forever remind me of Da.

"Hello, Da," I whispered, trying not to cling to him.

"It's good to see you," he said. "I never thought you'd leave and not come back to us."

I flushed and looked down.

"Ah, Clarissa, you've returned to us," Mrs. Smythe said. She frowned, the fine lines around her eyes crinkling and highlighting her displeasure. She tapped her pale green silk fan against her thigh in agitation as we entered the room. "By now I'm sure you have seen the error of your actions and wish to move home."

I took a deep breath to calm my roiling emotions at seeing her again. "Actually, no."

"No? No? You're not to move home? I'm surprised you don't know your sense of duty. Duty to your family first, yourself always second. You are a selfish girl."

"Mrs. Smythe, I have no interest in your proclamations on my person. I came to see my da and brothers before my journey."

"Journey? Where are you going? Why have we not been consulted?"

"I am of age and able to decide what I would like to do."

"It is that sort of belief that will cause you to remain a single, unwanted spinster for the rest of your life."

"I am traveling to Chicago and then on to Minneapolis tomorrow with Mrs. Chickering and Aunt Betsy to attend the annual suffragist meeting. It is proper due to their presence."

"I hardly believe going to a meeting with firebrand women who haven't the sense to realize their good fortune to have men govern for them is acceptable for a young, impressionable woman."

"I believe there are those who hope it will fulfill all of her suffragist tendencies and she will come home with an equal fervor for other interests," Lucas said.

"You shouldn't be going at all, young lady. If you were living at home, where you ought to be, if your unscrupulous uncle hadn't taken you in and given you shelter after your horrific display of disobedience, then this would not be happening. You would be here now, with us, learning what you need to for your future life."

"I believe I will learn important skills and information at the convention."

"On how to scare decent, God-fearing men away! On how to continue to live your life as an unwanted, unloved spinster! How I despair for you. You have no sense, Clarissa. If you would only listen to those of us here, in this room, who wish the best for you." She let out a dramatic sigh and then fanned herself as though it were all too much for her.

"Yes, I must always be certain to listen to the counsel of those who have my interests at heart," I said.

Colin gripped my hand tightly. "It's good to see you, Rissa," Colin said. "Are all of your plans settled then?"

I shared a long look with him, his blue eyes showing their concern. "Yes, they are. We leave on the train tomorrow from South Station."

"And all is to plan?" he murmured. We had spoken alone once after I received my letter from Gabriel of my plan to travel to Montana, and he had insisted on traveling with me.

"Yes." I squeezed his hand, and he nodded in understanding. I swallowed a lump in my throat, thankful for his support.

"When do you return?" Mrs. Smythe asked.

"We return in a little over a month."

"I hope when you return, you will have seen sense and will be more amenable to those who have shown you interest."

Lucas and Uncle Martin moved to converse with Colin, and I rose to speak with Da. I wanted to spend a little time with him this evening and resented Mrs. Smythe's presence.

He patted the settee next to him, and I sat down. "Tell me, Clarissa, how have you been? The house is too quiet without you in it."

"I am well, Da. I have enjoyed having the liberty to do what I want and need."

"I see now it was wrong to deny you of your freedoms…"

"Sean!"

"Hush, Rebecca," he admonished. "I understand it was like trying to cage a songbird and expecting it to sing. Forgive me, Clarissa."

"Da…" I said, unable to say more as I choked up.

"Any word from your Gabriel?"

"Sean!"

"He is well, enjoying life in the wilds of a mining town in Montana."

"I always thought he'd come back for you."

"Sean! That is completely inappropriate. She needs to focus on more acceptable men," Mrs. Smythe sputtered.

"Well, I always thought he was an appropriate young man. A little forward, mind, and I would have appreciated him speaking with me about courting Clarissa. I want you to understand, Clarissa. Even though I wanted you separated from him for a little while when he lived in Boston, I never wanted him to leave." He studied me as I nodded my understanding. "I wish him well."

"Thank you, Da."

"Clarissa, darling, when are you coming home? I had hoped, after my letter, you would return to us."

"I am uncertain, Da," I said. "I shall consider it after the convention."

"Do. I want you home where I can ensure you're safe."

"I'll let you know, Da," I said, clearing my throat so that I would not cry. I stared around the room, the one room I would never feel safe in again and stifled a shudder. "I should leave soon as the train departs early tomorrow morning."

"Take care of yourself, my Clarissa," Da said, rising to envelop me in a strong embrace. "Come back to us."

"'Bye, Da," I whispered, fighting tears.

CHAPTER 21

"OH, GABRIEL, I AM SORRY," Amelia murmured as she rocked baby Anne in her arms, trying to settle her. Nicholas sat in a corner near the dilapidated sofa, chastised for pinching Anne. Amelia's hair was tied back in a lose braid, and faint traces of flour clung to her hair and clothes. The scent of baking bread wafted from the kitchen mingling with the scent of drooping day lilies and carnations from the funeral and wake.

"I don't know what I am going to do, Amelia," Gabriel said as he paced the small living area. "I need to work."

"I know, Gabriel. What happened?"

"Jeffers thinks I have a poor work ethic. According to him I missed too much work. Between the wake and the funerals, I was away for four days. He didn't think mourning for friends warranted such time away."

"And who is this Jeffers?" Amelia asked, a fiery glint to her hazel eyes.

"My foreman. And that's not the worst of it." Gabriel continued pacing. "He's informed the other bosses that I should not be hired."

"Gabriel."

"I know he never liked me after my questions about politics. Well, and for being a Northerner, but it's too much! I need to work."

"Gabriel, I'm sure you have some money put aside. You'll be able to bide a little time and then find work. This Jeffers can't have this much clout."

"He's a very forceful member of the union, Amelia." He sighed. "But Ronan needs money for the hospital. And I must have work with Clarissa coming."

"Clarissa's coming?"

"I received a letter a few days ago from her. It seems that she and her brother Colin will be arriving soon."

He saw Amelia flush and look away.

"What is it, Amelia?"

"Haven't you heard the talk?" At his quick shake of his head, no, she sighed. "Why do you think that you are one of my only visitors? The neighbors and community at large are whispering that you have a lovely widow on the side."

Gabriel spun to look at her, shocked and angered.

"My neighbors shun me because they think I don't show consideration to the memory of my recently departed husband."

"Idiots!"

"Some say, if we were just a little more circumspect, it would be acceptable."

"We have nothing to hide, Amelia," Gabriel ground out. "Why can't people understand friendship?"

"To them it's unseemly. And I worry your Clarissa will hear the talk and…"

"Clarissa's not like that," Gabriel insisted. He continued to pace, lost in thought. After a few more turns around the room, he stopped, turning toward her. "I know I could find a job in one of the mines. They need carpenters, and I could work there." He closed his eyes as though in pain. "I just can't imagine that work. I never wanted to work underground, as though the outside were a distant memory."

"Is there no other option, Gabriel?"

"Do you ever dream of living in a place where you can see the mountains? Breathe fresh air? Not hear the whistle signaling shift change or read about the latest mine disaster at every turn?"

"What are you saying?"

"Do you want to remain in Butte?"

"Not particularly. But I have nowhere else to go. I have no family. Soon I won't be able to live here," she whispered in a broken voice. "It's Company property, meant for miners. Since I'm no longer married to a miner, I need to move on."

"Amelia," Gabriel said.

"I don't want to end up in the Cabbage Patch, Gabriel," Amelia said in a harsh, low voice.

"You'd never live there. I wouldn't let you," Gabe hissed. "You may not have family, but you have friends."

"Gabriel, what are you saying?"

"Let's leave Butte. Start fresh in a smaller town."

"Butte is the place to live in Montana. Butte *is* Montana. Why would we leave it?" Amelia asked confused.

"Because we need to live in a place where there aren't memories around every corner. Where I won't have an agitated union man preventing me from obtaining work. Even if it's temporary, I can't wait. And I can't work in a mine. Not after hearing so many stories and losing my friends in a mine. I can't."

"Where would we go?"

"I don't know. I just thought of leaving at this moment. I've heard of a town called Missoula. It's a ways west but still in Montana. Let me look into it." At Amelia's nod, he said, "Thankfully we had a decent collection for Ronan at the wake and funeral. So, even after helping Ronan with the rest of his hospital bills, I should have enough money set aside for the short train ride."

"And I have the money from the death benefit," Amelia said. "That will keep the children and me going for a little while as I determine what I can do in this new town." She paused for a moment as though uncertain how to broach the topic. "Gabriel, it may prove awkward for me to travel with you as an unmarried woman. There may be a lot of talk. And talk may follow us."

Gabriel sighed, closing his eyes. "I know, Amelia. But I can't imagine leaving you here alone. Of not being able to help you. Of not seeing little Nicholas and Anne grow."

"I want them to know their uncle Gabriel. Will you let me consider what I would like to do? Can you visit again tomorrow?"

"Of course. I won't abandon you," Gabriel said. He gripped her hand, leaning forward to kiss her gently on the forehead. He brushed away her tears as he crouched in front of her. "I promise that I'll always be there for you, Nicholas and Anne."

"I know, Gabriel," Amelia said. "But this isn't the life I envisioned. I need Liam so badly. Why did he have to die? Why?" she cried, burying her face in Anne's swaddled clothes.

"Amelia," Gabriel soothed.

"No, Gabriel," Amelia choked out. "There are no words of comfort.

There is nothing you can say to bring him back so that he can hold me in his arms and tell me it was all a bad dream. To take this pain away. To…" She began to sob.

Gabriel gathered her close, rocking her and baby Anne in his arms as he tried to offer solace. "I know, Amelia. I know there is nothing to say to soothe your pain. I just wish there were."

"Oh, Gabriel. Why did he have to go away from me?" she cried.

Gabriel merely continued to rock her, rubbing soft circles on her back.

After a few minutes, she eased away, refusing to meet Gabriel's eyes. "Forgive me, Gabriel."

"There's nothing to forgive, Amelia," he said. "If you didn't mourn Liam, then I'd be worried." He wiped her cheeks once then reached out for Anne. "Here, let me take her for a few minutes." He stood, holding her against his chest and cooing in her ear as he walked around the small living room.

***

"RONAN, HOW ARE YOU recovering?" Gabriel asked. He walked toward the chair by Ronan's bed, noting that most of the occupants in this hospital room were either sedated or unconscious. One man in the middle bed on the other side watched them, as though nothing of interest had happened in days.

Ronan struggled to a sitting position, gasping with pain. His arms shook with the exertion of pushing himself up. His brown beard had filled in and thickened, masking his recent weight loss. "Slowly."

"What's the doctor say?"

"That the pain'll go away, but I'll probably never walk again."

"Ronan, no," Gabriel moaned, grasping his nape. "What will you do?"

"I've no idea. There isn't much work a cripple can do at a mine."

Gabriel winced at the word *cripple*. "There'll be something for you to do. They'll find work for you."

Ronan shook his head. "How is Amelia?"

"Suffering. Missing Liam," Gabriel murmured.

"I wish I could have been at the funeral. Who kept vigil at the wake?" Ronan asked.

"I did."

"Was there a good showing for the funeral?"

"More than you could imagine. I stood next to Amelia at the cemetery and held Nicholas during the burial."

"And for Matthew?"

"I threw on the first soil. And I wrote his family. I don't expect to hear from them. He told me once they couldn't read." Gabriel sighed.

"What is it?" Ronan asked. At Gabriel's shake of his head, Ronan became more curious. "You seem worried. What's bothering you?"

"There's gossip about Amelia and me. And she has been blacklisted by the women of the Guild."

"What? How are you stopping it?"

"There's little I can do. I can't stop seeing Amelia, Ronan. She needs help with the children, and she needs company."

"Is there any truth to the rumors?"

"Of course not!" Gabriel glared at Ronan for a moment before he sighed. "No, Ronan. I received word from Clarissa that she is planning on joining me here in Montana."

"Seems your patience was worth it. But if you and Amelia aren't to marry, I don't understand what you can do to stem the gossip here in Butte if you continue to spend time at her house."

"We're thinking of leaving Butte."

"Leave Butte? Why?"

"I've lost my job due to the amount of time I was absent from work for the wake and funeral. I need work to support Clarissa." Gabriel massaged his hands. "Besides, it's too painful to walk around the streets, with the memories of all of us together. I need a fresh start, Ronan."

"And you think it's acceptable to leave me here? Alone?"

"Ronan, I can't stay here," Gabriel rasped out.

"Take me with you," Ronan begged. At Gabriel's silence, Ronan whispered, "Please, don't leave me here with no close friends and only self-pity for company."

"I can speak with Jed at the railroad station. I know him from when I arrived last fall. Let me see what can be managed. If you want to come with us, Ronan, I won't leave you behind."

Ronan sighed. "Thank you, Gabe."

"One day, you may wish you had stayed in Butte, Ronan."

"When that day comes, I'll let you remind me that you told me so. Right now I can't be separated from you, Amelia and the children. You're my only family," he whispered. Gabriel nodded, gripping Ronan's shoulder as he left.

"I'll return tomorrow, hopefully with plans."

CHAPTER 22

"SOPHIE, I CAN'T BELIEVE the convention is already over," I said as I leaned against an overstuffed chair upholstered in a steel-gray silk damask pattern in her well-appointed room in the West Hotel in Minneapolis. Potted ferns flourished beside the large arched windows, sheer curtains preventing the glare of the late afternoon sun from shining on the thick red rugs. Sophie sat on the matching settee, its button-tufted back cushions curved at the top in a serpentine manner forming a camelback shape and finished with rosewood carved in an elaborate floral pattern. Small tables were scattered around the room, and the cream-colored wallpaper held pictures highlighting the beauty of Minnesota.

"Nor can I, although I am ready to return to Boston. It has been a wonderful few weeks with you, my girl, between the time in Chicago and the convention. What did you think of the convention?"

"I liked Mrs. Catt and her plan to have us organize and then work with the legislators. I think Miss Anthony chose a good successor in Mrs. Catt."

Sophronia *harrumphed* but then smiled. "Yes, she will lead us on well, but she mustn't become too enamored with all of her organizing. Sometimes change comes from chaos."

"Don't you think we need to have a better understanding of our opposition in order to attain our goal of the Sixteenth Amendment?"

"I'll never argue against understanding the myopic views of those who would rather choke on tradition than accept that change is coming. However, you should not become so entrenched in your beliefs on how to accomplish something that you can't see another way to obtain your goals."

I nodded for a moment as I thought through her words. "What did you think of Mr. Blackwell?" I asked.

"I found him as fascinating here as in Boston."

"Do you think it possible for a man to truly be in favor of women having the vote? Can there really be a partnership between men and women like he had with Lucy Stone?"

"I can't answer for their marriage, but I believe it can happen, yes." Sophronia watched me. "You're thinking of your young man in Montana."

"Yes, I am. I hope he is like Mr. Blackwell, although I don't know as I want my wedding to be referred to as a marriage protest."

"You say you don't want a marriage protest, but I imagine you would like a marriage like theirs. Like equals," Sophronia said with a piercing stare. "I can envision you wanting to omit the word *obey* from your marriage vows."

"Yes, I would like to feel like my ideas and beliefs matter. That I have rights as an individual even though I am married. And I've never liked the word *obey*."

"Did you know that Lucy Stone was the first woman from Massachusetts to earn a college degree?"

"Yes, I had heard that."

"It seems to me there are men who aren't afraid of educated women."

"And I remain hopeful Gabriel is one of those men. Sophie, I can't thank you enough for insisting I come to this convention." I sighed with delight as I clasped a throw pillow to my chest.

"Have you learned anything useful, my girl?"

"Yes. I must continue to champion this cause, and, although it may seem daunting, we will obtain our goal."

"Very good," Sophie said with a small smile. She settled herself in her comfortable chair before pinning me with the gaze of her intense aquamarine eyes. "Have you learned anything about yourself and what you need?"

"No."

"No?" Sophie asked.

"Sophie, please listen. I knew when I left Boston I wasn't returning."

"You have this planned?" At my quick nod, she directed her stare at me. "What of the tea?"

I flushed, but met her eyes. "All is as I had hoped," I muttered.

Sophie gave a satisfied nod. "Who will travel with you?"

"Colin. He helped me and plotted it all with me. He'll be here tonight, and we'll travel together to Montana tomorrow while you return to Boston. In fact he wishes to stay with me."

"Wonderful news," Sophronia said. "About time you took your life into your own hands. I had never thought to visit Montana, but now I might have to."

At the quick knock on the door, I knew it would be Aunt Betsy. Sophie rose to answer the door, calling out as she opened it, "Clarissa has wonderful—" She stopped short.

"News?" Aunt Betsy said. "I too have a ... surprise." I turned toward her with a lightness of spirit and gave a hoot of happiness at seeing Colin. He wore a simple suit of gray pants, waistcoat and jacket. The light blue of his shirt enhanced the sparkle in his blue eyes.

"Col!" I flung my arms around his neck. He laughed as he picked me up and swung me around once.

"Rissa," he said, patting me softly on my back when he set me down.

"Would either of you care to tell me why Colin is here?" Aunt Betsy said as she maneuvered her way to a chair, her cane making a loud *thunk* with each step. She settled into my recently vacated chair and turned her blue-green eyes, lit with concern, on us. "I suspect he isn't here to escort us home."

I exchanged a worried glance with Colin but decided to trust Aunt Betsy. "I'm not returning home with you, Aunt Betsy."

"What do you hope to accomplish?"

"A future with Gabriel."

A slow smile spread across her face. "It's about time. I'm thankful you have the sense your mama did to grasp at happiness and not allow others to dictate how you should live your life."

"Thank you, Aunt Betsy," I whispered, attempting not to cry.

"So that is why you have traveled here to be with us?" She turned toward Colin. At his nod, she looked at me and then toward Sophronia. "When are you traveling?"

"We ride out of town on a Northern Pacific train tomorrow, Aunt Betsy," Colin said.

"Why don't you rest a few days?" Sophronia asked.

"I'm concerned that Cameron may follow me. Savannah warned me that she heard him speaking with Jonas about traveling to the west," Colin said.

"Then you need to leave as soon as possible. Clarissa, do you have comfortable travel clothes you wish to wear for a few days?" Aunt Betsy asked.

"I plan on wearing my eggshell-blue shirtwaist."

"How have you managed to purchase your tickets?" Aunt Betsy asked.

"I have money saved from my teaching."

"And I have some from the smithy," Colin said.

She snorted as she rose. "Clarissa, will you accompany me to my room?"

"And you can keep me company, young man," Sophronia said. "I shall enjoy speaking with you about the goings-on in Boston."

I shared an amused glance with Colin as I walked slowly beside Aunt Betsy toward her room. Upon entering her lavish suite, I relaxed on the chaise longue in the nook by the window, curling up in the sun like a cat.

"Clarissa, I am surprised you did not share your plans with me."

"I couldn't risk anyone ruining my chances with Gabriel." I watched her as I lay on my side.

"I know you cannot have saved what you need," she said as she walked to a chest of drawers. "Take this, my dear." She held out a sack that jingled and crinkled, and I realized it was filled with money.

"Aunt Betsy," I said in protest, sitting upright as I grasped the bag.

"I have no need of this money, Clarissa. I fear on your journey to Gabriel, you may need more than you have saved. Take this and allow me to help in my own small way."

"Thank you, Aunt Betsy," I whispered as I rose to enfold her in a gentle hug.

"Be happy with Gabriel, and that is all the thanks I need," she said as she leaned away from me to brush the tears from my eyes. "Clarissa, you have always been my favorite niece. I know I shouldn't say such things, but I may never have the chance again. Be happy. Be honest with Gabriel. Do not be afraid of sharing with him your deepest fears, for, if he is the man you think he is, he will still love you."

I nodded, my eyes welling again with tears.

"No tears, Clarissa," she said. "We'll have letters. Never forget, you are doing what your mama would have wanted you to do. Living out your dream, not the dream that others had for you."

"Thank you, Aunt Betsy," I said.

CHAPTER 23

GABRIEL THRUST OPEN the workshop door, allowing fresh air to slowly permeate his workplace. He raked his hand through his hair, shaking out wood dust. He continued to gently massage his right shoulder with his left hand, attempting to relax his muscles and ease some of the tension that seemed to have permanently settled there.

After a few more moments spent enjoying the sun and fresh air, Gabriel returned inside to continue with his work. A small rectangular room, his workshop was adequate for his needs. The sun continued to shine in through large windows on either side of the door, allowing him to work at his bench along the far wall with no need for additional light. A cabinet was fitted along the wall to the left of the entrance holding Gabriel's tools. On the wall to the right of the door, a staircase led up to his living quarters above the workspace. Scattered throughout the room were pieces of furniture in various shapes and stages of development. The thick brick walls of the building prevented his neighbors from becoming annoyed when he worked long into the night.

He walked toward an angled drafting table, sat at his stool and tapped his pencil on the edge of a blank sheet of paper. He sketched a design for a small chest of drawers for one of his customers and soon became lost in the act of creation.

A short time later, a knock at the door interrupted his work. He set aside his pencil before walking toward the door.

"You're early today!" he said with a broad smile. Upon opening the door, he stopped short, staring with momentary confusion at a tall, well-dressed gentleman. "Excuse me, may I help you, sir?" Gabriel asked.

The gentleman appeared well-to-do, with freshly pressed black pants, a starched white shirt, crisp red checkered tie, black waistcoat, with matching overcoat and top hat. His shoes were brightly polished to a shine so bright that one's reflection was visible. He turned fully to face Gabriel, and studied him for a few moments with his head tilted to one side. Suddenly, he beamed.

"Yes, I do believe you'll be able to help me," the man replied, in a deep, cultured voice with a hint of Boston in it.

Gabriel squinted, a whisper of a memory teasing him. He peered at the middle-aged man.

"Uncle Aidan?" Gabriel asked.

"Yes, Gabriel," Aidan replied, unable to stop smiling. "I've finally arrived. And what a journey it was!"

Gabriel reached out to embrace his uncle but was afraid that would be improper and dropped his arms to his sides. Aidan nodded, seeming to understand his confusion, and grabbed him into a big hug, clapping him on the back. He released him and then gave a short *whoop*, hugging Gabriel again for another quick embrace.

"Ah, Gabriel, I never thought this day would come," Aidan admitted with a wide grin. "Since I learned you had not perished, I hoped for it, prayed for it, but I always feared something would occur to prevent our reunion." He looked up and down the street, and then peered into Gabriel's workshop. "Is there somewhere we can go for a visit?"

"Yes, please come inside." Gabriel waved toward his workspace, inviting Aidan in. Gabriel had not cleaned for a few days and realized a fine sheen of dust covered every flat surface. "Please pardon the dust, Uncle." He walked to one of the chairs he had recently finished and wiped it off with a rag.

"You have beautiful pieces here, Gabriel. Is your business growing?" Aidan wandered the workshop, delight and awe on his face as he beheld the pieces created by his nephew.

"Yes, even though I arrived recently, my reputation is growing. I continue to sell more of my work. I don't mind the long hours. New homes are being built, and I have a few commissions for finish work and cabinetry. I arrived a little over a month ago, but it seems there wasn't a reputable cabinetmaker in town. I was fortunate." He sighed and turned to his uncle, studying him.

"I can't believe you're here. I can't believe you're really alive." He collapsed into the chair he had just cleaned for Aidan.

"Gabriel, it's as though a dream to me too. You look so much like your father. So tall and broad, with serious eyes, though with a smile ever lurking. You even speak like him."

Gabriel watched his uncle walk around his workspace, studying his tools. He was tall and dark-haired like his brothers. Like his da. Yet Aidan was more lanky, long boned and trim. He had intense blue eyes with laugh lines at the corners that seemed to take in everything he saw in one quick glance. His voice was cultured, polished, gentle. Different from the booming, vivacious voice of the uncle he remembered as a child. However, the changes were subtle, and Gabriel could see in him the uncle he remembered.

"Uncle, please sit and tell me about your trip here." Gabriel motioned toward one of the chairs, belatedly realizing it was dusty. However, Aidan sat with no apparent concern for his fine clothing.

"Ah, a well-made rocking chair." He sighed, starting to rock to and fro. "This is one of my favorite types of chairs, where I often get my best thinking done."

After a few moments, he cracked open his eyes and said, "I assume you made this?" At Gabriel's nod, Aidan continued to rock. "A remarkably comfortable chair. I can see why you'll be a great success."

Gabriel smiled.

"You have your mother's smile. Did anyone ever tell you that?" Aidan murmured, pain and sadness deep in his eyes.

"No, no one ever spoke of my parents in a positive way after they died," Gabriel said. "I had to ignore what my aunt said about them, how she wanted us to remember them, and instead to remember what life truly had been like when they were alive. To tell Richard and Jeremy stories so that they would remember our parents as they were."

"Ah, so that's how it was then." He watched Gabriel with an angry intensity in his blue eyes. "Richard didn't care to talk much about your aunt. I'm more sorry than I can say that she had a hand in raising you three boys. She's a truly vile person." He looked toward Gabriel with anguish. "I thought I'd lost all of you that night. I was told you were dead. I couldn't believe it. When I went to see your aunt, she met with me in her formal parlor and confirmed what I had heard."

"Who told you that we had died? I thought everyone on the street had seen us alive, huddled in the middle of it, screaming out for our parents to the point of hoarseness."

"I spoke with a neighbor of yours, across the street. I can't remember her name, but she had a houseful of little ones. A widow, I think. Or her husband was out to sea. I can't recall." Aidan looked down, his eyes squinted, a distant look in his eyes as though deep in thought.

"But how can that be?" Gabriel exclaimed, causing Aidan to look up. "She took us in, took care of us after our parents died. She was the one who sent for Aunt Masterson. She…" Gabriel stopped speaking.

"I'm not sure, Gabriel, but I do know she told me that you were all dead and to seek out your aunt. Thus, I did, and, when it was confirmed you had died, I fled Boston. I had lost everything that had any true value to me. I never wanted to return. I was bitterly angry that I had lost my entire family that night."

There was a period of silence, as Gabriel attempted to understand what his uncle had just told him. "You can't know what it is to learn that there existed someone who wanted us. Loved us," Gabriel whispered.

"Always, Gabriel. Always. Even when I thought you were lost to me, I loved you boys and never ceased mourning the loss of you."

"Uncle, what do you remember about visiting my parents' house?"

"Ah, Gabriel." He sighed. "It's not a simple thing for me, remembering those times." He paused for a moment before meeting Gabriel's eyes. "Returning to your parents' house, your house, after my journeys was the closest thing I had to going home. I would go to sea, travel the world, and know that I could come home and be with family. Always be welcome." He sighed again, closing his eyes with a half smile on his face.

"I remember the smell in the kitchen. Your mother was a terrible cook, so she always had spices brewing on a pot on the stove to cover up some disaster in the oven. She would laugh over it, then try again. Your father and I would discuss politics, his work or my travel. You boys would be in the kitchen, attempting to do your studies, but would really just be listening to us. After supper your mother would read to all of us from her latest book. Poetry or mysteries or novels. She loved to read and wanted her boys to have a proper education. It was a wonderful, welcoming place."

Gabriel stared at him, unable to speak, overcome by memories. "Da never became upset that Mum was a horrible cook. We somehow never went hungry," Gabriel murmured.

"Well, you all had stomachs of iron," Aidan joked. "I agree, though your father never became upset with your mother in front of me. He knew she was not of that world and did the best she could." Aidan paused for a few moments, then continued, "Understand this, Gabriel. Your father truly loved your mother, and they cherished and adored all three of you boys."

Gabriel nodded. Gruffly clearing his throat, he asked, "Will you tell me more about them, some other day, Uncle?"

"Yes, of course, but I think we should wait for a time when we are both ready." They sat for a few moments in companionable silence. Finally Aidan spoke. "Now, on to happier thoughts, my Gabriel. Any news of your Miss Sullivan?" He leaned forward, anxious to hear the recent updates.

"I am worried, Uncle."

"Why?"

"Am I interrupting?" A soft feminine voice came from the doorway.

Both men immediately rose to their feet, with Gabriel walking to the door to open it fully. "Amelia, how wonderful to see you and the children," Gabriel murmured, his eyes lighting with pleasure. "Please come in."

***

"UNCLE, WHERE ARE YOU STAYING?" Gabriel asked, after his visitors departed.

"At the Florence Hotel. I like being in the midst of the town. I had thought I would need to stay in a rustic hotel. I rather enjoy those, but this is quite nice. It's very modern, and I haven't had to do without the conveniences I've become accustomed to in San Francisco." Aidan's expression turned serious as he faced Gabriel, studying him. "Gabriel, what do you mean to do about Mrs. Egan?" He waved toward the door as though to indicate Amelia who had just left.

"I don't know what you mean. Amelia and I are good friends."

"Don't be so disingenuous, Gabriel. I think you know exactly what I mean. She's a young widow with a baby and child to take care of. She needs a man in this harsh world, and she's set her sight on you. How can you not see that?"

Gabriel sighed, massaging the back of his neck. "You misunderstand our relationship, Uncle. I like her, maybe more than I should. I enjoyed a wonderful friendship with her while her husband, Liam, lived." He met his uncle's eyes. "We've discussed what you are saying, and she knows I am committed to Clarissa."

"I'm amazed you can't see the bond that has formed between you and Mrs. Egan, Gabriel," Aidan insisted.

"It's one forged of loss and pain," Gabriel said. "You know what it is to lose those you love. But, through it all, I've never stopped loving Clarissa."

"This sounds like a lengthy story. Why don't we cool off by the river, rather than remain indoors on this nice afternoon?" He pulled on Gabriel's arm, ushering him out of the workspace.

Gabriel locked up, and they walked toward the Missoula River. He nodded occasionally to passersby, smiling that the number of people he knew continued to grow daily. They walked down Main Street passing various shops including a chemist, a small grocer and a lady's apparel shop until reaching Higgins. As they walked on the boardwalk along Higgins, Gabriel noted that the Missoula Mercantile—a large two-level redbrick building filling half a block—continued to do a roaring business. They made their way past the old Missoula mills and his competitor's shop, crossed the wooden Higgins Street Bridge and walked alongside the river on the other side of town.

"If Clarissa were truly traveling toward me, why hasn't she arrived? It's mid-June." He attempted to hide the anguish and fear from his voice, but knew he had failed. "I read the papers each day, ensuring there's been no train derailment. And every day there is no word from her."

"What were her last letters to you like, Gabriel?"

"Sad. Mournful. As though something precious had been lost. And yet she seemed happy when she wrote of traveling to me. I worry that I read what I wanted to see, not what she was truly feeling."

"That's nonsense, Gabriel. If she were planning to travel to you, then I believe you were both feeling the same emotions."

"Then where is she?"

"She knew you moved here?"

"I wrote her, and Richard always delivered my letters."

"Well, then, I would suspect she will arrive at any time," Aidan said. "You'll hold her in your arms again soon, Gabriel."

CHAPTER 24

"WHAT DO YOU MEAN, he doesn't live here anymore?" I looked toward Colin with horrified eyes.

I turned my attention back to the boardinghouse manager as he spoke. His left cheek bulged with chewing tobacco; his shirt had spit stains down the front; and his yellow decaying teeth looked as though they'd crumble at any moment.

"That's right, miss. He paid up an' moved out a few weeks ago now, maybe e'en a month ago. Can't rightly say when. But he's not here now. Good day to you." He nodded with no real measure of regard in my direction.

"Wait!" I grabbed his dirty coat sleeve. "Do you have any idea where he went, sir?"

"No, miss. They don't tell us nothin'. An' as long as they pay up's all I care 'bout." He freed his shirt from my grasp and turned away, spitting into a spittoon with amazing accuracy as he left the room.

I would have collapsed had there been a chair available. I remained standing, although I swayed like a tree about to be felled. "Say something, please, Col," I entreated as I looked toward him. "What are you thinking?"

"Let's go to the post office, see if there's a forwarding address," he said with a weak smile. "It's a start, at least."

I nodded, feeling a stirring of hope. I knew that Colin would help me find Gabriel. After a few inquiries about the location of the post office, we made our way from Centerville toward Butte's main post office on East Broadway in Uptown Butte.

Upon entering the post office, I waited with veiled impatience for my turn to speak with the postmaster. "Excuse me, sir. We are looking for a forwarding address of a man who used to live here."

He glanced at me over his spectacles, nodding a few times. "Good mornin' to you, miss," he replied, making me feel churlish. "Did he know you would be comin' to look for him?"

"Excuse me?" I asked, flushing.

"Did he leave you a message 'bout where he was movin' to?" the postmaster asked, looking me up and down, then glancing at Colin with an amused expression over his spectacles.

I blushed a rosier red, straightening my shoulders. "Sir, I expected to meet my fiancée here, yet have found that he has moved on. I'm inquiring to determine if you know where he went." Colin placed his hand on my arm, as though to calm me.

"Well, miss, it appears he don't want you to know where he went. If there ain't no letter here for you, there ain't no way of knowin' where he went, and there ain't no way I can help you," the postmaster replied, in a condescending manner. "Out of pure curiosity, what is the man's name?"

Colin squeezed my arm, and spoke up in his deep, authoritative voice, "Gabriel McLeod."

The postmaster shook his head. "I don't have nothin' for you 'bout him. Sorry, miss, sir." He nodded and looked past me toward the other customers in line waiting their turn.

I turned away, dazed, unsure what to do. We went outside into the bright sunshine. "Where is he, Col? He knew I was traveling to him. Why wouldn't he leave me word?"

"Well, we can ask around, see if anyone knew him. And if that doesn't work, I'll send Richard a telegram," Colin replied, deep in thought.

"I don't want to use the meager amount of money we have on a telegram," I said.

"Don't be foolish, Rissa. It's better spent on a telegram than nights at an expensive hotel."

I nodded, blinking away tears. "What if he has decided he doesn't want me here?"

Colin brushed the tears off of my cheeks. "He'll be over the moon to see you at last, Rissa. Never doubt that." He glanced around the city for a moment. "For my part, I'm hungry. Let's find a decent café before we continue our search."

I stared out at the barren hills of Butte, wondering where we would be headed next.

***

"COLIN, QUIT GRUMBLING about sitting in the ladies' section," I hissed. I gave him a gentle kick under the table, and, rather than glaring at me, he winked.

"At least it served a purpose," he said.

"How can you, being grumpy, serve a purpose?"

"It made you think of something other than Gabriel's whereabouts," Colin said. "Besides, you looked so morose, it were as if I were leading you to the gallows in the morning. I don't care to garner any more interested stares than necessary."

"I do not look that miserable!" I protested.

"Finally a flash of color on your cheeks," Colin said as he stared around the room. Booths lined the wall with tables along the middle of the room and in front of the windows. Cream-colored walls reflected the light streaming in through the tall windows. An oak sidebar stood in one corner of the room. He smiled openly at the other patrons. "At least we arrived early enough to receive a booth. I like the privacy."

"I like the tall windows letting in the sun. It's almost seven, and there's still so much light."

"Maybe it's because we're a mile high and that much closer to the sun?" Colin mused.

"Maybe it's a sign we are truly insane to be in such a city."

"Rissa, it's not that bad, once you get past the aesthetic."

"The soot and dirt and overwhelming brownness? I never thought I'd long for trees and green the way I do after one day here, Col. What would a year be like?"

"Could you ever have envisioned a mining city so grand, Rissa? One with opera houses, electric streetcars and women dressed fancily enough to impress even Mrs. Smythe?"

"No, Col, I couldn't. And the brawls in the middle of the night are entertaining too."

"Oh, so you heard that?"

"Yes, and you calling out encouragement to Iron Fists Flanagan! You should have been rooting for Poor Jimmy Slims," I said. "I'm just thankful I didn't hear you placing a bet."

Colin laughed. "Ah, what an introduction to Butte. I think it would take close to a year to visit each saloon if I went to one a day. Isn't that extraordinary? And they never close. How is that possible?" He shook his head in wonder.

"You've never been one for the saloons."

"No, I haven't. But imagine all the tales you would hear if you spent time there. Well, it worked for a few moments at least," Colin murmured as he glanced at the menu. At my quizzical stare he said, "Distracted you for a few minutes."

I nodded, looking at the menu but not seeing it. "How could Gabriel have moved without informing me?"

"Focus on the fact that you're here now. We will find him. You'll have your adventure with Gabe."

"Pardon me, are you ready?" a nasally voice interrupted the conversation.

I jerked, glancing up at the waitress. I glanced at Colin to order, as I had not even looked at the menu. Colin quickly ordered two sirloin steaks, with coffee and tea.

"Rissa, I'm going to telegram Richard, see what he has to say," Colin said in a hushed, determined voice. Then in a lower voice, "I want to see you with Gabriel, and I worry about Cameron."

"I can't see him, Col."

"And you won't," Colin agreed.

"Please, can we try one other place before sending the telegram?"

"What do you have in mind?"

"I remember that Gabriel found work at a new hotel under construction," I said, thinking aloud. "Could we find the foreman?"

"Clarissa," Coin said, sighing and leaning away from the table. "You know he'll have as little information as everyone else. And be as unwilling to help."

"I know. I just want one more day without resorting to a telegram," I said in a firm, resolute tone. "I don't want to have to admit defeat to anyone yet."

"I wouldn't call sitting in a café with its booths for ladies in Butte, Montana, *defeat*, Rissa," Colin said, glancing around him.

The waitress returned with our dinners. "All this?" I stared at the two plates each piled high with potatoes smothered in butter and a huge steak.

Colin winked at me as he devoured his meal. "Miner's portions, Rissa."

After dinner, we wandered toward our hotel. I looped my arm through Colin's, enjoying the short walk in the long summer evening. Our hotel was a few blocks over from the restaurant but still on Broadway, and we did not have to traverse the steep hill to return to our rooms. The majority of the brick buildings were two and three stories tall with businesses such as grocers, saloons and bakeries on the street level with private residences above. Men mingled outside some of the bars, enjoying the pleasant evening.

"Can you believe how light it still is?" Colin marveled, tilting his head up to the sky.

"I never would have imagined such a thing," I said. As we neared our hotel, we walked past a crowd of men loitering in front of the California Saloon, relaxing in the cool evening breeze.

"Ahem," cleared a deep voice behind us. Colin turned to address the man while I peered around Colin's shoulder. It was a man we had just passed, in worn clothes with patches on the elbows of his jacket with no tie, waistcoat or collar in sight.

"Yes?" Colin asked, raising one eyebrow.

"I heard you were asking about Gabriel McLeod," the man said.

I dug my fingers into Colin's arm, and I felt him grimace in pain. He reached up to my hand on his arm as though to pat it but, in reality, was prying my fingers from it.

"And if we were?" Colin asked, waiting to see what the man offered.

"I'm not sure where he went, but Mr. Jeffers might. I'm Larry Ferguson, and these are Niall and Morgan," he said with an engaging smile, pointing to two of his companions who sat on the steps of the saloon. "We used to work with him, and we'd come here every once in a while for a pint."

"Nice to meet you, Mr. Ferguson," Colin said with a grin. After a short pause, Colin asked, "And if I were to look for this Mr. Jeffers, where would I go?"

"If he's not at the Thornton ordering us around, I'd go to the M&M on Main Street. He tends to spend most of his time there." He pointed down the hill as he spoke. "The Thornton's kitty-corner to the McDermott."

Colin nodded, appearing to think through what he had just heard. He reached out his hand to Larry, shaking it with a firm grip. "You say you worked with him?" At Larry's nod, Colin asked, "And yet you don't know where he went?"

"He always was a private man. Never liked discussing himself much." Larry glanced toward me and smiled. "Kept a picture of that woman there on his nightstand and never told us why. Seems a shame you've come all this way and can't find him now."

Colin nodded, releasing his hand as he nodded toward Morgan and Niall. "Thank you for your help, Mr. Ferguson." Larry smiled, turned and walked back to his friends at the pub in a long lope.

Colin and I continued our slow walk toward the hotel. "Just think, tomorrow we'll be able to speak with Mr. Jeffers and determine where Gabriel is," I said as I squeezed his arm in excitement.

Colin continued our sedate pace, shaking his head and laughing. "No, Rissa. *We* won't do anything of the sort. You most assuredly should not go into a saloon," he said, turning his head to watch me with raised eyebrows.

I blushed yet refused to be swayed. "But, Col…"

"No, Rissa," he said in a firm voice that brooked no argument. "I will speak with him tomorrow, and then we will determine what should be done."

"Fine, but I refuse to wait in the hotel. I'll wait in a place acceptable for ladies. Like the café we were just in."

***

THE NEXT MORNING, we went to the same café where we had eaten dinner, and I ordered breakfast. Colin left me after only finishing his coffee to search out Mr. Jeffers. I waited impatiently, biding my time by writing a letter home I knew I would not post until I had my reunion with Gabriel.

After finishing a second cup of tea, I began to worry that Colin had been unsuccessful in meeting with Mr. Jeffers. I itched to leave the café and wander to the nearby M&M but knew Colin would be furious with me.

Finally after another fifteen minutes Colin returned, seeming flustered and out of sorts. He scanned the room before sitting down with me in my booth. He signaled for the check, pulling coins from his pocket to pay.

"Col?" I asked. "Are you all right?"

"Not now, Clarissa," he whispered in a low, angry voice. "Let's get back to the hotel."

"Colin, talk to me," I begged, fear stealing inside me at his actions and tone.

"Not now, Rissa," he said again, pausing to smile engagingly up at the waitress, making small talk while he quickly paid the bill. He rose, expecting me to follow his lead. "Rissa?" he said.

"Col, no," I said. "Talk to me."

"Not here. If you want to talk, we'll talk at the hotel." He strode out of the café.

I slid out of the booth, almost slipping onto the tattered carpet covering the wooden floor in my haste. I caught myself just before I landed there, causing a few patrons to gasp in alarm. Unfortunately my clumsiness slowed me down, and I knew I had no hopes of catching up to Colin and his long strides.

I raced after Colin as quickly as I could, dodging the barber next door as he washed his front window. I kicked his metal bucket, but only a small amount of water sloshed out of the top of it.

"Watch where you're going, miss!" the barber grumbled as he reached for his bucket and damp cloths.

"Col, wait," I gasped, quickly losing my breath. He appeared not to hear me, and continued to march away. I gave up trying to keep pace, slowing down to a brisk walk. After I crossed Main Street, I stumbled as I ascended the stairs onto the boardwalk and was grabbed by a young man to prevent my falling.

As I righted myself and absently thanked the man who aided me, I glanced ahead, but Colin was nowhere in sight. I continued, passing a tailor shop, a bakery, a cobbler and numerous saloons. After a few minutes, I walked past the Thornton and then crossed the street to the McDermott. I entered the hotel lobby, its parquet floors glinting in the late morning sun from the tall windows.

After nodding to the man at the front desk, I made my way upstairs to the rooms Colin and I shared. I found him pacing in front of the windows in the sitting room. The forest-green sitting room suite was pushed aside so he had more room to pace, reminding me of Da. I collapsed onto the settee, now pushed against my bedroom door, in an attempt to catch my breath and remain out of his way.

"Colin, why are you upset?" I asked as I glared at him.

"I must inquire at the front desk about the train schedule to Missoula," Colin said as he continued to pace.

"Missoula?"

"Yes, Missoula. That's what that Mr. Jeffers told me," Colin said, the tempo of his pacing increasing.

"He must have told you something else to have put you in such a black mood. What did Mr. Jeffers really tell you today that bothered you?"

Colin paused for a moment as though thinking through his response. "Fine, I'll tell you. But remember that you wanted me to." He watched me with a stern expression. "I went by the M&M, but he wasn't there so I then went to the Thornton. We should have had you just wait here, Rissa." He began to pace again, and he rubbed his hand through his auburn hair in agitation. "I spoke with Mr. Jeffers. He wasn't inclined to aid me at all at first but finally decided to help."

"Why?"

"I honestly have no idea. But, when I was nearing the end of my patience and worried I would do him bodily harm because he seemed to take joy out of my distress, he admitted that he had heard that Gabriel had moved to a place called Missoula." At this Colin paused, causing me to wait in a near breathless state for what he would say next. "And he didn't go there alone."

"What?"

"Gabe traveled to Missoula with a woman, Rissa," he said.

"No, that Mr. Jeffers must have been mistaken," I argued, shaking my head in denial. I paled and met Colin's furious eyes while I fought panic at the thought of having lost Gabriel.

CHAPTER 25

TWO DAYS LATER I walked arm in arm with Colin into Butte's train station. Until today there had been no available seats for the short journey to Missoula. The redbrick building had large oak double doors leading into a two-story foyer. After Colin purchased our tickets and discovered our train was delayed, we walked down the platform toward the porter's storage room. Every bench along the hallway was filled with delayed passengers.

"Sir, we have tickets booked to Missoula and would like to ensure our trunks join us on our journey."

"Never fear, young man. Old Jedediah will see they make the train." Frayed suspenders stretched over his paunch covered in a crisp white shirt with his formal jacket and waistcoat draped over a nearby chair. He squinted at Colin. "Ah, you'd be the lovely lady and brother from the East. I just spoke with the young lady's betrothed. I'll be sure to inform him I've seen you when he returns." He turned away toward a desk at the back of the room, his irregular gait forming an offbeat tattoo as his shoe heels clicked on the tiled floor.

I reached out and gripped his right arm. "Sir. He's not my betrothed. He's not my anything. I've no wish to see him ever again."

"He seemed confident of his welcome here, miss." Jedediah raised his eyebrows as he studied me. "You running away from the young man?"

"Sir, I don't believe it's any of your business what we are or aren't doing," Colin said.

"Seeing as you're trying to rope me into your shenanigans, it just became my business."

"I was to meet the man I hope to marry here, but he has left for Missoula.

I … I need to travel to him. This other man is…" I broke off.

"Delusional," Colin said.

"Dangerous," I said at the same time.

"The dangerous, delusional ones always give you the most trouble," Jedediah said with a rueful shake of his head. "I'll watch your trunks, and I won't tell him that I saw you. But you'd better hide, as I'm sure he'll find his way back here, 'specially seen' as you're delayed a while here."

I stiffened when I heard an imperious voice shouting, "Old man! I want to speak with you!"

"It's Cameron." I stifled a shriek as Jedediah grabbed my arm and pulled me toward the back room. His off-kilter gait made me stumble, and I reached out a hand to the doorjamb to steady myself.

"Hide," he said pointing toward the storage room filled with trunks. Colin had followed, and we huddled behind a row of trunks. I sank to kneel among them in an attempt to find a comfortable position.

I heard the squeaking of the door as it was partially closed. I leaned against the trunks as far forward as possible to better hear the conversation.

"Hello, again," Jedediah said in a welcoming voice.

"I was told you know everything about the coming and going of everyone who arrives and departs on trains. I'm beginning to doubt my sources. Tell me." Cameron's loud commanding voice and his footsteps carried on the wind as he paced back and forth. "Have that young man and sister I spoke with you about been seen here?"

"Were they not at the hotel?"

"They had just departed. I can't have come so far to have just missed them. You told me they were at the McDermott," Cameron demanded as a slapping sound of a hand hitting a wooden surface reverberated to the back room.

"As far as I know, they were," Jedediah said. "Last I heard of the fancy brother and sister from Boston, they were staying there."

"They checked out this morning. It means they must have come to the station."

"Or they met someone in town and are staying with them now."

"That damn McLeod," Cameron muttered. "If he's touched her, I'll…"

"Better not to say something incriminatin', son."

"If you hear anything, send word to me. I'll pay you handsomely,"

Cameron ordered. "I will rent rooms at the McDermott, the only decent hotel in this wretched place." The pacing stopped.

"As you say, sir."

"If you play me false, I'll discover it. You'll find I am not on good terms with mercy."

"Good day, sir."

"At least someone out here knows their place." I heard the rapid staccato of Cameron's shoes as he strode away from the room.

I exchanged a long glance with Colin and agreed with him by a silent nod to remain where we were until Jedediah came for us. After a fifteen-minute wait, he entered the trunk room.

"All right, you can come out now," he said.

I groaned as I rose from my position behind the trunks. I tried to massage my back as I arched it in an attempt to stretch it. Colin and I remained in the shadows of the room until Jedediah flung the door open and waved us out.

"I wandered to the front desk area as though I were making inquiries about a late-bound train. I watched to make sure that man left." He sighed as he shook his head. "He's gone for now, although I'm sure he'll be back soon enough. He'll want to know where McLeod went once he realizes he's gone."

"Why did you help us, Mr. Maloney?" I asked.

"I don't like outsiders coming here and acting like they're better than us." Jedediah studied me with inquisitive eyes. "I imagine he meant Gabriel McLeod?"

"Yes, sir," I said.

"Well, he's in Missoula. At least that's where his train ticket was booked. Anyone in town who knew him could tell your not-betrothed-suitor that. I can't keep that secret for you."

"I understand. I just want a chance to arrive in Missoula. Without him."

"You do realize Mr. McLeod didn't travel alone?"

"I know."

"Hmm ... Well, I wish you the best of luck. Your train just arrived, earlier 'n expected. It'll leave in about thirty minutes. I imagine you could board now if you wanted. While I was out poking around, I ensured your trunks will travel with you."

"Thank you, sir," Colin said. He shook Jed's hand before ushering me toward the waiting train.

"Whatever you gotta do in that town of Missoula, do it quickly. I fear that man is a bit fixated on you, miss." Jedediah nodded toward us as we handed our tickets to the conductor and boarded the train.

CHAPTER 26

GABRIEL LOOKED UP from his workbench at the quick tapping on the frame of his open workshop door. He rose to greet the wiry man who stared into his room with blatant curiosity.

"What do you have that could tempt me?" the man asked as he glanced around Gabriel's workspace. Half-completed projects lined the back walls, while two pieces of maple were clamped together at the vise. Small blocks with different chiseled patterns lay on his workbench. A thin board hung above his workbench with sketches nailed into it.

"I'm Sebastian Carlin, the foreman at the local lumber mill, and I heard we had a new cabinetmaker in town. I just hope you're better at your craft than the other one." He roamed the room, picking up pieces of wood, nodding his approval as he studied the grain and cut of each piece.

"Why don't you try this?" Gabriel said with a smile his hands on the back of the rocking chair his uncle had found comfortable. "I'm Gabriel McLeod. Nice to meet you."

"Ah, a good chair." Sebastian sighed as he sat. "Would you be able to make one to fit my frame?" Sebastian was a lanky six feet four inches tall, with long, limber-looking arms and legs. He had a deep, commanding voice, although he generally spoke in a soft tone.

"I already commissioned and bought another chair from your competitor, but it was a rickety thing. Fell apart after I sat on it a few nights," Sebastian commented, rocking to and fro. He seemed incapable of remaining still. When animated, his pale complexion became flushed, highlighting his freckles and making his red hair seem brighter. "I hope you can build them better than he did."

"I will build you a solid chair that you will be glad to sit in after a long day of work," Gabriel promised, then motioned for Sebastian to move toward Gabriel's workbench where he pulled out a blank piece of paper. He sketched a chair similar to the one Sebastian had been sitting in but with dimensions to match his frame.

"I want it sturdy, but attractive. I think maple would be the best choice. And not too much ornamentation. I want a good masculine piece."

"Hmm. Something like this," Gabriel said as he drew a new sketch with simple, elegant lines in the Eastlake style.

"Exactly," Sebastian said. "You really do know what you're doing."

Gabriel grinned. "I am a Master of the craft, Mr. Carlin. Never fear."

"You should call me Sebastian, as I hope to do plenty of business with you. It's a pity we don't have wood at my mill for you to purchase."

"Of course," Gabriel said. After haggling over the price, Sebastian departed.

After a few hours, Gabriel needed a break and was thankful for the knock at his workshop door.

Aidan poked his head in, a broad smile lighting his face. "Are you ready for our outing?"

"Yes, I'm tired of being inside on such a nice day." Gabriel locked the workshop door and walked beside his uncle on the boardwalk. "I'll finish my work tonight."

Aidan's pair of worn faded pants and rough cotton shirt were the most casual clothes Gabriel had ever seen him in. His uncle's new cowboy boots were stiff and free of the scuffs common from frequent wear, and he was unable to hide a slight limp as he walked.

Gabriel smiled, remembering his discomfort when he first wore a pair in Butte. He flashed a quick grin, his dimple showing in his right cheek. "It's good to see you. I don't know as I'll ever become tired of having you here."

"I'm sure happy to be here, Gabriel. This is beautiful country. I went on a ride this morning and had a look around. Have you gone on any rides since you've been here?"

They walked down Main Street toward the corner of Higgins before turning left to walk toward Pine Street, their boot heels sounding on the planks of the boardwalk as they walked on the shady side of the street. A horse-pulled streetcar rumbled along beside them at a sedate pace, with

Gabriel and Aidan nearly keeping abreast with the horses.

"No, not yet." Gabriel flushed, looking uncomfortable. "I come from the city, Uncle."

"Yes?"

"Let's just say, I don't get on well with horses, unless they are pulling a carriage. I haven't ridden many, growing up in Boston," Gabriel said, looking abashed.

"Well, nephew, you're going to have to learn. You live in Montana now, and there's no way around it." Aidan laughed, pointing at the Johnson Livery, Feed, and Sale stables they now stood in front of. "We'll take it slow, but it'll be fun, don't worry. I'll enjoy exploring this area with you. I've hired a pair of horses, and there's no time like the present for you to become more accustomed to horse riding. It's a beautiful day, and you shouldn't spend all of your time cooped up inside. I spoke with the stable master. He has a horse he usually hires out to the ladies, called Star. I thought he might be docile enough for you." Aidan evaded Gabriel's good-natured jab as he walked over to a pair of horses tied to a post in the stable yard.

"I imagine you have a beast fierce enough for a Buffalo Bill production." Gabriel studied Aidan's horse. "His name matches his coloring. He sure is a pretty horse."

"Flame is a beauty, although he's temperamental." Aidan and Gabriel laughed as they watched the horses.

"I'll enjoy watching you struggle to control him," Gabriel said. "Ah, there's the star." He traced the mark on his horse's haunch. Star looked back at him and shifted his behind before settling.

"I told you that he was calm. You couldn't do that with Flame without threat of losing your teeth." Aidan took a firm hold of Flame's bridle. "All you have to do is get on that saddle, and you'll be fine. Star is a born follower."

"Are you sure about this?" Gabriel asked, gently petting Star's nose. Star nickered, nudging Gabriel's hand in encouragement. Gabriel laughed, enjoying being near the horse. "Ah, I'd forgotten the smell of horses. It's all their own, isn't it?"

"Yes, it is, and pleasant in its own way." Aidan smiled as he easily mounted Flame. His horse whinnied and trotted in a circle, tossing his head a few times, trying to throw his bit, but finally calmed. Aidan spoke calmly to Flame, maintaining a firm hand on the reins, patting Flame's neck a few times, never showing any sign of weakness or fear.

"Gabriel, it will be time for supper by the time you get on that horse." Aidan gave him a pointed look with feigned impatience.

Gabriel patted Star's neck and nose once more, and then moved to the left side to the stirrup. He took another deep breath, placed his booted foot in the stirrup, vaulted upward toward the saddle, nearly falling off the other side due to his excessive force. Aidan laughed, Flame raised his head, whinnying in agreement, and Star moved his backside as though concerned about the caliber of his rider for the first time. Gabriel righted himself and looked at his uncle in annoyance.

"I'd like to think I'd be more compassionate to you, Uncle, if I were ever to help you overcome one of your fears," he hissed. Star moved his hind legs from side to side, so they moved in a circle.

"Relax, Gabriel. He can feel your tension. If you don't relax, you won't see more than this paddock."

"I'm trying, Uncle. It's harder than I remembered." He inhaled and forced his body to be limp. Star stopped moving in a circle and focused on Flame. At Aidan's *click-click*, Star moved toward him.

"Remember my quick lesson to you on the way here, and you'll be fine. Let's get a move on. The day is passing us by."

Aidan turned Flame with an expert flick of his wrist and left the stable. Star, a born follower, trotted after Flame. They walked down Higgins, crossed over the bridge and left the city. There were a few homes on the south side of the bridge, but it was not long before they entered meadows.

The more they rode, the more Gabriel began to understand the beauty of the place. He thought back to the valleys he had seen on his train ride west. He had liked Bozeman's wide-open valley with numerous distant mountain peaks. The high, windy valley of Deer Lodge had also been pretty, though sparse. As he paused to look around the Missoula Valley and fully appreciate it, he realized that, for him, this was his ideal valley. Plenty of room on the valley floor for farms and for a growing city, with the mountains forming an intimate backdrop.

Gabriel paused, his sweeping glance taking in the untouched mountains, the forests in the distance, the rolling hills leading toward the Bitter Root River. Now, during a rare peaceful moment outside of the town, he understood he had underestimated the wildness of Montana. Everywhere he looked, he saw mountains covered in pine trees, and meadows with wild grasses and flowers blowing in the wind. He heard birdsong, watched swallows flitting about just above his head. The cool, crisp air carried a hint of pine. He inhaled, enjoying the fresh air after the smell of wood smoke in town.

"Isn't it marvelous, Gabriel?" Aidan asked, settling himself, at ease in his saddle.

"It's wonderful. I always knew there was a place I yearned to travel to. I can't believe I actually found it. I'll have to become a better horseman so I can do this frequently, especially on my days off. Have you learned the names of any of the mountains or valleys, Uncle?"

"All I know is that way leads toward mountains, the Bitter Roots," Aidan said pointing south. He continued, now pointing north, "And if you go that way, you go to the Mission Mountains and the Flathead area. I hear both sets of mountains are quite majestic. I imagine trying to learn more about the area will be a good conversation to have with the locals at the saloon."

"Uncle, can you tell me more about my parents?" Gabriel asked as he gave a small *click-click* to spur Star into walking next to Flame.

"What would you like to know, Gabriel?" Aidan asked.

"How did they meet? Why did her family dislike my da?"

"Well, they met at a Peace Jubilee in Boston in 1869. Your father finagled a few hours off of the construction site to be able to go and see what the to-do was about," Aidan said.

"The Peace Jubilee?" Gabriel asked.

"Oh, it was a grand exhibit and concert put on to celebrate the end of the Civil War. It happened a few years after the conclusion of the War," Aidan said. "I remember going to the Jubilee. You've never seen a building so big or a concert so large. Even just reading about it afterward in the papers was a thrill, but actually attending the Jubilee was unlike anything you could imagine. There were over a thousand people in the band and around ten thousand singers."

"Surely you exaggerate. How was such a thing possible?"

"Oh, you know Boston. They put their mind to having a grand gesture for peace, and they did," Aidan stated. "I was too young to fight in the war. Ian could have gone by the end, but he never did. At any rate, everyone knew someone who had died or been maimed, and we all longed to celebrate peace. Your father went and met Geraldine there." Aidan glanced at Gabriel, smiling. "I've never seen a man so smitten in my life."

"Was my mum as taken with Da?"

"She must have been because she started concocting reasons to meet with your father. I wouldn't call it lying, but bending the truth for her benefit. Eventually her sister, Patricia, your Aunt Masterson, found out about your father and their meetings, and your father was heartbroken."

"Why?"

"Well, your mother was of a much higher class, much better educated than he was. Ian had ensured that I continued to go to school, so I received an education, but, to do that, he had to leave school to find work. He could barely read or write. He was a construction laborer, working on the filling project of the Back Bay. Decent work, good-enough pay, but hardly the type of man I imagined the Sanders wanted their daughter to bring home."

Aidan paused, looking around the valley, watching the birds flying above. He smiled upon hearing the lilting call of a meadowlark. He seemed lost in thought but then turned to Gabriel and met his gaze.

"I imagine Ian thought he'd lost her. But neither of us reckoned on your mother's stubborn nature. She had decided on Ian, and she was going to have her way." Aidan smiled at Gabriel.

"Why did Aunt Masterson continue to dislike my da so much?" Gabriel asked.

"Well, I can't answer for her, but I have an idea. She's extremely concerned about social standing and appearances. I've never seen her equal in that regard, though I imagine there are plenty just like her in Boston. She felt her sister had brought ridicule on the family and had hurt the family's social aspirations by not marrying well."

"Why should my mother's marriage reflect on her?" Gabriel asked.

"You know well enough how society is, what its expectations are. Your mother was expected to make a brilliant match. Instead, she married a poor day laborer for love. Not at all what her family wanted. Her parents never spoke to her again. As far as I know, they never met you three."

"Until my parents died, I thought Mum's family had all died," Gabriel said.

"Well, *they* hadn't. But for all intents and purposes, *she* had for them. And then she really did die."

"I can never forgive Aunt Masterson for her treatment of us."

"That's your right, Gabriel. I just hope, at some point, you stop thinking about her and focus on your future rather than the past."

CHAPTER 27

"DO YOU THINK HE'LL BE at the station?" I asked. I attempted to hide my anxiety, but Colin discerned it easily.

We sat facing forward in a fancy Pullman train car. Rows of banquettes large enough for two faced each other, with an aisle of sturdy green carpeting to one side of the train car. I stared at the vacant green velvet seats with mahogany accent detailing across from me, thankful we had a small amount of privacy as we headed toward Missoula. Every other seat in our car was occupied. Colin sat near the large window and stretched out his long legs.

"I hope so. But it's hard to know if the letter you sent him from Butte will arrive before we do. We were only delayed a few days."

"I need to see him, Col. I need to know this journey was not in vain."

"Remember, Rissa, it will never have been in vain because it saved you from Cameron." He gripped my hand, attempting to encourage me. "I think we should be arriving soon, once we travel through this canyon."

I closed my eyes, taking deep calming breaths. Colin stared out the window commenting on the passing scenery. The narrow mountain valley covered in thick pine trees. The winding river sparkling in the sunlight. It sounded more inviting that anything I had seen in Butte. I opened my eyes as the train exited the mouth of the canyon and entered a wide valley with a small city at the base of the mountains.

"I think this is it, Clarissa, our new home," Colin said. "Welcome to Missoula."

I peered out the window at the wide expanse of open valley and the small town. "Why would Gabriel choose this over Butte?" I whispered.

"I thought you didn't like Butte?" Colin asked on a chuckle.

"Well, it's ugly, but at least it's a city. This is, this is nothing more than a village," I stammered. "How are we to live in a place so small?"

"As long as Gabriel is here, I am sure you'll do just fine."

The train came to a lurching halt at the base of a hill. The long golden-bricked station came into view as I looked out the window. I sat immobile as though carved in granite.

"Rissa, there's only one way to know," Colin said as he heaved me to a standing position. He grabbed our day bag and led the way off the train.

The bright sun momentarily blinded me as I descended the stairs. I reached out for Colin's arm, desperate not to lose contact with the one person I knew in the sea of strangers. We slowly made our way down the platform, peering into one unknown face after another. As we reached the end of the platform, my shoulders slumped, and I collapsed onto a bench.

"Courage, Rissa. I need to see about our trunks. Will you be all right?" he asked as he crouched in front of me.

"What will we do, Col? I was sure he would be here."

"We'll find him. Don't worry." At that moment he jerked around as though listening attentively to something. "Do you hear that?"

I started to shake my head, but then stilled, closing my eyes to listen better. "Col..."

"Hush."

"Clarissa! Colin Sullivan!"

I opened my eyes, almost afraid to hope. I stood, peering around the mingling crowds in an attempt to see who sought us.

"Gabriel!" I screamed though I didn't know where he was. I tried to yell his name again, but I had started crying and no sound came out. Suddenly he was in front of me, his clothes dust-covered and his ebony hair wind-tousled, even more handsome than I remembered. "Gabriel!" I cried, throwing myself into his arms. He gripped me in a tight embrace, a safe haven.

"Clarissa, you brave, crazy woman," he murmured into my ear, kissing my head a few times, caressing my hair with his big hands. He leaned away, gently wiping away the tears that fell unheeded down my cheeks. "I only just received word that you were to arrive today." He stared at me and then at Colin with absolute wonder. "I thought..."

"There's enough time to talk about that," Colin said. "First, we need to see to our trunks and find a place to stay."

"Of course," Gabriel said, although he refused to release me from his embrace as he hugged me again, kissing my hair and resting his cheek against my head. "Colin, the porters are over there." He nodded to the far side of the platform.

"I'll be back soon." Colin smiled the first genuinely happy smile I had seen since we had met in Minneapolis.

"Clarissa, I can't believe you're here in my arms." Gabriel leaned away, framing my face with his hands to study me. "You came to me."

"I had to," I whispered. "I yearned…" I couldn't go on as tears continued to fall. I traced his jaw with my fingers, and he turned into my touch, kissing my palm. I took a moment to study him. "You're covered in dirt."

He laughed, gripping my hand. "Yes, I was just on a horseback ride with my uncle. I received your letter when I returned home and came here, afraid I'd be too late."

"I just hope I'm not too late," I whispered.

"Clarissa?"

"Well, sir," the scrawny porter said with a strong slap on Gabriel's shoulders. "Looks like you really are a ladies' man."

"Pardon me?" Gabriel said with a warning note in his voice as I stiffened in his arms.

"You know what folks are talking about. Just remember, polygamy ain't allowed in these parts," he said with a grin and a wink.

"It isn't allowed anywhere in the United States," Colin said with a frown.

"They might argue with you in parts of Utah," the porter said with a grin. "Now, where am I taking these trunks?"

"Take them to the Florence," Gabriel said. "They'll be there for a few nights at least."

"Won't this be an interesting tale to tell my aunt, Mrs. Vaughan?" he called over his shoulder as he began to whistle as he loaded the trunks.

"Gabriel, what did he mean about polygamy?" Colin asked.

"And who is Mrs. Vaughan?" I asked.

"Let's talk at the hotel," Gabriel said, holding out his elbow so I could loop my arm through his. "It is just a short walk."

At first glance Missoula was very different from Butte. There were no smokestacks pumping ash into the sky and no piles of tailings strewn about. Missoula did not seem to be as advanced as Butte, as I saw no electric street-cars, only horse-drawn ones.

"Where are you staying, Gabriel?" I asked. "I should like to stay near you."

"I have a small workspace with a loft overhead that I live in," he said. "It's down Main Street, not far from the Florence. But don't worry, everything's pretty close here in Missoula." After a short stroll down a boardwalk, we entered the hotel.

The Florence Hotel was an impressive three-story building that filled half a city block. The lobby had numerous seating areas near a large fireplace. Off the lobby area I heard the click of pool cues and the muffled low tones of male voices. The wood floors, covered in thick red rugs, did not creak with our steps. The chandeliers glittered, and the pale gold wallpaper highlighted the lush red fabrics, drapes and floor coverings.

"Gabriel, this seems a bit grand," I whispered. I edged away from him as I turned to study the room. I stilled as he touched my shoulder and flinched when he stroked a hand down my arm. He grasped my clammy hand, and I blushed.

"Clarissa, are you all right?"

I met his worried gaze with a stiff smile. "Of course. I still can't believe I'm here with you after all this time." I glanced toward Colin and the man at the desk. "And I'm concerned this hotel is too fancy for us. We stayed at the McDermott in Butte, and I worry about a similar expense here."

"For a night or two, it should be fine," he murmured as he tucked a piece of hair behind my ear. I jumped at his touch. "Besides, my uncle is staying here too." He watched me for a moment as though contemplating my reactions.

"Your uncle is here?" I asked.

"Yes, he arrived last week," Gabriel said with a broad smile. "He will be delighted to see you again."

A man at the front desk interrupted our discussion. The area to register consisted of an imposing mahogany desk with key boxes nearby. A short, wiry man stood behind it perusing a newspaper, muttering to himself as he read, although looking up frequently to keep an eye on the lobby area. "Hello, Mr. McLeod," he said with a broad smile.

"Hello, Tommy. Do you have rooms for my friends who just arrived?"

His alert glance stole over Colin and me, taking in our appearance from our shoes up to our hats. He must have assessed that we were acceptable patrons, as he set aside his newspaper and grinned. "Of course, Mr. McLeod," he said. "Would be a pleasure. And a good thing you came now as we're al-most filled up."

He pulled out a form and asked Colin questions. "Well, I say. You must be from wherever Mr. McLeod is from," Tommy said with a chuckle after he listened to Colin speak.

"We are all from Boston," Colin said with a grin.

"Imagine! Boston," Tommy said as he grabbed two keys out of the wooden key boxes behind the desk. He began an impromptu tour. "There's a pool room with billiards and a bar, both for the gents," he said waving in their direction, "and a reading and writing room on the first floor. Those are acceptable for the ladies." He nodded in my direction.

He cleared his throat loudly as he continued. "Upstairs"—with this word he waved over his head—"there are parlors, the dining room and the guest rooms. There is electricity for the hotel from a plant in the basement, and, if you stay so long as to need it, we even have steam heat," he finished with a smile. He walked us upstairs to our rooms. "When your trunks arrive, I'll have them brought up."

"Thank you, Tommy, that is most kind," Colin said.

After Tommy left, we moved to a small parlor. Colin closed the door for privacy. As I entered the room, I became increasingly nervous to be with Gabriel after wishing to be with him for so long. I paced toward the window, looking down onto busy Higgins Street.

"Colin, do you think I could have a few moments with Clarissa?" Gabriel asked.

I tensed. I turned to watch them, attempting to appear calm and col-lected. Colin studied me before replying. "No, I'm afraid that won't be pos-sible, Gabriel. Not until I understand why that porter mentioned polygamy to you."

"It's because of Amelia."

"Amelia?" I asked, my voice cracking.

"Amelia Egan. She's a very good friend of mine who…"

"A good friend? How good a friend, Gabe?" Colin demanded.

"Now calm down, Colin. Let me explain," Gabriel said on a long sigh as he reached to massage his neck. He paced the small room. "I wrote you about my mining friends." At my quick nod, he continued. "Well, two of them died last month." He paused for a moment as though collecting his thoughts.

"Since then I've been trying to help one man's widow, Amelia."

"Aid her how, Gabriel?" Colin asked.

"I help her with her children, with the bills. Spend time with her when she is lonely."

"Have you married her?" I choked out.

"No, no, not at all," Gabriel said, a flush spreading up his neck. "I've always made it clear that I would wait for you, Clarissa."

I shared a long, intense glance with Gabriel.

"Others in the community must think you are working your way toward marriage to make jokes about polygamy or to call you a ladies' man," Colin said, interrupting our long silent exchange.

"I know. It's part of the reason we left Butte."

"What?" I gasped. "You left Butte to avoid rumors about the two of you?"

"Listen, please, I'm not explaining myself well at all," Gabriel said, turning toward me, begging me with sincere eyes to understand. "Amelia and I have been friends almost since I arrived in Butte. Her husband, Liam, Matthew's partner in the mine, became a close friend too." He closed his eyes a moment. "She reminded me so much of you, Clarissa."

"How?"

"She was a teacher before she married. She loved books. And I saw in her marriage with Liam a parallel to my relationship with you. She was more educated, better than he was in social standing, and yet they married and had a successful life. I hoped for the same for us." He watched me with intense blue eyes.

"Why would others think you were interested in her?"

"Not everyone is charitable. And when I spent more and more time at her house after Liam died, helping with little Nicholas or doing chores, people began to talk."

"Isn't running away with her proof of what they accused you of?" Colin asked.

"Well, I knew I wanted to try a new place to live. A place where I didn't have a memory of my dead friends around every corner. And I imagined it was much the same for Amelia. So I invited her to come with me. She and the children and our crippled friend Ronan, who said he wouldn't be left behind."

"Quite a menagerie you have collected, Gabriel," Colin said with a hint of a smile.

"I'm afraid our arrival hasn't gone as unnoticed as I had hoped. I realize now that people love to gossip everywhere, and I have garnered the attention of this town's worst. You met her nephew today," Gabriel said.

"You knew I was coming to you," I whispered. "Why didn't you write me to tell me you had moved?"

"I did write, when I knew I was to leave Butte. You're the one who didn't write me."

"I never received your letter. We spent days in Butte looking for you," I said. I shared a long look with Colin. "It must have arrived after I traveled for my convention. We left earlier than had been planned to spend time in Chicago."

"And Richard must have kept it for your return," Colin murmured. "He wouldn't have known to give it to me."

Gabriel moved toward me, framing my face with his palms. I tensed but soon relaxed under his gentle touch. "There has not been a single day since I left you that I have not dreamt of you," he declared, staring into my eyes.

I nodded, crying as I leaned into him. I could no longer fight my tears and sobbed as he held me tenderly against his chest. "I have missed you, missed you so much, Gabriel."

"Shh ... we are together again," he whispered into my ear. "There's nothing that can keep us apart now."

CHAPTER 28

"AFTER WE FINISH BREAKFAST," Colin said, "why don't we walk around Missoula? I'd like to have a better sense of this small town, especially if we're to settle here." The tip of Colin's auburn hair remained wet from his recent bath, and he appeared relaxed and invigorated. He wore casual black pants with a matching jacket and a white shirt, having foregone the formality of a waistcoat and tie on the hot summer day.

"I'd like that, although I want to see Gabriel too."

"Of course, Rissa," Colin said with a smile.

After we finished our hearty meal, we walked through Missoula, a neat little town laid out in a grid pattern. The locals casually referred to the main thoroughfare through town as Higgins.

"Colin, look at that building," I said as I marveled at the beautiful Higgins Bank building. "Mr. Higgins must be someone important."

"It is nice to find beautiful buildings in this town, although they don't rival Butte," he said as he looked at the bank with its corner entrance and granite columns supporting a gracefully curved two-story cylindrical tower and cupola. "The granite and brick buildings give the town a sense of permanence, don't you think?"

I nodded in agreement, my spirit lightening as we walked.

We continued our stroll down Higgins Street, passing many small stores including drug stores, grocery stores, barbershops, bakeries and even a bicycle repair shop. The awnings over the boardwalk provided shade for passersby. I looked toward the unpaved streets and shivered at the thought of the mud when it rained or snowed. Men rode by sedately on horses, a few carriages passed, and numerous men on bicycles weaved in and out of the horse traffic causing a few of the animals to start.

As we meandered down Higgins, and then onto a few of the side streets called Cedar and Pine, I glanced toward Colin, trying to gauge his mood. "Any thoughts?"

"I think it's a glorious place," he said, smiling. "Look at the mountains. And the river is quite beautiful. The bridge is impressive. I wouldn't have thought they'd have a bridge. It's a place of great industry." He sighed with contentment as he turned a slow circle, studying everything around us. "A man could really make something of himself here."

"Colin," I said, unable to hide the concern in my voice. "What are we going to do for work? We can't continue to live off of my savings or the money Aunt Betsy gave us."

"Don't worry, Rissa," he reassured me with a wink. "It will sort itself out. There are at least two forges here, and I'm sure I'll be able to find employment."

"What should I do?"

"Teach, of course," he replied with supreme confidence. "You have great training. They'll get no better here."

I shook my head. "I doubt they want a woman teacher. Maybe they'll need help at the new University of Montana here in Missoula." I found myself dreaming.

"That's it, Rissa!" Colin said. "Let's see Gabe and hear what he thinks." He turned us down Main Street and toward Gabriel's workshop. "I think this is it," Colin said as he peered up at a small sign hanging over a doorway. He poked his head through the open door into the workspace. "Gabe!"

"Hi, Colin," Gabriel said.

I heard a *thunk* as though Gabriel had dropped a tool and then footsteps as he moved toward us. I squinted as I tried to adjust to the darkened interior of the room.

"Clarissa," Gabriel murmured as he stopped in front of me.

I looked up to find him standing a few feet in front of me, my eyesight suddenly crystal clear. I studied him with a hungry gaze. He wore his jet-black hair longer than in Boston, just past collar length. His work clothes were similar, though more casual, and his beautiful blue eyes watched me warmly.

I continued to stare at him, cataloging minute changes. He seemed thinner, taller, simply *more* than I had remembered. I searched for an aspect of him that had not changed and focused on his eyes. Oh, his eyes! They had not altered. His intense blue eyes with the studying looks. I found myself the subject of the same perusal, the same intense logging of changes. However, Gabriel seemed to look for the changes in me, not physically, but through my gaze. We continued to stare at each other for extended moments, until Colin cleared his throat again.

"Yes, of course," Gabriel murmured to us. "Welcome." He flashed a mocking half smile as he turned toward someone else in his workspace. "Uncle, Clarissa and Colin Sullivan whom you met in Boston."

"Miss Sullivan, it's wonderful to see you again," Aidan said as he rushed toward me to give me a warm embrace.

A faint hint of his cologne wafted about me, and I paled as I smelled a hint of bay rum.

As he released me, his blue eyes remained lit with joy as he turned toward Colin and clasped his hand. "I never would have imagined we would meet again in Montana." While he spoke with Colin, I studied him for a moment. He had a bit more salt in his salt-and-pepper hair, but, other than that, he did not appear to have changed much from when I had first met him. Even on this warm day he wore a full suit, his cream-colored shirt enhancing the deep navy of his waistcoat and suit.

"Nor I, sir," Colin said.

I nodded, unable to say anything but gripped Colin's arm as I became momentarily overwhelmed by emotions.

"How long have you been here, sir?" Colin asked Aidan.

"A little over a week. And I am able to stay as long as I want. Though I plan to leave before the weather changes," he said with a smile. "Winter in San Francisco is much more appealing than winter in the mountains."

"We'll have to see if we can convince you to stay," Gabriel said. "I don't like talking about any leave-takings, especially when you've all just arrived." He looked toward me with tenderness.

"How is your family, Miss Sullivan?" Aidan asked.

"I believe they are well," I said. "I have been away from them for a while. I attended a convention in Minneapolis recently."

"Oh, which one?"

"The National American Woman Suffrage Association Annual Convention."

"And your family approved?" Aidan asked.

"Yes, though I believe Da and my stepmother would have preferred me to remain in Boston."

"Though they didn't have much say as Rissa was already living with Uncle Martin when she made the decision to go to Minneapolis," Colin said.

"You left your da's house?" Gabriel asked.

"Yes. I had to. I needed more freedom than they were willing to allow me."

Gabriel chuckled. "That's my Clarissa."

He moved toward me, and I inadvertently jerked away from him.

I saw him share a surprised glance with Aidan. Gabriel paused his movement for a moment, before continuing, reaching down to clasp my hand. "Would you like me to show you the workspace and the loft overhead?"

In an instant, I had the sensation I was in a long dark tunnel and knew I needed to escape as soon as possible. "No, not today," I murmured. I threw an alarmed glance toward Colin.

"Clarissa and I were just discussing our lack of employment. We have limited savings and need to begin our search," Colin said. "Perhaps some other day you can show us around?"

"Of course," Gabriel said as he released my hand and moved away from me.

I tried not to gasp for air, but my panic at this moment would not abate.

"I will see you soon, Gabriel," I whispered as I turned to flee outside.

When I was in the full sun, I tilted my head up to its warming rays, wishing the sun would warm me all the way to my icy core.

Colin emerged from the workshop, gripped my elbow and propelled me into motion. "What was that?" he demanded in a harsh whisper. "I thought you wanted to see Gabe."

"I do … I did," I said on a shudder. "Just stop, Col. Please, give me a minute." I paused to look into one of the shop-front windows, happy to see it was a store filled with knickknacks that a woman would be interested in and not a barber shop or saloon. "I'm sorry I panicked."

"Why did you?"

"It reminded me too much of Boston. Of Cameron." My voice broke, and I blinked furiously to ward off tears.

Colin swore. "This isn't fair to Gabe. You have to tell him. How do you think he feels?"

"I have no idea," I whispered. "I can't tell him yet. I don't know how."

"Well, too many scenes like this and you may no longer have a chance," Colin muttered as we continued our walk toward the hotel.

CHAPTER 29

"SO, SHE'S HERE," Ronan said from the bed in his room. He lay propped up on two pillows on a single bed, his features becoming more gaunt every day. Beneath the light sheet that covered him, Gabriel noted Ronan's legs growing more spindly and weak.

The second-floor room was a brightly lit corner room with two windows, a closet, washstand, one chair and the small bed Ronan remained confined to. A gentle breeze riffled the red-and-white checkered curtains.

"Yes," Gabriel said as he paced. He moved from the chair to the wash-stand in two strides, his movements jerky.

"What are you going to do about Amelia?"

"I don't know. She needs me," Gabriel said as he sat in the chair by Ronan's bed. He clenched his jaw as Ronan rolled his eyes.

"Maybe not you. But I agree, she needs help. No need to engender any more talk, especially now that your woman is here."

"What do you mean, Ronan?"

"Why do you think that you must somehow make everything better for Amelia? Or for me? You can't, Gabe. You need to go on as you mean to live. With your Clarissa."

"Amelia's my friend, as was Liam."

"But Clarissa is the woman you love," Ronan argued, pushing himself higher onto his bed with his knuckles. "Your first loyalty should be to her." At this, Gabriel lowered his head as though in pain. "What is it, Gabe?"

"I don't know what happened in Boston. Clarissa flinches every time I approach her. It's as though she doesn't trust me. That she fears I'll hurt her." He rubbed his face. "The only time she showed any joy at seeing me was when she arrived, but since then…"

"Maybe she's just a skittish female."

Gabriel snorted. "You wouldn't say that if you knew Clarissa. I think she regrets coming here. To me."

"Or it could be what happened in Boston was damn awful."

Gabriel looked up sharply to share a long, tortured look with Ronan.

"And I know whatever befell her is my fault," Gabriel whispered.

"How? You didn't hurt her."

"I left her."

"Then find some way to let her know, no matter what, you want her. But you have to believe it too, Gabe," Ronan said. "Show her, now that she's here, why you're the man she should still choose."

Gabriel nodded. "Are you improving, Ronan?" Gabriel asked, turning his attention away from his concerns. "I know the journey here was too much so soon after your injury."

Ronan grimaced as he again shifted his upper body against the pillows. "Slowly, though the doctor is certain I'll never walk again."

"Ronan," Gabriel said, unable to hide his anguish for his friend. "There's no hope?"

"I could be dead, Gabe," Ronan said. "At least the blast threw me far enough that I wasn't crushed."

"Are you doing anything to keep up your arm strength?" Gabriel asked. "You know I saw men, wounded from the War, crippled like you, but who were able to do things because they were strong. You must stay strong."

Ronan closed his eyes, letting his arms slump down in the bed. "I'm as strong as I'll ever need to be, Gabe."

"I doubt that, Ronan. Your life shouldn't be wasted, feeling miserable and sorry for yourself simply because—"

"Because I'm crippled. Just like you were so kind to say."

Gabriel glared at him as he rose to pace the few steps in front of the window. "Ronan, you can't give up. You aren't eating. It's like you don't care." He moved toward Ronan and gripped his shoulder. "I know the nurse we hired brings in food in the morning, and I bring in your supper at night, but we can't force you to eat it. Please try, Ronan."

"My life is over, Gabriel. I've accepted it. You need to also."

"Never," Gabriel rasped. "I lost Liam and Matthew. But, dammit, you still live. There's more left for your life than laying in this bed." Gabriel kicked one leg of the bed and continued pacing.

After a tense silence, Ronan said, "Do you think I don't want more from my life? To not be a shell of a man?" He shook his head slowly. "I have nothing to offer her, you see." At Gabriel's quizzical stare, he said, "Amelia. If I were whole, I'd marry her. Protect her and the little ones. But who would want me?"

"Ronan, you'll heal. You'll find work." Rather than emerge as a command, the words sounded more a prayer.

"So you say. At this point, I don't know how I'll survive."

"You know I'll find a way to help you," Gabriel said.

"Gabe, you need to look to yourself and Clarissa. And if there is any left over, to Amelia and her babes. I realize now it was foolish of me to leave Butte. And I know I told you that it would be all right if you said 'I told you so.' But if you do, I'll belt you." He paused for a moment. "If I had remained there, the miners would have seen to me, helped me through this." He waved at his immobile legs as he spoke. "They might have even found me a job at the surface. But now?" He stilled, his despair overwhelming him. "Now I'm stuck in a second-floor apartment on Pine Street in Missoula with few visitors. No one will miss me when I'm gone."

"Dammit, don't even think it, Ronan," Gabriel snapped. He sighed and paced toward the window. "I understood your desire for a new place, a new start."

"It's too bad you didn't leave me behind, Gabe, and ignore my wishes. That would have been more charitable."

Gabriel remained silent.

"What am I good for in this town? I can barely see to my own needs without help," Ronan growled.

"We'll find something, Ronan. I promise," Gabriel said.

"I'm sorry, Gabe."

"For what?"

"You have enough to worry about with Clarissa without having to concern yourself with me."

"Now you're talking nonsense," Gabriel said with a half smile. "I'll be by again to visit you later today."

"Bring your fancy lady. I'd like to meet her."

"I will," Gabriel promised with a smile. He gripped Ronan's shoulder and left.

***

"HELLO, UNCLE," GABRIEL SAID as he entered the billiards room on the first floor of the Florence next to the saloon. "I thought I'd find you here." Stale cigar smoke scented the air of the dark paneled room. Wooden shutters covered the lower part of the windows, allowing for privacy while slivers of light played across the cobalt-blue carpets. Two billiards tables upholstered in red stood in the room with pool-cue racks hanging on the walls.

"I often do some of my best thinking when I'm focusing on something else," Aidan said with a smile. "Care to join me?" His hair was disheveled as though he had run his hands through it a few times. He bent over the table, eyeing the perfect shot, his shirtsleeves rolled up to his elbows.

"If you don't mind a novice," Gabriel said with a grin. He took off his jacket, unbuttoned the buttons at his wrists and rolled up his sleeves, mimicking his uncle. They began to play, silently harmonious for a while.

"What happened to Clarissa, Gabriel?" Aidan asked.

Gabriel's head jerked up, and his pool cue flew off the intended ball, causing it to careen haphazardly around the table. "I don't know, Uncle. She just arrived, and we haven't spoken much."

"What do you know?"

"Little more than what she told us today," Gabriel said. "And now she's here and doesn't want me near her."

"I think she wants you near her, Gabriel. It's simply that she needs to become accustomed to you again. From the sounds of it, for a woman to leave her father's home, she was poorly treated by many of those in her life and now may be afraid of trusting you."

"I would never hurt her."

"I know that. And at some level, I am sure she knows that, or she never would have traveled here. But some fears make us irrational. You must understand that."

"I hate that she flinches from me. That she would ever fear *me*."

"Be patient, kind and gentle with her, Gabriel, and I am sure your patience will be rewarded by her love in the future."

"What do you think happened to her, Uncle?"

Aidan shook his head. "Let's just say that I hope I'm terribly mistaken." He cleared his voice that had grown hoarse. "Do you want to continue to play?"

"No, I don't. Let's go to the saloon and get a drink," Gabriel said.

CHAPTER 30

I SOON CAME TO REALIZE that finding a job would be much harder than I had expected. All the teaching posts were already filled in Missoula, although the school board seemed genuinely disappointed to have nothing to offer me other than an unpaid position as an aide. I had heard there were open teaching positions outside of Missoula in towns called Florence or St. Ignatius, yet I did not want to live alone away from Gabriel and Colin. Colin had suggested advertising in *The Daily Missoulian* as a tutor. However, even with a finely worded advertisement, there had been no interest. My spirits drooped as each day passed, and I continued with no prospect of having an occupation.

I finally wandered into the Book Depository one afternoon on a hot, still day in late June. As I entered the business on the second floor of a two-story brick building above the Allenstein and Company's Grocers store, I began to relax due to the presence of so many books. I had missed my mama's extensive collection in Boston and the easy access to any book I wanted at the Boston Public Library. I scanned the room to see piles of books on tables in no apparent order. It was a medium-size long rectangular room with bare brick walls and plank floors that creaked as I walked. The front of the building had three large rectangular windows. There was a door-way at the rear of the room that appeared to lead to a small room or office. I noted no desk for a librarian.

I perused the front room, empty save for tables piled high with books, self-conscious of the noise I made on the creaky floors. I tried to walk sound-lessly but found that impossible. There was a faint musty smell to the area, and I sneezed a few times. I longed to open the windows to let the warm, dry air flow in. However, the front windows were draped in drab puce curtains and firmly shut, allowing very little natural light into the room. Two overhead chandeliers emitted a dim light. I wandered the low tables of books, attempting to find a method to their placement, finally realizing they were arranged haphazardly by genre, although no further attempt at organizing the books appeared to be in use.

An elderly man tottered out of the back room, wheezing slightly with each breath. A loud *thunk* punctuated every step as his cane struck the ground. I glanced up, smiling as I remembered Aunt Betsy and her cane. He stopped, swaying near a stack of books, placing one hand on the books to stabilize himself, then smiled fully with an almost toothless grin. "How may I help you, dear?" he asked in a whistlinglike voice.

"Good afternoon, sir. This is my first time here, and I am finding my way around," I said, in an attempt to explain my confusion as to the book placement. "Are you the librarian, sir?"

He laughed, sounding like a bagpipe filling with air, screechingly harmonious. "Oh, no. I don't know enough 'bout books to be a librarian."

"Do you need a librarian? I'm looking for work and would be interested in working with these books. Although I'm uncertain as to how they are arranged."

"Ah, if you figure out how old Bessie left this lot, explain it to me," he said, winking at me. "I don't know much about books myself, but Bessie, God rest her, did. She passed on last month, and I haven't had the heart to find a replacement for her." He stopped talking, as though lost in thought.

"I'm sorry for your loss, sir. Were you close to Miss Bessie?"

"Ah, you ain't from around these parts then," he said. "My Bessie and I were married fifty-three years. Yes, indeed." He nodded. "Her great love was books, you see. So this book depository was started." He closed his eyes, holding out his hand as though in acknowledgment of his next statement. "She and the other ladies hate the word *depository*, and I know I should call it a library. But it ain't yet," he said, a twinkle of defiance in his eyes. He sighed a long rattling noise as he continued to speak. "I know it weren't hers, but it sure felt like it. She was so dedicated to it, spent more time here than at home." He opened his eyes to peer at me, nodding. "Now there are other women who come in to help, but none like my Bessie." He seemed wistful for a moment, then focused on me with keen dark brown eyes that appeared almost black.

"You seem like a young lady who knows a thing or two about books," he said in as authoritative a manner as possible between occasional wheezes. "I think you might be just what this place needs."

"Oh, well," I stammered and felt the heat of a blush overtaking me. "I hope so, sir."

"You sure are formal, wherever you come from," he said. "My name's Mr. Pickens, Mr. A. J. Pickens. I don't care much for my name, so I go by A.J."

I held out my hand, and replied, "I'm Clarissa Sullivan, sir, from Boston."

"Wowee, Boston!" he said, wheezing so much he nearly fell over.

I think he might have tried to whistle, but I only heard the sound of rustling air. I looked around for a chair but failed to see anything.

He regained his balance. "What's the city life like?" he asked. "It's been years since I've seen a proper city."

"Big. Busy. Bustling," I replied.

"Hmm … Sounds to me like you're a bit homesick."

He furrowed his brow, and moved it up and down a few times, as though trying to see if I would agree with him or marvel at his intuition, I could not tell. I smiled, waiting for him to continue.

"Why in the world does a pretty girl like you come all the way out here?"

I blushed, shook my head slightly and did not answer.

"A story for another day. Come, let's find me a chair and you can *pa-rooose*." After noticing my smile, he said, "Ah, I see you like my fancy words. My Bessie was always tryin' to teach me more high-society words."

He tottered over to a pile of books on a low table that was really a chair. He knocked them to the floor and sat down heavily.

I rushed to where he was, picked up the books and began to put them in order. "Mr. Pickens," I asked. "Is this really the way the books should be sorted?" I kept my voice gentle, trying not to criticize the dear departed Bessie.

"My Bessie thought people would like to have books by type," he said. "That's not the word she used. She used some fancy French word. But the meanin's the same. Do you object?"

"It's not that I object to the plan," I said. "I believe that once you have them in an area by type or genre…"

"That's the word!" he stated with glee.

"Yes, well, once they are in their area, they should be arranged some way for library patrons. Alphabetical by author or title. Something like that," I suggested. I looked at a table of classical literature with a mixture of frustration and confusion.

"Well, Miss Sullivan," he said, smiling fully, displaying his remaining teeth, "I am not the person to arrange, as you say."

"If you don't mind me asking, sir——" At his gentle nod, I continued, "Why are you here, if you don't arrange the books?"

He wheezed again and then gave another bagpipelike laugh.

I smiled in response, realizing I had not smiled this much in months.

"Ah, if that ain't what my Bessie asked me!" He laughed a little more, almost falling out of the chair.

I realized any height off of the floor posed a potential danger to him.

"She liked my company, see, and, now that she's gone, I feel close to her here."

"I am terribly sorry about your loss, Mr. Pickens," I repeated. I knew the words were inadequate yet felt the need to say something.

"It's A.J., missy. I knew she was dyin', see, and there weren't nothin' I could do to stop it," he said, looking away. "But we had fifty-three years together, and they were wonderful years. My Bessie ordered me, she said, 'No sadness!' So I'm tryin'."

"I think you are doing a marvelous job. I haven't smiled this much in weeks."

"Now that's a shame, a pretty girl like you," he said, a twinkle back in his eyes. "Just be thankful I'm no younger."

I laughed.

"I have a question for you, now, Miss Sullivan," he said.

I looked toward him with an expectant expression.

"You asked me, when you arrived, if we needed a librarian. And, yes, we do. Would you like to arrange the books?"

"I would like to, sir, very much. Are you certain?"

"I know you like books," he wheezed out. "You picked up the ones I threw to the floor as quick as could be. You have a look about you like you want to arrange things here. You seem a tidy sort, just the type we need 'round here." He glanced at the haphazardly arranged books, the dusty corners.

I blushed at having been seen through so completely.

"The pay is terrible," he continued. "Not enough to live on alone."

"But there is pay," I said. I turned toward him, with hope in my eyes. He nodded, studying me.

"I would very much like to work here, but I need to earn some sort of salary. I live with my brother, and I want to contribute to our household."

Mr. Pickens studied me, with a confused expression. "Most women don't want to work, missy. You should allow your brother to take care of you," he admonished.

"I know that is the normal way, sir," I acknowledged. "However, I used to teach school in Boston. Not because I had to, but because I wanted to. I need to continue to maintain some sense of independence."

He laughed, slapping his thigh with his hand. "Don't you sound like my Bessie!" He continued to wheeze, which then turned into a rattling cough. He waved away my concerned expression. "No need to worry about me. The doctor assures me it'll be a while afore I die." He chortled some more, causing me to smile.

"Are you serious, Mr. Pickens, about me working here?" I asked.

"Very serious," he said. "I'll just need to speak later with a few of the ladies that come by." He sighed. "Now don't get worried. They tend to carry on some, but none of them have the time to work here like they should. Families and homes to run, you see."

He winked at me. "They have a soft spot for this old gander," he said, with a touch of pride. "Come back tomorrow around eleven, and we'll see how things are."

I nodded, my spirits uplifted at the thought of having a job. "Thank you, Mr. Pickens. I look forward to working here."

CHAPTER 31

"READY, RISSA?" COLIN ASKED, as I stood nearly breathless. I nodded and Colin tapped on the door. It creaked opened, and I looked inside as I heard a small boy yelling.

"Nicholas Egan, you behave when our guests arrive," I heard a woman command.

"Amelia, let me."

I heard Gabriel's deep baritone and then his gentle murmurings as I peered around the doorjamb to see Gabriel on his haunches in front of an irate toddler. Suddenly he scooped him up and held him upside down. The boy shrieked with joy.

"Put me down, put me down, put me down!" he yelled, holding onto Gabriel's legs tightly. Gabriel turned him upright, holding Nicholas in his arms.

"No more fuss tonight, Nicholas," Gabriel said as he brushed the boy's russet-colored hair into a semblance of order.

"I won't like her. You can't make me," Nicholas said.

"No, I can't make you. But I would like you to be nice to my friends. Can you do that for me, little man?" Gabriel asked with a soft pat on his head.

"Maybe," Nicholas mumbled.

"Good lad," Gabriel said as he turned toward Amelia. He finally noticed the door was ajar. "Clarissa! Colin," Gabriel said with a broad smile, his dimple flashing in his right cheek. "I want you to meet Amelia and her children." Nicholas had attached himself to Gabriel's leg like a third appendage, although Gabriel didn't seem bothered by his antics.

Colin and I entered the tiny apartment. Near the front door was the living area with a small sofa and a rocking chair. A table with a worn cloth separated the living space from the kitchen along the far wall. One little window in the living room faced the street. There was a closed door off the living room, which I imagined to be the bedroom.

Gabriel reached to place his hand on the small of my back. I tensed involuntarily, before relaxing. I sensed Gabriel stiffen next to me, and I turned toward Amelia.

"Hello, Mrs. Egan," I said, moving forward to shake her hand. "I've heard so much about you."

She moved with an innate grace, her honey-blond hair wispy, giving her a casual beauty rather than a harried look. A worn apron covered a tan shirtwaist. "Miss Sullivan. It's very nice to meet you. That's my Nicholas, and this is my Anne," she said pointing to a small bundle in a well-made crib near the dining room table, a tightly swaddled bundle with only a patch of red hair visible.

"That's one of yours, isn't it, Gabriel?" I asked.

"The crib, yes," Gabriel said as Colin chuckled behind him.

I turned to watch Gabriel elbow Colin.

"I gave it to Amelia and Liam for Christmas."

At Liam's name Amelia turned away, moving into the kitchen. "I hope you like stew. It's only root vegetables tonight as it's Friday," she said.

"Of course," I murmured. "It was very kind of you to invite us. Is there anything I can do?" I asked and then immediately wished the words away as I was a horrible cook.

"You could help me set the table."

"Yes, yes, that I could do," I said as I moved toward the small dining area.

"Nicholas, do you have marbles?" Colin asked. "I haven't played them in far too long, and you have the look of a master about you."

"Mama, Mama, Mama," Nicholas said in his excitement, letting go of Gabriel's leg, nearly bouncing up and down with excitement. "Can I..."

"*May* I," Amelia interrupted.

"May I get my marbles 'n play?" Nicholas asked.

"Not now, Nicholas. Go wash for dinner. After dinner, if Mr. Sullivan still wants to play, then we'll see."

Nicholas ran to Colin. "Will you still want to play, Mister Sullie?" He grabbed Colin's hand in his excitement.

"Of course, little man," Colin said, ruffling his hair. "Now show me where to wash up for supper." Nicholas held on to his hand, pulling him toward the sink area in the kitchen.

"He's made a friend for life," Gabriel murmured into my ear from behind. "Colin will have no peace now every time he visits."

"I think Colin will enjoy it," I whispered back, turning to smile at Gabriel. He watched me with an arrested look on his face. "What?"

He shook his head. "Amelia, the stew smells delicious," he said as he moved away.

"I added plenty of pepper, Gabriel. I know how fond you are of it," Amelia said with a grin.

I stood rooted to the side of the room, watching them interact, realizing all of the time I'd lost with Gabriel. He had much more of a history with Amelia than he had with me. Why should he prefer me to her?

"Clarissa?" Colin asked, and I noticed they were all seated for dinner. I sat in the vacant chair next to Colin.

"Sorry," I murmured. I saw Gabriel and Amelia share a quick glance and wanted to scream. Instead, I took a taste of the stew. "This is delicious, Mrs. Egan."

"Thank you."

"You are a fine cook, ma'am," Colin said. "Gabe, tell me about your and Clarissa's visit to see your friend, Ronan."

"I think he enjoyed meeting Clarissa," Gabriel said with a smile in my direction. "He was surprised she was as beautiful as her picture."

I blushed. "He seems a very nice man, though it's a shame he has lost the use of his legs. Is there nothing to be done for him?"

"Very little. I'm still trying to think of some sort of work for him," Gabriel said.

"How did you meet him?" Colin asked as he blew on a spoonful of stew to cool it before taking a bite.

"Through Matthew. They were friends back in Ohio. I met him on my first day in Butte," Gabriel said. "He found work for Matthew with Liam, and soon we were a close-knit group of friends." Gabriel paused, clearing his throat. "They told us he had died too. But, in reality, he had been only half buried in rubble. So he lived."

"It's just tragic he won't walk again," I said. I sat fidgeting with my spoon, not eating.

"Yes, it is. But it's worse for those who emerge only for their funeral," Gabriel murmured, reaching out to gently grip Amelia's hand.

"I beg your pardon," I said to Amelia. "I never meant to sound unfeeling."

"Of course not, Miss Sullivan. You are not used to the ways of the mining camp."

"Though we are no longer in one," I said. "If you will excuse me, I am feeling unwell." I rose and turned to leave with Colin on my heels. I heard him murmur something to Gabriel, but I was out the door with such alacrity, I failed to hear what he said.

"Rissa!" Colin called out. "Rissa!" he said as he gripped my arm and pulled me to him before I barged down Front Street alone. "What's the matter with you?"

I continued to look away from him, staring at the mountains in the dim twilight. "Can't you see, Colin? I'm too late. Gabriel wants Amelia."

"No, he doesn't," Colin argued, spinning me to face him.

"Colin, I want to return to the hotel," I whispered. I blinked rapidly as I fought tears.

He nodded, understanding my need for solitude. He offered me his elbow, and I leaned into him as we walked the short distance to the hotel.

CHAPTER 32

AMELIA SAT, CUDDLING a morose Nicholas. "Hush, love. Don't carry on so. He'll be back soon to play marbles with you," she whispered with a gentle rub to his back. He nodded and pushed out of her arms.

"I'll play on my own, all right, Mama?" he asked.

"Fine, Nicholas," she said. She picked up her spoon to finish eating the stew. "Your Clarissa is … high-strung, Gabriel."

"I don't know what's going on," he said as he tapped his fingers on the dining room table. "She says she's happy to be here with me, but she doesn't want me to touch her and rarely looks at me with any joy."

"Are you sure you remember how things were last year?" Amelia asked.

"Yes," Gabriel said on a long sigh. "I know I didn't imagine it. And she traveled all the way here with her brother."

"Hmm…" Amelia said looking away.

"Amelia, tell me what you're thinking," Gabriel said in a low voice, watching her closely.

"You aren't going to want to hear it, Gabriel."

"Tell me anyway."

Amelia paused as though trying to find the words. "Imagine the worst thing that could have befallen your Clarissa." She paused sharing a long, intense stare with Gabriel. "How else would you expect her to act?"

"You can't mean…"

"Yes, I do. I've seen it a few times, and it's a difficult thing to behold."

"Amelia, you're speaking nonsense," Gabriel argued.

"Maybe I am. But whatever happened to your Clarissa is enough to make her as prickly as a porcupine. You need to determine why. And show her you love her no matter what," she said.

"Ronan said something similar the other day," Gabriel mused.

"Then he is a wise man. I wouldn't have expected it of him after all of his wild antics with Matthew."

"I think their deaths and his accident have really changed him, Amelia."

"It changed us all," she whispered as she rose to clear the table.

"Amelia," Gabriel said.

"Gabriel, there is nothing you can do for me. I value your friendship. I would be lost without your help with Nicholas. But I don't know as it is right of me to expect your continued presence in my life."

"Amelia, no matter what, I'll continue to support you and the children."

"Is that fair to Clarissa? You saw how she reacted when she saw us together tonight."

"That is between Clarissa and me. It has nothing to do with you."

"I think you're wrong, Gabriel. Women don't like other women around their men."

"And men don't like other men around their women. But I put up with reading about Cameron's visits for months. She can damned well understand my friendship with you," Gabriel hissed.

"You are much angrier with her than you've demonstrated, Gabriel," Amelia said with a raised eyebrow.

"Of course I'm angry. How could I not be?" he asked as he stood and paced. "I wrote. I waited. I behaved myself when there were a multitude of distractions in Butte."

"Don't even think of mentioning that wretched street," Amelia said.

"I worried myself sick that she had been in some train accident. And now that she's finally here, she doesn't want me anywhere near her. As though she thinks I would hurt her. How could she think I'd hurt her?" he roared, nearly waking baby Anne. He walked to her cradle, gently rocking it with his foot to settle her.

"All that you say is true, Gabriel," Amelia said in a soothing voice, pushing Gabriel aside and picking up Anne to rock her in her arms. "And you have the right to your anger. But you have to decide if you are going to allow your anger to separate you. Or are you willing to set it aside and be the man she needs you to be?"

"I must go, Amelia. I need to..." He did not finish.

"Yes, Gabriel. Go to Clarissa," she murmured, watching his hasty departure.

CHAPTER 33

I HEARD A GENTLE TAPPING at my door and nearly threw a pillow at it. Colin knew I needed time alone. "Go away, Col!" I gasped between my sobs.

"Rissa?" Colin asked with another gentle knock. I refused to budge from my protective cocoon of blankets and pillows, and knew he would leave soon. However, the door creaked open, and someone entered.

"Oh, darling." A gentle murmur in Gabriel's voice came.

"Go away," I pleaded, looking at him for an instant, letting him see my horrified red-rimmed eyes. "Leave! I don't want you to see me like…" I broke off, turning away and burying my face into a pillow, sobs wracking my body.

"No, no, my Clarissa. I will not leave you," he whispered. I heard him dragging a chair toward the bed and then sitting heavily. I felt a gentle touch to my back and soon he had begun to trace a soothing pattern. Although initially I had stiffened at his touch, I gradually relaxed into his caress and began to calm.

"Why are you here?" I whispered around a hiccup.

"To see you. To hold you if you'd let me. To ask you to forgive me for being so thoughtless."

I took a shuddering breath, my back toward him. Suddenly I needed to be held. I turned, and he was able to see the full extent of my sorrow and grief. I scooted toward him, not giving myself time to think through my actions. I clambered onto his lap. "Hold me. Please," I asked. Another shudder rippled through me, and I sighed as his arms clasped me firmly, yet gently.

"This is what I missed most," I murmured. "Being held by you. Feeling safe in your arms."

"I hope you understand that now, Clarissa. I'm sorry you felt unwanted or threatened at Amelia's. But it is you I love. You I want," he murmured into my ear.

I nodded, beginning to stroke his nape.

He eased me back so he could look into my eyes. "I'm sorry that you have such pain inside, darling. But you know we must speak of it."

My eyes welled again, and he chased away the tears with his thumbs. "Not tonight, Gabriel. Please."

He nodded as he eased my head back onto his chest. "Soon, my darling, soon." The soothing caress continued over my spine, a balm to my bruised spirit.

CHAPTER 34

"IF YOU ARE GOING to work with me, missy," Mr. Pickens said, "stop *sir*ring me."

I noted an amused twinkle in his eye and hid a smile. "My name's A.J. Been good enough for ever'one else, good enough for you." He stood by the chair he'd cleared off by a table covered in cookbooks and others highlighting the home arts. Sunlight streamed in through the windows at the front of the room, the rays dancing on pieces of dust. Yellowed wallpaper with green flowers covered the walls, the edges toward the ceiling peeling away and rolling toward the floor. Patches of plaster could be seen in certain sections and a water stain marred a small section of the ceiling near the window farthest from the door.

I wandered among the scattered tables and nodded my agreement. "I'll try, Mr. Pickens."

He frowned at me and my persistent inability to call him A.J.

Mr. Pickens wheezed a sigh at the sound of a slamming door downstairs and then heavy footsteps on the stairs leading to the depository. "Ah, here it is then, the final hurdle to working here. You better be ready to run the gauntlet. A bit like good ol' Coulter!" He laughed with glee, nearly falling over again.

I walked toward him, pushing him into the only available chair. I looked toward the door with a pleasant, impersonal smile. I realized I was emulating Mrs. Smythe and grimaced, but pasted the smile on once more. I tensed as I heard the footfalls growing louder as the people approached.

A rotund woman emerged through the doorway into the depository. I blinked in surprise once, hoping she did not note my momentary shock at seeing only one person after the amount of noise from the stairwell.

"A.J.," she bellowed out in an authoritative, booming voice akin to a drill sergeant's. "Good morning!" She inhaled a few times, catching her breath. Her bosom heaved with her laborious breaths, and I feared her dress might give way from the exertions. She had reddish-blond hair tied back in a tight chignon, causing her forehead and eyes to be pulled back from the pressure of the pins in her hair. Her dress style was fashionable, yet more colorful than expected. Her rich hazel eyes glowed with intelligence.

"So this is the young miss you want me to meet," she said in her loud voice. "What's the matter, dear?" she called out in a louder voice. "You hard of hearing?"

"No, ma'am," I replied, attempting to cover up my laugh with a small cough, speaking as demurely as possible.

"*Hmmph*," she replied. She started to walk toward me, causing the floorboards to creak. "Let's have a look at you then." She perused me up and down, frowning. "Not much to look at, is there, miss?"

My head shot up, color tingeing my cheeks with anger. "I beg your pardon, ma'am?"

"You need sharper clothes, need a better sense of style," she said, holding one hand at her waist, as though to show off her jade-colored suit with gold-tinted buttons. "We want our patrons to believe only the most refined are here to care for them. Your hair is a drab, nondescript brown, and your face is freckled from the sun. Don't you know better, to wear a hat? And you're too thin by half. Don't you eat?" Her bosom heaved more and more with each noted transgression, and her voice became louder. "I can't imagine you have the strength to stand for long periods, never mind to put this place to rights," she finished with a wave toward the disordered room.

I breathed out in an attempt to control my temper.

"Well, girl, can't you speak?" she asked in her booming voice.

"Yes, ma'am, I can. I will do the best I can to meet your exacting fashionable standards on the limited salary. And I believe my figure is fine the way it is."

She jerked, clearly taken aback at my words. Mr. Pickens sounded like a bagpipe as he laughed, and I blushed beet red at my impertinence.

"Ah, so you have a bit of a bark," the woman said with a small frown, before smiling. "I like that. Well done, A.J." She turned to survey the room, giving a small sniff of disapproval, before turning back toward me.

"What's your name, girl?"

"Clarissa Sullivan, ma'am."

Her brow furrowed as she studied me. "Sullivan, hmm … Your brother works at the smithy on Alder now?" She said it as a question, but I knew she required no answer. "And you're the one who jilted your fiancée, then ran across the country with nary a word to your family and is trying to steal that cabinetmaker from the poor widow." Her voice held a note of barely restrained curiosity.

After an appallingly long silence, I stammered, "That is one way of looking at things."

"I can tell there is an entertaining story here, and we need good tales to survive the long winters," she said. "Well done, A.J.!" She beamed again. "You are learned? You know your letters?"

"I was a schoolteacher in Boston," I said.

"A schoolteacher! In Boston!" she gushed. "And now in little old Missoula." She watched me. "I wonder how long you'll stay."

After a moment's pause, I spoke. "If you don't mind me asking, what is your name and what is your role here?"

"Oh, I am Mrs. Bouchard," she preened as she said her last name with an attempt at a French accent. "I helped found the library with Bessie. I try to help out when I am able, but I can become so busy at home. I'm sure you understand." Then she looked at me as if to say, "Maybe not," with a dismissive shrug of her shoulders. She waved her hand as though to indicate "No matter" and continued at a near bellow. "I will be so thankful to have the day-to-day burden of running the library off my shoulders. You have no idea how much of a concern this has been for me." She sighed in a dramatic fashion to emphasize her worries.

I heard Mr. Pickens snicker, before muttering, "You wouldn't know what a burden was if it sat on yer head."

I attempted to hide my smile but knew I had failed when Mrs. Bouchard stared at the two of us. She cocked her head to one side, squinting at Mr. Pickens for a moment. At our continued silence, she shook her head in frustration.

"Good luck, Miss Sullivan!" she called out as she pivoted her large girth toward the doorway. "A.J." Then loud footsteps could be heard down the stairs, and she was gone.

I realized I was holding my breath and exhaled loudly. Mr. Pickens laughed, slapping his thigh in merriment.

"Oh, you did well, missy," he said with glee, making that strange bagpipe noise. "She didn't know what to do with you!"

"I wonder," I said.

"No need to worry about her. All bluster, very little bite," he said. "And she married well. You know what her name means, don't ye, missy?"

I shook my head, smiling fully at him, enjoying his contagious good mood.

"Well, she used to drive my poor Bessie insane, with all of her demands and comments and need to impress the townsfolk. Now, never mind she was never willin' to lift a finger." He sighed out a wheeze. "So, one day, my Bessie was fed up. She never was mean, mind you, just dubious." He looked at me, lifting his eyebrows up and down, proud to have used another big word.

"Dubious?" I asked. I thought through the conversation. "Oh, you mean *devious*!"

He slapped his leg, laughing silently. "Yes, that's it, missy. *Deeevious*." He liked the sound of the *E* and overemphasized it. "So, my Bessie looked into what her proud French name means. Any guesses?"

I shook my head again.

"Someone with a big mouth!" he exclaimed with glee.

I couldn't help myself. I laughed out loud, nearly doubling over with it, and I soon had tears coursing down my cheeks. I finally gasped out, "No, you must be making this up."

"On my poor Bessie's grave." He raised one hand as though swearing an oath, though his eyes continued to twinkle with merriment.

"Do you think she knows?" I asked.

"I doubt she'd let on to somethin' like that," he said, wheezing out a new noise, an accordion-sounding laugh. "I'm sure she's off to give a report to Mrs. Vaughan. They'll be chatterin' away worse than two magpies soon about you. Never doubt that, missy. You are too mysterious for their likin'," he said with a knowing quirk of his eyebrows.

"Mrs. Vaughan?" I asked. "Who's Mrs. Vaughan?"

Mr. Pickens heaved a sigh, rolling his eyes heavenward. "She's the one the good Lord sent us as penance for any misdeed we might have done or contemplated doin' at some point in our lives."

My eyes widened.

"She's the biggest—and I do mean that laterally, missy—biggest busy-body ye'll ever have the misfortune of meeting."

"She likes to gossip?" I asked. I looked around in vain for another chair to sit on. I felt ill at the thought of all these faceless people talking about me without my knowledge. I located a stool hidden in a corner, pulled it out and perched on it for a few moments near Mr. Pickens's chair.

"Gossip? Gossip?"

I thought this time he would faint onto the floor.

"Oh, missy, there ain't been no word invented yet to describe how that woman likes to talk. I ain't never seen nothin' like it in all my years. And I've lived plenty o' years," he said, twitching his eyebrows at me again for empha-sis. "At times I think she'll get lockjaw, she talks so much."

"Lockjaw?" I asked weakly, but then giggled.

"Yes, missy, you will do fine," Mr. Pickens said.

CHAPTER 35

"HELLO, MR. O'BARA," I said as I poked my head into his room. "Is this a bad time for a visitor?" Midmorning sun had begun to peek in through his windows enhancing the shadows on the side of the room near his bed.

He turned his head toward me, welcoming me with a faint smile. He was propped on a pile of pillows, his upper body covered in a long- sleeved blue cotton shirt. He lay under a white sheet that was pulled up to midchest. "No, Miss Sullivan. I'm not going anywhere."

I bit back a smile but couldn't prevent the humor in my eyes. "I always thought you'd be a bit of a rascal from what Gabriel wrote about you in his letters." I entered the room, moving around the confining space. "May I open a window? There's a lovely breeze today." At his nod, I pushed on one of the windows by the washstand, but it refused to budge.

"That's why it's not open," Ronan said. "The nurse isn't much bigger than you, and she couldn't get it open either."

"Well, let's try again," I said. I put my shoulder into pressing on the window frame, and the window flew open. It opened with such a start that I found myself half dangling out the opened window. I screeched in dismay and then with laughter, as I pulled myself back into the room.

After collapsing into the only free chair in the room at the foot of the bed near the corner of the room, I tried to quell my giggling. "That was more of an adventure than I had bargained for."

"I can see how you leveled that ladder on poor Gabe when you first met," Ronan said.

I flushed at his words.

"You are not grace personified, Miss Sullivan."

"No, and I never will be. But the window's open, and the breeze is welcome," I said with a triumphant tilt to my head.

"No wonder Gabriel insisted on waiting for you," Ronan said with a half smile. "No matter how hard I tried to lead him down the road to ... well, a road well traveled, he refused."

"I'm glad to hear that." I gave him one of my best schoolteacher looks. "I'm sure you were a hellion in Butte."

"The only way to be in such a city." He looked toward his legs and grimaced. "Until ... until the accident that is."

"You are still an attractive man, Mr. O'Bara. You don't have to consign yourself to living your life confined to a bed."

"What would you have me do, Miss Sullivan? I can't move about. I can't make my living as a miner. I can't help my friend's widow. I can't do anything for myself."

"I'd do what Gabriel said to me once. Stop focusing on what you can't do and focus on what you can." I watched as he huffed out an irritated breath. "Forgive me, Mr. O'Bara. I didn't come here to argue with you."

"I know you didn't, Miss Sullivan. I'm thankful for the company."

"Do you read?" I asked and then flushed at the question.

"I do, yes."

"If you tell me what you like, I can bring you books from the depository."

"That's very kind of you. Thank you."

I rose and wandered his small room. I moved from the chair in the corner to his bureau in three steps and then back again. "Why did Gabriel rent a room for you on the second floor?"

"It's the most affordable room he could find."

"Would you object to moving?" At the shake of his head, I paced a few more times and then sat again. "If you were on the first floor, you'd have more of an opportunity to go outside."

"In what? I can't walk, Miss Sullivan. I am confined to this bed."

"Hmm ... we'll think of something."

"You're like him, you know," Ronan said. At my inquisitive stare, he said, "You seem like someone who's trying to fix things and make things right. Just like Gabe."

I smiled my agreement.

"Some things can't be made right, Miss Sullivan. Sometimes things can be so awful that there's no way to right the damage that's been done."

I paled at his words. "Surely you don't mean that," I whispered.

He tilted his head to one side as he studied me. "Who hurt you?"

I shook my head with too much force. "No one. It's nothing."

"It's clearly not nothing when you are keeping at arm's length the man you traveled thousands of miles to see."

My eyes flashed as I met his gaze. "Is that what you do together? Gossip?"

"I have little else to offer Gabe but my advice. And you seem to be running him ragged with worry."

My expression softened as I registered his words. "I'm sure all will be settled soon."

"Is that one of those things you believe that, if you tell yourself the lie often enough, it will come true?"

"I traveled all this way to be with Gabriel. I will be with him."

"Then you need to trust him, Miss Sullivan. With whatever haunts you."

I rose to stand in front of the opened window. "You know what fear is Mr. O'Bara. You know what it is to live, every day, with a different future than the one you'd planned."

"Yes."

"So do I. And coming to terms with my new reality has been difficult."

"Are you saying you don't want Gabe?"

"Never." I spun to face him. "Never. I've always wanted to be with Gabriel. I just hadn't imagined it would be here. In Montana. As I am now."

He pushed himself up with his fists to sit higher in the bed. "Well, he's never been happier to have you here. In Montana. As you are now. Never doubt that man's love for you, Miss Sullivan."

I nodded as I again turned toward the window, tracing the checkered curtain with my fingertips. "He's following me, you know."

"Who?"

"The man in Boston who wanted to marry me. Cameron Wright. He followed me to Butte. I don't know when he'll arrive in Missoula."

"What will happen when he does arrive?"

"He'll claim I'm his. That I broke a betrothal with him."

"Did you?"

"No. I never betrothed myself to him again. Not since he failed to show on our wedding day three years ago. But there are those who will believe his tale. And I worry…" I took a deep breath. "I worry Gabriel will believe he would do better to marry someone such as the widow, Mrs. Egan."

"Why would you believe that?"

"She can cook. Knows how to run a proper house. She can most likely starch his shirts just right without making his collar itch. All the things I wouldn't know the first thing about." I sighed as I stared at my clenched hands. "I'm rather useless with the domestic arts."

I turned to study him again. "I can see why Gabriel comes to talk with you. I had no intention of speaking with you about anything remotely personal, and, yet, here I am. Discussing all this with you. You have a soothing presence."

"Ah, yes, the soothing crippled confessor," Ronan said with bitterness.

"Don't speak of yourself thus," I chided. "There'll be something for you to do yet. You have friends, Mr. O'Bara, and we'll think of something." I walked toward him and clasped his hand. "And never discount the power of truly listening to another's fears."

I gripped his hand once more before releasing it. "Now, I must be off to the depository. Mr. Pickens will be looking for me. I'll come by with some books for you," I said.

"Thank you, Miss Sullivan. Remember, Gabe's one of my best friends, and he's stood by me through everything. Tell him about that man following you. I would hate for him to hear about it from someone other than you."

I paled as I nodded. "Thank you, Mr. O'Bara."

"It's always a pleasure to see you."

***

"RISSA!" I TURNED TO SEE Gabriel approaching. "Where are you coming from?" He looked up and down Pine Street, noting I was blocks away from the center of town and the apartment I shared with Colin. In a few long strides he stood in front of me, towering over me. My long indigo skirts brushed against his black pants as he faced me. The gentle breeze ruffled his black hair, making strands of it stand on end.

"I went to visit Ronan. I thought he might like some company before I headed into work."

"That was very kind of you. Thank you for visiting with him." He reached out to stroke my hair, but I leaned away from his touch. He dropped his hand, his fingers near mine. He flexed them, the tips of his fingers brushing against the tips of mine. I stilled at the contact before I moved my fingers toward his and clasped his hand.

"He's a nice man," I murmured in a husky voice.

"Yes, although he's suffering, living the way he is."

"Thanks to you," I said.

Gabriel reared back as though I had struck him.

"What could you be thinking, having a crippled man living on the second floor? He should live on the ground floor so he would have the opportunity to move about more."

"I know, Rissa," Gabriel said. He released my hand and moved a pace away from me. He rubbed his hands through his hair, tousling it further. "It's the only way I could think of to make the money he has last the longest."

"He's a capable man. He can work if he's not spending his days bemoaning his life, lying in a bed."

Gabriel nodded his agreement. "I know, Rissa. I'm trying to think of something that should help him. If you have any ideas, other than belittling the help I've already given my injured friend, I'd welcome them."

I blushed at his gentle, yet forceful, chastisement.

"As for you, let me walk you to the depository." He offered me his arm, and I slipped my arm through his. "What else did you talk about with Ronan?"

I stopped our slow progression down the boardwalk, thankful there were few mingling during the midmorning lull. "Gabriel, I have to tell you something. I don't want it to influence you in any way."

"Are you sure this is the place to speak of it?" he murmured as he looked around the boardwalk.

I took a deep breath as I gripped his arm tightly and garnered all my strength. "Gabriel, Cameron followed me to Butte."

"He what? Why?"

"He wants to marry me. I don't know when he'll realize I'm in Missoula."

Gabriel had bowed his head over mine, and I felt cocooned as though in his embrace. My body remembered his presence—his musky, masculine smell so different from Cameron's—and I relaxed as I leaned toward him. We jerked away from each other at a loud, imperious voice.

"Mr. McLeod!" Loud footsteps and a portly woman stood in front of us. She gripped a large basket in one hand, the other she propped on her protruding hips. The crimson blue of her satin walking dress highlighted her size rather than diminished it.

"Mrs. Vaughan," Gabriel said. "Always a pleasure to see you."

"I would have thought you would be at the library by now, Miss Sullivan."

"I was on my way there."

"When I met you yesterday, I thought you had more sense than to cavort with men of the town."

"I hope to someday merit such gossip," Gabriel said with a wry smile. "I've yet to be considered a cavorting sort of gentleman. However, I know Miss Sullivan from Boston and wanted to speak with her of common acquaintances as I escorted her to the depository."

"Miss Sullivan, my sister and I expect great things of you. You have the future of our library in your young hands."

I nodded as I fought a smile. "Of course, Mrs. Vaughan. It's why I'm so thankful to have Mr. Pickens's guidance." I bit my lip as she sputtered at the mention of Mr. Pickens.

"If you will excuse us, Mrs. Vaughan, we don't want your charge to be any later than she already is," Gabriel said. He nodded toward her and I walked beside him, arm in arm.

"Clarissa, now is not the time to speak of it. Yet we must speak of Cameron."

"There's nothing more to discuss, Gabriel. I only wanted you to know that he maintains an interest in me. He may arrive at any time in Missoula."

"You must know such news is unwelcome," Gabriel murmured.

"I know no such thing, Gabriel." I turned to him as I reached the depository. "Thank you for the walk. I hope you have a good day."

"Rissa! You can't mean that." He gripped my arms, forcing me to face him.

I paled as I thought through my words. "Gabriel—"

"Hello there, missy. 'Bout time you showed up for work."

I glanced up to see Mr. Pickens watching me from the open window at the front of the depository. Gabriel released me, and I stepped away from him.

"I must go to work. I can't lose my job. I'll see you soon." As I opened the door to the stairs leading to the depository, I glanced over my shoulder to find Gabriel watching me with a deep intensity.

CHAPTER 36

"CLARISSA, CAN'T YOU TELL ME what is wrong? It seems like so much has changed, and yet what is important hasn't." Gabriel stood, studying me from across the small living room in the apartment Colin and I had found on Pine Street. It had two bedrooms, dilapidated yet comfortable furniture and was perfect for our needs. Gabriel had come to see me because I had not seen him since we had spoken on the boardwalk a few days ago.

I moved away from him. The comfort I had felt with him the night of Amelia's dinner and the morning afterward had disappeared as readily as an early dawn mist exposed to bright sun. "What do you mean?" At his quizzical stare I asked, "What hasn't changed?"

"I still love you."

"How do you know that? You haven't seen me in nearly a year."

"If you are at all like the woman I left in August last year, you are the woman I love."

"What if I am not? What if..." He moved toward me, and I braced myself.

"Clarissa, you are. You traveled all the way here to me, fulfilling my dreams that we would be together, here in this marvelous place," Gabriel said, a touch of wonder in his voice, his eyes lit with a deep happiness. He traced the edge of my hairline, his gentle touch a balm. "Though you somehow don't see it, you're the brave, intelligent, beautiful woman I have always wanted."

"If you truly believed that, the entire time you were separated from me, why did you wait so long to ask me to join you? Why, Gabriel?"

He paled as he watched tears course down my cheeks. "I was afraid you'd say no. That a life outside of Boston, away from your family, would be unimaginable to you."

"Did I ever give you a reason to doubt me?"

"No, never." He closed his eyes and whispered, "It was my own cowardice. I could only envision a life with you. If you wrote, refusing to join me, I don't know what would've become of me."

"Gabriel," I gasped out, my throat closing up as I fought tears.

"Is this why you are so angry with me? Because I didn't ask you out here sooner?" His smile faded as I pulled away from him. He tipped up my face to his, forcing me to meet his now troubled eyes. "Why won't you be honest with me, darling?"

"I have never lied to you," I rasped.

"No, but you've never told me the whole truth. I need to know. I need to be able to mend whatever is between us."

"Gabriel, I'm so afraid that you can't."

He frowned, and I sensed him searching for a way to encourage me to speak with him. At that moment, Colin entered the living room, and I sighed, uncertain if it was with relief or frustration.

"Hello, Gabe, Clarissa," he said, watching us. "Is all well?"

"Colin, I think it would have been if you had given us a few more moments alone," Gabriel said.

"Well, I'm sorry to disappoint, but I'm filthy and tired from a day at the smithy. Besides, I'm sure Rissa should have a chaperone," Colin said.

"When did you start caring that Clarissa be properly chaperoned?"

"While you were away, playing in Butte," Colin said with a steely undertone. "I'm going to wash up."

"Why is it that Colin is willing to allude to what happened in Boston, and you don't even like to mention it?" Gabriel asked.

I shook my head.

"Do you regret coming here? Regret having to leave your family behind? Is that why you are upset with me?"

"No, of course not. I made the decision to come here."

"Are you waiting for Cameron to come for you? Is that why you don't want me near you?"

"No!" I paled at the thought. "I don't want him. I never did."

"Are you sure? You seemed to think his arrival to Missoula would be welcome news." He glared at me.

"It won't be to me," I whispered as I paled further.

"And it won't be to me," he snapped as I met his stormy blue eyes. He took a deep breath. "So you're saying you want to be here? In Missoula? Away from your family?"

I nodded.

"That you're not mad at me for causing you to leave all of them behind?"

I blinked my agreement.

"That you don't want Cameron?"

I nodded my head vehemently.

"Then why won't you decide to have a full life here? You chose to come here. Can't you choose that?" At my persistent silence, he asked, "Why don't you want to have any type of relationship with me?" He watched me with anguished eyes while I stood there, incapable of responding.

"Damn you," he whispered in a tortured, low voice. "Damn you for coming all this way if you never envisioned what I dreamed." He turned, striding out the door.

I collapsed onto a chair, shaking. Colin emerged from his room in freshly laundered clothes and with damp hair.

"Did Gabe go?" Colin asked with a raised eyebrow.

I nodded as I rose, scrubbing my eyes as I headed to the kitchen area. I opened the oven and began coughing uncontrollably as a waft of black smoke emerged. I reached in and pulled out a burnt chicken from within and began fanning away the smoke with a towel.

"You expect me to eat that?"

"It's not that bad, Col, I promise. The meat inside will be nice and tender," I choked out on a cough as I attempted to blink away tears.

Colin flung open a window and watched me with a dubious gleam in his blue eyes. He grabbed the towel from me and took over the attempt to fan the smoke out the window. After a moment, he stuck his head out the window and gulped some fresh air. "We'll be lucky if the fire department doesn't come, seeing all this smoke."

He turned toward the kitchen again. "For Pete's sake, Rissa, can't you cook?" He swiped at his cheeks at an errant tear from the smoke.

"It's edible, Col, I promise," I said as I attempted to carve the chicken.

"It's red in the middle and charred on the outside. How do you have such talent?"

I glared at him as I dropped a plate in front of him. "I'd eat and stop complaining when you come home to a cooked meal every night."

"If you call this a meal," Colin muttered.

I sat with a thud and stared at my plate. "This part isn't bad," I said as I took a bite of the chicken that had been between the charred and raw sections.

Colin took a long sip of water. "Not as long as you can get past the charcoal taste." After a few minutes of pushing our food around our plates, Colin said, "You need to tell him, Rissa." At my mutinous silence, he said, "He has a right to know."

"I told him about Cameron following us to Butte."

"And?"

"He was upset, although he seems to think I'd welcome Cameron's arrival here."

"Why would he think that?"

I flushed and looked away.

Colin growled, "Did you give him that idea Rissa?"

"I didn't mean to, Col. I wasn't sure if he'd be upset. I thought he might be relieved so he could be with Mrs. Egan."

"Stop it, Rissa, right now. He's been nothing but faithful to you."

"I don't know what to do! How do I talk about what happened?" I asked in an anguished whisper. "Why would he want me once he knows? I don't want him to hate me. To look at me differently."

"Tell him, Rissa. You must have trust in his love for you. Besides, if you aren't honest with him soon, he just might start to look to another for comfort." He watched me intently. "And I want to see you happy. Fully happy again." He gripped my hand for a moment.

"Well, I know what will make you very happy," I said, trying to dispel the serious mood and turn the topic off of myself. "I worried my most recent recipe might be a, well, a, ah…"

"A bloody, inedible disaster," Colin continued.

I shot him an exasperated look at his accurate description. "Anyway," I continued, "I went to the bakery and bought a treat for dessert. I hoped it would last tonight and tomorrow, but…" I sighed as I saw Colin gobble up a quarter of the rhubarb pie I had bought. "Or, we can eat it all tonight." We devoured the pie, finishing off the milk. "Oh, that was delicious." I sighed in contentment, finally feeling full.

"Is there a reason you never learned to cook, Rissa?" Colin asked, leaning away from the table on the back two legs of his chair. He let out a groan, showing his exhaustion after a long day at the smithy. "'Cause I need to eat if I'm going to keep up at the smithy." He sighed again, stretching farther.

I worried he'd fall over, but knew Colin had more grace than I would ever possess.

"We always had a cook!" I protested. "But I'll try to learn. I'm looking for a beginner's cookbook at the depository."

Colin rolled his eyes in exasperation. "You don't need a book, Rissa," he said. "You can read just fine. Somehow everything you make comes out awful. I wish we had money for a cook now." He sighed and yawned.

I frowned at him, upset that my feeble attempts in the kitchen were so lacking.

"Besides," Colin continued, "when you do fully reconcile with Gabe and marry him, he'll need to eat too. I know you never cared about keeping a proper home for Cameron, but you must want one for Gabe." Colin watched me.

"Well, yes, but why must I cook?" I asked, panic-stricken at the thought of having to prepare three meals a day.

"It's the way of things, Rissa," Colin said with a mischievous grin.

"So like a man," I muttered, thinking of Sophie.

Colin laughed, stood and stretched. "'Night, Rissa."

"Good night, Colin," I grumbled as I tried to banish the image of myself in an apron, daily pulling charred, smoking objects from an oven. Then I envisioned Gabriel laughing and embracing me from behind, and it didn't seem an undesirable future.

CHAPTER 37

"I'LL BE EVEN OLDER than Mr. Pickens before I finish organizing these books," I muttered to myself as I put my hands on my hips and glared at a pile on one of the tables. I sighed, and then nearly choked on the dust from the subsequent deep inhalation. I moved toward the window, cracking it open to let in fresh air.

Mrs. Vaughan had been adamant that the windows remained firmly shut to protect the books. She wished she could have the windows permanently sealed, but, as this was rented space, it was not possible. Between the dust, the heat and the occasional pungent visitor, I sometimes worried I would faint dead away. I often had to open the windows to survive.

I perched on the windowsill, breathing the relatively fresh air. I listened to the sounds of the town around me—the horses nickering, the wagons rolling by, the people walking on the boardwalk below, their voices muffled as they carried on conversations. I smiled, feeling like I had finally begun to be a part of this town.

I reached into my pocket to reread part of the letter I had received from my da yesterday.

> *While your stepmother cannot understand your desire to travel to Montana to be with Gabriel, I do. It always seemed to me that you should be with him. He appeared to suit you much better than Cameron. And I know I shouldn't be surprised that you, my brave daughter, was the one to travel to him. I miss you, Clarissa. I hope to hear of your wedding soon.*

I jerked from my reverie as someone cleared his throat. "Ahem." I bumped my head on the window sash, causing myself to nearly topple onto the floor. I caught myself but knew it had been a less-than-graceful moment. I blushed, looking toward the man in the doorway.

"Gabriel," I whispered with a soft smile. I stuffed my letter into my pocket and rubbed my head, trying to ease the ache.

"Hello, Clarissa," he said in his gentle baritone. He studied me for a few moments. "I've wanted to see you. I'd hoped you would come by the workshop."

"Oh, I don't know as that would be proper," I stammered out.

He frowned, his blue eyes showing his confusion while his long, elegant fingers traced the edges of a brown felt hat. A slight sheen of wood dust clung to his faded gray workpants and blue shirt. "When did you begin to worry about what was proper?"

He moved toward me, his boot heels making a resounding *click* on the floor. I backed away a step, and he stilled his movement. His expression chilled. "Why don't you want me near you?"

"Gabriel, I'm sorry."

"For not trusting me? For thinking I would harm you?" His eyes sparked fire as he glared at me and spun on his heel.

"Gabriel!" I called out, but I heard his boots as he descended the stairs.

"That was poorly done, missy," wheezed out Mr. Pickens as he *thump*ed into the room with his cane. "Even if you didn't plan on askin' my opinion, I'm givin' it. Poorly done indeed. That man come here to see if you still wanted him, and you repuffed him," Mr. Pickens said.

I half smiled, realizing he meant *rebuffed.* "I don't mean to act as I do," I croaked out.

"Then tell him, you simpleton," he said. He collapsed into his chair, as though speaking to someone with such limited reasoning ability took more energy than he had.

I shook my head.

"You got to fight for what you want, missy," he said. "It don't just get given to you." He gasped a few times, though I suspected out of exasperation rather than true breathlessness. "Ah." Mr. Pickens sighed. "So that reasonably intelligent brain of yours is finally workin'."

He smiled, clamping his teeth together like I had seen men who smoked pipes clench their jaws.

"What're you goin' to do, missy?" His curiosity and concern lit his face.

I shook my head, thinking things through. "I honestly don't know," I murmured.

"Pshaw!" Mr. Pickens said, waving one hand at me in disgust, rolling his eyes heavenward as though trying to obtain divine help. "You go over there now, missy, and speak with that man. That's what yer goin' to do."

"It would seem impertinent."

"Impertinent my foot," he tried to roar, but it came out weakly on a gasp. "You have to grasp at happiness, missy. No one else will help you grab at it. Go. Go on now. I'll hold down the fort for a while." He smiled his nearly toothless grin.

I walked toward Mr. Pickens and gave him a quick hug. "Thank you, si— A.J.," I whispered, tears choking my throat.

I left the Book Depository and hurried toward Gabriel's workshop. The warm, dry air caressed my cheek as I walked down Higgins toward Main Street, avoiding the restless antics of teenage boys racing on bicycles as I crossed the street.

I arrived at Gabriel's door to find it wide open. I peered inside, allowing my eyes to adjust to the darker interior, looking around for Gabriel. I heard a low muttering off to one side, and the loud *thunk* of metal as a tool hit another tool. I watched as he bent over the workbench, gripping the sides of it as though he were in pain.

"Gabriel," I called out.

He reared up, glancing over his left shoulder before spinning around to face me. I saw happiness flit across his face before he controlled his emotions and pasted on a neutral expression. "Clarissa."

I stood there, uncertain what I wanted to say.

"Come in, Clarissa," he spoke again, in an even gentler tone. "Let me show you my workshop." He held out his hand toward me in welcome.

I nodded, smiling, and entered the room, looking around for the first time. The space was similar to his workshop in Boston, though much smaller. There were two workbenches with tools hanging nearby, a table and furniture in various stages of completion. The main difference I noted was the staircase to the living area overhead, which he did not show me.

He leaned against one of the workbenches, allowing him to be closer to eye level with me. He waited for me to speak, watching me with guarded tenderness, the way he used to when I was with him in Boston.

I smiled at him, gathering my courage to speak. "I'm sorry I reacted to you the way I did, earlier today," I said in a soft voice.

"I want to understand, Clarissa. Help me to understand."

"Gabriel," I said in a low, quivering voice, "I don't..." I broke off at a loss for words. I stared at a place over his shoulder. "I don't know how to explain to you my life in Da's house this past year, especially the past six months." I took a deep breath and then met his eyes. "And Cameron. Cameron was horrid. Worse than you could imagine." I closed my eyes, as though in pain.

"Why didn't you write me the truth?"

"I ... I tried. Some things can't be written," I whispered.

"What was in the letter you were reading today?"

"It's a letter from my da. He was wishing me well. Hoping I found happiness in Montana."

"Why does that make you sad, darling?"

"Because I know I might never see him again. Because he won't be here to share in any aspect of my life. Because I left his house with such anger."

"I'm sure your father understands why you are here. What compelled you to travel such a long distance."

I choked back a sob and bent my head. I brushed away a strand of loose hair from my neck.

"Where is the necklace I gave you?"

"In my room. At the apartment."

"Is it because I took so long to ask you to join me that you removed it?"

"No, Gabriel. My life might have been very different had you invited me sooner. But most likely not. I've been thinking a lot about it, and I know I wouldn't have traveled here until after the convention in Minneapolis even if you'd asked me earlier."

I reached out to stroke his arm for a moment. "I've come to realize what really matters. You did write me. And I'm here now."

Gabriel's eyes flashed with a deep emotion, but he did not reach for me. "It saddens me that you aren't wearing my necklace."

"I never wanted to take it off. You can't imagine what it was like to..."

"To what, Clarissa?" He reached out toward me, and I became rigid in anticipation. He encased my arms with his hands, caressing my upper arms.

I relaxed against his soothing embrace, shock coursing through me.

"Clarissa? Why the tears?"

"No, Gabe, it is nothing," I replied.

A small, pleased smile flickered over his face. "That's the first time you've called me *Gabe* that I can recall." He again caressed my cheek, wiping away an errant tear. "You won't get out of this so easily, Clarissa. Please tell me why you no longer wear my locket. Let me share the burden of this memory. I wasn't there to help you at the time, but I can help you now to forget it."

We shared a long look until I nodded in agreement. I took a steadying breath and reached out to clasp one of his hands with both of mine, holding our hands between us.

"It's all right. Tell me," Gabriel urged, gently massaging the side of my neck with his free hand.

I took another deep breath. "Cameron believed that I would marry him. When he saw me wearing your necklace, he became enraged and ripped it off me."

"I'll kill him if I ever see him again," Gabriel said in a low, lethal voice. "How dare he treat you in such a way?" He gently cupped my face, looking into my eyes. Then his expression turned distant, as though remembering a nearly forgotten fact. "The scarf," he whispered.

"What?"

"Jeremy wrote me about you wearing a scarf when you visited him once at the warehouse. He thought you had an injury because your neck looked red, but you left soon afterward and seemed fine the next time he saw you. It was one of the many allusions from Jeremy about his concern for you." Gabriel's voice and eyes hardened. "That occurred right after Cameron ripped the chain off of your neck."

I nodded.

He looked at me, anger, hurt, regret flitting through his eyes. Finally he closed them for a moment, before opening them to watch me again. "What aren't you telling me, Clarissa?" He continued to study me with his intense blue eyes, daring me to remain silent.

I swallowed once. "I told you why I'm not wearing your locket."

"No, there's more to this that you aren't telling me," Gabriel demanded.

"Don't ask me," I begged. "Not today."

"You must believe, you must understand, that no one, no man, has the right to hurt you, threaten you, make you feel less in any way."

I smiled leaning into him for the first time since my arrival, hopeful for a kiss. At that moment, there was a loud *clunk* on the door as something or someone barreled into it. I jerked away from Gabriel, looking toward the noise. Gabriel glared at the door, appearing upset to have this moment disturbed.

"Uncle! What brings you by?" he asked with a glower.

Aidan stood at the workshop door and glanced at the two of us with a slight squint, studying the scene and the mood. He looked down, seeming distressed to impart whatever news he had to tell. "Well, Gabriel, I hate to ruin the, ah, moment." He paused, and I felt Gabriel tense next to me. "Mrs. Egan's daughter, Anne, is very ill. She sent a message to me at the hotel, after word here went unanswered, and I came to find you."

"Anne? Ill? With what?" Gabriel demanded, dumbstruck. "She was fine yesterday."

"Appears a severe case of dysentery, from the sounds of it," Aidan responded. Gabriel and Aidan stared at one another, as though frozen in place.

I interrupted their silent communication. "We must go to her, at once, to offer whatever help and support we can." I looked toward Gabriel. "She's alone here with a sick baby. She needs help from those she knows. And that would be the three of us, Gabriel."

He nodded. "Is there anything from here we should bring?"

"For now, let's visit, and, if we need something, we can fetch it. It's not that far," Aidan reasoned. "I just hope we aren't too late for that little girl."

CHAPTER 38

WE RACED TOWARD MRS. EGAN'S rented rooms, my mind filled with the rudimentary medicine I had learned during my mama's illness. "Should we call for a physician?" I asked Aidan, trying to keep up with their long strides, the storefronts a blur from the rapid pace of our walking.

"Why don't we see how sick the baby is before deciding," Aidan said as we ascended the rickety stairs.

The smell of illness assaulted my senses the minute I opened the door to the living area. Toys lay sprawled over the floor, dishes were piled in the sink, and the dining room table was covered with cleaned but unsorted laundry.

"Whew," I gasped, blanching and trying not to gag at the stench. I glared at Gabriel who seemed unaffected. "Mrs. Egan, we're here," I called out as I watched Gabriel and Aidan stand by the door, waiting for her to appear. "Mrs. Egan?" I moved toward the sounds of quiet sobbing coming from the bedroom and rushed into the room.

I nearly wretched from the smell upon opening the door, and it took a few moments for my eyes to fully adjust to the dark room. When they finally did, I saw Mrs. Egan huddled in the corner of the room with her baby in her lap. I rushed toward her, but she held up her hand.

"Don't come too close," she whimpered. "Don't become ill yourself." She continued to sob, clasping her baby to her breast, rocking forward and back. "I can't lose her too," she whispered, kissing the baby's forehead.

"Does she live?" I asked.

"Barely."

I turned toward Aidan. "Get a doctor, please, Aidan." He nodded, appearing relieved to leave the sickroom.

I turned toward Gabriel, "Boil water, find clean cloths. Open the windows." I was telling him this but also walking around, doing much of the same. I went to the lone window in the front living area, thrusting it open. Little air entered, but I realized if I left it and the door open, I could sense a bit of a draft.

"No, no, no," cried Mrs. Egan. "The air is bad for her!"

"Mrs. Egan," I said from the doorway, "she needs fresh air. This air is stale and putrid. It needs to be freshened. We had to air my mother's room when she was ill. Trust me." After a moment I asked, "Mrs. Egan, where is Nicholas?"

"I sent him to play with the other children. He'll come home soon," Mrs. Egan sobbed, keening in the corner.

I moved into the living area, to find Gabriel pacing the small space. "Can you find Nicholas, make sure he goes somewhere safe?" I asked. "He can't come here."

Gabriel nodded. "Playing with children? I have an idea where he is. I'll be back as soon as possible." He gripped my arm once before leaving in a rush, and I found myself alone, with a distraught woman and a deathly ill baby.

I returned my thoughts with reluctance to my mother's sickroom. I tried to remember everything that we had done for her. I recalled one eccentric doctor with flaming red hair reprimanding us to frequently wash our hands. Other than that, all I could remember were numerous doctors, useless tonics and advice to "hope for the best." I didn't want to have to resort to the last yet, and I had no tonic to give. I hoped there would be a competent doctor in town.

Gabriel returned twenty minutes later. "Amelia," Gabriel said as he entered her room and crouched in front of her. "I have Nicholas staying with a friend of mine. He'll be fine." He caressed her arm as she rocked Anne. "Amelia?"

"Gabriel, you shouldn't be in here. You could become ill," she whispered.

He squeezed her arm, again rising to join me in the main living area.

"Where do you have him?" I asked, as I moved to stand near the stove, waiting for a pot of water to boil. "I thought Colin might be able to care for him at night, but, during the day, his job at the smithy would pose a problem."

"I brought him to Seb," Gabriel said.

"Seb?" I asked.

"Yeah, Sebastian Carlin. He's the foreman at the local mill. He has the freedom to take on the little tyke and keep him entertained."

"Will he be safe?" I asked.

"He'll be fine. Safer there than here," Gabriel said, a grim light in his eyes.

I began to pace again while Gabriel sat in one of the small chairs, drumming his fingers in a nervous tattoo on the tabletop. After nearly an hour, Aidan returned with the doctor. He seemed young to me, but I reminded myself that youth did not preclude competence.

I watched from the doorway as he coaxed Mrs. Egan to allow him to examine baby Anne. He placed her on the bed and proceeded.

"She seems so tiny to me," I whispered to Gabriel.

"Well, her mum and da aren't all that big," Gabriel said with a half smile.

The doctor murmured a few words to Mrs. Egan and then came out to speak with us. "It's a severe case of dysentery, just as suspected," he stated. "There's not much I can do, I'm afraid. All that can be done is to provide as much fluid for the baby as possible, and hope that she'll maintain a modicum of strength to be able to suck. If she can't, I'm afraid she won't…"

I reached out to hold onto Gabriel's arm, feeling his mounting tension.

"There must be something that can be done for her, Doctor," Gabriel pleaded.

"There is no medicine. She just needs time," the doctor replied. "But, if she can't obtain enough fluids, well…"

"What do you suggest, Doctor, to help us ensure she obtains fluids?" I asked.

"If you can afford it," he said with a quick glance around the impoverished rooms, "I would recommend bringing her to the hospital so that she can be cared for by the nurses. They may attempt a newer treatment for her."

Gabriel moved to Amelia, sitting cross-legged in front of her. "Amelia, did you hear what the doctor recommends? He wants us to bring baby Anne to the hospital. So that they can help her there."

"No, no hospital," Amelia said. "I want her here at home, with me."

"Amelia, don't worry about money—"

"No, Gabriel," she screeched. "I will not have her poked and prodded, and then taken from me when I'm not with her. No."

Gabriel glanced toward me with a shake of his head, then rose and walked toward us in the living area.

I turned toward the doctor. "What can you suggest that we do here, Doctor?"

"Damn stubborn woman. The nuns would take excellent care of her. Better than you will be able to," he hissed. "At this stage, I'd pray for the best."

"No," I snapped, shocking him. "Tell me something useful. Tell me something that might help us keep that baby alive," I growled, waving my hand toward Amelia and baby Anne in the other room.

"Find some way to get fluids into her," he sighed. "Drops from the end of a spoon, a wet cloth, a dropper if you can afford to buy one. Anything to keep her hydrated." He watched me intently. "And if you can, talk sense into that woman and get the baby to the hospital."

"I've heard people say that, when you have dysentery, it's better to dry out, so that then it resolves sooner," Aidan argued in his quiet way.

"Well, those are the lucky ones. Most who would argue that, they either never had dysentery or are dead," the doctor responded.

Aidan grunted his agreement.

"If she is still here, I'll come back tomorrow to check on the baby," the doctor promised as he left.

"Aidan, can you go to the Merc, buy cheap cloth we can use as diapers and cleaning cloths? Cloth that we won't mind throwing away, but that isn't too rough for a baby?" I asked. Aidan nodded his agreement and was gone. Gabriel watched me.

"What?" I asked.

"Why do you always send him on errands first?" he asked.

"Would you like to go on them?"

"Hell, yes. The last place I want to be is in a sickroom."

"Do you think I relish being here?" I asked. I looked up from the stove, tilting my head to one side, studying him.

"No, but it's more of a normal, common thing for women. To be in the sickroom. More normal than for men," Gabriel said.

"That's a weak reason, Gabriel," I retorted. I turned away for a moment, raising my arms in frustration. "Argh!"

"Clarissa?" Gabriel asked.

"Why is it that men always think women are better suited to something simply because it's something they don't want to do? Why can't you just say, 'I don't like doing this. Will you do it for me?' Why is it always couched as 'women do it better?'" I demanded. "I *hate* the sickroom. I loathe it. But I'll be here because I know this is where I need to be. For that baby and that mother. I'll be here. And so should you."

I turned away, entering the room with a ratty basket in which to put the dirty diapers and linens. I planned on burning them, if possible. If that proved impossible, then boiling them in vats of hot water ten times. I saw a window in the far corner of the room—on the opposite side from where Mrs. Egan was seated—and hastened to open it.

"The doctor recommended lots of fresh air for a return to health," I called out, failing to mention that the doctor who recommended that had lived in Boston and had advised it years ago. "Let's see if we can't get a little more air in here." I managed to pry open the window, only to see that it opened onto the back of another brick wall. However, a small draft of air entered, for which I was thankful. I moved hastily around the room, picking up dirty cloths, stowing them in the basket. I decided to leave the basket for the moment until I knew what I was going to do with its contents. It felt like progress to have tidied the room.

I used a portion of the boiled water to clean up a little more. I scrubbed the floor, the walls and the furniture in the sickroom, trying to console Mrs. Egan all the while. Upon exiting the room, I remembered to wash my hands, considering it could not hurt to be a little cautious. Throughout all of this, Gabriel remained silent, following my lead. He tried to help where he could, tidying the main room and continuing to boil water so there was a readily available supply.

"Where is Aidan?" I whispered to Gabriel in the kitchen area. "He should have been back by now."

"He'll be here soon," Gabriel said as he rubbed my back. I arched into his soft caress, the soothing touch easing the ache between my shoulders.

"That feels wonderful," I murmured.

He leaned forward, kissing my nape. "Thank you," he whispered as he released me. I realized it was one of the first times I had not cringed away from his touch. He turned toward the doorway. "Hello, Uncle."

"My timing is terrible, as usual," Aidan said with a smile. "I have what the doctor suggested." He piled cloths and a dropper onto the table. "I also stopped in at the Book Depository to see if I could find a book on home remedies." A thick tome clunked down next to the cloths.

"A dropper! You remembered," I said with a smile. "Let's see if this will work."

I placed some water in the dropper and walked into the bedroom. "Mrs. Egan," I said softly. "Let's try this."

Gabriel leaned over and cradled Anne's head, tilting it back. I sighed as the water dribbled out of the side of her mouth and down the front of her clothes.

"Here, let's try this," Gabriel said as he tickled her throat.

"A few drops," I whispered. I exchanged a long glance with Gabriel. "This is going to take time."

He nodded. "Yes, but we can do it."

CHAPTER 39

GABRIEL MOVED AROUND Amelia's kitchen, making a cup of tea for them both. As the water boiled, he poured it into the pot and sat at the scarred table, waiting for it to steep.

"Amelia, Anne will be fine. The doctor was very reassuring on his recent visit," Gabriel said, smiling as he gripped her hand. "You are fortunate that she didn't have to go to the hospital."

"I can't thank you enough, Gabriel. You, Clarissa and your uncle took such good care of us. And you ensured that Nicholas remained well."

"I told you that I would continue to care for you and the children, Amelia. I meant what I said in Butte. Your friendship is very important to me, and I will find a way to care for those I consider as part of my family."

"I couldn't lose her, Gabriel."

"Nor could I. Not after…" He gripped her hand for a moment longer before releasing it to pour a cup of tea. "Can you do me a favor?" At Amelia's nod, he said, "The next time a doctor recommends the hospital, heed his advice." She smiled and nodded again. Gabriel changed the topic. "When will Nicholas be home?"

"Soon, I think. Your friend, Mr. Carlin, has taken very good care of him."

"Yes, and Colin too," Gabriel said. "I hear they have had many marbles matches."

"Nicholas will be delighted," Amelia said on a long sigh before taking a sip of tea.

"More delighted to be back here with you. He's missed you."

"He's been clingy since Liam. I thought the separation from me would scare him. It couldn't be helped though."

"Better scared than ill," Gabriel said.

Amelia nodded. "Your Clarissa is a fighter, Gabriel."

"I know."

"Have you discussed with her yet what makes her so edgy?"

"No. Though when I do, don't expect me to share it with you," Gabriel said with a lift of one eyebrow.

"Gabriel, I wouldn't. I merely wanted to know, as a friend, if the two of you have begun to find your peace yet."

"We were starting to, the day little Anne got sick. I thought I was finally making headway with her when Uncle interrupted us."

"I'm sorry, Gabriel."

"Never be. We worked together to help baby Anne and you. And I realized again that I don't love Clarissa just for her beauty. I love her for her strength, her determination. You can't know what it means not to have lost her, Amelia."

"I think I can," she murmured.

Gabriel paused for a moment before sighing. "Yes, I know you can. I miss him too." Gabriel gripped her hand. He jolted as the front door flew open, and Nicholas barged in.

"Mama, Mama, Mama!" he called, throwing himself into Amelia's arms. "I'm home!"

"I can see that, little man," she said, kissing his forehead and caressing his face. "It has been too quiet here without you."

"We played marbles an' I beat them most of the time," Nicholas proclaimed as he wriggled out of Amelia's arms and started moving around the apartment. "Where's Annie, Mama?"

"She's resting in her crib in the bedroom," Amelia said.

His shoulders relaxed at that, and he moved toward his toys, pulling out the wooden horse Gabriel had given him for Christmas.

Amelia focused on the man hovering in the doorway. "I will never be able to thank you enough, Mr. Carlin."

"No thanks needed, ma'am. He's a fine boy," Sebastian said. He stood by the threshold, tapping the frame with his fingers as he watched her with intense light brown eyes. "I must be returning to the mill."

"Won't you have a cup of tea?" Amelia asked, a soft blush rising on her cheeks as she looked toward the dishes in the sink. She swiped at her hair in an attempt to brush back strands into her wayward bun.

"No, thank you, ma'am. Good day." He stared at her for a moment more before disappearing.

Gabriel watched Amelia as Sebastian left, marking the racket he made as he descended the dilapidated stairs. "He's a good man, Amelia."

"I'm sure he is or you never would have left Nicholas with him. Thank you again, Gabriel."

He studied her agitation for a moment but shook his head as exhaustion overtook him. "I must return to my workshop. I'll be by soon to check on you all."

***

"RONAN, I CAN'T STAY LONG," Gabriel said as he burst into Ronan's room. Ronan lay on one side toward the sunlight streaming into his room. A pile of books lay on the chair next to his bed, and he looked up from reading one of them. No breeze blew in through the open windows, the still air hot in the second-story apartment.

"Hi, Gabe." Ronan put the book face down. "I haven't seen you in a few days." He scratched his face; his beard was shaggier than usual.

"I'm sorry, Ro. Have you had enough food? Has the nurse continued to come? I can't remember if I asked Colin to check on you." Gabriel looked around the small room, noting its tidy state.

"I'm getting by." He rubbed his stomach as it grumbled. "She only comes in the morning, and I tend to get hungry again by evening."

"I'll go out for food in a moment. I wanted you to know that little Anne is recovering."

"Recovering? Was she ill?" Ronan pushed himself to a sitting position. He brushed unwashed, greasy brown hair out of his alert eyes as he watched Gabriel.

"When's the last time the nurse was in?" Gabriel asked as he focused on Ronan's unkempt state.

"She comes by every day to tidy the room and ensure certain necessities are taken care of. However, she says there's some outbreak of illness, and the hospital is busier'n usual. She hasn't had time to bathe me for a few days."

"Damn," Gabriel said. "We are paying her a decent wage to see to your care, Ronan. I had no idea this was occurring."

"I'm fine, Gabe, just a bit unclean. I'm thankful your Miss Sullivan hasn't visited in a few days. I'd be embarrassed to be seen by her in such a state."

"You know she wouldn't care."

"But I would." He looked away from Gabriel's intense stare. "How is little Anne?"

"Better. At home with Amelia. I won't lie to you though. We almost lost her. I can't imagine what that would have done to Amelia."

"I wish I could have done something to help."

"Yes, well, she's recovering now."

"I wish there was something I could do besides lie in this bed all day long, Gabe."

Gabriel leaned against the windowsill, his long arms crossed against his chest. "Can you think of anything you could do that wouldn't require…"

"Walking?" Ronan said. "Even if I did, Gabe, I'd still need some manner of moving about."

"I'm too tired to think of anything besides finding you some food. We'll talk more about this soon, Ronan. You won't be in this second-floor apartment for long. I promise." He reached over and gripped his arm as he left Ronan's rooms.

CHAPTER 40

A TAPPING ON MY DOOR stirred me from a fitful sleep. I clung to my dreams, even though I was hungry.

"Rissa?" Colin called and tapped louder. "Rissa, wake up. I have food, and, if you aren't hungry, you should be."

"I'm coming, Col, give me a minute," I called out. I rose, nearly tripping because one of my feet had fallen asleep. I stumbled toward the door, crashing into the doorjamb before successfully opening the door.

Colin watched me with a mix of humor and concern in his eyes. "What's wrong with you?"

"Oh, ouch, ouch, ouch!" I hopped to the bed to sit while I massaged my foot. I grimaced as the circulation finally returned.

Colin chuckled, leaning against the doorjamb. "You all right, Rissa?" he asked.

I detected no note of sympathy in his voice and glanced at him, annoyed. "No, I'm not all right," I snapped. "But I will be as soon as my foot wakes up." I continued to massage it, wincing at the pins-and-needles feeling. After a few minutes, it felt normal again, and I paid full attention to Colin. "What did you get for dinner, Col?"

"Dinner?" Colin asked. He moved into my small room, standing near the bed and me. "Oh, well, that was a ploy to get you up. We're going out for dinner."

"Col, I don't want to go out," I groaned as I collapsed back onto the bed.

"Brush your hair, change your dress. Gabriel is anxious to see you."

"How is Anne?" I asked on a huge yawn.

"Anne is fine. I went by a little while ago, and she was sleeping soundly with her mother after having eaten a big meal. And no sign of dysentery."

After hastily washing and donning a light floral calico dress, I walked out to the living room, stopping abruptly at the sight of Gabriel. He stood in the living room in a fresh set of clothes, watching the hallway for my entrance. His eyes lit with pleasure when he saw me. "Gabriel," I whispered.

"Hello, Clarissa," he said moving toward me. I barely flinched as he reached to touch my arm. "You are well?"

"Yes, though still tired."

"I feel I could sleep a year."

"You haven't rested yet?" I asked, grasping his arm, my gaze moving over his weary expression. I raised my hand to his cheek, caressing the three days' worth of stubble. He leaned into my embrace, and, before I knew what had happened, I was in Gabriel's arms with my head tucked under his chin.

"Ah," he murmured, "you have no idea how I have longed to hold you. It hurts that you're afraid of me, darling."

"I'm sorry," I whispered. "It's instinct. I know you wouldn't hurt me."

"I don't understand what could have happened to you to cause you to fear me," Gabriel said. He leaned away, fingers braced along my neck, massaging my tense muscles.

"I'm sorry," I whispered again, lowering my eyes.

"Are we ready?" Colin called out as he entered the room.

"Give us a minute, Col," Gabriel said with a glare at the interruption. Colin moved to the small kitchen area and began whistling. Soon he started singing an offbeat song I had not heard before.

"*Eaaahh aaaaah*," Colin sang with gusto, causing me to glare in his direction, before I bit on my lip to stave off a nervous giggle.

"I realized when we were at Amelia's that I was being unfair to you. I saw you again, against all my hopes and dreams, and began to plan for our future. What if you don't want that future?"

I clung to his hands gently massaging my neck. "I do, Gabriel. I do. Please be patient."

He smiled as some of the tension left him. "Shh ... don't fret. I also realized how unfair I was thinking we could begin again where we left off." He traced a solitary tear down my cheek. "Let me court you again."

"Court me?" I asked. "You would be content with courting?"

"For now, my Clarissa, for now," he murmured. "Though I need you to promise me something." At my long stare where I neither agreed nor disagreed, he said, "I need you to tell me all that happened in Boston. When you are ready."

"I will," I whispered with a jerky nod.

"Good. Let's celebrate. Colin? Do you want to finish your caterwauling and join us?" Gabriel yelled to be heard over his song. The noise from the kitchen ceased, and Colin joined us in the living area.

"What was that horrible song, Col?" I asked.

"Oh, just a new song from the smithy. They're trying to make me into a Westerner by teaching me cowboy songs." Colin's big grin showed his delight at the prospect.

"It's awful," I complained.

"Well, it's only awful 'cause I don't know all the words yet. But I like the yodeling," Colin said.

"I'd hardly call that yodeling," I muttered.

Colin grinned, unperturbed by my comment. "And you think you know how to yodel better? Would you like to come down to the smithy and yodel for the boys?"

I smiled, shaking my head at him.

"Are we ready to meet Uncle Aidan?" Gabriel asked.

We walked to our favorite restaurant, the Buttercup Café, to find Aidan awaiting our arrival. I sat with Colin to my left and Gabriel to my right and across from Aidan. I sighed with contentment, reaching under the table to grip Gabriel's hand.

Early evening light poured into the room, casting shadows on the floor. The assortment of circular, square and rectangular tables were nearly full, with hearty homemade meals such as chicken and dumplings, and steak and potatoes being served every few minutes from the kitchen, situated to the rear of the café.

Partway through our meal, a loud voice bellowed, "Mr. McLeod!" I stilled, my fork halfway to my mouth, dreading having to speak with Mrs. Bouchard tonight.

"Mrs. Bouchard," Aidan said in an elegant French accent, causing her to flutter her eyelashes and giggle at him. He wiped at his mouth with the thin cotton napkin before pulling on the tailored cuffs of his white shirt. His impersonal smile did not reach his eyes as they shone with wary amusement as she neared.

Heavy footsteps heralded Mrs. Bouchard's approach. Tonight she wore a crimson satin dress with silver buttons. Lace at her wrists, neck and hem highlighted the bright red. Aidan turned to smile absently at her, in no way welcoming her to join us.

"Do you have a good reason why this young lady has been absent from the library?" she demanded in her carrying voice, thrusting her hands on her well-endowed hips. She lifted a hand as though to chastise me but then raised it to her neck to itch around the lace. A bright red mark, matching her dress, bloomed there from her scratching.

I cringed as other diners became interested and listened to our conversation. "I sent word with my brother, Mr. Sullivan"—I waved in his direction—"to Mr. Pickens about what detained me."

"Mr. Pickens? Mr. Pickens?" she gasped, placing one hand on her now heaving bosom though the only exertion she had done was breathe. "Why on earth would you entrust such vital information with that man?"

"If that is all, Mrs. Bouchard?" Aidan asked in his most solicitous tone. "I'm sure your young assistant will return to her post tomorrow, none the worse for wear," he said, in a mild tone that brooked no argument.

I nodded in agreement.

She flushed with indignation before flouncing away in a huff. I momentarily pitied her companion until I realized it was Mrs. Vaughan and any sympathy vanished.

"The old bat," Aidan whispered. "Though she isn't a bat, because she's so deaf she has to yell all the time." He shook his head in wonder. "All she wanted was a better look at the two of you together," he said, nodding at Gabriel and me. "She's been most curious about you."

"I wish we could have avoided her," I said.

"There's one like her in every town, Clarissa. At least she's not malicious," Gabriel murmured, playing with my fingers under the table. We finished our meal, but remained at the table, enjoying each other's company over cups of coffee for the men and a cup of sassafras tea for me.

"Ah, it's grand we are all together," Gabriel said.

"I just wish Richard and Jeremy were here too," Aidan replied.

Gabriel was on the verge of replying but was interrupted by the arrival of a tall, wiry man with shocking red hair and a deep booming voice. "Gabriel." He was not quite as tall as Gabriel, but taller than Colin.

"Seb," Gabriel replied with a grin and a quick handshake. Gabriel's voice, nearly as deep, was much quieter and sounded only like a hum in comparison. "Mr. Carlin, may I introduce Miss Sullivan and my uncle, Mr. McLeod? You know Colin."

More handshakes and nods, and then he pulled up a chair to join us. "How are things, Gabe?" Sebastian asked.

"Well enough."

"Good, good. I was happy to see that all was fine now with the missus and little ones this afternoon," he said.

I choked on my sip of tea at the word *missus*, and Colin helpfully pounded on my back. I glanced between the two men, unsure what was going on.

"It's not seemly, Gabe," Sebastian said in his deep voice. Even though seated, he appeared to be in constant motion. His hands gestured; his hips moved from side to side or rocked forward in his chair; his head bobbed when he made a point. But his eyes were the most expressive aspect of him because they were a rich honey brown that eloquently showed his feelings.

"She's no one's *missus*, Seb," Gabe said, taking a small sip of coffee. "Not anymore."

"But if she's to be yours..." he started, with another long look.

Gabe just watched him with a curious expression. "What is it, Seb?" he asked. When he saw Sebastian hesitate, he said, "You're among friends. The restaurant is virtually empty. What is it that you want to say?"

I saw Gabriel's jaw twitch, betraying his tension.

Sebastian spoke in a fast, low voice. "I'm saying that it ain't right to play that good woman false just 'cause your other lady love come to town."

I gasped. Colin started pounding me on the back again, though for no reason because I'd not had a sip of tea, and Aidan started to laugh. I glared at Aidan as I tried to edge away from Colin and his overzealous desire to aid me.

"Young man, if you want her so badly, then go ask her if she'll have you," Aidan said to Sebastian.

I saw Gabriel smile, then Colin's arrested expression and realized belatedly the reason for Sebastian's concern.

Sebastian fidgeted worse than before. Tapping his foot, running his hand around the brim of his hat, moving around on his seat. "I didn't mean that," he protested.

"I think you did," Aidan said, watching him, a grin playing around his mouth.

"She'd never want the likes of me when she could have someone like..."

"She can't," Gabriel said, watching his friend. "She can't have me, Seb. She's always known that. It's only the gossips of this town that made it seem we were ever more than friends." He glowered toward where Mrs. Bouchard and Mrs. Vaughan had sat. "So all that's stopping you is you."

"How's Nicholas?" I asked, joining the discussion.

"He's a pistol." Sebastian glowed as he spoke of him. "Such a great kid. I'm teachin' him songs from the mill."

"Do you play marbles?" I asked.

"You bet," Sebastian said with a smile. "Nicky and I are to have a tournament."

"It's nice you have a nickname for Mrs. Egan's children." I took a sip of the sassafras tea as I hid my smile with my teacup. "You seem quite taken with little Nicholas."

"Who wouldn't be?" Sebastian asked. "Mrs. Egan's doing a fine job raising those two youngsters on her own."

"Hmm ... yes, on her own," Colin said with a wink in my direction.

"Think about it, Seb," Gabriel said. "She'll be needing support and protection again soon, from the likes of..." He broke off, and they shared a long stare. Sebastian nodded, seeming to be lost in thought.

I yawned. "I must beg your pardon." I stifled another yawn. "Colin?" I looked toward him.

"Hmm ... oh, yes," he said, hopping up, offering me his arm.

I wished I could walk on Gabriel's arm, but now that I had accepted Colin's, I needed to walk home with him.

Colin leaned down and whispered to me, "Less talk this way, Rissa, if you walk with me," followed by a small wink.

Gabriel joined us as we walked home talking companionably, with Gabriel and me only sharing a long look before I retired for the night.

CHAPTER 41

"MR. PICKENS!" I CALLED OUT as I entered the Book Depository the following day, opening the windows to attempt to refresh the stale air.

"Missy," he replied in a wheeze, poking his head out of the back room. "'Bout time you came back. That youngun's on the mend?"

"She's getting stronger every day," I reassured him.

"Good," he said, each step resonating with a loud *thunk* from his cane. "But that ain't all that's put such a bloom in those cheeks of yours, missy," he said, watching me with a twinkle in his eyes. He collapsed onto his chair, winded from his short walk.

I blushed, meeting his gaze. "Of course not. But I'm sure you've heard all about it by now."

"You bet," he said, laughing his bagpipelike laugh. "Heard all about the shameless young woman we'd hired having dinner with that feckless carpenter at a restaurant last night. Seems you were entirely too circumference for them, missy."

"Circumference?" I asked.

"Yes, you know, missy. Too tight-lipped for their liking. You've gotta learn to give them a bit of gossip here and there if you want to have your share of peace," he said, nodding.

"*Circumspect!*" I said, after puzzling out his word.

"That's it, missy! You're a walkin' dictionary," he said, thumping the floor once with his cane for good measure. "Now, missy, you ain't 'bout to get me off of my topic of choice," he watched me with knowing eyes. "What happened between you and that strapping young man who came here mooning over you a few days ago?"

"Who you sent me after," I retorted.

"Naturally. One of us has to have some sense."

"Well, in any case, it has all turned out well." I was unable to hide my broad smile.

"When's the weddin'?"

"Sir!"

"Well, that's why you came all this way, ain't it?" he asked, enjoying my reaction.

"Of course, but nothing has been discussed yet," I said, turning away toward one of the tables in an attempt to conceal my anxiety at the thought of marriage. "If you must know, we are … courting again."

"Courtin'," Mr. Pickens said. "Hmm … well, I wouldn't dither too long if I was interested in a young pretty girl like you. Doesn't do no good to waste time when you already know what you want." He laughed aloud. "I sure didn't let my Bessie wait! Best not to let her come to her senses, that's what I thought." He wheezed out a few more laughs.

"Mr. Pickens, can you tell me stories about what life has been like here in Missoula?"

"It's A.J., missy," he chastised before continuing. "Ah, it was a great place to be young," he wheezed. "My Bessie 'n' me came out here from St. Louis in '69. It was a small town, much smaller than now. Only a couple hundred or so people. My uncle Pete lived here, worked at one of the local stores, Wordens and Company, and said it was a good place to live," he said. He closed his eyes, lost in thought, smiling. "Ah, those letters home, writin' about the glories of this place. Well, it just set a fire in my blood, to come out here and see what he was seein'. An' poor Bessie had to come along or be left behind. She was none keen on that, so she came. But it was some journey."

"How did you travel here?" I asked.

"There was no train then, missy," he said, looking at me over the rim of his reading glasses. He had moved his chair to the table where I was working, pretending to help me sort books, and so had put on a pair. "How d'ye think we got here?" He nodded as he watched me. "Wagons. Good ol' godforsaken wagons." He sighed again. "God, they hurt your, er, nether regions by the end of the day!

"You laugh, missy, but it was torture." He frowned. "And the heat, comin' across the prairies. Praying you'd have enough food, enough water. I hated it," he said. "It seemed endless, as though we would never cross the prairie. Then there was the added fear of an Indian raid." He shook his head ruefully. "Though there was less chance in '69 than before, but still a chance."

"Yet you still decided to come," I remarked. "You couldn't have been a young man in 1869."

"I ain't as old as I look, missy," he retorted. "An' Bessie, bless her, had a frontier spirit," he said with pride. "Though I never would've known that living in St. Louis. Ah, she was a one. Organizin' the women on the journey, rationin' our food and water so we always had enough. Not plenty, mind, but enough."

"Were you happy when you arrived?" I asked. "Did it seem worth it?"

Mr. Pickens let out a rattling laugh, slapping his knee in his enjoyment. "Lord, no, not at first. We arrived, an' I couldn't believe what a small, inconsequence town it was."

"Inconsequential?" I asked.

"Exactly," he wheezed out another laugh. "I couldn't imagine all the fuss over a few small buildings and dirt roads." He sighed. "But then we'd made the long journey, and there weren't no goin' back. Winter was coming, and we had little money. So we stayed."

"But you like it here?" I asked, fighting down my unspoken doubts.

"Oh, missy, it's grand now. Nothin' like the town I came to over thirty years ago."

"What are some of the exciting things that have happened?"

"Plenty of saloon fights. There was the unfortunate shooting of Mr. Higgins's son, God rest 'im."

"Mr. A.J., there must have been other more interesting things to have happened in the past twenty years than brawls and murder."

He watched me and then smiled his near toothless grin. "Ah, missy, you wish to hear tales of the old days."

"I do."

"Well, there was the time we all acted like a herd of sheep, scared of our own shadows, hidin' in Wordens or the Merc 'cause we heard rumor that the Nez Perce were comin' to pay us a visit," he said, watching me over his glasses, shaking his head in disgust. "Which they never did. They just wanted to go their way, find Canada, a bit of peace. 'Course, some here got a fire in their blood at the thought of killin' some Indians." Another shake of his head followed.

"You have different ideas about Indians than others I've met," I said. "I'd have thought it rational to be scared after the stories I've read and heard."

"Well, fear is a strange thing, missy, and makes some people act in ways you never thought they would. And I s'pose I don't have the same mind as others 'bout the Indians 'cause my father was a trapper as a young man before he settled in St. Louis and married my mother. He met plenty of Indians, always had good things to say about 'em. Got him out of a fix a time or two. Fierce negotiators. And wanting to protect their home, but then don't we all?" he asked me.

"A few years back, old Chief Charlo and his people were hauled off their land down the Bitter Root. They moved on up toward the Flathead Res, but I can't imagine that could be takin' the place of being on your own land, the land of your ancestors and seeing those mountains every day," he said.

"The Bitter Roots?" I asked.

"Don't you know nothin' about geography, missy?" He waved his arms around as though drawing a mountain range with his hands. "South of Missoula. Beautiful valley, big mountain range. Quite pretty." At the quick shake of my head in denial he again looked heavenward as though for help. "Ask that young man of yours to take you there someday."

I nodded.

"Well," Mr. Pickens continued, "one day some years ago, they had to leave their land. They marched as proud as could be through downtown. All done up in their Indian clothes, beads flashin' in the sunlight, men with their face paint on, herdin' whatever animals they had. About two hundred of 'em. All peaceful. Scared some silly ninnies senseless, but, for those of us who watched their march, it was beautiful. But it made me sad. All those people, dispossessed, an' walking with such pride. Reminded me a bit of the War."

"What else do I have to look forward to here?" I asked after a few moments, wishing to turn the topic and lighten the mood again.

"You'll see plenty of parades. It seems people like any excuse to march about. And the men always like a pretty lady waving at them as they do," he said with a grin.

He sat up as he continued talking. "But, missy, I'll tell you 'bout my favorite memory. It occurred one dark, cold night, when I waited outside the theater to see Mr. Mark Twain." He sighed. "Now I may not like books much, missy, but that man can make me laugh."

"You met Mr. Twain?" I set down the books I had been sorting to pay full attention.

He nodded, his eyes full of mischief and glee. "I remember that night like it was yesterday." He closed his eyes as though to more accurately recapture that moment in time. "The hint of wood smoke in the air, the stars shinin' overhead." He opened his eyes, piercing me with an intense gaze. "Ah, missy, I felt so alive!

"I was standin' outside the theater, hopin' for a glimpse of the man," he continued. "There was a small crowd of us there, those of us who either couldn't get tickets or couldn't afford 'em. We could hear the crowd, laughin' and guffawin' at the man's talk. Some would try to pass on a story out to us, but, by the time it got to me, it was so wrangled, I saw no humor in it."

He sighed. "But then it might have just needed to be told by a man like Mr. Twain." He glanced over my shoulder, lost in his recollection. "I remember standin' there, enjoyin' the night sky, wishing I could hear him speak, when all of a sudden I was grabbed and pushed into the theater."

I gasped, gripping my hands together.

"I sputtered and attempted to break free of the arms, but I wasn't as strong as I used to be," he admitted. "Mr. Twain had said he would like to have a drink with any man who had worked the Ol' Miss, and friends of mine knew I had. They had called out my name and then pushed me forward.

"Next thing I knew, there I was, in the front of the crowd, with Mr. Twain. He seemed right pleased there was a man in Missoula who had worked the Mississippi. I was pushed, prodded and propellered up to the stage, all the time thinkin' I must be in a dream. Just like one of Mr. Twain's stories." Mr. Pickens's eyes shone with a brilliant light, emanating excitement. "An' there I stood, little ol' me, in front of himself, Mr. Twain," he said in awe.

"I felt a right fool, standin' on that stage with nothin' clever to say. I felt like a mute, but Mr. Twain didn't seem to mind. No, not Mr. Twain. He clapped me on the back, as happy as could be to see a former river rat so far from home," he said, beaming his nearly toothless grin at me.

I stood still, mesmerized by his tale.

"Mr. Twain spoke a few moments on the splendor of the river, and then I left the stage." He closed his eyes again, as though imagining the moment. "But Mr. Twain made sure I stayed inside, missy, so as to hear what he had to say rather than count on those hooligans tryin' and failin' to get it right."

He watched me for a moment. "I never did get that drink with Mr. Twain. No, those men from the Fort wanted their own time with him and whiskered him on out of the hall as soon as he finished." He gave a long sigh, as though imagining what having a drink with Mark Twain would have been like.

"An' my poor Bessie." He sighed again, this time with contentment, shaking his head from side to side, his voice filled with no discernable remorse. "Had to live with a trumped-up ol' goat like me for weeks afterward. I don't know how many times that woman listened to me tell the same story, but she never complained, not my Bessie." A peaceful silence remained between the two of us for a few moments.

"Thank you for sharing that story with me, Mr. A.J."

"You're welcome, missy. Now my Bessie's gone, and I'm alone in the world with my memories for company. Some good, some bad. But what's done is done, an' there ain't no goin' back. Least not for the likes of me," he muttered.

I shivered at his words and knew that I needed to speak with Gabriel. For Mr. Pickens was correct: there was no going back. Not for me.

CHAPTER 42

AFTER LEAVING THE DEPOSITORY, I wandered along the Higgins boardwalk in the direction of the Missoula Mercantile—or Merc as the locals called it—interested to see if it would compare to the stores in Boston. It stood on the corner of Front and Higgins, about a block from the river and across the street from the Florence Hotel. I wandered inside, impressed at the number of clerks eagerly awaiting my arrival. Everything I could imagine wanting or needing appeared to be available for purchase. Although it didn't have the grand style of the Hennessy Building in Butte, I was delighted to find such a store in Missoula.

I passed through the children's department. My eyes lit upon a small baby's rattle, and I immediately thought of Anne. I decided to buy it for her and opted for a set of tin soldiers for Nicholas. I left the Merc content with my purchase and strolled toward Amelia's.

While walking down the west side of Front Street, I saw numerous saloons and *hurdy gurdy* establishments, as Mr. Pickens would call them. I kept my eyes downcast after seeing one female in a shocking state of undress.

I knocked on Amelia's door.

"Clarissa, Miss Sullivan," Amelia said, startled at my arrival.

"Hello, Mrs. Egan. May I come in?" I fidgeted with the bag from the Merc. "I'm sorry to intrude. I know I wasn't invited."

"Yes, yes, of course you are welcome. It's always a pleasure to see you," she said, opening the door fully. She blushed as I noted the unkempt state of the kitchen.

"How is Anne?" I asked.

"On the mend," she said with a bright smile as she blinked away tears.

"Nicholas has been very demanding and clingy after his days with Mr. Carlin."

"I imagine he feared losing you too."

"I know you're right, but it's hard to accomplish anything with a toddler attached to your leg."

"It seems you were finally having a moment's peace, and I've interrupted it," I said looking around.

"Anne is settled in for her nap, and Nicholas is off playing marbles again with Mr. Carlin. They are having some sort of tournament. He has been very kind," Amelia said waving toward a dining room chair. She looked toward the kitchen area with distress. "Might I offer you a cup of ... a glass of water?" she asked.

"Oh, yes, a glass of water would be lovely," I said with a smile.

After settling at the dining room table, I opened the parcel I had purchased. "I was walking by the Merc on the way here and thought I'd like to find a little gift for Nicholas and Anne. I saw these and thought they'd like them." I held out the small rattle I had bought Anne.

"Oh, Anne will love this," Amelia said with a sigh.

"I found this for Nicholas," I said, holding up the box of tin soldiers.

She smiled again, gently touching the objects.

"Last I bought a nice packet of English Breakfast tea for you. I thought it would be a nice pick-me-up for you after the worry about Anne." I gave her a smile, watching hers become more tremulous as tears threatened. I reached out to grip her hand.

"Thank you," she whispered. "You can't know what it is like to have a woman's friendship. Gabriel is wonderful, but..." She sniffled as she fought tears.

"Amelia, I think I can. I left all of my friends behind when I traveled here." We sat in a companionable silence for a moment. "May I ask you something?" I blurted out. At her nod, I asked, "Why did you not pressure Gabriel to marry you after your husband died?"

"Gabriel is a good man and a wonderful friend. But I know what it is to feel cherished and beloved by a husband. Although I must admit, there have been times, like when we were leaving Butte, that I wanted to marry him to stem the gossip. And yet I knew it would be wrong to snare him into only half a life. Half a marriage." She paused. "And I'd like more for myself."

"I would too," I murmured. I glanced toward the kitchen, deciding to change the subject. "Amelia, you know how to cook."

"Cook? Yes. Yes, I do. My mother was a great cook and taught me," she said with a touch of pride.

"Do you think you could teach me?" I asked. "I'm trying to run a house with my brother Colin, but I can't cook. I'm afraid one of my concoctions someday will do us bodily harm."

Amelia giggled and sounded girlish for the first time.

"What if you helped me cook by teaching me very basic recipes to start, and, when I learn how to make those, I'll graduate to more difficult things." I paused for a moment, thinking further. "We can cook in our rooms, Colin's and mine, and then we could all have dinner together! I'm used to larger family dinners."

"That sounds a lovely idea," she said. "When would you like to start?"

"Is tomorrow too soon?" I asked. "Poor Colin comes home nearly faint with hunger every night, and we can't continue to go out for meals."

"Tomorrow is perfect," she said.

"I leave the Book Depository by four. Why don't you come by sometime after that?"

"The Book Depository?" she asked. "You work there?"

"Yes, I do. I think you'd enjoy Mr. Pickens. He's the best thing about the depository. Well, except for all the books."

"Oh, I'd love to be surrounded by books again. I had to leave almost all of mine behind in Butte, and I miss them. I was a schoolteacher in my old life, and I loved it."

"So was I!"

"I remember Gabriel talking about you. How proud he was of your teaching. Who is Mr. Pickens?"

"Stop by some day and I'll introduce you."

"Mama, Mama, Mama!" Nicholas shouted as he barged into the room. He threw himself against Amelia's legs. "I won!"

"That's wonderful, darling," she murmured with a quick stroke of his hair at the nape of his neck.

"Hello, Mr. Carlin," I said as I turned to watch Sebastian. He leaned his beanpole frame against the doorjamb, a slight sunburn enhancing the freckles on his face and neck. His light brown eyes shone as he watched the reunion between Amelia and her son.

"Mr. Carlin," Amelia gasped, standing.

"Mrs. Egan. Always a pleasure to see you," he said in his deep voice. "Now that Nicky's home, I must be gettin' back to the mill. Miss," he nodded toward me. "Mrs. Egan." A deeper nod and a longer look, and then he was gone.

Amelia collapsed onto her chair as Nicholas wandered over to play in the small living room near the door.

"Amelia, are you all right? You look like you're going to faint dead away," I whispered.

"I'm fine. I just hate that he saw such disorder in my house. I keep a fine home."

"I'm sure no one worries about such things," I soothed. "Besides, caring for your daughter was more important than washing dishes." After an awkward pause, I murmured, "He seems a nice man and has taken to Nicholas. And he's friends with Gabriel."

"Are you matchmaking?"

"No, merely pointing out the obvious," I said with an impish smile.

"I feel disloyal to Liam even considering marrying another man," she rasped. "He died so recently. And yet I can't raise them alone. I'm not someone who ever wanted to be alone."

"Amelia, from all I've ever heard about Liam, he was a kind, devoted man who loved you dearly. I like to think such a man would want you happy." I clasped her hand as she tried to blink away tears.

"Then you don't think I'm shameless to consider marrying again?"

"No, not at all. Though I hope you can take the time you need to mourn Liam."

"I will never stop mourning him," Amelia said with a grief-thickened voice. "And yet I know I can't live in the past. It's not fair to the children."

"Nor to you." I squeezed her hand and rose. "I'll pass by the grocer's tomorrow. I'll see you around four?"

"That works well. Thank you, Clarissa. I have desperately needed a female friend."

"So have I, Amelia."

***

I KNOCKED ON RONAN'S DOOR, hitching a heavy basket from one hand to the other.

"Come in."

"Hello, Mr. O'Bara," I said as I entered. "I haven't visited recently and wanted to see how you were before I returned home for the evening. I just visited Amelia, and then remembered I had books for you, so I went home to collect them."

He smiled at me as he pushed himself up on his knuckles. "Thank you for all the books you've brought me. They help pass the time."

"Oh, you're welcome. I brought a few more I thought you might like. I found books by H. G. Wells as I was organizing yesterday, and I thought you might find them interesting."

"Thank you, Miss Sullivan."

I set the heavy basket with books next to him on the bed and then turned toward the empty chair. I unpinned my hat, set it at the foot of his bed and sat for a moment.

"Are you well, Miss Sullivan?"

I threw him a nervous glance and then rose to pace the small confines of his room. My heels clicked on the pine planks with each step. "I've just invited Amelia to my apartment tomorrow afternoon. She's to teach me to cook."

"You couldn't have picked a better instructor. She always made the best meals in Butte."

"But that's just it. I'm a disaster in the kitchen! I'm lucky the entire building hasn't burned down already with the dinners I've attempted to cook." Ronan laughed and I grinned at him before giggling.

"I have a hard time imagining you're that bad."

"Picture the worst cook you can. Then multiply it by ten. That's me."

"What has you so worried, Miss Sullivan?" Ronan asked as he continued to chuckle.

I collapsed into the chair in the corner. "I knew what my role was in Boston. Well, until it was taken away from me. I was a teacher and a daughter and a sister. I wasn't expected to cook or clean or sew. My sewing's even worse than my cooking if you can believe it."

"I saw your socks," Ronan said with a half smile and a shake of his head.

I threw him a disgruntled glare before grinning. "Well, you see what I mean? What do I have to offer Gabriel?"

"Besides your love and friendship, your loyalty and affection?" He raised an eyebrow and watched me with amused humor glinting his brown eyes.

"Mr. O'Bara—"

"No, Miss Sullivan. Anyone can cook and clean and do all those domestic things. Well, almost everyone because you can't. But you are the only one who makes his heart sing with joy at the mere mention of your name. Don't discount that. Don't try to change yourself into something you think he wants when all he wants is the woman you already are."

I blinked rapidly to prevent tears from pouring down my cheeks. "Thank you, Mr. O'Bara."

"I don't believe you could be as horrible a cook as you describe."

"Just to test that theory, would you like to come to dinner with all of us tomorrow? It would give you a chance to get out of this room and see something different."

"How would I get there?"

"I imagine Colin and Gabriel could manage," I said. "Will you come? I'd love to have you to our place, and I know it would do you a world of good to leave these rooms, if only for a little while."

"Yes, Miss Sullivan. I accept. I look forward to eating your first edible meal."

CHAPTER 43

July 8, 1901

My dearest Clarissa,

I received your letter today informing me of your journey to Montana. I have been terribly worried about you, and I am delighted that you are finally reunited with Gabriel. Has this turned out as you had wished, Clarissa?

I should warn you that Jonas has had word from Cameron, and it appears that he is headed to Missoula. Somehow he traveled to San Francisco, but he is headed back toward you again. Take care, dearest.

Jonas is irate, stating that your behavior reflects poorly on us and demanding I have no further contact with you. I, on the other hand, could not be more thrilled that you have eluded one such as Cameron. Be happy, dearest cousin.

I feel well, although many of my clothes are becoming too tight to wear. I am very excited about this pregnancy. I know Jonas says he would like a boy, but I am secretly hoping for a girl.

I miss you, dear cousin. Write me when you have the opportunity, though it would be best to mail your letters to my parents. Give Colin a big hug for me. I hope he has enjoyed his adventure and is finding that the trip to Montana was as much for him as for you.

Your Loving Cousin,
Savannah

At a knock on the door, I shook myself free of thoughts of Boston. "Gabriel," I said with a quick smile as I moved backward to allow him to enter.

"I thought I would see how you were today as you didn't come by the workshop."

"Oh, I stopped to see Amelia and Ronan after work," I said, turning toward the living room.

"Why are you upset?" He stopped my movement away from him with a gentle hand to my arm.

I stilled, thankful I did not flinch.

He lowered his hand with a questioning look.

"I received a letter from Savannah. She is well."

"What did she write that you found unsettling?"

"Cameron is traveling to Missoula. He was in San Francisco, but now he's coming back here," I whispered unable to hide the panic from my gaze.

"Why is he so intent on you, Clarissa?"

I shook my head.

"What aren't you telling me? Why does the thought of Cameron coming here terrify you?"

"Gabriel, I told you about the locket…" I said.

"Yes. There's more though, isn't there?"

A long silence.

"Why won't you trust me?" he asked in an anguished whisper, moving toward me. I flinched, causing him to curse. "Dammit, I thought we were past that."

"You would never…" I said, my face contorting with pent-up tears as I tried to turn away.

"You're right. I'll never understand until you tell me," Gabriel said with a fierce tenderness, grasping my face between his palms. "Make me understand."

I had lost all strength and crumpled to the floor, a shivering, sobbing mess. Gabriel sat beside me, eventually pulling me onto his lap, enveloping me in his warm, soothing embrace. "Tell me, darling. I can't help you until you tell me."

"I don't want you to hate me," I whispered.

"I could never hate you. I love you," he said, kissing my cheeks and brushing away my tears. He nuzzled the side of my face, waiting. As I remained silent, he murmured. "Do you want to know what I think happened?"

I shrugged, words beyond my ability at the moment.

"I think Cameron did more than rip a necklace off your neck. I think he tried to break your spirit. Attempted to make you think that no man would ever want you but him. And he … he…" At this Gabriel stopped, not wanting to say the words. "And he forced you. He did the unthinkable."

"Yes," I breathed out, burrowing into Gabriel's embrace.

"How did it happen?"

"At my house. Mrs. Smythe had invited him for tea and then had left us alone in the parlor. When he realized I had no intention of accepting him, of marrying him, he said he would make me realize I was his only option. Oh, Gabriel, it's all my fault! If I had paid closer attention. If I'd fought harder…" I wailed, tears continuing to fall. "I couldn't stop him. He was so strong, and he wouldn't listen to my pleas to stop. Why did he do that, Gabriel?" I sobbed into his neck.

Gabriel's grip tightened but never to the point of pain. He was silent for a long moment, and I worried he was disgusted by me. Then he took a deep, steadying breath. "Clarissa, you are not to blame," he said in a low voice.

"How can you not blame me when I blame myself?" I asked, turning devastated eyes to him.

"Because you should never have been in that position," Gabriel said with tear-brightened eyes. "Your stepmother knew what she was doing. And there was no way you could fight off a grown man, darling." He caressed my cheek. "If I hadn't left. If I'd stayed…" Gabriel closed his eyes for a moment before opening them and looking at me with unutterable torment. "Will you ever be able to forgive me, Clarissa?"

"I was so afraid of losing you. Of telling you the truth. And yet I had to come. I had to escape."

"Thank God you did," he murmured into my hair, stroking my back in a soothing pattern.

"It's why I had to leave my da's house. I couldn't stay there, be anywhere near that room."

"Darling," Gabriel groaned as he kissed my head and rocked me.

"Can you be patient with me?"

"I can wait forever, now that we are together again," he said, leaning back to meet my eyes. "I need you to do something for me." At my nod, he continued. "I need you to tell me when I have upset you or reminded you of something that bothers you."

"I will try, Gabriel," I murmured as I collapsed against his chest. "I'm sorry. I'm so tired."

"Then sleep for a few moments. Let me hold you," he said, kissing my head as he leaned against the wall with me on his lap.

I don't know how long I slept, but I awoke to hear Gabriel speaking with Colin. "Quiet, Col."

I jerked in Gabriel's arms, but then relaxed as Gabriel continued to stroke my back.

I heard Colin sigh and then collapse onto one of the chairs. "So she's told you?"

"Yes. Though I have a question for you." Gabriel's voice rumbled, amplified in my ear by my check against his chest. "Why is that bastard still alive?"

"Because Clarissa needed my help to escape. First Da's house and then to Montana. She didn't need me in jail for murder."

"If I ever see him again…"

"You'll get in line," Colin growled.

"And now he's headed to Missoula," Gabriel said with a gentle kiss to my head.

"Jedediah didn't head him off then?" Colin asked.

I gave up pretending to be asleep and joined the conversation. "Savannah sent word that Jonas said he's on his way here. And Mr. Maloney must have done something as Cameron ended up in San Francisco." I heard Colin snicker and Gabriel snort.

"Good ol' Jed," Gabriel said. "I didn't know him well, but a kinder man you couldn't find." I tried to rise from Gabriel's protective hold, but he murmured, "Let me hold you a little longer, love."

I relaxed into his embrace and kissed his cheek as I settled.

"What are we going to do about Cameron?" Colin asked.

"You can't shoot him," I mumbled, a complete enervation having overcome me in Gabriel's arms.

"Now, Rissa," Colin said.

"I won't have either of you going to jail," I said in as strong a voice as I could muster.

"Then you'll have to do something else to foil him," Colin said.

"Colin…" Gabriel warned.

I snuggled closer as he spoke.

"What are we eating for dinner?" Colin asked.

"Why don't you cook?" I asked, finally turning to look at him.

"I wouldn't muck it up any worse than you, Rissa. I just wish you'd learn someday," he said.

"As it so happens, I'm going to learn to cook from Amelia," I said with a small smile.

"Are you?" Gabriel asked with a grin, watching me with frank amusement. "Whose idea was it?"

"Mine. I realized she might know quite a bit about cooking, and she could teach me. When I visited her today, I knew I needed to find some way to help her that didn't seem too much like charity."

"And how will you manage that?" Gabriel asked.

"She'll teach me to cook, then she and the children will have dinner with us," I said, smiling as I thought through my plan.

"Well done, darling," Gabriel said with an approving nod.

"It's too bad we couldn't get your friend Ronan up here," Colin murmured. "I imagine he'd like a good home-cooked meal."

"The stairs would be too much for him," Gabriel said.

"But surely, between the two of us, we could carry him the short distance from his place and up the stairs," Colin said with an arched eyebrow.

"I'm glad you agree, as I've already invited him."

Gabriel chuckled and gave me an affectionate squeeze. "That would be grand. To have us all together for dinner. And we'll invite Uncle Aidan too."

"A family dinner like we used to have in Boston, Col," I said.

"Yes, but this one with our Western family," he said.

I sighed with contentment as I snuggled into Gabriel's embrace.

CHAPTER 44

I CLAMBERED UP THE STAIRS to the Book Depository, making more noise than usual, looking forward to focusing on the arduous task of arranging books rather than on tonight's dinner and Cameron.

"Mr. A.J.!" I called out. I pulled off my hat and light coat, setting them aside with my gloves. "Good morning!"

"Hello, missy," he said in his wheezy voice, slowly making his way to his chair. He plopped onto it, taking a deep, rattling breath. He watched me for a few moments, seeming curious about my frenetic movements around the room. "You sounded like a herd o' buffalo comin' up those stairs. What's got you so riled?"

"Nothing. I'm fine," I said, slamming down a stack of books with a loud thud.

"It's plain for anyone to see, missy," he said, concern in his gaze. "You haven't fought with your young man, have you?"

"No, we didn't fight, no," I said. I collapsed onto the miniature wooden stool I had found for myself, ready for a small chat.

"If you're confused by somethin' he did or didn't do, missy, I've always found it best to go straight to the horse's mouth. But he ain't here. Tell me what happened."

I looked behind me to ensure we were alone and no other patrons had entered. I was confident I could hear the heavy footsteps of Mrs. Vaughan or Mrs. Bouchard if they decided to pay us a visit. "I am to make dinner tonight, and I'm nervous he'll realize how unsuitable I am to all things domestic."

"Haven't you cooked since your arrival?"

"Nothing edible," I muttered.

"Don't they teach young ladies nothin' of use out in that big fancy city?" He wriggled his eyebrows at me.

I laughed. "No, nothing of use. And I didn't learn well the lessons they attempted to instill, so I have very little of practical use to offer."

"Now I doubt that, missy," Mr. Pickens protested. "You were a teacher. That's valuable."

"Maybe valuable, but not practical," I countered. "Doesn't help me at night when I can't cook chicken or bake bread. I nearly had to call the firefighters to put out the roast I cooked the other night!"

At Mr. Pickens's guffaw, I giggled. "How in blazes are you cookin' tonight?"

"I found someone to teach me," I said.

"Who?"

"Amelia Egan."

"You're tellin' me that you got the woman—who everyone says he jilted so as to return to you—to teach you?" he asked.

"Yes, that about sums it up," I said with a broad smile.

"Well, I'll be," he said as he tried to whistle. He moved to the back room while I began to work.

By midafternoon, I was tired of my own thoughts and wanted some company. "Mr. A.J.," I said as I moved onto another stack of books. I had successfully sorted about one-fourth of the stacks, but much hard work still lay ahead. I glanced longingly at the bare walls, wishing I were arranging the books on shelves. My gaze veered over to the doorway, watching Mr. Pickens make his way out of the back room. I waited for him to settle on his chair before I continued.

"You wanted me, missy?" he asked. "You done broodin'?"

"Yes, Mr. A.J.," I said. "What would you think about asking Gabriel to build bookshelves for that wall?" I waved toward the long, barren brick wall.

"Gabriel?" he asked with a twinkle in his eyes.

"My, um, friend," I said, blushing a rosy red.

"You mean that strapping man who wants to court you?"

"Yes, him."

"Hmm ... well, I don't know, missy," he said. I started my argument, but he waved away my words, his movement almost causing him to tip out of his chair. He caught himself by balancing on his cane. "I wouldn't get any delusions of ganderer, if you know what I mean."

"Delusions of..." My mind raced. "*Grandeur?*"

"I hear tell, when Mrs. Vaughan or Mrs. Bouchard come by, that Mr. Carnegie himself might give us money for a new library. So there'd be no need for the likes of bookshelves here, missy. 'Cause we wouldn't be here."

"A real library?" I asked with wonder. "When will we find out?"

"Soon enough, I expect," he replied. "We'll have to find another way to keep that man of yours occupied," he teased, moving his brows up and down.

I blushed, laughing as I moved onto another stack of books.

***

I RETURNED HOME AFTER a visit to Allenstein's Grocers, tripping on the boardwalk planks and nearly spilling the food I had purchased for dinner in my agitation. Mr. Allenstein had packed the baskets well, and little except a potato and a carrot escaped. As I trudged toward home, my arms ached from the heavy baskets. The dry, hot summer weather had caused the streets to seem dustier than usual and each passing carriage, horse or bicycle raised a funnel that seemed to swirl in the middle of the street. As I neared my apartment building, I saw Amelia waiting outside, holding Anne and a basket, while little Nicholas played marbles in the dirt. "Amelia!" I called out. I smiled down at Nicholas. "Hello, Nicholas, Anne. Let's go in."

I put down my baskets for a moment and brushed off Nicholas. He squirmed and squealed but seemed to enjoy the attention. When I finished, I rubbed down his hair, dust sprinkling out with the movement. He giggled and moved to clasp Amelia's leg. Amelia smiled her thanks, and I picked up the baskets to move toward the apartment.

Upon entering our rented rooms, Nicholas started to play marbles on the floor, and Anne was placed in the middle of my bed for her nap. "Clarissa, you seem out of sorts. I'm here to help you," Amelia soothed. She pulled out a pair of clean aprons from her basket, tying it around her waist to protect her lavender floral calico dress. She reached up to repin a few strands of hair, waiting my response.

"Gabriel's invited Aidan, and I invited Ronan." I bit my lip as I tried not to wring my hands. "I've never cooked an edible thing in my life."

"Well, I have, so this dinner will be a success," Amelia said as she unpacked the baskets and laid out the food to be prepared.

"Now, Clarissa," Amelia began, "it isn't hard to roast a chicken and vegetables."

I watched her as she walked me through the process of cooking. We stood side by side, and I mimicked her movements. We had the same ingredients, and we each prepared a chicken and vegetable dinner. Although it all seemed natural and second nature to her, I wanted to write everything down. I scribbled a few notes on paper at the kitchen table to expand on after she left.

I had hoped we would converse and become better acquainted as I learned to cook. However, I needed to concentrate so hard that I had no ability to think about anything else. At last the meal was placed in the oven, and I took a deep breath. "That's it then?" I asked.

"Yes, though it always helps to stir up the vegetables some as they are cooking," she said.

I collapsed onto a chair. "I like to think I am not an envious person by nature. But I do envy your composure and confidence in the kitchen." I drank from my glass of water. "I never thought I would admit this, but perhaps my stepmother was correct. Maybe I did need to learn how to properly run a house."

"Did she cook?"

"No, we always had a cook."

"Then how were you to learn? It takes time to become proficient in the kitchen."

"I have begun to fear that. I worry Gabriel will be upset with me," I admitted.

"I've rarely seen a man as in love as he is," Amelia reassured me with a smile. "If he had to eat at a café every meal for the rest of his life, he would, as long as he were with you." She rose to go into my bedroom to check on Anne. "Ah, there you are, darling," I heard her say. A few more murmurings and Anne was with us at the table area, sitting on Amelia's lap.

"There's the little angel," I said. Amelia offered her to me. I brushed at her silky, wispy red hair, holding her tightly swaddled form in the crook of my arm. She gurgled at me, the corners of her eyes crinkling as I tapped her chin. "Ah, who's a good girl?" I said, talking with Anne and sharing a smile with Amelia.

I looked up, surprised to see Colin entering. "Lord, that smells good," he said on a long sigh, his eyes closed as he inhaled. He rubbed at his stomach, his blackened hands adding sooty patches to his sweat-streaked shirt-front. "Did you find a book then, Rissa?"

I laughed, and he opened his eyes.

"Hello, Mrs. Egan. Are you cooking for us?" he asked, unable to hide the eagerness from his voice.

"No, I'm teaching Clarissa," Amelia said on a giggle.

"As I told you last night," I muttered.

"Bless you," he said with a wink. "Nicholas, prepare yourself. Once I have washed up, you owe me a marbles match."

Nicholas looked up with glee as Colin strode toward his room. "He remembered, Mama," Nicholas said.

"I told you he would."

Soon Colin had washed and changed, and he and Nicholas were sprawled on the floor, a fierce marble battle underway.

Amelia watched the proceedings with a warm glint in her hazel eyes. "I can't tell you how happy I am that Nicholas has these amazing men in his life."

"He is a wonderful boy."

"How are things between you and Gabriel?" she murmured, taking Anne from me to soothe her as she became fussy.

"Better every day. I still have trouble believing I have his love and support after..." At Amelia's long stare, I flushed.

"He's only ever wanted you," Amelia said.

I nodded, smiling fully as Nicholas threw himself in Colin's arms with a whoop as he won the marbles match.

"Best of seven!" Colin yelled, kneeling, holding Nicholas upside down. Nicholas giggled as Colin laid him on the floor to tickle him. Amelia and I laughed too, the boy's joy infectious.

"Colin, quit torturing Nicholas and help me with Ronan," Gabriel said from the doorway. He grinned, flashing his dimple as he looked at me and winked. He wore clean black pants and a burgundy shirt with no wood dust in sight. He turned and disappeared down the stairs. They were gone for a few minutes and then I heard groaning, a few muttered words, and I busied myself readying a chair for Ronan.

"I think the armchair, don't you?" Gabriel asked on a grunt as Colin tripped and almost dropped Ronan.

Ronan gripped them tighter around their necks, nearly strangling them in the process.

"Let go of my neck, you bleedin' idiot," Gabriel hissed. He gasped as Ronan relaxed his hold, and they settled him in the chair. Gabriel and Colin fell to their knees on either side of Ronan.

Ronan's spindly legs folded in front of him, and he pushed backward with his hands to keep from slipping out of the chair.

"Gabriel?" I asked.

"Water," Colin rasped as Gabriel nodded his agreement.

"You don't look to be such a heavy ba…" Colin began but stopped as he remembered Nicholas. He ruffled the boy's hair.

"Sorry to be such a nuisance," Ronan said, flushing with embarrassment. His bright blue shirt was at least two sizes too big, as was the black jacket washed to gray. The slight flush on his cheeks and neck emphasized his now protruding cheekbones and slender neck.

"Nonsense," I said as I approached with two glasses of water. "It's about time you visited, and those two were in danger of wasting away into decrepit old men from lack of physical exertion." I moved toward him, gently touching his arm. "I'm very happy you are here."

"Uncle Ronan, Uncle Ronan!" Nicholas said, crawling onto his lap. "I beat Mr. Sullie twice in marbles." He chortled with glee. "Why can't you walk?" he asked as he played with the buttons on Ronan's shirt collar. His weight acted as an anchor, preventing Ronan from sliding to the floor.

"I was hurt in an accident, Nicholas."

"What do you do all day?" Nicholas asked. "If you laid on the floor, I could play marbles with you."

"Thank you, Nicholas, but I am looking for work."

"What happened to your beard?"

"It's too hot for a beard this summer, Nicholas. I shaved it to cool off." Nicholas reached up to pat his cheeks, tracing his sharp cheekbones.

"Any leads for work, Ronan?" Gabriel asked as he stood. He moved toward me, leaning down to casually kiss my forehead.

I brushed a lock of ebony hair off his forehead and he tilted his face into my touch.

"Not yet."

Aidan poked his head into the apartment, the door left ajar.

"Well, something will turn up. Uncle," Gabriel exclaimed as he turned toward the door.

"Hello, everyone," Aidan said. "I'm sorry if I am late." He stood next to Gabriel, equal in height although his shoulders were slightly stooped. He was the most formally dressed in a brown suit, waistcoat and tie. He handed me a loaf of warm bread.

His affectionate smile boosted my confidence as the time to serve dinner neared.

"I thought this would go well with dinner," Aidan said.

"Thank you," I murmured and then sighed. "Well, no use postponing dinner. Find a seat everyone, and let's see how it tastes."

After everyone was arranged at the cramped table, I pulled out the matching pair of roasted chickens and vegetables, closing my eyes in appreciation at the delicious smell, and saw that they appeared to be cooked perfectly. The vegetables looked soft and flavorful, and the chicken was moist. I could detect no difference between Amelia's meal and the one I had prepared. I heaved a sigh of relief as I attempted to carve one of the chickens. However, my abilities at carving were even worse than cooking, and I worried I would soon mangle a perfectly cooked meal. I glanced around, uncertain what to do, and met Aidan's concerned gaze.

"Here, Clarissa, give me that before you harm yourself," Aidan commanded, taking the knife from my hands. He winked at me as he carved. "I used to help the ship's cook, and I think I still remember how to cut up a chicken."

I watched with envy as he easily separated the meat from the bone.

After serving everyone, I saw Colin eyeing his plate of food. "It won't bite," I muttered.

"With your cooking, you never know," he said as he ate a forkful. His eyes closed with delight. "Ah, finally. Mrs. Egan, thank you."

I smiled my thanks to Amelia as Gabriel clasped my hand under the table. I watched as everyone ate.

"When do you think Cameron will arrive?" Colin asked in a lull in the conversation about the day's activities.

"He's coming then?" Ronan asked.

"Who?" Amelia asked.

"Clarissa's ex-fiancée," Colin said.

"He's chasing after Clarissa," Gabriel said.

"Why is that?" Aidan said as he studied me. When I shook my head, Aidan said, "It's about money, isn't it Clarissa?" At my jerky nod, Aidan looked around the table. "When Gabriel told me of his concern about Clarissa, and the other man interested in her, I made inquiries."

"And what did you discover?" I whispered.

"That Mr. Wright's family is near financial ruin due to hazardous speculation on Wall Street. He looks to you to replenish the family's coffers."

"That's absurd," Colin said with a snicker. "Rissa has little more than the money she saved from teaching."

"Col, I'm afraid I haven't told you everything," I whispered. "I have a dowry."

"A dowry?" Colin and Gabriel asked at the same time.

Ronan watched me with frank curiosity, Nicholas balanced on his lap.

"From the grandparents. They wanted to ensure I would marry someone acceptable. They maneuvered Sav into marrying Jonas, and I was to be manipulated into marrying Cameron."

"Their definition of *acceptable* is perverse," Gabriel growled.

"By going against their wishes, I won't receive their money," I said.

"I wouldn't want it anyway," Gabriel said as he gripped my hand.

"So this Mr. Wright is en route intent on marrying you," Aidan said. He looked toward Gabriel.

"Yes," I said on a wavering breath, battling my fear.

"We'll marry. Remove any possibility that Cameron can force her into marriage," Gabriel said.

"Good," Aidan said with a nod.

I glanced around the table to see that everyone had finished eating. "Gabriel," I whispered.

"Clarissa," Gabriel murmured. "Walk with me?" He smiled at me, running a finger down the side of my face to my chin.

Gabriel rose, plucked my shawl from the peg by the door and wrapped it around my shoulders. He turned to the room, sharing a long glance with Colin before nodding to Aidan, Ronan and Amelia. He gripped my hand, leading me from the room.

As we emerged onto the boardwalk, I glanced toward the hills surrounding the town. It was my favorite time of night, with the light softly glinting off the hills, making them seem to shimmer like gold. I closed my eyes for a few moments, taking a deep breath of air.

Gabriel kept a firm grip on my hand, urging me to walk with him by the river. "It will be cooler there. The air is fresh, and we will hopefully have a bit of privacy," he said. "We need to talk."

Gabriel turned left on Front Street, and we walked alongside the Missoula Mercantile, continuing along Front Street a few more blocks before cutting over toward the river. A small, informal path wound through the knee-high grass, and we followed it to the river's edge. Gabriel finally stopped as we approached a large log, leading me around to sit on it.

He remained silent, giving me time to relax as I listened to the water, inhaled the mossy, earthy, elemental smell of the river, and heard the birds trilling in the nearby bush as they prepared for dusk.

"Thank you," I said. I squeezed his hand. We studied each other for a moment. "Gabriel, I don't want you to feel that you have to marry me. To marry me in haste."

"Clarissa," Gabriel said, gripping my arms and leaning forward so our eyes were level, "you must know we have to marry. There is no way I'm going to leave you unprotected."

"This is what you truly want?"

He beamed at me, his dimple shining in his right cheek, his beautiful blue eyes filled with joy. "Think back to my letter I wrote you, darling. The letter I wrote you after you had written me about your dreams for us."

"Remind me," I whispered.

"*I dream of exploring this new world with you, finding delight in new experiences. I dream of holding you in my arms. I dream of listening to you talk about your day, your exuberance and interest about the world around you infectious. I dream of having a family together, growing old together. Spinning new dreams out day by day. Dreams grow and change, and I'd like to grow and change with you.*"

"Gabriel," I whispered, fighting tears. I rose to stand in front of him.

"Is this what you want, Clarissa?" He watched me with a searching look, before he closed his eyes and whispered in a tortured voice, "I hate to think that I am acting no better than Cameron in taking away your choice by deciding that we would marry." He opened his eyes again. "Do you want to marry me?"

"Yes," I said in a strong voice. "Yes. I love you, Gabriel. I want to marry you and be your wife."

A wondrous smile bloomed over his face as he caressed my cheek with his fingers. "Finally, you said the words."

"I've loved you since last summer but was afraid to say it out loud. It seemed too soon, and then you were torn away from me. But, I am reclaiming you, my love."

I placed my palms on his cheeks, leaning into him for the first kiss in nearly a year. I heard his soft inhalation. I had closed my eyes and hoped my lips would successfully meet his. His gentle lips were soft under mine, and I kissed him tentatively a few times. Suddenly he groaned, gripping me tighter and all thought fled. My hands dropped from his cheeks, and I flung my arms around his neck. His passionate response and kisses caused me to lose my breath, and I never wanted the moment to end. Unfortunately after a few more intense kisses with Gabriel caressing my back, he eased away from me.

"I..." Gabriel gasped, cheeks flushed, deep-blue eyes passion-filled. "I would beg your pardon except you started it," he said in a teasing tone.

I blushed beet red and leaned into him for a hug. He kissed me gently on my forehead, gathering me close for a long embrace. I shuddered in his arms, amazed and grateful that I had not thought of Cameron while I had kissed Gabriel. I had felt no fear. Just joy.

"Are you all right?" he whispered. I nodded against his chest. He eased me away from him and gazed into my eyes in the fading twilight.

"I am fine, Gabriel," I whispered. I paused, breaking eye contact.

"But?"

"I know we must marry." I met his eyes. "I *want* to marry you." I leaned into the palm cradling my cheek and kissed it. "But I'm terrified of what comes after the wedding." My voice broke as I choked down a sob.

His eyes darkened for a moment. "I know, darling," he murmured. "I wish I could give you all the time you need before our marriage, but I can't allow any chance that Cameron could harm you again. Could attempt to claim you as his." He paused, staring into my eyes and letting out a long sigh. "I know that makes me sound a hypocrite as I want you as my wife too."

"I know you won't hurt me," I whispered.

"I promise to be patient."

I sniffled and took a deep breath. "But that's just it, Gabriel. I know it is completely irrational, but I don't want you to have to be patient. I don't want to be filled with fear. I want to feel only joy and impatience as our wedding approaches."

"Life isn't always kind, love."

I took a deep breath, closed my eyes and then forced myself to meet his patient gaze. "I want a full marriage with you. And I am so afraid."

"There is nothing I can say that will calm those fears. Only time. And only as you begin to trust again will you be free of such fears." He wiped away a few errant tears. "I have something for you."

"I don't need anything."

"Ah, but I have a need to give this to you," he said in a teasing voice. "I asked Colin to find this in your room and to repair it for me." He extracted my locket from his pants pocket, and I saw where the two pieces of the chain had been forged together. "This is like you, love. With patience, time and care, you will mend. This locket and the repaired necklace will be a sign of your strength and resilience. And of our love."

"Gabriel," I whispered, standing on my toes to kiss him. I had no words.

"Let me," he murmured, turning me and clasping the locket around my neck. "At last, it is back where it belongs." He kissed the nape of my neck and then turned me to face him again.

I stepped into his arms, content to remain in his protective embrace for long minutes. "Shall we return to tell the others?" I whispered as night descended.

"They know we are to marry, love," Gabriel murmured with another kiss to my ear. "But, yes, let's tell the others, and hopefully Colin has saved us some dessert."

CHAPTER 45

GABRIEL POKED HIS HEAD into Colin's smithy, the blast of heat causing him to gasp. He glanced toward the back of the room to watch Colin hammering with small well-placed strokes on a piece of iron balanced on an anvil. Holding one end of the iron with metal tongs, he thrust the long piece of metal into the fire to heat up the end, shrugging his left shoulder at the same time in an attempt to wipe away some of the sweat running down the side of his face.

"We need more air, Eddy," Colin yelled over the sound of other blacksmiths working, the sound of metal on metal ringing throughout the forge. He pushed the piece of iron around in the now cooling coals, raising one arm to wipe at his forehead.

Gabriel looked toward a young man manning a large bellows. Eddy reached for the long wooden pole attached to the bellows, pulling air into the bellows and then pushing it onto the coals. The coals glimmered to life, each puff of air provoking a glow until they appeared bright yellow.

"That's great!" Colin yelled as he yanked the piece of iron out of the coals and, in a fluid movement, turned toward the anvil and quickly began hammering again before the iron cooled.

He repeated the movement again from anvil to coals, and then to vise, where he clamped the iron, clasped the heated part and bent it in a graceful loop, forming an attractive arc.

"Colin," Gabriel said and realized he wouldn't be heard over the hammering in the smithy. "Colin!" he hollered.

Colin looked up, startled at the interruption. He lowered the pincers, left the iron clasped in the vise and moved toward the doorway. "Gabe, good to see you." He mopped at the rivulets of sweat streaming off his forehead with his shirtsleeve and reached for a cup of water from a bucket by the door. "Let's step outside, where it's cooler."

"And quieter," Gabriel murmured. "I'd think you'd go deaf."

"I probably will," Colin said as he leaned against the brick wall of the smithy. "Everything all right?" Though his posture conveyed a relaxed mood, his eyes were alert.

"Yes, fine. Everything is settled for the wedding. I wanted to speak with you about a project for my friend Ronan. I need your help."

"What can I do?"

"I think he would improve if he were able to leave his rooms more. And yet he is unable to because he can't walk."

Colin nodded, waiting for Gabriel to continue.

"I want to make him a type of wheeled chair, like I saw once in Boston. I could make the chair with sturdy wood from Seb, and you could make the metal wheels."

"It would be expensive, Gabe," Colin said.

"I know, but I can't stand to see him squander his life laying in bed all day long. And I have some money saved."

"I would think you'd want to use that with Clarissa."

"She's as concerned for his welfare as I am. I'm sure she'll agree with my plan."

"You didn't cause the accident at the mine," Colin murmured. "Why do you feel this need to help him?"

"If we hadn't left Butte, he'd have been looked after by his mining friends."

"He chose to come here," Colin said as he stretched, leaning away from the side of the smithy.

Gabriel merely shrugged.

"Do you have a drawing? Dimensions?"

Gabriel pulled out a sketch, showing it to Colin.

"This looks a bit grand."

"It may be, but if he is going to spend his life in a chair, he might as well be comfortable," Gabriel said.

"I have to finish the project I'm working on. After that, I can start on this. Probably day after tomorrow."

"Sounds good. Thanks, Colin." They shook hands and Gabriel walked toward the mill.

***

"WHAT'S GOT YOU SO PENSIVE?" Sebastian asked Gabriel as he approached to stand next to him by the river. Gabriel stood staring at the mountains, a far-off look in his eyes.

"I'm imagining a design."

"I thought you sketched all your visions."

"Some I do. Others I picture in my mind before picking up a pencil." Gabriel shook his head and met Sebastian's curious gaze.

"Who's it for?"

"My friend from Butte. Ronan."

"The cripple."

"I worry that he believes he'll be bedridden for life, something I can't accept. I need sturdy wood that will survive constant use. I mean to make him a chair. I need to order more maple from the East."

"A chair ain't going to improve his life none, Gabe."

"A chair with wheels," Gabe ground out. "He'll have more freedom that way."

"In his home, maybe. But he can't get around town in that contraption."

"He could on the streets," Gabriel argued.

"And then, when he wants to go into one of the stores, how do you expect him to get up onto the boardwalk? Float up?"

"Listen, quit making this harder than it is," Gabriel hissed. "I want Ronan to feel like he has a life yet to live. And he never will feel that way stuck in a bed."

"Hmm ... well, it's your vision," Sebastian said with a wry smile. "As for your friend, don't get his hopes up too high, Gabe. Sometimes false hopes are worse than death."

Gabriel glowered at him, nodded and strode away.

***

"RONAN, SEE SENSE, MAN," Gabriel argued as he paced around Ronan's small room and thrust open the window. "You need to get out of this room." He leaned against the window frame, crossing his arms over his chest as he glared at Ronan.

"I'm not taking your money when you're about to be married. You need to think about Clarissa now. Stop worrying about me."

"If our positions were reversed, would you consign me to a life of bedsores, slowly wasting away until I lost the will to live?"

"Of course not."

"Then don't expect any different from me, Ronan. I know Clarissa, and I know she'll agree with me. She was furious with me for even renting you a second-floor room to begin with. She'll be delighted to search for a new home for you."

"And when I'm down on the first floor? What will I do?"

"I've already made plans to build a wheelchair for you. You'll have more freedom of movement once I have it built."

"Gabe, it's too much," Ronan protested.

"What was your father? Did he teach you a trade?" Gabriel spoke over Ronan, ignoring his protest.

"I haven't done it in years, and I don't have the tools." At Gabriel's silence and intense stare, Ronan half smiled. "He was a cobbler. A good one, too. But there wasn't much need for four cobblers in our small town, so I left."

"So your brothers would have a chance," Gabriel said.

Ronan nodded.

"Well, I have room in my shop. I'll see about building you a bench you can work at, and I'll ask around about tools. If you'll be working in the shop, we should look for a rental room nearby."

"Gabe, it's too much. I can't ask you to do this."

"You haven't. I'm offering. And I know you and I will have one of the busiest storefronts in town." Gabriel grinned as he scratched his chin. "We'll have to see if Clarissa or Amelia can think of a name for our business. One that will pique the interest of the passersby."

"Gabe, I'll be renting workspace from you, nothing more."

"You'll have a chance at a decent future, Ro. That's what counts. I'll get to work on the chair and workspace after the wedding. I won't be able to do much until then."

"Thank you, Gabe. I couldn't ask for a better friend."

"I know you'd do the same for me," he said as he clapped Ronan on the shoulder. "Now, start eating. You'll need your strength if you'll be working every day."

Ronan nodded, a smile breaking out.

Gabriel glimpsed hope in his eyes for the first time since the accident.

CHAPTER 46

I STOOD IN FRONT of the mirror in my bedroom, staring at myself. I banished thoughts of Boston and my mama's vanity, of my dreams of having seen myself reflected there on my wedding day. The ice-blue of the satin A-line dress highlighted my pale complexion. I twisted and pulled at my chestnut brown hair but was unable to force it into a fashionable style today. I let out a huff of frustration as I dropped my hair, watching it swing nearly to my hips.

"May I come in?" Amelia asked as she poked her head into my room. "Oh, you look lovely." She frowned a moment. "Though your hair is a mess. Give me that," she said, grabbing for my comb. "Did you never learn to do your hair?"

"Only simple styles," I said as she shoved me into a chair so she could work easily. "I generally had a maid."

"Hmm … quite a life you had in Boston. A maid, a cook," she murmured.

"Maids," I muttered, then bit my tongue. "Yes, life was different there. Not better though."

"I hope you continue to feel that way after winter rolls in," Amelia said as she styled my hair into the fashionable Gibson Girl hairstyle. "There, that should do it." She looked at me affectionately. She wore what I imagined to be her best summer dress, a striped yellow-and-cream-colored cotton dress with a red belt.

"I can't believe today is my wedding day," I whispered.

"Be thankful it is," Amelia said. "You never know when that horrid man might show up. It's better to have Gabriel's protection."

I glanced away.

"Why the face, Clarissa?"

"I hate that I have to look to a man to protect me," I said. "I would think, by now, a woman would be able to live the life she wanted without a man."

"Are you saying you don't want Gabriel?"

"No, of course not. He's the reason I'm here. I don't want to imagine my life without him. It's just that I hate anyone thinking I am marrying him solely for protection."

"There are a lot of reasons for marrying, Clarissa," Amelia said. "Not everyone is so fortunate as to marry for love while also knowing that the man will do all in his power to protect and honor you." She watched me for a moment. "I would think you'd be thankful to have such a man."

"I am," I whispered as I blinked away tears. "I just wish I had more time."

"Well, time is the one thing there is never enough of. And no matter how much or little money you have, you can never make more of it," Amelia said. "And with that, we must be off to church, or Gabriel will think you aren't coming at all."

***

BRIGHT LIGHT SHONE in through the clear windows and onto the stone floor. Incense scented the air, and the walls and ceilings were painted in a soothing pale rose. Scattered murals depicting scenes from the Bible had been completed with others still in progress. Pillars—painted with white paint to resemble marble—rose to support high arches, the barrel-vaulted ceiling soaring above, awaiting its mural. The altar at the front of the church stood below a half dome, the priest already there awaiting my arrival.

Rows of wooden pews were mostly vacant, although I recognized the flamboyant plumes of the hats worn by Mrs. Vaughan and Mrs. Bouchard. Mr. Pickens sat next to Aidan, his rough patched coat a contrast to Aidan's refined tailored suit.

I watched Gabriel pacing the nave of the church and could not suppress a smile. "He seems a bit nervous," I whispered to Colin. He wore his best suit with a pink wildflower in his breast pocket.

"No matter how much a man says he wants to marry, it's still hard for him to give up his independence, Rissa," Colin murmured back. "If you look closely, I think most of his nerves come from Ronan's ribbing."

I giggled. At this Gabriel looked up, saw me and grinned.

"Ready, Rissa?" Colin asked. At my nod, we walked slowly down the aisle, the only music a gentle humming from Amelia.

I moved toward Gabriel, unable to break eye contact with him. As I watched him, I thought fleetingly of Savannah's polished society wedding where no true emotion, other than horror at my clumsiness, had been expressed. In comparison Gabriel's eyes shone with love and devotion; Colin beamed as he placed my hand in Gabriel's; and Amelia cried next to Sebastian and Ronan as the priest said the wedding mass.

Afterward I was not able to recall the ceremony. Or what I had vowed to do. I only remembered Gabriel, his gentle clasp of my hand, the feel of the simple gold band sliding over my finger. The firm, swift kiss at the end of the ceremony. His soft murmur, "Finally, we are wed." The trace of his finger down my cheek a few moments before we turned to face the small group of friends and family gathered to witness our wedding. The tremendous sense of joy blooming inside me as we walked down the aisle after the priest called out, "I present Mr. and Mrs. McLeod!"

***

I PACED THE APARTMENT over Gabriel's workshop. I had imagined a loft area, open to the downstairs workspace. Instead, it was a separate living quarter, closed to the downstairs except for the staircase against one wall.

I moved from the top of the stairs, turning to face the large rectangular room. The kitchen was at my right against the solid brick wall, opposite one of the windows. It consisted of a small stove, sink and cupboards. I moved into the room, tapping my fingers on the rectangular dining room table, tracing small grooves and nicks on its scarred surface. Toward the middle of the room, a rocking chair and a tattered oversize gentleman's chair made up the living area, with a lamp on an overturned crate between the two chairs. Three windows lined the outside wall, covered in thin white cotton curtains. No pictures or paintings adorned the walls.

I continued to pace, resolutely avoiding the sleeping area on the opposite side of the long room. I wandered toward a small bookcase nestled between two of the windows and near the rocking chair. Knickknacks and a small box rested on the second shelf, and I reached out to open the box.

"I can't believe the day is finally over," Gabriel said with a long sigh as he walked up the stairs.

I jerked away from the bookcase and turned to face him.

"So, you've already found the box?" He smiled at me with tenderness. "It's where I've kept all of your letters."

I blushed as I moved toward him. "It was a lovely reception," I murmured.

"Uncle wanted to celebrate," Gabriel agreed as he moved toward the small kitchen area. "Would you like a cup of tea?" he asked. At my nod, he put the kettle on. He busied himself with preparing the pot and cups, and I settled into the rocking chair.

"This is like Boston," I said. "This chair is just like the one you made me. And here I sit again, watching you make me tea."

He glanced toward me and smiled. "No, this is better. Now we are wed, and I don't have to worry about whether or not you'll visit me again."

I rocked, hoping the motion of the chair would soothe me. However, my stomach was tied in such knots; I feared any motion would cause illness. I stilled my rocking, my hands clenched in the skirts of my gown. I watched as Gabriel poured the boiling water into the teapot.

"Clarissa," Gabriel said. "Nothing need happen tonight. I can sleep on a cot."

I nodded in an attempt to express that I understood what he said. I feared Gabriel interpreted it to mean I agreed with him as he closed his eyes and gripped the edge of the table for a moment. "Gabriel." At my tortured whisper he walked toward me, pulling a chair out so he could sit facing me. "I know you said you would be patient. That you could wait forever."

"Yes."

"I don't want you to." I grasped his hand. "If I insist on postponing … my fear will only continue to grow. I am so tired of being afraid."

"Clarissa—"

I interrupted him with a finger to his lips. "I trust you, Gabriel. I trust in my choice of you. Of us. Unless you can't imagine…"

"Darling Clarissa, look at me." He tipped my chin up with two of his fingers so that I would meet his eyes. "I have imagined for over a year now what we will have. I will stop at any time."

I nodded, my breath coming out in a near pant.

He leaned in slowly, tracing my hairline. "I love you so." He lifted my left hand, kissing my wedding ring. His first kiss was tentative, soft and soon had me leaning so far forward in the rocking chair I was almost on the floor.

He lifted me carefully from the chair and cradled me on his lap. As I settled, he traced a palm down my back, and I arched into his caress. "Show me what you like," he whispered. He finger-combed my hair, tangling it, but freeing most of it from its pins. "Ah," he said as he leaned away for a moment to stroke the long, chestnut-colored strands. "I've dreamt for so long of seeing your hair down."

I moaned, leaning forward into his embrace. I was desperate for more of his deep drugging kisses that erased all fear. Soon I was past thought as I tangled my hands in his soft ebony hair and kissed him back.

A loud crash sounded outside the window, and I jolted. "Ignore it," Gabriel said, kissing the skin below my ear. The crash was joined by a cacophony of pans clanging together, a honking noise and whistles.

"What the hell?" Gabriel asked as he placed his forehead against mine for a moment before he pushed me to a standing position and moved toward the window.

"What are you doing down there?" Gabriel called out in exasperation.

I peeked out beside him, peeved at the momentary reprieve.

"Yer bein' chivareed, young man," Mr. Pickens hollered with glee as loud as he could as he gave a good wallop to a pan with a metal spoon. He stood with about twenty men, and they were making as much noise as possible. "'Bout time too after you stopped yer dillydallyin' an' all that lunarcenary 'bout courtin' an' finally married Missy."

"Missy? Lunarcenary?" Gabriel asked me with a quirk of his eyebrow.

"Hello, Mr. A.J.! And you mean *lunacy*. What will it take for you to go away?" I yelled as I covered my ears from the discordant din.

"Yer young man can buy me and the lads a drink. We'll try not to send him home to you too enerviated!"

"Enerviated?" Gabriel asked. "Is he senile?"

"I think you mean *inebriated*, Mr. A.J.," I called out with an elbow to Gabriel's ribs.

"There you go, missy! Never was one for those big words." He banged on his pan a few times. "Son, you buyin' me an' the lads a drink or not?"

"Clarissa, I think this is the only way to silence them," Gabriel said with a cringe as nearby dogs howled.

I giggled and then laughed so hard I had tears pouring down my cheeks.

"Oh, Gabriel, of course this would happen to us," I gasped through my laughter. I leaned over and kissed him. "Go, buy them all a drink, and come home to me."

He watched me, arrested for a moment. "There it is," he whispered. "That joy that glimmers from within that has eluded you for so long. If I had known it would take your fool friend banging on a pot outside our window, I would have had him do it weeks ago."

I laughed again as I pushed him toward the stairs. "One drink, mind," I whispered.

"One. And don't change from this dress," he whispered back. "Wait up for me." He kissed my knuckles and then ran down the stairs. I raced toward the window to watch him emerge. When he did, he received a few comradely slaps on the back, but the noise stopped.

"Night, missy!" Mr. Pickens called.

"Night, Mr. A.J. Enjoy that drink."

I watched the small mob of men depart, noting that Colin, Aidan and Sebastian had joined in at the end. I glanced up toward the full moon, remembering my letters to Gabriel where I had written to him that, although we were apart, we had the moon in common. I sighed in momentary contentment that, finally, we were together under the same moon.

CHAPTER 47

I WOKE IN STAGES to the feeling of something tickling my shoulder. I twitched my arm away, but it continued. I didn't have the energy to swat at it, thinking it a fly. However, I jerked awake, rigid with fear, when I felt a muscled arm wrapped around my waist and a strong leg hitched over mine.

"No, no, no!" I cried, trying to break free.

"Clarissa, shh … it's me, Gabriel."

My legs and arms were instantly freed, and the tickling sensation, which I now realized was Gabriel stroking my shoulder, stopped.

I sat up, taking in the fact I remained fully clothed and was covered by a light blanket. I looked around, and, rather than a formal sitting room, I was in a dilapidated apartment over a workshop in the pale moonlight. *In Missoula, Montana*, my mind whispered. I turned toward Gabriel, trying to quell my gasping breaths.

"I'm sorry to have frightened you," Gabriel whispered, sitting up on his knees. He continued to caress me, hands gently stroking down my arms, fingers playing in my hair. "I would never mean to…" His voice broke.

"Gabriel," I groaned and leaned into him. "Forgive me," I whispered. I opened my eyes to meet his worried gaze. "It terrifies me to feel overpowered."

"I will remember. I just wanted to hold you. You were so peaceful when I came in from the saloon, asleep in that lovely dress underneath the coverlet. I didn't mean to wake you."

"Gabriel," I murmured again, pressing into him, wishing I were different.

"Do you want me to go?"

"Never." I gripped his shoulders and kissed him. "Never, my darling."

"Good because I don't know how I'd ever leave you after holding you," Gabriel whispered, letting out a sigh of relief, leaning into my kiss.

Soon Gabriel had pulled me tighter, his hands digging through my hair. He deepened the kiss, bringing me flush against him, and, before I knew what had happened, I had my legs wrapped around him. I had only ever imagined a kiss so intense that I lost all ability to think, not caring if I had enough air. I gripped Gabriel tightly, lost to the passion of the moment.

I flinched when his hand covered my breast. "Shh ... darling, we won't do anything you don't want to." Gabriel raised both hands and caressed my head softly, leaning in for another kiss. "I want you to trust in this. In us."

I took a shaky breath in an attempt to relax. "I do. Help banish my fears, Gabriel." I reached for one of his hands and held it to my heart. "I want a full marriage with you."

Gabriel kissed me with a soft growl, moving and rolling until I was under him. "If you want me to stop at any moment, I will. All you have to do is ask." He traced my cheek. "I will not be angry with you, darling. Frustrated, yes, but never angry."

I gifted him with a tremulous smile. "I know I don't know much about what we're going to do." My smile faded as I fought memories. "But I believe I am overdressed for the occasion."

Gabriel's blue eyes shone with tenderness as he bent to kiss my neck. He kissed the area around my collar where his necklace hung. A trail of kisses followed the movement of his hands as he undid the buttons along the front of my dress. I gasped as he kissed my upper chest.

"I agree, darling. We both are. I must unfortunately admit I am unfamiliar with how to remove all of your attire." He blushed as he stroked his hands up and down my arms.

"Here, I'll show you," I said, as I wriggled from under him and stood by the side of our bed. I lifted my hair, pointing at hidden clasps on the back of my dress. A moment later it lay pooled around my ankles.

"That was simple enough, but now there are the other thirty layers to remove," Gabriel teased.

Soon my corset cover, then corset, joined the dress on the floor. I flushed as I stood in my undergarments.

"I'm feeling decidedly overdressed," Gabriel murmured. He unbuttoned and dropped his waistcoat to the floor. He pulled the straps of his suspenders so they dangled at his waist. "Help me?" He reached for his shirt, and I brushed his hands away.

My fingers shook as I released each button. I took a deep breath and stepped closer to him as I pushed his shirt off over his shoulders. It snagged on his wrists, and I kissed his right shoulder. I traced my hands down his arms to his wrists where I unlatched the cuff links and freed his hands. His shirt joined his waistcoat at our feet.

I traced his wrists for a moment before gripping the edge of his cotton undershirt. It had no sleeves but covered his chest. I tugged it free of the waistband of his pants and pulled it upward. "Lift," I whispered. He raised his arms and his upper body was bared to me. I traced my hands down his chest causing gooseflesh to rise.

"Clarissa," Gabriel whispered. "I love you so."

"I know," I said with what I hoped was a seductive smile. I faltered as I rested my hands on the waistband of his pants.

He chuckled as he kissed me to distraction. "Lift," he murmured as he pulled my shift over my head. He bent to kiss my belly as he pushed my drawers down my legs.

Embarrassed by my nakedness, I dove toward the bed, burrowing under the covers. I heard his carefree laugh and the sounds of him disrobing. I peeked over the edge of the sheet as his side of the bed dipped with his weight. He lay on his back with his head resting on a bent arm.

He turned toward me, a half smile lighting his face. "Hello, darling. You seem too far away."

I clutched the sheets to me and moved toward him, inadvertently stripping the bed as I moved.

"You'll be rolled up like a caterpillar soon," Gabriel teased. He reached out with one hand and touched my cheek. "Let me hold you, love."

I released my grip on the sheets and inched toward him. I settled against his side, gasping at the feel of him against me. "You're like a furnace."

"That's one way of looking at things," Gabriel said with a humor-laced voice.

"You smell good," I said as I leaned forward to kiss his neck. "Woodsy and musky and male." I kissed his ear. "My man."

He groaned, and I felt him tense beneath me. "I'm trying to behave here, Rissa."

"Maybe I don't want you to." I kissed his flexed bicep resting by his head and moved down toward his shoulder and his chest. He reached forward and brushed my hair away from my face, tangling his fingers in the long strands. "Love me, Gabriel."

He moved, flipping me onto my back. I tensed, fighting memories of Boston. I closed my eyes and a tear leaked out. Gabriel kissed it away.

"Clarissa, look at me." He traced my eyebrows. "Open your eyes."

I did, meeting his concerned stare.

"It's me. Gabriel. You're here with me, in Missoula."

I nodded, releasing a stuttering breath. "I'm trying, Gabriel."

He kissed me as he rolled me onto him. "You have all the control, darling. You decide what we do and don't do. I will not frighten you again."

After a few moments, I squirmed on him, rubbing against the light coating of black hair on his chest.

He groaned, gripping his hands into my hips. "This reminds me of when you fell on top of me after knocking me off the ladder. Even then you knew how to torment me."

"Gabriel! You couldn't have thought of me in such terms."

"I admit, I was more concerned with not blacking out or becoming violently ill in front of you. But believe me, I was aware of your feminine charms." He stroked a hand down my back, and I arched into his caress.

"I love your touch," I whispered as I kissed his jaw. "I love how you've only ever touched me with respect."

"Always, my darling. Always."

I took a deep breath and hitched one leg on either side of his hips. He groaned and released his hold of me to grasp the mattress.

"Show me, Gabriel. Show me what we can have."

He stared into my eyes, while I saw love and hope reflected in his. "With pleasure, my darling."

***

I AWOKE TO BRIGHT SUNLIGHT filtering through the thin curtains. I lay on my side, cradled next to something warm. I pushed back against that warmth, gasping as I heard the gentle snore in my ear turn into a grunt and realized in my half-conscious state that I was abed with Gabriel. Naked. And, most wondrous of all, happy.

I started to ease away, but his arm around my belly tightened for a moment.

"Let me hold you a bit longer, love," Gabriel said in a voice slurred with sleep. He kissed my nape after mumbling those words. I attempted to relax against him, and his arm tightened reflexively for a moment. "Sorry," he said as he loosened his hold.

I felt a huff of breath against my nape. "If you think any harder, you'll hurt yourself," he whispered. "Relax, Rissa."

"I can't."

Suddenly he released me, and the protective cocoon I had felt in his embrace disappeared. "Forgive me for being selfish and wanting to hold you. I didn't mean to scare you again."

I turned toward him, seeing him laying on his back with one arm flung over his forehead and with his eyes staring dully at the ceiling, the blankets and sheets tangled around his belly. I reached out to him, softly tracing the contours of his chest. He flinched, but I hoped not in a bad way.

"Gabriel, it's not what you think," I whispered. "I admit, when I woke last night, I was frightened. But I'm not now, and I wasn't afraid a few minutes ago when I woke up."

He turned wounded eyes to me. "Then what is it? I'm trying my best to be gentle and patient, and all I seem to do is hurt you."

"No, no, you don't! Hurt me, I mean. I started thinking, and I couldn't stop, and it made me nervous."

He watched me. "Nervous about what?"

"Did I please you last night? Is it normal to want to lie in bed and hold me in the morning? Or is it because you can't bear to do it all over again?"

He watched me with a fierce frown for a moment before breaking into a huge grin. If he laughed, I knew I would start crying. He reared up, gripped my shoulders, and soon I was laying on my back with him looming over me. He traced my cheek, my eyes and my forehead with reverence, a fierce joy enhancing his blue eyes.

"I only ever dreamed I would be able to hold you like this," he whispered. "I began to worry it would forever remain a fantasy." He leaned in for a tender kiss.

"I hold you because I can't imagine you sleeping anywhere but beside me. I love the feel of you. I wanted a few more minutes so I could regain my strength and hopefully convince you to make love with me again."

He watched my eyes the entire time he spoke, and I found I could not look away.

"I would think, after last night, you would have no doubts as to your desirability or *our* ability to find pleasure together."

"Gabriel," I whispered. "I love you so much, and I don't want to disappoint you."

His eyes flashed with a deep emotion. "I will never tire of hearing you tell me that you love me." He leaned in for another kiss, before he eased away with a teasing smile. "Why would you ever think you would disappoint me?" he murmured as he kissed my collarbone.

I tried valiantly to continue with the conversation, though it was becoming increasingly difficult. "Because I'm ... I was..." I trembled as he nipped the soft skin underneath my ear.

"Clarissa, you were exactly as I dreamed you'd be," he whispered. "Giving, loving, passionate. I know there were a few moments when ... when you were reminded of what happened before," Gabriel said in a husky voice, looking up to meet my eyes. "And I am sorry for that. I tried for it to be as good"—a gentle kiss to the underside of my chin—"as wonderful"—another kiss to my shoulder—"as I had always hoped."

"It was, Gabriel." I reached down, threading my hands into his hair. "It was. Thank you for understanding when I—"

"Screamed like a woman possessed and took a few minutes to calm?" he asked with a chuckle and a kiss to my breast.

I realized he had begun to work his way down my body. "Gabriel," I said.

He looked at me again. "Let us find a way to banish him from what we have, darling. And if that is with humor, that is good. Passion would be even better," he murmured as he bent to kiss my belly button.

I gasped and, after a split second, arched into him. "Gabriel." I sighed. "You have no idea how amazing that feels."

"Besides, my love," he said with a grin, "I think you have your concerns backward. You should worry that I disappoint you, not the other way around." At another of my gasps, he leaned in toward me, kissing me again, and all need for conversation became secondary to our need to touch each other.

***

I LAY SPRAWLED across Gabriel's chest as he lazily drew circles on my back. "Are we expected anywhere today?" I murmured.

"No," Gabriel said. "Though, if we don't leave these rooms, people will talk."

"I'm too tired to move. And I find I no longer care about gossip."

"Sleep, love," Gabriel said with a soft kiss to my hand.

He continued to play with my fingers as I hovered between wakefulness and sleep. I bolted upright as I heard a loud crash downstairs in Gabriel's workroom.

"If they think they can scam me into more damn chivaree-drink-buying a second time…" Gabriel growled as he moved to slide out from under me.

"Goddamn it, I said don't go up there!"

I heard Colin's voice and then another dull thud. Was he fighting someone? I shook my head from side to side in an attempt to wake up.

"She is the woman I plan on marrying, and you can't tell me what to do."

I froze in place. All pleasure leached away at the sound of that refined voice.

"I'm going to kill that son of a…" Gabriel hissed as he pushed me off him and jumped up, looking for his pants. He had just buttoned them, and was bare from the waist up, when a clatter of footsteps came up the stairs.

I sat with the blankets drawn around me, my hair framing my face, and my eyes so large I thought they would pop out of my head. I tried to calm my breathing for fear I would faint. I watched as Cameron burst into the loft, coming to a halt as he saw me across the room on the rumpled bed. His shaggy blond hair hung limply to his collar and a large tear rent one of his jacket sleeves. He watched me with a wild look in his eyes—lust, scorn and rage emanating from him.

"You bastard! How dare you touch her, turn her into nothing more than a common whore. You worthless swine," Cameron snarled.

I paled at Cameron's words as bile rose in my throat. Gabriel moved around the bed to stand between Cameron and me, shielding me as best he could.

"I'd thank you to speak with more respect toward my wife, Cameron," Gabriel growled.

"That marriage is not binding," Cameron argued. "She is bound to me."

"We were married at St. Francis Xavier Church yesterday, with Father McInninny saying the mass. And I can assure you, we"—a quick glance at me and my disheveled state—"had a splendid evening."

"You couldn't possibly want her," Cameron sputtered. "Not after…"

In a few long strides, Gabriel gripped Cameron around the throat and pushed him against the far wall. Gabriel's long arms prevented Cameron from inflicting any real damage on Gabe, and soon Cameron focused on just breathing.

"Not after you so brutally attacked and raped her?" Gabriel growled. "Not after you tried to break her spirit?" Gabriel shook him so that Cameron's head *thunk*ed against the wall.

"You never understood that her spirit was too great to break. That she was always too good for your little inconsequential world. And you will never understand that my love for her is boundless."

He released Cameron, feigning to the left to dodge Cameron's intended blow to his midsection. Gabriel backed up to stand beside Colin, whose right eye was swelling shut. "I will not give you the satisfaction of killing you and ending your misery. I will not allow you to take me away from Clarissa now that I'm finally reunited with her." He shared a long look with Cameron filled with loathing.

"I would like you to leave," Gabriel said. "Leave Mrs. McLeod and me alone. You have no business here, and no claim to anything."

"No," I called out from the bed. I clambered out of it, wrapping the sheets around me protectively. "No, not yet." I marched over to them to stand next to Gabriel with Colin backing up a step to stand behind me. As I approached them, I nearly tripped on the long sheets. Thankfully Gabriel reached out to prevent me falling and possibly stripping myself naked in front of them.

I turned to face Cameron, flushing from my clumsiness and from the nerves fluttering in my stomach. I studied him, any polish and charm chipped away from his long journey across the country.

"How dare you presume to interrupt my honeymoon?" I asked, causing Cameron's jaw to tighten. "If you never understood I would escape you and come to the man I love, then you are as dense as Sophronia thought."

"You will never get their money," Cameron rasped as he massaged his throat.

"When will you learn that I never wanted it? That I never desired to be a part of that constrictive society? I only ever wanted Gabriel and a life I could be proud of." I watched him for a moment, taking a deep breath as I forced myself to remember that horrible afternoon.

"I want you to know that, no matter how hard you tried to ruin me—" At this my voice broke. I felt Gabriel's hand at the small of my back and was comforted by his support. "To ruin my chance for happiness, you have not succeeded. And you never will. I refuse to allow you to tarnish what I have with Gabriel."

"I need that money," Cameron claimed.

"When will you learn that I don't care?" I stared at him a long moment with scorn and derision lighting my eyes before I turned away, into Gabriel's arms.

He tucked the sheets around me tightly and kissed my head.

I realized in that instant that I had not understood fully how fortunate I was to have married Gabriel until now. He was willing to fight for me, but also willing to stand beside me and support me as I fought my own battles.

"This isn't over," Cameron said in a low, angry voice.

I turned to look at him, standing tall with Gabriel behind me. Gabriel placed his hands on my shoulders, and I reached up to link one of my hands with his. "But it is over, Mr. Wright. I am a married woman. There has been nothing between us for three years," I said with a tilt of my chin upward.

Gabriel squeezed my shoulders. "Leave, Cameron, while you can still walk." Although his voice sounded calm, the vicious undertones caused Cameron to pale.

I watched as Cameron moved down the stairs with Colin at his heels and then heard Colin leading Cameron out the door. I trembled but fought back tears.

"Clarissa? Gabe? May I come up?" Colin called out.

"Yeah, for a few minutes," Gabriel said as he moved toward the living area and collapsed into the large oversize chair. He pulled me down so that I sat on his lap. "Let me hold you," he murmured, and I realized some of the trembling came from Gabriel.

"That was pleasant," Colin said.

"What the hell were you thinking?" Gabriel asked. "Bringing him here?"

"I didn't. I was on my way to Ronan's and saw him walking this way. Must have come in on the train today or yesterday and asked about you. Anyway, I raced after him and tried to get him to stop."

"I would think you would be able to fight better than receive a facer from a pansy like him," Gabriel said, taunting Colin.

"My hands were full of baskets, and he caught me off guard. If I'd been prepared, believe me, he would never have bothered you," Colin said in a regretful voice.

"Well, at least he's gone," Gabriel said with a sigh.

"But he's not," Colin said, and I stiffened in Gabriel's arms. "When we were fighting, I told him to leave, that he wasn't wanted here. But he can't. He doesn't have the money to return to Boston. He's stuck here."

"Christ," Gabriel muttered. "I barely stopped myself from killing him today. If I have to see him on a daily basis…"

"That is something to worry about another day." I whispered into Gabriel's ear, "Last I heard, we were honeymooners."

Gabriel chuckled and rubbed my back. "Colin, if that is all?" Gabriel said with a shake of his head toward the door.

"Actually I have some food, if you'd like it?" At Gabriel's swift nod, Colin ran downstairs and came up with a basket. "Amelia thought you might not have thought to get food in and that you probably wouldn't want to go out. She sent over some cold chicken, rolls, potato salad," Colin said as he rooted around in the basket. "I also have one for Ronan."

"Thanks, Colin," Gabriel said. "Now go."

Colin laughed. "'Bye! See you in a few days!"

I heard him clamber down the stairs.

"Clarissa, will you wait for me in bed? I just need to make sure it's locked up downstairs," Gabriel said as he eased me off his lap. "I don't want any more interruptions."

"No, I'll wait for you in the kitchen. I'm hungry," I said as I stood.

Gabriel rose, gripping my shoulders and kissing me for long minutes.

"Can we compromise?" At my quizzical stare he said, "Can you please not put on any clothes? Just remain wrapped in the sheets?"

I beamed at him and nodded my agreement.

CHAPTER 48

I WANDERED AROUND the small kitchen area, finding chipped plates and dulled silverware. After I wiped off the table, I found a dilapidated, wrinkled tablecloth and covered the table before setting it. I continued to trip over the long sheets, and tried to envision the pictures I had seen of togas. However, from what I remembered, they did not look too comfortable, nor in any way romantic, so I decided to continue with my shuffling, slow gait around the kitchen wrapped haphazardly in sheets as I prepared our cold feast.

As I brewed a pot of tea, I heard hammering from the workshop. I could not imagine that Gabriel had a sudden inspiration for one of his projects, but he had been gone for much longer than I had expected to lock a door. I sat, relaxing into the rocking chair with a cup of tea as I waited for him. As I glanced around the sparsely decorated loftlike living area, I understood for the first time why women liked to go shopping. I envisioned all sorts of improvements for the small space. First and foremost, I wanted a screen to shield our bed from the rest of the living area and unexpected guests.

"Idiots," Gabriel muttered as he climbed the stairs. "The world is full of idiots." I watched him over my teacup, hoping he would calm soon so we could eat. "They broke the damn door when they barged in."

I gasped in response.

"It was hanging on one hinge. Anyone could have walked in, robbed me blind."

"Gabriel, why didn't Colin tell you?"

"I imagine he didn't want me to take out my anger on him," he said with a rueful laugh. "He knew I was close to killing someone with Cameron here."

He sighed. "Though it would have been easier to repair had I had another set of hands."

"You should have called me," I said. "I am your wife. We are to share everything. The good and the bad."

Gabriel grinned, cupping my cheek and bending for a swift kiss. "You're right. Next time I'll ask you for help, love." He cleared his throat as he looked at the small feast on the table. "Amelia sent all that?"

"Doesn't it look wonderful? Although I think we should try to save some for supper tonight."

"I feel like I could eat it all right now," Gabriel said as he looked at the pile of fried chicken, heaping bowl of potato salad, sliced beets and at least half a dozen rolls. "Are you ready to eat?"

"Almost," I whispered. I stood, balanced on my toes and kissed him. His arms wrapped around me, and I had to remember to hold onto the sheets rather than him. After a few minutes I leaned away. "Now I'm ready."

He kissed my forehead and helped me to one of the three chairs at the table.

"Three chairs?" I asked and then could have bit my tongue. Of course. There had always been three of them: Gabriel, Richard and Jeremy.

"It's habit, I guess," he mumbled.

"I miss them too, darling. We'll see them again someday."

"It feels like that day will never come soon enough. Hard to believe that two of us are married now."

"Two of you?" I asked. "Did Richard and Florence marry?"

"Yes, in mid-May. I thought you knew."

"No, not at all. I was traveling in mid-May. I was in Chicago with Sophronia and Aunt Betsy, before heading to Minneapolis." I attempted to eat a piece of fried chicken with a knife and fork but it nearly flew off my plate.

Gabriel winked at me and picked up a piece with his hands. "Finally they are together. That should be what they write in the paper for both couples. 'Finally, they are together.'" Gabriel said as he gripped my hand. "Although Richard and I were damn fools to take so long to marry either of you."

"I thought you didn't like Florence."

"I didn't, not when I heard she and Richard were first together again. But I had a lot of time to think in Butte, and, as I thought more and more about her story, I began to understand why she had acted like she did. Because no matter how bad my life was, I was never alone. And there was always some comfort in that."

I blinked away tears as I gripped his fingers.

"And I remembered how much I liked her years ago, before the deception."

"Jeremy likes her too," I said as I gave into what I considered Western manners and licked my fingers. "He said he could think of no better woman to consider as a wife for Richard."

"That sounds like Jer. He always was the best one of us all."

"I wouldn't agree with you, although I am thankful to be able to call him brother. He protected me from Cameron, threw him out of my uncle's home once."

"I'll have to be sure to thank him," Gabriel said with a smile. "How is he, darling? I worry about him now that he's returned from the war."

"From what he told me, he suffered quite a bit. And was expected to do any number of acts that we would consider unthinkable. It appeared to me that he was having a hard time coping with all he had seen and done."

"That is what I feared," Gabriel murmured.

I nodded and squeezed his hand. "What did you think of Mr. A.J.?"

Gabriel nearly choked on a bite of potato salad. "He's an ornery old goat, but, underneath that prickly exterior, he's a good man."

"He's not ornery."

"That's 'cause he likes you. And he's not so sure he likes me. Thinks I'm a 'damn foolerin' idiot' to even think of 'wasterin' my time courting a girl so fine as his missy.'"

I blushed as Gabriel mimicked Mr. Pickens.

"I enjoyed him even though I often had trouble understanding what he was trying to say."

"Well, that's Mr. A.J. I have fun trying to decipher the meanings of his mangled words."

"Must be because you were a teacher," Gabriel said, and suddenly he had become very serious. "Clarissa," he murmured as he wiped his fingers and face with a napkin. "I know you had a full life in Boston. You were a suffragette, a teacher, a woman of standing in society." He sighed, breaking eye contact.

"What has you concerned, Gabriel?"

"I worry that, now we have married, life will seem very small to you. That you will come to resent this life that I can provide for you. For us."

I stared at him dumbly, mouth agape.

"I make a decent living. You'll never have to worry about hunger or having a roof over your head. But look around you. This is hardly the elegant home you are accustomed to living in. You won't have the fine clothes or the—"

I reached out and placed my hand over his mouth. "Gabriel, stop. Stop right now." My voice was harsher than I had intended, but I couldn't bear to listen to him speak this way. "How can you possibly doubt what I want? I am sitting, wrapped in a sheet, in *our* kitchen, learning to eat fried chicken with my fingers, the day after our wedding." I turned my hand to caress his cheek and run my thumb over his eyebrow.

"I meant what I said to Cameron. I never wanted that life out there. I want this life with you." I stared into his eyes for a few moments. "I admit I will miss teaching, but I have found contentment while working at the Book Depository. I imagine there are suffragettes here as well as in Boston. I should think they'd welcome another to their cause."

I paused a moment. "You have not limited my life in any way, Gabriel. You are allowing me to live it as I have only dreamed I could live. With love and understanding and encouragement for me to be me. Not how you wished I were, but how I truly am. And that is a miracle for me." I blinked away a few tears.

"Thank you," he murmured as he kissed my palm. "Thank you for being that brave, amazing woman I knew you were and coming to me. When I left Boston, I truly thought I would return to you."

"I'm only sorry it took me so long to make the journey."

"No regrets, Clarissa," Gabriel murmured. "We are together. And no matter what happens in the future, we will face it."

"Yes," I murmured as I leaned in for a kiss. "Together."

AUTHOR'S NOTES

Thank you for reading *Reclaimed Love*. Never fear, dear reader, the third book in the series, *Redeemed Love*, will soon be forthcoming with the next installment of the Banished Saga. I hope you will continue to join me on their journey.

Would you like to know when my next book is available? You can sign up for my new release e-mail list, where you'll be the first to know of updates, cover reveals, and special giveaways at http://www.ramonaflightner.com

Follow me on twitter: @ramonaflightner

Like my Facebook page: http://facebook.com/authorramonaflightner

Reviews help other readers find books. I appreciate all reviews. Please consider reviewing on Amazon, Goodreads or both. Most people learn about books by recommendations from their friends.

Please, share *Reclaimed Love* with a friend! Look for *Redeemed Love*, Book Three in the Banished Saga, in Winter 2014/15.

ACKNOWLEDGMENTS

Thank you, Molly Morrison, for your musical genius and encouragement.

Thank you to Dick Gibson for giving me a wonderful walking tour of Butte on a sunny Sunday afternoon. The walking tour, along with his indispensible book, *Lost Butte*, aided me in envisioning Butte as it would have been in 1900.

Thank you, Katie B, for sharing your great fashion knowledge with me.

Thank you to David Emmons for his book, *The Butte Irish: Class and Ethnicity in an American Mining Town, 1875-1925,* without which I would never have been able to form such a complete picture of Butte society.

As always, thank you to my family and friends for your love and support.

HISTORICAL NOTES

Those of you familiar with Butte, Montana will recognize many of the landmarks I cite. Some, such as the saloon in Centerville, I created, envisioning what a saloon in Butte in 1900 was like.

As with all works of fiction, there are areas where I fudged the facts. When I took the "Underground Mine Tour" at the World Museum of Mining in Butte, I learned that a rock falling on one's head was called a "duggan" after the undertaker. During my research, the Duggan funeral parlor was just opening around 1900. I'm uncertain if that term would already have been in use in 1900-1901, but I felt it added a sense of what made Butte, Butte.

I also know Matthew, a relative greenhorn, would never have been partnered with Liam, a well seasoned miner. However, for the purposes of the story and the friendships formed, I altered Matthew's traditional trajectory as he began working in the mines. I hope the readers forgive me.

As for historical places in Butte, the hotel where the Hotel Finlen currently stands used to be called the McDermott Hotel in 1900-1901. It was bought by Finlen in 1902 and renamed the Hotel Finlen. During my research I discovered that the Chequamegon Café had two locations. In 1900, it was on Park Street, near the Curtis Music Hall. It later moved up past the M&M on Main Street, the site of the historical commemorative plaque.

In Missoula, Cedar Street is now known as Broadway, the Missoula River is now the Clark Fork River, and we now refer to the Bitter Roots as the Bitterroots.

I refer to the Public Library as the Book Depository in Missoula for a few reasons. One reason is that it was referred to as such in one of my sources during my research. The main reason is that Mr. Pickens is a cantankerous old goat and that's how he'd refer to it. I mean no offense to anyone involved with the wonderful library in Missoula. For the purposes of my story, I continue to refer to the Library as the Depository until they move into their formal building in 1903.

Made in the USA
Charleston, SC
19 June 2014